G000320723

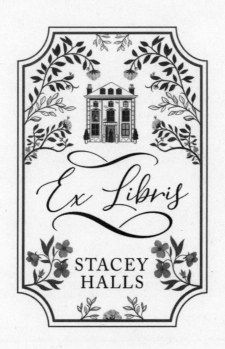

Ex Libris

STACEY
HALLS

Mrs England

ABOUT THE AUTHOR

Stacey Halls was born in 1989 and grew up in Rossendale, Lancashire. She studied journalism at the University of Central Lancashire and has written for publications including the *Guardian*, *Stylist*, *Psychologies*, the *Independent*, the *Sun* and *Fabulous*. Her first book, *The Familiars*, was the bestselling debut hardback novel of 2019 and won a Betty Trask Award. *Mrs England* is her third novel.

Also by Stacey Halls:

The Familiars
The Foundling

www.staceyhalls.com
@stacey_halls
@staceyhallsauthor

Mrs England

STACEY HALLS

**MANILLA
PRESS**

First published in the UK in 2021 by
MANILLA PRESS
An imprint of Bonnier Books UK
80–81 Wimpole St, London W1G 9RE
Owned by Bonnier Books
Sveavägen 56, Stockholm, Sweden

Copyright © Stacey Halls, 2021

Internal illustrations © Lucy Rose Cartwright

This is a work of fiction. Names, places, events and
incidents are either the products of the author's
imagination or used fictitiously.

A CIP catalogue record for this book is
available from the British Library.

Hardback ISBN: 978–1–83877–286–4
Special edition hardback ISBN: 978–1–78658–107–5
Export ISBN: 978–1–83877–287–1

Also available as an ebook and an audiobook

1 3 5 7 9 10 8 6 4 2

Typeset in Dante by Palimpsest Book Production Ltd, Falkirk, Stirlingshire
Printed and bound in Great Britain by Clays Ltd, Elcograf S.p.A.

Manilla Press is an imprint of Bonnier Books UK
www.bonnierbooks.co.uk

This novel is dedicated to NHS workers.
Thank you for all you've done and continue to do.

How doth the little crocodile
Improve his shining tail,
And pour the waters of the Nile
On every golden scale!

How cheerfully he seems to grin,
How neatly spreads his claws,
And welcomes little fishes in,
With gently smiling jaws!

Alice's Adventures in Wonderland
Lewis Carroll

Fortis in arduis
(Strength in adversity)

Norland Institute motto

The woods at night were far from silent. Nightjars and owls called their strange solos, and my boots crunched on the stones littered across the track. All around was the sound of water: noisy little brooks and streams made their ceaseless descent to the river, bubbling, chattering, murmuring. The rain had stopped, and the moon peered out from behind her misty veil. I pulled my cloak more tightly at the neck, closing my shawl around my face.

The way was easier without a lamp, which rendered everything beyond its range even darker. The glimpses of moon were guidance enough, and my eyes adjusted without difficulty. I left the mill yard and paused on the bridleway that passed the outbuildings, looking left to the moors and right towards town. I turned left, passing the millpond, its surface smooth and glassy, like a mirror held up to the night. Pines climbed the hillside above the track, which wound like a ghostly ribbon along the valley, and I tried to remember how to reach the low, lonely cottage on the moor.

I'd locked the children in the nursery; this time there would be no escapes. All being well, I could slip inside, unnoticed. If I returned after the master . . . *No*, I told myself, *don't think about it. Just keep walking.* My legs carried me upwards, the crags looming like a spectre to my left.

'Ruby?' A whisper, unmistakable.

The shock almost tripped me. I froze, looking out at the slim trunks and black branches. I could hardly hear above the blood pounding in my ears. Seconds later it came again.

'Ruby? Is that you?'

CHAPTER 1

London, August 1904

I took Georgina the usual way home, east through Kensington Gardens towards Hyde Park. She had fallen asleep with a fistful of daisies, and I pushed the pram along the bridleway, nodding at the other nurses. Her shoes nudged the end of the cushioned carriage; she would soon outgrow it, and I felt a distant stab of mourning for the baby she had been. She could sit up herself now, which she did on fine days with the hood folded down; she loved to see the Household Cavalry with their piped uniforms and plumed hats, and ladies would put down their parasols to admire her.

I crouched to retrieve a woollen bear lying on the sand beside a pram. The baby's nurse sat on a bench reading a novel and had not noticed. Behind her a tangle of small boys tore about the grass, bashing one another with sticks.

'Oh, thank you,' the nurse said as I passed her the bear. She took in my uniform, distinct from the other nurses', designed to set Norlanders apart from the rest. Beneath a smart brown cloak I wore a fawn drill dress with a white cambric apron edged with lace. At my throat a frothy cream tie completed the summer uniform. In winter we wore light blue serge, and all year round we did our heavy work in pink galatea, cleaning the nursery and making up fires.

'I wish she went off like that,' said the nurse. She nodded at the occupant of her pram: a slim, serious-looking child a little older than Georgina, who glared at me from beneath a white sun hat. 'How old?'

'She's seventeen months,' I replied.

'And look at her lovely curls. It's a shame this one's hair's so straight. She pulls out her rags when I put them in.'

'You could try setting them when she's asleep. If you wet the rags first, it'll dry like that.'

The nurse brightened. 'That's an idea.'

I said goodbye and she returned to her book. We passed through Albert Gate, where black stags stood guard on the park railings, and I smiled at the old woman who sold windmills and toy balloons. The windmills waited rigidly in their crates for a breeze to stir them that August afternoon, and the woman spun one half-heartedly. She never smiled back, but I supposed I looked much the same to her as all the other nurses. We flocked to the park after lunch with our charges, occupying the lawns and benches, spreading blankets on the grass, feeding the ducks and pushing prams through the rose gardens. An hour or two later we'd pass her again, heading home for naps and paste sandwiches before taking the children downstairs to see their parents.

Georgina was the only child of Audrey and Dennis Radlett, though Mrs Radlett was expecting again. I'd laundered Georgina's linens in readiness and circled cots in catalogues to show Mrs Radlett; Georgina would still be in hers when the baby came. The new arrival excited me, though I was yet to find a monthly nurse for feeding, and the prospect of sharing my nursery even for a few weeks caused a distant flutter of anxiety. For the top floor of number six Perivale Gardens was my kingdom, my domain: my office, schoolroom and workshop. Sometimes it was a tea room, if Georgina wished to give her toys refreshment; occasionally it was a jungle, and the two of us would crawl on our knees on the carpet, hunting for lions and tigers.

Georgina's hand opened, causing the daisies to scatter over her blanket, and deftly I swept them up and put them in my pocket. On the nursery windowsill I'd arranged in jars the flowers we'd picked in the park, and I was teaching Georgina their names. Georgina already had an impressive vocabulary, quietly absorbing as I pointed at plates and spoons and toys and stamps. 'Tag!' she'd declared one afternoon a few weeks ago, straining out of her pram to point at the Albert Gate stags. I'd felt a rush of pride and love for this cheerful, confident little girl, who everybody adored when they met, and who reflected adoration back at them.

On Knightsbridge, motorcars growled past carriages and choked the road with fumes. I glanced about at the red brick apartment buildings, the hot potato man, the green Bayswater omnibus and the Chinese laundryman unloading fresh linen from his cart. Crossing sweepers stepped aside for ladies in wide hats on their way home from department stores, tailed by their maids laden with boxes. Perivale Gardens was a large, quiet square a few minutes from the busy thoroughfare. A score of houses stood around an oblong lawn, guarded by black iron railings and planted with cedars and rhododendrons. The Radlett home was tall and stuccoed, with smooth white columns flanking a glossy black door. At the top was the nursery, which overlooked the long and sunny garden, and the neighbours' gardens either side. The Bowlers next door kept hens, and sometimes let Georgina collect the eggs.

The hall was empty and silent, and I carried Georgina upstairs, where she allowed me to remove her cream leather shoes and settled in her cot with a sigh. I closed the blinds and pulled the curtains, glancing into the street for a moment and seeing the butcher's boy on his rounds with his basket. He went down the area steps and a kitchenmaid examined its contents at the basement door, piling packets into the crook of her elbow. My father did his rounds with Damson, our docile pony, *A. May, High Class Fruiterer & Greengrocer* painted in large white letters on the side of his cart. My brothers and I would fight over who sat at the reins with him as he steered us through the streets, waving at people. 'You take the reins, Rhubarb,' he would say, putting them in my hands.

I closed the curtains.

At half-past three, Ellen brought me a ham roll and a pot of tea, and I gave her a copy of *Young Woman* I'd read and a penny dreadful I hadn't. I took a seat at the table beneath the eaves to eat, looking about to see what needed dusting; in summer, within hours of my morning clean, a thin layer of grime drifted in through the window and coated everything. On the bookshelf, the golden letters of my testimonial book winked from the black spine. On graduation day, the Norland Institute principal, Miss Simpson – who we fondly called Sim – handed them out from a gleaming stack. The books contained everything we would need for our fledgling careers, from uniform materials to blank pages for references. My photograph was pasted in the front, larger than I would have liked; I appeared stern and unsmiling, one hand resting nervously on the table beside me. At the end of my three-month probation, Mrs Radlett had marked my needlework very good, punctuality excellent, neatness excellent, cleanliness excellent, order excellent, temper excellent, tact with visitors very good, tact with children excellent, tact with servants very good, power of amusing children excellent, power of managing children excellent and general capability excellent. I was awarded my certificate in the autumn and kept it inside my trunk. Some nurses had sent theirs home for their parents to frame, but I imagined handing it to my mother, could picture her bemusement that there was such a thing as a certificate for caring for children.

I'd finished my roll and begun tidying when there was a light knock at the door. 'Come in, Ellen,' I called, moving the miniature globe an inch to the right and setting its equator. There was no reply.

'Mrs Radlett!' I straightened at once. She was a young mistress, only a few years older than me at twenty-three or four, and so gentle and feminine. A wide smile was the natural shape her mouth took, and pretty gowns and gleaming brooches showed her plump figure and creamy skin to its advantage. Her hair was the colour of toffee cooling on the stove, and she wore it in all the latest styles copied from magazines. My own hair was thin and dark and would not be coaxed to any height. My skin turned brown easily, and since the Norland hat offered no shade, I took care to keep out of the sun.

'Good afternoon, Nurse May,' said Mrs Radlett. She was good-natured and liked to tease; one of her favourite games was play-acting at being grand and proper, though the joke was slightly lost on me. 'Would you join me in the parlour when you have a moment?'

'Of course, ma'am, I'll come now. Miss Georgina's having her nap.'

I followed her into the house. The downstairs was far removed from my own quiet storey, with its own rules and codes and timings, from which I was happily exempt. Nurses were not servants, existing in that tricky place between domestic and family, belonging to neither. Sim warned us it could be a lonely profession: friendless, she had called it. But I'd been friendless most of my life, and found only joy in the busy hours, and peace in the quiet ones. Every morning I took Georgina to the dining room, every evening to the drawing room, where Mr and Mrs Radlett devoted an hour to entertaining her before supper. Mr Radlett played the piano while Mrs Radlett danced with her daughter, lifting her into the air and guiding her fat feet around the carpet. They were as delighted to see her as if they'd been away a week, and sometimes Georgina sobbed as I carried her back to her nursery, reaching backwards for her mama. 'Up the wooden hill and down Sheet Lane,' I would murmur as we climbed the stairs, and by the time the nursery door was closed she had often forgotten her anguish. She sucked her thumb when she was tired, and I always removed it from her sleep-soaked mouth when Mrs Radlett came to kiss her goodnight.

The parlour was at the front of the house, seldom used

and stuffy in summer, with the windows fastened to keep out the dust from the street. The blinds were closed against the heat, and the lace curtain hung flat against them. The Radletts' house was tastefully decorated and filled with antiques; the mistress even had her own library. As a couple they were intellectual and political. They entertained often and friends called frequently at the house, filling it with cigar smoke and leaving sticky rings of sherry on the sideboards, decorating the hat stand with feathers and ribbons, like a strange tree of exotic birds. In the eaves of the building there was little to disturb me, but occasionally Mrs Radlett asked me to bring Georgina down to kiss and pass around before bed. She always deferred to me, and was politely inquisitive about her daughter's diet and routine; there was no doubt whatsoever who was in charge.

'Do sit down,' she said now. I took a seat in a stuffed armchair beside a potted fern.

'I have some thrilling news.' Mrs Radlett placed a hand on her rounded stomach. She had recently begun to show beneath her waistband, and Ellen had let out her skirts. 'I've been longing to tell you for weeks, but Mr Radlett forbade me until it was all agreed and finalised, which it was last night, so now I can share it with you.'

I felt a glimmer of excitement and straightened my apron.

'As you know, Mr Radlett is doing splendidly at Dalberg and Howard. So splendidly that' – she spoke slowly, pausing as if for dramatic effect – 'the firm is sending him to Chicago, to work there as their senior architect. He's going to design a *university*, Nurse May, isn't that wonderful?' She clapped her hands, barely able to contain herself.

She went on quickly: 'Of course, we want you to come with us, to be Georgina's nurse out there. I hope you wouldn't imagine for a *second* that we would go without you! Oh, please say you'll come. Mr Radlett is searching for a house for us now; you wouldn't believe what you can get in America – positive mansions for practically *pennies*! And there are wonderful parks and shops, and new buildings going up all the time. Heavens, our next child will be American. How about that? I hadn't thought of that until now. How strange.' An expression of childlike wonder moved across her face.

'Chicago,' was all I could say. Even from my mouth, the name sounded foreign and glamorous. Coming from a smoky suburb of Birmingham, I thought London the most exciting place on earth, but Chicago was as distant to me as Mars. I calculated how long it would take for a letter to reach me there, how long it would take to return home, and a small, hard shape like a pebble formed in my stomach.

'Yes,' Mrs Radlett was saying, 'we must pack the house and ship our things, so that will take some time. But we hope to be on a steamer ourselves in a month or two; I know Dennis is eager to get started. The passage goes to

New York and we can take a train from there. I expect we'll stay in New York for a spell, wouldn't that be something? I've always wanted to go there. Nurse May, are you quite well? You do look queer.'

'Yes, ma'am.'

'Oh, do say you'll come. You will come, won't you?'

'I'm afraid I can't do that.'

Silence. The carriage clock ticked, and the porcelain spaniels observed tranquilly from the mantelpiece. Mrs Radlett had not been expecting my reply and attempted to recover herself, stroking her stomach automatically. 'Why ever not? Of course, you must take a few days off before we go, to bid your farewells.'

I could not meet her eye and stared at the carpet.

'Nurse May? I thought you'd be pleased.'

'Oh, I am, ma'am. I'm thrilled for you and Mr Radlett.'

'But not for yourself. Are you unhappy with us?'

'No. I'm very happy here.'

'Then why on earth won't you come? I simply can't fathom going without you, Nurse May. I hadn't even considered it! I *won't* consider it. You are like a family member to us, and Georgina adores you. *I* adore you, and Dennis does, too.' Her voice trembled and grew higher, and I realised with horror my mistress was about to cry.

My own throat thickened, and my nose stung with tears. 'Thank you, ma'am. You're so good to me, you and Mr Radlett. And I am so fond of Miss Georgina.'

14

'Then why won't you come? Is it your salary? I'll speak to Dennis about increasing it, if that's the case.'

I shook my head. 'It's not that.'

'Are you unwell, then? Or . . . *betrothed*?' Relief flooded her. 'Are you engaged to marry?'

'Nothing like that.'

'Heavens, what is it, then?'

'It's my siblings,' I said. 'I can't leave them.'

She burned with alarm and curiosity. 'Forgive my indelicacy, but I thought your parents were alive?'

'They are, ma'am.'

'Has one of them been taken ill?'

'No.'

'Out of work?'

'No.'

'Then why ever can't you leave them?'

My voice cracked with sorrow. 'I'm dreadfully sorry, Mrs Radlett.'

She sat back in stunned silence. Across the square a carriage discharged its passengers, then continued on its circuit; the horse hooves reached a crescendo outside the window, then faded. I thought of Georgina asleep upstairs, and the jam jars lining the windowsill, and the daisies in my pocket, ruined now. I thought of the tea cooling in the pot Ellen had brought me, and the half-finished copy of *Woman's Signal* I'd folded beside the armchair for later, and how the nursery on a rainy evening, with the hiss and flicker of the gas jets, was the most comfortable place I'd ever known. Georgina would wake soon and call out for me, safe in the knowledge I would lift her from her cot and give her a clementine or a sugar biscuit. I could not look at her mother, because tears were blurring my vision. The room was so quiet I could hear my heart breaking, and it sounded like a daisy snapping at the stem.

CHAPTER 2

'Nurse May.' The principal's tone was neutral; she
had answered the door herself.

Nine months had passed since I'd seen Sim, when she
attended me at Perivale Gardens for my inspection: Ellen
served coffee and madeleines in the sitting room as the
principal made notes and Mrs Radlett hovered. Now, faced
with her, that time vaporised to dust; I was as damp and
nervous as when I'd started, and resisted the urge to mop
my brow. I followed her inside and closed the heavy black
door behind me.

Inside the whitewashed entrance the familiar smells
rushed to greet me: fresh bread, carbolic soap, clean linen
and pencil shavings. The scent of femininity was overpow-
ering, of girls moving through the rooms, perfumed and

17

perspiring. To me, it smelt like learning. The house at Pembridge Square was a gleaming palace compared to the schoolhouse in Balsall Heath, a dull, miserable place, where chalk dust danced in the light that struggled through the dirty windows. At home, my education ended with the school bell; my parents were too busy with the shop to teach us, so I sat down with my brothers and our books in the evenings. At three and five years younger than me, Ted and Archie were willing enough but bickered through my lessons. Robbie, fifteen months my junior, was slow and reluctant, and even now his letters were riddled with errors.

The Norland Institute was situated in a large white villa on Pembridge Square, ten minutes north in a cab from Perivale Gardens. I'd left that morning, and would have preferred to walk there myself through Kensington Gardens, but the Radletts had insisted on waving me off in a cab; my trunk was to follow me to my new address. The farewell had been just as awful as I'd expected, with Georgina's forehead wrinkling in confusion in her mother's arms. Mrs Radlett raised one of her daughter's hands and made it wave, and she'd bawled as the cab pulled off. That had been too much to bear; I'd turned away and pressed my handkerchief to my face.

The institute was the first place of its kind: a school, home and agency for children's nurses. A little over two years before, I'd sat the entrance exam for the Maud Steppings scholarship and, by some miracle, passed. I'd barely understood any of the questions: *tell the story of*

Enoch Arden; describe the whereabouts of the following streets and shops in London; write the recipe for marmalade. Enoch Arden was unknown to me, and I had left Birmingham only once in my life, so the locations of Gooch's and Harrods and Urquarts were as unfamiliar to me as the Palace and Tower. Though I did know how to make marmalade: I shared my grandmother's recipe before setting the pencil on the desk and glancing with bleak devastation at the other girls, all of whom were writing vacantly, as though they constantly sat exams. That after-noon I thought I'd never see London again. My chaperones were Mr and Mrs Granville, who lived in the next street and looked after us once or twice as children; they bought me a sarsaparilla at Whiteley's before taking me back to the train, and it was with a leaden heart I returned to the Midlands. Nobody was more surprised than I when the letter arrived on the mat at Longmore Street, informing me that the tuition fee of £36 was *gratis*, a word I had to look up at the public library. I also had to order, at my own expense, the fabric for my uniforms from a clothier named Debenham & Freebody; for that I used my savings and had just enough left over to buy copybooks and pencils. I soon found out that all the other girls used pens.

My nine months at Norland were almost excessively happy. At first I'd been anxious and withdrawn, nowhere near as well educated or self-assured as my two-dozen classmates. The only person at Norland who had an accent like mine was one of the maids. I shared a bedroom at

19

the back of the house with an Irish girl named Bridget, who had black hair and a severe hooked nose, like a jackdaw. She was friendly and straightforward, and as we settled in beside each other, the unease melted away.

But it returned now, as familiar as an old cloak, as Sim shut the door behind me. She was small and slender, almost doll-like, but her countenance was not; her curly brown fringe was streaked with steel and so was her demeanour. Yet she was a fair and generous principal, not above tidying stray teacups and distributing the post. She was the only member of staff who lived at the institute, though I had only ever seen her in her neat serge dress with the gold watch at her waist; it was a mystery to the students when she bathed. Her parting advice was that we ought to display our silver hairbrushes at our new homes, for the servants to see. I had only a comb, but Sim didn't miss a thing; the week before graduation I found a box from William Comyns on my dresser. Nestled inside was a silver-backed hairbrush, heavy as a pistol, with bristles as stiff as pins.

She led me towards the back of the house and her office, passing a pair of students in uniform coming downstairs. They took in my cloak and hat and gave shy smiles. To the left was the refectory, where more girls in fawn and white bent over books and chewed pens. With a pang of nostalgia I realised it was exam season. There were no lessons on Saturdays, and the door stood open to the lecture hall: a high-ceilinged room with glass-fronted bookcases and fresh flower arrangements, threaded in the springtime with blue speedwell, the Norland symbol. Behind the desk a map of the British isles spread across one wall, beside it an upright piano. A tapestry hung above the bookcases, four or five feet high, of a lion climbing a hill.

A brass plaque, bearing: *M. Simpson, Principal*, identified her office, and she closed the door behind us. The window was open to the yard beyond, and the desk cluttered with teacups, newspapers, candle stubs and pen nibs. A begonia wilted in a pot beside a painted ceramic paperweight. On the wall hung a map of the London boroughs, studded with red pins for the nurses' locations. Beside it was a map of the empire, with pins as far as India, and as near as Paris. Books and journals were piled haphazardly into bookcases lining the walls, and I saw on a shelf a framed picture of the first Norland nurses, five sheepish girls in caps and aprons, flanked by Sim and Mrs Ward, the institute's founder, whose round face peered benevolently from beneath a wide hat. The overall atmosphere in the principal's office was one of bohemian chaos. Sim had studied at university and was unmarried, and inspired in me a mixture of fear and envy. She was the person I admired most.

'It disappointed me to receive your letter,' she said, removing that morning's newspaper from her seat and getting straight to the point. 'We don't take resignations lightly at Norland. I look forward to hearing your reason, but before I do' – she pulled the bell cord beside her desk – 'we shall have some tea.'

This was a first for me: I had been inside Sim's office once or twice before but never been offered refreshment. Part of me had expected that now I was no longer a probationer, she would see me in the drawing room, where client visits took place and where the furniture was for show, out of bounds to students except for at Christmas, when carols were sung around the grand piano in the window. Despite this, the maids dusted it down twice a day.

We spoke of the heat, and my route to Pembridge Square that morning, and a minute or two later a maid brought a tea service, and by some miracle found space on the desk.

After she had poured, Sim said: 'Now then, Nurse May. You resigned. Would you care to tell me about it?'

I took a sip, and the saucer rattled. 'Mr and Mrs Radlett are emigrating. To Chicago. In America,' I finished lamely.

Sim's blue gaze was direct. 'And you don't wish to go.'

Weakly, I shook my head.

'As you know from your peers' placements, a significant proportion of Norlanders are sent abroad. The foreign families want English nannies even more than the English ones. You understood travel was a possibility when you undertook your studies, did you not? It's one of the *draws* for some students: a free ticket to live in another country and expand your world view.'

'I don't wish to emigrate.'

Sim's posture was excellent; she brought her chin down to look more closely at me. 'A fair statement, but what are your reasons?'

I said nothing and looked into my cup.

'A new life in America could be a marvellous thing, Nurse May. It is a young country, relatively liberal in its morals and politics. It isn't a shabby place for a young woman. I've sent many nurses over the Atlantic who have settled remarkably well. Just last week one went to Boston, and we have two or three in New York. In fact, a girl from the class of '97 is on a steamer to North Carolina as we speak, for a placement with the Vanderbilts.'

I stared at the paperweight. The speedwell was badly painted; no doubt a gift from a nurse's charge.

'But you are unmoved.'

'I'm afraid so, Miss Simpson. I hoped you might find me another position.'

She appeared conflicted, then rearranged her features into weary resignation. 'To speak frankly, Nurse May, it's rather a thin time for me to find you a new situation. Many people are still at their country houses and won't return for another month or so, or else they're travelling. You're up against the girls who'll soon be finishing their exams, and I must secure places for them, too, to maintain our graduate employment levels. Mrs Radlett wrote to me for another nurse, and I have one in mind. Still, her testimony was glowing. Speaking of which: your testimonial book.' She held out a small hand.

I'd prepared for this, carrying it beneath my arm for the journey. I passed it over the desk. A dog barked distantly as she turned the leaves, finding Mrs Radlett's entry and reading with the page held between finger and thumb. Despite her education, Mrs Radlett littered her prose with exclamation points and underlined words and phrases for emphasis, which made her appear breathless and girlish. She had given me a parting gift: a silk handkerchief embroidered with my initials, and a crisp new copy of *The Wonderful Wizard of Oz*.

I tried not to think about the nurse who would hang her uniform in the press and sleep in my bed. Perhaps Georgina wouldn't even know the difference, and it wouldn't be long before she'd forget me altogether. My eyes filled again. My handkerchief was damp and streaked with dust from the road; Sim passed me a clean one, which I accepted, blowing my nose and sighing.

'I'm sorry,' I said. 'I don't know what's come over me.'

'Your old room is empty for the time being; Nurse Jenkins is on her kindergarten placement. You may stay a night or two, and we can go through the applications this afternoon, if I have time' – she checked her watch – 'or else tomorrow morning. After that you must go home until we've found you a family. Where is it again? Birmingham?'

'No. I mean yes, it's Birmingham, but no, I can't.'

She blinked. 'Well, I'm afraid you must. Nurse Jenkins returns at the end of the week, then my new students arrive on the first of September.' She studied me for a moment. 'No one enjoys going home with one's tail between one's legs,' she added more gently, 'especially when one has struck out on one's own and gained some independence, but it will only be for a short while. A break will be just the ticket. How much holiday allowance do you have left this year?'

'All of it.'

This displeased her. 'I am continually reprimanding nurses for neglecting to take their holidays. The allowance is generous for a reason; rest is necessary in this line of work. A wrung-out nurse is a wretched nurse.'

'I can't take a holiday,' I said. 'I need to find another position. Please, Miss Simpson. I send half my wage home each quarter, and I can't afford to miss next month's.'

She softened and sighed. 'What is your father's occupation?'

'They've a grocery business. And my siblings are at home, all four of them. The boys work and my sister Elsie – she's eleven now – she's at school another year. But she misses a lot because she has problems with her limbs. It's her spine, you see. She can't walk far and she has a limp. Most days she's fine, but it comes on, so she's no good at carrying things, or working the till. She drops things and gets frustrated, and . . . well, I'd like her to carry on at

25

school. She can write with both hands; she learnt, in case her right one stops working.'

Sim seemed to make her mind up, setting down her saucer and opening one of the desk drawers, taking out a small pile of letters. 'Earlier I took a swift glance at our applications, but as I said, summer brings more of a trickle than a stream. People get their affairs together around Michaelmas, and for a nurse of just a year's experience . . . What have we here . . . ?' I squeezed my gloves in my lap as she fell silent, sorting through the papers. 'There was a letter from a lady in St John's Wood . . . Where is it . . . ? Ah yes, offering a salary of thirty pounds per annum. *That* won't be suitable. I shall reply with our rates.'

'Does the college advertise?' I asked.

'Heavens, no. We never have, and Mrs Ward does not wish to begin. Let's see, here is one from a divorced actress. Well, that won't be suitable at *all*.'

'I don't mind,' I said.

'Well, I'm afraid I do.'

Another letter fell from its folds.

'This one from a Mrs Charles England in Yorkshire.' I waited. '*Please send photograph and fullest particulars and advise the salary your nurses command* . . . That's more like it, but where was the . . . ?' She leafed through the remaining papers with their elegant penmanship. 'I saw one from a lady in . . . ah yes, Edwardes Square. Mrs Askew-Laing. Why does that name seem familiar, Askew-Laing? *My dear friend Mrs Henry Cadogan recommended your institute of learning as* . . . Askew-Laing, Askew-Laing. Could it be the auctioneers?' Sim wet her lips and frowned hard at the letter, reading again. 'I shall have to consult Mrs Ward, but I'm almost certain they have the auction houses.'

I brightened and sat straighter.

'Yes, they have the premises at Piccadilly, and New York, I think. Oh,' she said, for my face had fallen, and Sim understood why. 'No foreign travel. I should think a family like that only spends part of the year in London, and it would be foolish of me to ask. Tell me, is it emigration you take exception to, or travel at all?'

'I don't mind getting on trains and things, I just can't move to another country.' I was growing exasperated with Sim's condescension, as if I had an irrational, shape-shifting objection. But of course for her, work was a choice and not a necessity; she had never queued up to send a money order to her family, and would never understand.

'Then I'm afraid you're limited, Nurse May, as the families who apply to Norland expect flexibility. If you can hold fast a week or two, I'll see who else applies, but I must also consider this year's graduates. Mrs Ward has made enquiries in the usual circles and arranged several interviews already. In fact' – a flash of gold as she checked the time – 'I must dash for an appointment in Marylebone.'

'What about the Yorkshire one?'

'What about it?'

'Mrs . . . England.'

She found the paper and scanned it. 'Four children: two sons, two daughters. They are mill-owners.' They might have been acrobats, judging by her tone. 'Mrs England read about the institute in the newspaper, and their nurse recently passed away. She was the husband's nurse when he was a boy, *dearly beloved* . . . Experience with sensitive children needed; she mentions her eldest suffers with his health. *The nursery is in a separate wing with its own entrance, and we have accommodation in the night nursery or, if the nurse preferred, arrangements can be made in the main house.* Well, that's out of the question.' She turned the paper to look at the signature. 'She doesn't give her own name, but Mrs England seems quite eager to fill the position.'

'I'll take it.'

'Should you wish to live so far away? They might have a house in London, but I doubt it. There isn't much in the way of textile trading here.'

'I don't mind where I go, Miss Simpson.'

She regarded me and went back to the letter.

'You are, of course, equipped with the skills and training necessary, but a nursery of four children is a substantial undertaking. It appears there is no nursemaid or under-maid. And Mrs England doesn't elaborate on her son's condition; if he is an invalid, he may require expert medical help. I shall enquire this week.' She tucked the letter back into its envelope, as if she had decided on the matter.

'I'd appreciate if you could reply by tonight's post,' I

said, 'and tell Mrs England you have found a nurse for her.'

Sim gave me a long look, then sat back in her chair. 'Nurse May,' she said. 'Do you know why I awarded you the Maud Steppings scholarship?'

I felt the pinch of disappointment that she'd remembered, and shook my head.

'You might recall I oversaw the examination in the lecture hall. Part-way through the assessment, an applicant dropped her pencil. It rolled towards the front of the classroom. And without hesitation, you stopped writing, got up from your seat and retrieved it. You walked to the back of the room to find its owner and return it, at the expense of your own writing time. Without reading your paper, I knew you belonged at the institute.'

'Because I picked up a pencil?' I asked in dismay.

'What children need most are kindness, patience and attention. Those qualities can be taught, but it's better if they're instinctive. When I interviewed you after the exam, besides confirming you possessed those qualities, you were . . .' She narrowed her eyes and searched for the word. 'Determined. I could tell that you badly wanted a place here, perhaps more than any student I had met. You have life experience, Nurse May, which is far more valuable than an education when it comes to caring for children. Far more valuable, indeed, than an ability to recall the poem *Enoch Arden*.'

I found myself disarmed once again at her ability to

remember everything, and see through everybody. 'I thought Enoch Arden was a prime minister,' I said. 'That's what I wrote.'

'I remember.' A reluctant smile twitched the corner of the principal's mouth, and the atmosphere lifted slightly.

'You're sure about the position? Once I write to Mrs England, the offer is made. I'll remind you that nurses who fail in three situations are invited to withdraw from the institute.'

I bristled and sat a little straighter. 'I shan't fail you again, Miss Simpson. You have my word.'

'Very well. I shall reply to Mrs England on my return.'

'They sound like the perfect family,' I said, trying to be bright.

Sim gave a dry laugh. 'Nurse May, there is no such thing.'

Dear Elsie,

I am writing to you from Norland, from my old bed. It is strange to be back, and though I have fond memories, I am eager to leave already. My dormitory (Temperance) has not changed a bit: the cream and brown wallpaper is as hideous as ever, and the loose floorboard by the dresser is still not fixed, nor is the cracked tile in the fireplace. I've grown used to sharing a room with babies, who go at once to sleep and cry sometimes. I'm quite out of practice with girls my own age, who sit up reading with the lamp lit and whisper after lights out. I am sharing with a student called Nurse Banford, who works on a children's ward during the day. She gets home late and always misses supper, but we've had some pleasant conversations.

I am waiting to find out if I have a new family in Yorkshire. I will write next from there, if it materialises. Please say a prayer for me. Remember to keep my address safe, when you have it. It was difficult to say goodbye to the Radletts, who have been so good to me, and I so fond of them.

I hope you are keeping up your studies. Please give my love to the boys, and tell Mother I'll send September's wage as soon as I get it.

All my love,
Ruby

Within days, everything was arranged. I had not unpacked, not wishing to give anybody, including myself, the impression that my stay at Pembridge Square was anything other than temporary. Besides, Nurse Jenkins had left some of her things in the drawers: a half-eaten jar of pear drops, two or three dusty handkerchiefs and a spare exercise book. I kept to my room or wandered the streets, noticing how the trees were slowly turning to yellow and gold and caramel. Meanwhile, character references were sent, trains booked and my clothes laundered and pressed. The doctor pressed a stethoscope against my back and warned

me of the damp climate in the north and the smoke from
the mills.

The morning of my departure, I washed and dressed
and breakfasted, then made the bed a final time, though
a maid would strip it before a speck of dust could settle.
A cab waited at the railings, and going downstairs I was
embarrassed to see a little farewell party at the door: Sim
with a pair of students, and Mrs Ward herself, who clasped
my hand in her own soft one, and wished me farewell. I
felt grossly self-conscious, unused to being at the centre
of anything, and noticed the brief admiring glances of
the students, who looked forward to fastening their own
cloaks and going out into the world. The driver shut me
inside the cab, and I waved at the little band on the doorstep before retreating into the shadows, thirsty and already
perspiring.

Travelling east down the Bayswater Road, I couldn't
help but feel as though I was going the wrong way, like
a clock wound backwards. There would be no more trips
to the theatre with the other nurses, no more of Ellen's
scones. I realised I had left my copy of *Woman's Signal*
down the side of the armchair, half-read. I stared out of
the cab window at the glossy black carriages crawling and
shoving like beetles; the bright advertisements for cocoa,
soap, mustard; the variety of shops and street vendors:
flower sellers, crossing sweepers, blacking boys . . . I'd
been shocked, at first, to see so many children at work
on the streets, but they had become part of the tapestry,

and seemed a different species than the plump, milky children who I and my fellow nurses cared for, though of course they were not.

The traffic was slow to cross town, and everybody hot and irritable; by the time the cab arrived at King's Cross I had just twenty minutes to spare before the train. I paid and tipped the driver, never failing to find it remarkable that I was a person who did that sort of thing. The station ceiling was cavernous, enormously high and filled like a glass balloon with engine smoke. I asked for the platform and battled my way along the concourse, discovering with relief an empty compartment in second class, just as I was about to melt. I looked forward to the prospect of opening the window once the train had left the smoke-choked tunnels behind, and took my gloves off in anticipation, fanning myself and hearing, a minute or two later, the shrill whistle. The carriage doors slammed, another whistle shrieked on the platform, and the train slid along the rails, gathering momentum, with a belly full of coal and its eye on the north.

CHAPTER 3

The distant sound of a whistle woke me with a start. Night had fallen by the time I arrived in Yorkshire, and the oil in the ceiling lamp swung back and forth, shedding a rather feeble light. Though it had been a hot summer's day in London, here a chill seeped through the draughty window and the rain made patterns on the glass. I looked about for Elsie sucking her sweet, for Father peering out through the window, then remembered where I was, and realised the train was stationary. I checked my pocket for my purse, getting quickly to my feet and finding the conductor. The train had been full when I changed at Leeds, where I'd shared a compartment with a family with three children. But the carriage had emptied now, and in my panic I thought I had missed my stop. The conductor told me mine was next, and all at once I felt dread and relief, nerves and excitement. I retrieved my book from where it had fallen to the floor and began tidying my appearance, using my reflection in the dark window to pin up strands of hair and fasten my cloak.

Five minutes later the train drew to a halt in darkness so complete we might have been inside a tunnel. Nobody else disembarked, and the compartments I'd passed were all empty. Two cowardly lanterns glowed dimly at either end of the platform, as though they knew their chances of penetrating the night were slim. The rain had stopped but the air was thick and moist, like a laundry in winter. The guard whistled, and the train gathered itself and heaved off.

I looked up and down the platform, but found myself alone. Across the rails was the station entrance, with more lanterns and a porter's office. I picked up my luggage and began to find a way towards it when I heard hurried footsteps; there was a subway beneath the tracks, and somebody was coming up the ramp. A man appeared: hat first, followed by a lively face with a dark moustache, then a smart black coat and green waistcoat with a slim, elegant chain. His large hand held aloft a lantern, giving the impression of a convivial innkeeper. He was tall and powerfully built, and when he saw me a wide smile broke across his face.

'Nurse May.' He spoke with confidence and familiarity, as though we had met before. I approached him and set down my portmanteau to shake his hand. His grip was warm and energetic, his eyes black and shining like jewels.

'Yes,' I said. 'Pleased to meet you.'

'I'm dreadfully sorry I'm late, the horse needed a new shoe, and Broadley . . . Never mind, I am here now, and I shall take you. Let me unburden you; pass me your things, that's the ticket. I hope your journey was comfortable?' He said all this pumping my arm like a piston. Finally I extracted it and we descended into the subway, where more dismal lamps battled with the darkness, advertisements flaring in the lantern's path.

'Very comfortable, thank you,' I replied. 'Are you the coachman?'

'Ha!' His booming voice found every dark corner and came crashing back. 'Gracious, no. I neglected to introduce myself. I am Charles England.'

I almost expired with shame. 'I'm dreadfully sorry, Mr England. I didn't realise.'

'No harm done whatsoever, Nurse May.' He seemed thoroughly delighted by my mistake, and I followed him through the shut-up booking office to a yard where a piebald horse and carriage waited. 'This is Magpie, and please admire his new shoes, or he gets terribly offended.' He slapped the stallion's flank and held open the little door, tossing my portmanteau inside as though it was weightless. I thanked him and climbed in, and the carriage rocked as he leapt up and took the reins, while I withered and cringed. The coachman! What must he think of me?

That a more idiotic girl never lived, and worse, was here to care for his children.

I sat more neatly and pulled the little curtain aside to look out of the window, but it was as though a black blind had come down. The carriage was large and expensive, with leather seats, and I wondered why the Englands appeared to have no driver, and why the master himself collected me. Surely they had staff? I hoped very much they did not expect me to take on more domestic work than I was able to, with four children to look after, a nursery to keep clean and no nursemaid to assist me. No matter, I would establish everything with the mistress when I arrived.

The gradient shifted and we went uphill, turning slightly here and there, making me think of long, kinked passes up steep gorges. I closed my eyes and tried to push the image from my mind, tried to picture the place that would be my home for the next few years at least. I wondered if the children would be asleep or waiting for me in the nursery. Four of them: it seemed suddenly a lot, though I told myself it couldn't be all that different to being the eldest of five. For many years I had been a little mother to my siblings, with our parents busy in the shop; it was me they came to when they scraped a knee or had an empty belly, me who washed and dressed and chaperoned. It was me Mother asked where Ted was, or if I'd seen Archie's cap. I reassured myself with the knowledge I had done it before, and that skills, once cultivated, did not vanish.

After five or ten minutes, the carriage descended and moved more slowly, eventually drawing to a halt. But instead of silence, there was a loud rushing sound, like a train, or a great valve emitting steam. Mr England landed heavily, opening the door and swinging the lantern inside, and again the unseasonal chill found me.

'Good! I have not shaken you to pieces,' he said. 'I must bring you out now, I'm afraid, because the path up to the house is narrow, and I can't promise we wouldn't plunge to our deaths down the valley. If you wait a moment, I'll put the horse away and the carriage to bed.'

He left me standing on the cobbles and went with his lantern towards a dark mass of outbuildings. The strange hissing noise continued, and as my eyes accustomed to the darkness I could make out the blue-black sky, with a clouded moon. To my right was a tall, dense impression – an immense building or perhaps a wood, for among the dampness was a distinct smell, a *green* smell, that city dwellers like me detected easily. It was cold and fresh as spring water, entirely unlike the heavy smoke and dust I was used to, and I gulped it in. Mr England's lantern returned a moment later. He took my case and led the way, moving easily, as though the darkness was a natural habitat to him.

'You can't see it, but this is the mill yard,' he said. 'The house is just across the river and up a hill.'

Of course, the noise was a river, growing louder now, as though we had disturbed it. I found I had frozen in the dim light of my master's lantern, and he swung it up to look at me.

'Are you well, Nurse May? I'm afraid the way is rather primitive.'

'Sir, how will we cross the river?'

'In rubber boots. I have two pairs waiting on the bank,' he replied seriously. There was an awful silence, then a smile broke his expression. 'I am teasing: we are not *that* primitive in Yorkshire. Here we are.'

All that existed outside Mr England's halo of light was noise and darkness. He was striding quickly; at once we had left the yard behind and were upon a stone bridge, wide enough for a carriage, but with only an inch or two either side. It rose in a little hillock and stood perhaps fifteen feet above the water flowing powerfully beneath it. I fixed my stare forwards as we were briefly suspended, and in a moment we were across it. Mr England directed us left, along a rough track that led upwards, away from the river. Trees flanked us either side, their wet black trunks shining in the lantern's glow, as though we were entering a secret cave.

'The house has a private situation,' he told me. 'My wife's grandfather built it forty years ago to overlook the mill at the bottom. Do you know anything about the textile industry, Nurse May?'

'Very little, I'm afraid, sir,' I replied, trying to keep up, and panting rather.

'You might have noticed how damp it is. Ideal for keeping

cotton from drying out. Though wool is the thing this side of the border. The further east you go from Liverpool, the fewer cotton mills you'll find. Worsted, fustian, moleskin – that's what we make in this dank little corner of the world. And the mill we passed at the bottom – no doubt you missed it, but you'll see it in the daylight – that's mine. Though I'm a cotton manufacturer, haven't made the switch to wool. My wife's family are the wool makers, and her grandfather the king. He makes the rest of us look as though we're playing at it. Twelve hundred looms he has at Greatrex Mill; thirty thousand yards of cloth per day. Do you know how many miles that is?'

I struggled to keep up. 'I'm afraid not, sir.'

'Eighteen. My output is yards, not miles, though I have twenty-four workers now, up from sixteen when I took it on. Alpacas,' he said abruptly, turning to examine me with the lantern, and finding me nonplussed. 'That's how Champion Greatrex made his fortune. Almost sixty years ago he pioneered the use of alpaca wool in manufacturing. Do you know the beast I talk of?'

'I . . . I don't think I do, sir.'

'He found three dozen bags of it, piled against a warehouse in Merseyside, and said: "I'll take the lot." They couldn't give them away; the wool was too coarse, and nobody had ever done it. Champion was the first to attempt it, and now . . . eighteen miles. Next a baronetcy. Or so everybody says.'

'Goodness.'

'Do you know what country they are native to, alpacas? Take a guess.'

I hadn't even heard of the animal until a minute ago. 'Scotland?'

'Ha!' His laugh was like a gunshot tearing through the darkness. 'You're as likely to find an elephant. No, they are natives of Peru. Nurse May, you appear to travel light – do you have no trunk?'

'It's being sent on.'

'Splendid. Here we are.'

We were crossing another cobble-stoned yard towards a large, flat-fronted house cut into the hillside. To its left was a vague suggestion of outbuildings, and in front the ground fell steeply towards the river and was choked with more trees. The door was large and painted red, and Mr England unlocked it with a key attached to a chain at his waist and set my luggage inside.

'I shall put away the lantern in its proper place or Broadley will have me in the morning. Go straight up to the nursery. The children are asleep, but you will meet them in the morning. Are you hungry?'

'No, thank you, sir.'

How unusual this man was, meeting me himself, discussing his business and offering food. I was quite unnerved and could only mutter my thanks as he strode smartly off. He hadn't given me a lamp, and inside the house was entirely dark. A clock ticked faintly somewhere, and I stretched out a hand for the staircase, eventually finding the banister and following its smooth direction. There was a slightly musty odour of rugs that needed beating, or wet coats drying. The stairs were stone and my feet soundless on them. Upstairs was even darker. Mr England had told me to go to the nursery, but several doors led off the landing. I considered waiting for him to return, but no doubt he already thought me meek and ignorant, and stupid, too, if he found me standing here like a frightened child. I thought of Sim and my cool, direct roommate Bridget; neither of them would hover. They would go downstairs and look for a lamp, perhaps in the kitchen, which appeared to be closed for the night.

There was a faint click, and suddenly a light appeared in a doorway that was opening wider. A woman stepped out in a dressing gown hanging loose over a white nightdress. Her hair was long, falling to her waist and framing a small, round face with a delicate nose and wide, dark eyes. I froze, and the woman did, too, wearing an expression of such fear and bafflement I thought I'd got the wrong house altogether.

'Mrs England?' I said. She looked as though she had seen a ghost. 'I'm Nurse May. I'm dreadfully sorry for disturbing you. I just this minute arrived, ma'am.'

She gripped the lamp more tightly, pulling her dressing gown around herself. 'A nurse?' She sounded frightened. 'Did Charles send for you?'

'I thought you were expecting me, ma'am. I'm the children's nurse.'

'Oh,' she said. Then: 'Oh.' Her puzzled brow cleared, and I swallowed, my mouth dry suddenly.

'Mr England told me to come up to the nursery. Could you show me which room it is, please?'

'I thought you were coming tomorrow.' Her voice was almost a whisper. She was an inch or two shorter than me and much younger than I'd been expecting.

'Tonight, ma'am,' I replied, burning with mortification. 'Mr England collected me from the station. He's putting away the lantern.'

She glanced downstairs; the hall was still in darkness. 'I'll show you to the nursery,' she said, and took the lamp towards a baize door to the left of the stairs. Beyond was a corridor, with one door immediately to the left and another at the end. Cold and numb with embarrassment, I followed obediently through the furthest door. The curtains were drawn across both windows, and she made for the gas jets above the fireplace and turned them on. They hissed gently as she looked about her for a match. I noticed a box behind a candlestick on the mantelpiece and, eager to help, set down my case and retrieved them.

'Please, ma'am, allow me.'

The glass globes leapt to life, startling her. We were standing in a small, comfortable nursery, with papered walls and rugs covering the floorboards. A rocking horse stood in one corner beside a wooden cradle and a miniature painted house. Teddy bears sat stiffly around a small table before it. On a low cupboard a handsome boat with a white sail tipped to one side, surrounded by a menagerie of wooden animals. Against the far wall was a bath chair, with a checked blanket folded on the seat. I was better able to see the mistress; her long hair was a tawny gold colour, her dressing gown apricot silk. She fixed her dark eyes on me, as though expecting me to speak first. The house was cold, as large houses tended to be in summer, with the fires unlit, and as Mrs England had not invited me to take off my cloak or told me where to put my things, I felt quite the intruder.

'Do you prefer ma'am or madam?' I asked.

'Either is fine.'

'And shall I come to you with any queries about the children's clothing and diets?'

She looked lost, as though I had asked her to solve a complicated riddle. 'Yes,' she said without conviction. 'Or Mr England.'

I struggled to contain my surprise. 'I should ask the master?' I repeated.

'It would probably be best.'

Her voice was unrefined. She had a broader accent than her husband; his was more polished, though still unmistakably Yorkshire. There had been a Yorkshirewoman in Balsall Heath who did her shopping every Wednesday, and my new mistress sounded surprisingly indistinct from her.

'I'll leave you to unpack,' she said.

'Will I sleep with the children, ma'am?'

'Is that what you usually do?' Again she adjusted her dressing gown, closing it over her throat.

'Yes,' I said. There was a pause. 'I'm ever so sorry, ma'am. I thought my principal, Miss Simpson, had made clear when I would arrive.'

'Yes, I remember now. She did, of course. Goodnight, Nurse . . .'

'May,' I said.

She left quietly with her lamp and closed the door, making no noise in the corridor. I stood for a long time listening to the house and its deep, shroud-like silence, thinking how far away Perivale Gardens seemed, and how different its mistress to Mrs Radlett. I walked slowly to the chair by the window and lifted a stuffed bear to sit down. I could not help but think backwards, to my journey across London that morning – had it really been only that morning? – and the chaos and vibrancy of the city. I'd spent the best part of a week in a state of idle impatience, waiting for my life to begin again. Those few days seemed glorious now, and sitting in the cold and strange nursery, in a house so silent, even lifeless, I felt as though I'd made a terrible mistake.

A noise started up like a candle sputtering, and I looked about in alarm. Behind me was the window, and I took a moment to realise it was raining. I pulled it open and heard the river, and some night-time bird – an owl or a nightjar. I'd never lived in the country, had never spent a night in it, and thought it a stinging, biting, changeable place. I was used to flats and shops, busy roads and pavements. I'd never used a lantern outside in my life. But the air was clean, and perhaps there would be birdsong in the morning, and a wide, sunny sky. And there would be plenty to occupy the children: scavenger hunts, flower-picking and feather-collecting, and picnics and bicycle rides while it was still warm. Georgina's windowsill garden contained daisies and irises from the London parks; here the fauna would be more varied, and the wildlife, too. Perhaps there would even be deer, made of flesh and not iron. It didn't matter that the house was so quiet, with so much to explore outside.

I lit a lamp, turned off the gaslights and took up my portmanteau, going down the hallway to the night nursery. The room was dark; the curtains closed. In the shadows playing at the edge of the light I caught glimpses of iron bedsteads and wooden floorboards, white sheets and lumpen shapes beneath them. One shifted and stirred, and I turned down the lamp. In the far corner before the window, at the foot of an empty bed, was a cot, covered by a length of lace suspended like a veil. The floorboards creaked as I crossed the room, easing aside the canopy. The lamp threw its friendly glow over a fat baby lying on his back, his fists flung to each side. His chest rose and fell softly. This room, too, was airless, but not warm. I longed to open the window, but worried it might disturb the children, so sat on the edge of my bed and unbuttoned my boots. At Pembridge Square I'd slept with only a sheet, and the window thrown as wide as it would go.

One of my boots fell noisily to the floor, and I froze, waiting for the children to wake. From somewhere in the room came a deep and dreamy sigh, but that was all. I turned the wick all the way down and blew gently across the glass, and the stench of burnt oil swelled and settled. The sheets were cool and welcoming, and the counterpane smelt faintly of mothballs. I nestled into the gloom and waited for sleep.

CHAPTER 4

I woke at six before the children, lifting my clothes from the peg on the wall and dressing quietly. At the foot of my bed was the cot, and beside that another iron bed, the length of which stood against the wall. Two little girls were asleep in it, one fair-haired, one dark. By the far wall, closest to the door, was a third, occupied by a fair-haired boy. The room was small, with a fireplace to the left of my bed, covered by a fender, and a rag rug over the floor-boards. In the right alcove was a built-in press. Without opening the blinds, I passed the sleeping children and gently closed the door.

The nursery wing was on the west side of the house, separated by a green baize door studded with brass. The house beyond was silent, and I stood listening for a moment at the top of the stairs. The first floor was exposed to the hall below, divided by a balustrade that ran the length of the landing. Upstairs and down, the walls were decorated with enormous portraits in gilded frames, their subjects all men dressed in black, with sand-coloured hair and moustaches. I went in search of the kitchen, glancing in the rooms at the front of the house for any servants, but the curtains were still drawn, and there was the lingering scent of cigar smoke. I headed for the back of the house, towards the distant but promising clatter of saucepans.

'Nurse May.'

I froze in surprise and noticed an open door to my right. Mr England was sitting at a breakfast table with a pot of coffee and a newspaper. Though the blind was open, the room had a murky, underwater atmosphere, magnified by dark green walls.

'Good morning, sir,' I said.

'You're an early riser.'

'I've come for hot water for the nursery, sir. Do you know where the housemaid's box is?'

He raised his eyebrows.

'Sorry, sir. I'll ask the mistress.'

'No, no. Ah, Blaise will tell you. She's the general house-maid. I'll introduce you to the servants.'

'Oh, that's very kind, sir, but I'm sure you're busy. I can introduce myself.'

'Nonsense. Take a seat.'

After a split second's hesitation at the idea of the children waking alone upstairs, I pulled one of the slim mahogany chairs from the table.

'Coffee?' he asked. He wore a white shirt beneath a claret-coloured waistcoat. His jacket lay discarded beside him, and his hair was slightly damp.

I shook my head. 'No, thank you, sir.'

'Do you prefer tea?' He smiled, and his moustache turned up at the corners. 'Don't look so anxious, Nurse May, it doesn't come out of your wage. I'll fetch some.'

While he was gone I sat still, holding myself away from the chair. The room had taken on the gloomy presence of the forest; outside a breeze made the trees shiver. A moment later he returned and spread his napkin across his lap.

'I don't wish to disturb your breakfast, sir,' I said. 'I can ask the housekeeper.'

'There is no such person, I'm afraid. I apologise, we are rather a more modest operation than what you are no doubt used to. Tell me, how did you find it in London?'

He took a loud sip, and a moment later the door opened and in came a maid with a silver tray pressed against an enormous bosom. We caught one another's eye, and she set the tea things down before her master.

'For Nurse May, thank you, Blaise.'

Another glance, this one loaded with resentment. She was four or five years older than me, plump and a little matronly in appearance, with small dark eyes like currants.

I thanked her and, making no reply, she let herself out, closing the door with a firm thud.

'Where were we?' Mr England asked. 'Ah, yes, London. Did you like it? Young people do, I suppose.'

'I liked it very much.'

'And what brought you to the north?'

'This position, sir.'

'Quite right.' At once I worried I'd sounded facetious, though he seemed amused. 'Are you from London?'

'Birmingham, sir.'

'The Black Country. They should call this the Grey Country, what with all the chimney smoke. It's why we have to paint the rooms so dark.' He stood and moved to the sideboard, running a finger along the wall and showing me. 'Even with the windows closed it creeps in.' He rubbed it on his trousers and returned to the table, pouring tea and asking if I took milk or sugar. It was as though I'd stumbled into an upside-down world, where the master had taken the place of the mistress. I hadn't been alone with a master or even a man before, and hoped it would not show.

I took an obliging sip. 'Thank you.'

'What is it you want to know?' He folded his newspaper and placed both elbows on the table, clasping his hands.

'I'm sure I shouldn't trouble you with domestics, sir. I can speak to the mistress.'

'You can speak to me.' He smiled expectantly.

'Well,' I said. 'I should be grateful to know if there are any routines in place that I ought to stick to. Of course,

I can take over and ensure everything runs smoothly, but if there is anything you'd like to remain unaltered with timings, meals, that sort of thing . . .'

He grew thoughtful and placed his chin on his knuckles. 'The nurse who was here before you was mine from when I was a boy. I remember her being very old even then, so she was *ancient* when she passed away. I was very fond of her.'

'I'm sorry, sir.'

'Oh, don't be. The children are delighted to have someone closer to their age. I always think you have to *be* a child with a child.'

I could not help but smile in agreement.

'Nurse Nangle was *not* a child. In fact, I once overheard Saul calling her Old Dragon Nangle. Your arrival, I hope, will put an end to any fire-breathing in the nursery. Still, they were horribly upset. I suppose it was a dreadful shock for them, waking and finding she'd gone in the night.'

A beat of silence. 'She died here, sir?'

'Afraid so. Gosh, I hope I haven't spooked you.'

'I don't believe in ghosts.' I remembered the mothball scent of the counterpane and shuddered.

'Very wise.' He rubbed his right eye and looked tired. 'The nursery. Yes.'

At that moment Blaise returned with a rack of toast and a plate of eggs and kippers.

'Thank you, Blaise. Nurse May needs hot water for the children.'

'I'll take some up now, sir.'

'Thank you, Blaise.'

She left, and he covered the kippers in pepper and began to eat. 'Tell me: what's your usual routine?'

I smoothed my apron. 'I get up at six, clean the fire and blacken the grate, polish the brass and sweep and clean the nursery. Once a week I clean the carpet by hand. Then I get the children up for breakfast, then washing, mending, a walk before lunch, a rest after lunch. Late afternoon I'd usually bring the children downstairs, or I could do that after tea. I'm not sure what time Nurse Nangle put them to bed, but it might be best to keep it.'

'Seven, I think,' he said, eating. 'Earlier for the baby. All that sounds perfectly agreeable.'

'Should I go through everything with Mrs England?'

'No need.'

I blinked in surprise, then nodded.

'Saul has a tutor four times a week, from nine until one. Mr Booth. They work in the dining room.'

I nodded again and checked the watch at my waist.

'I arrive home at ten minutes after five. Perhaps you could have the children ready then.'

'Yes, sir. Do the girls have education?'

'They don't.'

'Not a governess?'

'The nursery would be too cramped, do you agree?' He mopped the yolk with some toast, and my stomach rumbled. 'The girls have no need of a tutor. They can read and know basic arithmetic. I taught them to play the piano myself.'

He sounded like my mother. Nurses did not involve themselves in their charges' education, and so I brushed it aside.

'Sir,' I said. 'Last night when I arrived, Mrs England didn't seem to . . .'

He waited.

'Well, she didn't seem to be expecting me.'

He cleared his throat and returned to his breakfast. 'My wife is, ah, forgetful.'

'Of course, we all are, sir, from time to time. Only it took me by surprise; I thought she booked my train.'

There was an uncomfortable pause, the length of which made me regret raising the matter at all. Mr England appeared to interpret this, and changed the subject. 'What made you become a nurse, Nurse May? Plenty of girls like you would prefer to become a clerk, or work in a shop or a factory, where you have your evenings free.' He seemed genuinely curious. I was not used to having my opinion asked and felt myself grow hot and twitchy.

'I have always loved children,' I said.

'Hmph. Can't know many.' Another smile.

'I am the eldest of five, and my parents were always working, so I suppose the role feels natural to me.'

He nodded, though I felt he was unsatisfied.

'As well, I . . .' I cast about for the right words. 'I suppose I wonder what employment could be more interesting than training a child's mind.' Now I had his attention, and went on self-consciously. 'My principal says that the material on which nurses work is more precious than canvas, more exquisite than marble, and more valuable to the world than both of those things. It's about the shaping of people into good human beings.' I flushed scarlet. 'That sounds awfully grand.'

'No, I'm very interested. And I agree: a good seed sown in fertile soil bears fruit from generation to generation. A bad seed, likewise. You're an alienist, Nurse May.'

'I'm sorry, sir, I don't know what that is.'

'They work with minds. Chiefly those of criminals who plead insanity.'

His tone was warm and good-natured, but I felt I had said too much and scrambled up from the chair. 'I must go to the children now, sir.'

'Of course. They are very much looking forward to meeting you. I read about the Norland Institute in *The Times* and thought: *I must have one of those.* I was impressed; it seems like a progressive endeavour.'

'Thank you, sir.'

'I hope the children behave well for you. You come to me if not.'

'Yes, sir.' He did not look like a smacking sort of father. With his humorous dark eyes and light, easy way of speaking, he seemed more likely to take them on his lap and issue a cautionary tale.

'I shall see you in the drawing room later.'

'Yes, sir. Will I tell the mistress?'

He took up his knife and fork and began slicing the kippers. 'You may. Oh, and one more thing,' he said, without looking at me. 'Please lock the nursery at night. You'll find the key in the back of the door.'

I blinked. 'Yes, sir.'

'Good day.'

'Good day, sir.'

The kitchen was large and high-ceilinged, tiled in terracotta, and I found the cook, Mrs Mannion, blacking a complicated-looking range with a stiff brush. Mrs Mannion was rather orange-coloured herself, short and round with hair the colour of marmalade. I introduced myself and asked for the water, and she replied that Blaise had already taken it up.

'Thank you,' I said. 'What time is breakfast served?'

'Eight.'

'And what do you serve the children?'

'Toast and porridge.' She spoke without looking at me, her plump figure folded at the knees on the stone floor.

'Would it be possible for them to have soft-boiled eggs as well?'

She paused with the brush held aloft, tipping an ear towards me and squinting. 'What were that?'

'Soft-boiled eggs,' I said. 'For the children.'

'You want eggs as well?'

'They might have a smaller portion of porridge, if that's more convenient.'

'Might they!' She blew orange hair from her face, but did not seem vexed. 'Very well. I'll add more eggs to the weekly order. Dinner's at twelve, tea's at six, but I do a nursery tea at four usually.'

'Dinner?' I repeated blankly.

She flung the brush in the pot and got to her feet. 'Lunch, dinner, whatever you want to call it.'

'Oh, so lunch is at twelve? And tea is in place of supper?'

'I've no time for riddles!' she cried. 'Dinner's at twelve, tea's at six, like I said.'

I thanked her and left. The kitchen door closed quicker than I expected and caught me from behind. On the stairs I met Blaise coming down with a slop pan. She stood aside for me to pass, saying nothing, her dark eyes fixed on mine.

'Thank you for the water,' I said. 'I would have fetched it myself. I'm Nurse May.'

'Welcome,' she said, with blistering insincerity. A door closed on the landing, and she moved past me down the stairs. Burning with humiliation, I hurried to the nursery and closed the baize door behind me, shutting out the house.

The children were awake. The older girl sat on her bed with the baby, holding him away from the edge while he pulled at her dark hair. Across the room, the younger girl stood at my clothes peg, examining my cloak.

'Good morning,' I said brightly, and she leapt a foot in the air. I strode to the curtains and threw them wide, pulling up the blind and opening the window. The boy sat straight up in bed. 'I am Nurse May.'

'You don't *look* like a nurse,' said the boy. 'You're too young.'

'Well, I am a nurse, and I'm *your* nurse. What's your name?'

'Saul.'

'Pleased to meet you, Master Saul.'

I turned to the others.

'The baby is Charley,' said the eldest girl. 'And that's Millie. I'm Rebecca, but everybody calls me Decca.'

'Nurse Nangle didn't,' said Saul. 'She said nicknames were for labourers.'

'I was only looking at your things,' said Millie. 'I didn't steal anything.'

'I should hope not,' I replied. 'You're welcome to look, but it's polite to ask.'

She put her hands behind her back, as if restraining herself.

'I told her not to,' said Decca. I studied her for a moment. I might have been looking at myself at that age; we had the same long, dark hair, and I realised she was a year younger than Elsie. She had her father's eyes, and there was a gentle seriousness about her, the sense of responsibility found in elder children. She lifted the baby onto her lap and he gurgled. I took him from her and set him on my hip.

'How old is Charley?'

'He was one last month.'

He pressed his fingers into my mouth and I pretended to bite, making the children laugh. The baby was pleasantly fat, with a pinky complexion and golden curls.

'Nurse Nangle *died* in that bed,' Saul announced. 'We woke up and she was a dead body.'

'That will do,' I said firmly, seeing Millie's distress.

'She was Father's nurse, so she *was* old,' Decca offered as compensation.

'She was fat and smelt of cabbage!' This was from Millie, who leapt onto her bed and began jumping.

'You mustn't say that.'

'She was asleep all the time,' Millie expanded. 'She didn't wake up even when I shouted in her ear, and then a black carriage took her away.'

'I expect she was tired after being a nurse for so long,' I said.

'Do *you* sleep, Nurse May?' asked Millie.

'Yes, of course. I woke up before you to get everything ready.'

'We didn't hear you come in. Do you snore?'

'Little girls shouldn't ask questions like that.'

'Can you play jacks?' asked Saul.

'Yes, though I prefer board games.'

'Draughts?'

'Yes. Now, that's enough chit-chat for the time being. Decca, if you'll show me where everything is, I'll help you all get dressed.'

The morning passed in a blur of chaos. I washed and dressed the children, noticing how their clothes fitted them badly and needed adjusting. The girls' petticoats wanted letting down, as did Saul's shorts, which showed his white thighs, and all of them except Charley needed new shoes. I enquired about the bath chair, and Saul told me it was his; he suffered from asthma and used it while convalescing. Both rooms were dusty and poorly ventilated. The day nursery window got stuck an inch from the sill, and I made a mental note to have it looked at.

Blaise brought breakfast in on a vast silver tray: porridge, eggs and toast. She spoke not a word when I thanked her, her jaw set hard. While the children helped themselves, I fed the baby, wiping his fat chin with a napkin. The table-cloth was crusted with ancient soup and oily stains, and had evidently avoided many wash days. I noticed an unpleasant smell and went to investigate, pulling forwards a cupboard where it was most pungent, and finding a stash of rotten food banked up against the skirting board. Saul turned beetroot and confessed: Nurse Nangle made him eat foods he did not like, of which there were many, with fish, aspic and tongue topping the list. As the old nurse's eyesight was poor, he would feign interest in something on the other side of the room and evict it from his pocket.

I fetched a pail and scraped up fishbones, bacon rind and a substantial amount of boiled cabbage, then took it down to the kitchen to empty into the waste. In the hall I met Tilda, the parlourmaid, coming in the other direction. She was plump and Germanic in appearance, with honey-coloured hair arranged attractively in coils. She told me where I could find what I needed and moved off with the dustpan. The breakfast room was empty, the crimson tablecloth cleared of crumbs.

I hurried back to the nursery to finish my morning tasks, dusting and sweeping the rooms and cleaning the fireplace, which had neither been lit nor swept in several months. The children watched me, intrigued by the novelty, and were enraptured when I changed my uniform afterwards, stripping to my shift in front of them and climbing into my fawn dress. I told them it wasn't polite to look, and they were obedient enough to turn away.

I thought Mrs England might call in after breakfast, but the morning passed with no interruption, and at nine o'clock Saul took himself downstairs for his lesson. I put Charley down for his nap and lifted the duster to the bookshelf.

'Does your mother come to the nursery?' I asked the girls.

'Sometimes,' said Decca.

'She *never* does,' said Millie.

'She does, Millie. She does sometimes, like on our birthdays,' Decca insisted. I felt a twinge of sympathy.

'And you two don't have lessons?'

'No.'

'Father taught us to read and write.'

I noticed Decca's use of the past tense. Things were different for the England girls; they were not like Elsie and me. For us education was like a gate, or a bridge leading from one bank to another. I thought about what their father had said to me: *girls like you*. I had not told him I did not wish for free evenings and holidays, had no desire to be home for dinner and sleep in my own bed. Free time allowed the mind to wander, and that was no good for me at all.

At two minutes before one, I took Charley downstairs to collect Saul. I'd left the girls reading, though it was becoming clear Millie had no patience for it, and preferred to play with her toys – every one of them, for a minute or two each, before moving on to another. Charley was teething and grouchy. All morning I'd had to prise things from his mouth: tin soldiers, the fire poker, even a wood-louse. The house, or at least the nursery, was infested with them; I'd seen several crouching at the skirting boards and kept gathering them up in my apron to toss from the window. I'd been half-listening for a knock from Mrs England, but still none came, and now the kitchen would be preparing lunch. Perhaps she would visit after lunch, or *dinner*, I thought, or perhaps she was out, was one of those social mothers who lived in a whirlwind of lace and calling cards. Her bedroom door remained closed all morning. I would ask the servants at dinner, I decided, reminding myself that it took time to learn the routines and customs of a house, and the people within it.

The long-case clock in the hall chimed once, and from the dining room came the scrape of chairs. I set Charley on the ground and held both of his hands; his legs bowed beneath him, and when his brother appeared he shrieked with delight.

'Hello,' said Mr Booth. 'You must be the nurse.' He pronounced it 'nuss'. He wore a tie and a brown cap, like an overgrown schoolboy, and there was a battered satchel at his hip. He was younger than I'd imagined, in his mid-twenties, and small, though his hands were large. His face was the kind that seemed determined to make the best of every situation, and his smile appeared a permanent fixture beneath a short brown moustache. I liked him at once.

Saul skimmed the banister with a long glossy feather and said: 'Nurse May sleeps in Nurse Nangle's bed.'

'Good afternoon, Mr Booth,' I said.

'Pleased to meet you. Thank you for the oranges. A nice touch.'

I nodded. I had asked Mrs Mannion to slice some and put them in a little dish for the lesson; Sim always said that children needed refreshment while learning, and I decided I would arrange fresh fruit each day.

'You're welcome. What do you have there, Master Saul?'

'I found it in the woods.'

'He wanted to use it for a quill, but I told him we use pens in this house, and this century,' said Mr Booth.

'Perhaps you should return it to where you found it,' I said. 'Its owner might be looking for it.'

Saul stared at me. 'Birds don't *look* for their feathers. Anyway, it's a pheasant. Mr Booth told me.'

Mr Booth plucked it from his fingers. Its pattern was complex and delicate, like the coat of a moth. 'Better in a hat than a school room,' he said, and gave it to Charley, who immediately clamped his gums around it. We all laughed, and at that moment Blaise entered from the kitchen.

'I wondered where you'd got to,' she said. At first I thought she meant Saul and wondered why on earth she would need him. I was even more astonished when Mr Booth replied.

'I'm coming. Tell Mrs Mannion I hope there's some brack in there, else it won't be worth my while.'

Blaise rolled her eyes, though she was smiling, and swung back through the door.

'Do you know the servants?' I asked, feeling oddly disappointed.

'Aye. Blaise is my fiancée.'

I laughed again, though he did not, and smiled at me

in puzzlement. Quickly I said: 'How lovely. When are you getting married?'

'Next month.'

'Congratulations.'

'Thank you.'

Saul hung from the iron banister, limp with boredom. 'Well, I've been summoned.'

'Pleased to meet you,' I said, lifting the baby. Mr Booth walked towards to the kitchen, whistling, his satchel banging against his hip. On the stairs, once I'd heard the kitchen door thud shut, I asked Saul if his tutor often stayed after his lesson.

'Sometimes.' He shrugged. 'What's for dinner?'

'It will be a surprise.' I hadn't yet drafted a menu with Mrs Mannion; our first meeting had made me decide to wait until the following day.

'What are we doing after?'

'I thought we'd go for a walk.'

'A *walk*! May I run?'

'You may run, if you wish.'

There was the soft click of a door opening, and Mrs England appeared on the landing. She wore a cream skirt and lace bodice, with a brooch at her throat. Her hands were bare, and she stood still when she saw us.

'Ma'am,' I said, curtseying, and hoisting Charley higher.

'Good morning,' she replied, though it was after one. There was a moment or two of awkward silence, in which I waited for her to make some remark or acknowledge her children, but she let herself into the bathroom and closed the door.

She'd left her bedroom open; through the gap I saw the corner of an iron bed draped with an ivory counterpane, and beyond, a window framing a wall of brown and green. The hillside rose steeply from the back of the house, and the trees leered in at the windows. The bathroom was silent, and I felt instinctively that she was standing on the other side of the door, waiting for us to leave. Peals of laughter carried upstairs from the kitchen. I paused, listening for a moment, before prising the feather again from Charley, and closing the baize door.

CHAPTER 5

The Englands were Roman Catholic, and on my first Sunday in Yorkshire I accompanied them to church. The seven of us squashed into the carriage to travel two miles to town, with the servants going before us on foot; they took their half-day on Sundays and had prepared a cold lunch for when we returned.

I'd met the scullerymaid, Emily, on my first morning, taking Charley's nappies down to the laundry room in a pail. Blaise leant against the light blue wall, picking her fingernails. 'Nurse Nangle washed them herself,' she said, indicating the bucket. Emily, a wisp of a girl who suffered badly with blemishes, glanced at her, then looked bashfully at me. I said nothing and set the bucket on the floor. Blaise raised her eyebrows, and with them the corner of her

STACEY HALLS
mouth in a snarl. 'Too good for washing work?' she retorted. I replied that I couldn't leave the children for any length of time. With that, she peeled herself from the wall and moved past me to the kitchen. Emily reached for the pail without a word.
We bumped along the track through dappled woodland. My daily walks with the children had revealed how remote the house was, with no neighbours on the hillside and the mill crouching like a secret at the bottom of the valley. I had expected Yorkshire to be a barren moorland hemmed here and there with grey stone villages, but here the land-scape was like something from a dream, or a fairy tale. Trees rose like columns of smoke wearing mossy lime jackets, and ferns burst from the damp ground like foun-tains. The ground was steep and creviced, with dark gorges and silvery waterfalls gushing into the fast brown river at the bottom. The high valley walls trapped smoke from the factories, which mixed with low clouds to make a gloomy, heavy atmosphere, but that morning the air had cleared and the sky was bright blue.

The children showed me their favourite places: large boulders, called crags, which were scattered across the forest and heaped in clumsy piles, some of them thirty feet high, which were naturally furnished with gaps and holes for hiding. They took me to see the stepping stones and begged me to run across the river. Saul skipped easily from one side to the other and back again, laughing when I refused to go closer than the bank. They told me Nurse

70

Nangle never took the children into the forest. Saul was acquiring a tally of my and Nurse Nangle's habits and preferences, but it was clear the catalogue tipped in my favour: the old nurse served leftovers from the previous meal at the next one, allowed them to read only the Bible on Sundays and dried them very hard after washing. How different life here was to the park lawns and creamy terraces I was used to; here the children scrambled up banks and hid behind trees, flitting in and out of sight. Saul was skilled at it, disappearing and leaping out to surprise us. Millie stayed close to me and the pram, bumping up against it, and Decca ambled beside us, gathering wildflowers. She was knowledgeable about the flora and fauna, showing me colonies of beech trees and little clumps of mushrooms. She knew the names of them all, and explained how only the hardiest grew in the close shadows cast by the trees that blocked the light.

Decca sat opposite me in the carriage, uncomfortable in her Sunday best. She was different to her sister; Millie had spent all morning choosing hair ribbons and insisted on changing the satin band around her hat. Their father sat with an arm draped loosely behind his son, their mother in the corner with a fussy little bag in her lap. Mrs England had not offered to take the baby, had not visited the nursery at all in the four days I had been there. Every evening I took the children to their parents in the drawing room, and every evening their father played with them while their mother looked on. She perched on the

71

arm of a chair, as though she had no intention of staying, and looked visibly relieved when half an hour passed and Tilda announced dinner.

So little interaction meant I barely had the measure of Mrs England, and I admit I was disappointed by what I'd seen so far. I thought often, in those early days, of Mrs Radlett, and how she would smuggle a slice of tart up to me from the kitchen or play with us in the garden, kneeling on the grass with no care for how it stained her skirts. Mrs England kept to her bedroom, taking her breakfast there each morning and surfacing around noon to eat with her husband in the dining room, when Mr England came home from the mill at a quarter past twelve each day. She often wore white and drifted about quietly, her slippers making no noise on the stone floors, as though she was made of crepe. Strangest of all was how Mr England acted like both master and mistress. He instructed me to direct all queries to him, and even came, on occasion, to the nursery to kiss the children goodnight. I showed him the weekly menu I designed before giving it to Mrs Mannion; I asked him for money to replenish the medicine cabinet; I told him the children needed new shoes. With each request and triviality, I worried I was a pain, that he'd come to resent the sight of me, but it seemed my anxiety was unfounded: he was always cheerful and high-humoured, generous with jokes and compliments. The previous evening he told me the nursery had never been so well organised, and I felt the warm glow of victory.

'Do your family attend church, Nurse May?' he asked me now. I had been looking out of the window at the trees, quite in my own world.

'No, sir.'

On Sundays we all washed the week's produce, while Father balanced the books. The large scrubbed table was the beating heart of our home, where we did everything: sewing, peeling, kneading, eating. Father sat in his shirt-sleeves, his eyebrows knitting together over the bookkeeping, while we worked around him and Mother cooked. If Ted and Archie made too much noise, he would send them out. He had no head for sums and often asked me to check them. I followed the columns with a finger, aware of his eyes flicking anxiously from the ink to my face. Half the time they were wrong, and I would gently correct them. 'What would I do without you, Rhubarb?' he would say, sliding the book back towards him with a sigh.

Mrs England glanced at me from beneath a wide hat. At her neck she wore a slim gold crucifix.

'I wish *we* didn't have to go to church,' said Saul. 'It's dull and smelly.'

Mr England's moustache twitched; our eyes met, and he looked away. 'Don't let's put Nurse May off. Have you ever been to mass before?'

'No, sir.'

'How's your Latin?'

'Poor, sir, I'm afraid.'

'Then you might find your attention wandering. Here we are.'

In the town, faces turned towards the carriage and peered through the window. The church stood on a wide, dusty thoroughfare opposite a small park. Beyond the neat lawns and flowerbeds, horses pulled heaped barges along a canal. The church was cool and musty-smelling; we found two pews at the front and sat down. Mr and Mrs England and Saul slid into the first, and I took the second with the girls and the baby. The children were on their best behaviour, and even Millie was quiet, though she fidgeted slightly as the priest droned on. The Englands were among two or three of the best-dressed families; the congregation appeared to be made up of ordinary working people, who glanced every so often at the children and me.

Ten minutes into the sermon, Charley began to cry. I put a finger in his mouth, and then, when he failed to suck, gave him a cloth mouse I'd made from a handker-chief. But he paid no interest, contorting himself in a way I knew would lead to screaming. As I gathered him up to take him out, Mrs England turned.

'I'll take him,' she whispered. Too surprised to protest, I passed him over the pew and she shuffled past her son and husband and swept down the aisle, leaving a faint scent of talcum powder.

I watched her retreat over my shoulder. Several pairs of eyes landed on me, and I returned my gaze to the front.

Both of the girls were daydreaming, staring vacantly. Decca yawned. After a few minutes the church door squeaked open and soft footsteps approached. Mrs England gave me Charley, who was red-cheeked but silent, and took up her place on the bench. I noticed she still had her silk bag; she set it down beside her and lifted her hymn book with spotless gloves.

The congregation rose and began exiting their pews to queue before the altar. I asked Decca what the priest was handing out at the front and she replied that it was communion, when adults were given bread and wine, and children a blessing. The three of them automatically followed their parents to join the slowly moving line. Mr England nodded at various people and a great number met my eye on their way past. I was quite the exhibit, displayed in my uniform for all to see, though one or two younger girls smiled shyly. I was relieved when Charley started up whimpering before the Englands reached the altar. I took him out at once, feeling a dozen pairs of eyes sweep over me; it gave me the sensation of walking through a cobweb, and I longed to shake myself free.

I carried Charley across the road to the little park, setting him down on a path that curved through pretty borders towards a war memorial. With it being Sunday morning, it was almost empty; the only other occupant was a man reading a newspaper on a green-painted bench. Charley toddled happily towards a bed bursting with pansies and marigolds, and I stopped him from planting his feet in the soil, taking his hand and wandering with him in the direction of the canal.

The man on the bench wished me a good morning, and I returned it.

'Determined little one, ain't he?' he went on.

'Yes,' I said.

'I bet you have your nurse running rings around you.' He spoke directly to Charley, who fell forwards, landing on his fists. At once he began to cry, and I lifted him and wiped his hands with the cloth mouse. The man sat forwards and rested his elbows on his knees. His skin was tanned and sun-cracked, and he had labourer's hands, the kind so embedded with dirt and oil they would never come clean. His fingernails were blackened at the beds.

'You must be the England nurse.'

'I am.'

'Have you lost the others?'

It took me a moment to realise he was joking. 'No, sir,' I said.

He smirked. 'You don't have to "sir" me.'

I lifted Charley to my hip and coldly wished him good day.

Mass had finished, and people were pouring from the church into the road. The Englands' carriage was drawn up against the railings, with their coachman, Broadley – a hardy, weathered old Yorkshireman – sitting up front, chewing something resistant and staring blankly at the road. I glanced about for the others. Mr England was talking to a smartly dressed man standing beside a woman wearing a large hat and a frothy gown. Two older girls lingered, with the children bunched around them, and Saul spoke to a boy his age in a green cap and suit. Mrs England, standing off to the right, was looking directly at me. She watched me cross the road.

'Sorry to keep you waiting, ma'am,' I said.

Her eyes flicked over my shoulder, towards the park, then she turned and climbed into the carriage. I followed with the children, and a moment later Mr England put in his head.

'I'm going to Laithe Hall,' he announced. Mrs England nodded and resumed gazing out of the window, her face obscured by her hat. 'Cheerio, cherubs,' he trilled to the children, and with gusto slammed the door.

That night, when the children were asleep, I locked the nursery door, took off my boots and sat on my bed to write to Elsie. My back ached; holding Charley made my muscles tense and tighten, and I pushed my knuckles into my shoulders, rolling them and settling against the wall as my bones rearrange themselves. Writing to my sister was like a treat I saved up for; I compiled little stories and anecdotes in my mind and took pleasure in recording them. I imagined her reading at the kitchen table, her wrist at her temple, and smiled. I spread out my blotting and writing paper, bought from a stationer's on the Uxbridge Road, and decorated with ivy and mistletoe; it was discounted Christmas stock, but so thick and creamy I used it all year round.

Dear Elsie. I blew gently on the ink to dry it, and reached for Elsie's bear Herbie, who she gave me when I left home. He was lumpy, made of wool, and somehow still smelt of her. I wondered if there was a word for homesickness not for a place but for people; I didn't miss the flat itself or our bedroom, only the warm, unique feeling of being around those who knew me best. Here nobody called me Ruby. Nobody knew me at all.

The nursery walls were decorated with framed pictures, and opposite my bed was a reproduction of a fair-haired little girl with a kitten and a ball of twine. As a girl I kept a scrapbook, cutting and pasting images of fat-legged children in nurseries with their pets. I longed for a dog or a cat, but our flat above the shop made it impossible to have either. We kept chickens in the yard, collecting their eggs for breakfast, and Damson the pony lived in a lean-to with a shabby iron roof. When I was ten, Robbie had pulled back the curtains one morning to find it empty. 'Damson's gone!' came his shriek from the bedroom. I looked up from the range, where I was frying dripping. The door to the staircase stood open to let out the fumes. 'Damson's got out!' Robbie came streaking through, flinging himself down the stairs. Mother was slicing a loaf at the dresser and did not look up. I hurried through to the bedroom and peered down at the yard, at the peeling privy and coal house, the stacked delivery crates, as though he might have been hiding behind them. The hens scratched indifferently in their coop. The gate to the alley was bolted.

'The horse isn't there,' I repeated to my mother's back. She went on slicing.

'Your father's sold it.'

'He *what*?'

'The pan's burning.'

I returned to the dripping, my mind wiped clean with shock. Ted thundered down the stairs after Robbie, pulling on his boots. 'Who's he sold it to?'

'I don't know.'

'But he's ours,' I said thickly, through the prick of tears. 'He *works* for us.'

'Hush, now, and serve breakfast. Your father'll be back in a minute.'

Damson was never spoken of again.

I hope this finds you well. More than a year had passed since I'd seen my sister. One Saturday in spring I caught the train to visit her and Robbie in Birmingham. We met at one o'clock by the statue of Horatio Nelson; I'd promised to take them to one of the nicer tea rooms off the Bull Ring, with gold-rimmed saucers and lace tablecloths. I saw my brother first, not recognising the lanky girl beside him in a checked blouse and a long, grown-up skirt. She'd tied gingham ribbons in her plaits to match her blouse.

Smiling, I took hold of one and gave it a tug. She beamed back. It was an old trick; I used to tell her she had lucky hair and pulled it to make a wish. Robbie, too, had transformed: standing before me was a young man with a fledgling moustache wearing Father's old clothes.

I wrote by lamplight as the evening drew in. The window was open, and a breeze moved the curtain and made the blind slap against the frame. I got up to close it so the children wouldn't be disturbed. Outside it was dim but not dark, though the trees absorbed the fading light, and across the yard I saw an outline. Mr England was standing where the ground dipped down with his back to the house, staring out at the valley. Yellow pinpricks from distant farmhouses studded the hillside, lighting it up like stars. The hot amber tip of his cigar glowed brightly, sweeping up and down as he smoked. He had a habit of leaving cigar tips wherever he cut them; the little brown nubs were scattered around the house like breadcrumbs, and I collected the ones the maids had missed, putting them in my pocket out of Charley's reach.

In one swift movement he threw down the cigar and turned, looking up at the house. I shrank away and let go of the blind, holding myself still as it tapped against the glass. A few seconds later I heard his tread on the cobbles, then the front door opened and closed. Quietly, I sunk to my knees and pulled my trunk from beneath the bed. It had arrived the previous morning, and the sight of it was like a friend. I held the lamp to it and rummaged for stamps, finding the booklet and fixing one to the envelope. Before I closed it, out of habit I felt for the black tea tin, where I kept my most precious things, and passed a hand over the lid. *Not tonight.*

A small sniff, a shuffle. I turned and saw Millie, propped on her elbows, watching me between the iron bars of her bed.

'What are you doing?' she asked.

'Nothing,' I whispered, pushing the trunk into the shadows. 'Go back to sleep.'

CHAPTER 6

Behind Mr England's mill was a flat, glassy pond, used now, in the age of steam power, only by ducks and other wildfowl. One blue and gold afternoon I asked the kitchen for some stale bread, returning to the nursery with a tea cloth of booty to cries of delight. They raced to finish their soup, and Decca saved her roll to determine whether ducks liked butter. The longer I spent with Decca, the more I found to like. She was thoughtful and intelligent, tender and shy, and she cared passionately for nature. She appeared at my side with a safety pin when I changed Charley's nappies and lit the lamps each evening before I could. She tidied away whatever she used or played with, unlike her sister and brother, who left trails of destruction; she tidied them, too. Each night

I read from *The Wonderful Wizard of Oz*, and though all of them listened, Decca was enraptured, but she never complained when I returned the book to the shelf, never asked for anything more than what was given to her. I wondered at her sometimes: her mother appeared to have been absent most of her life, but she did not seem marked by it.

It was quarter to two by the time we left the house. Charley was in his pram and cross about it, and I was attempting to push it through the gate when Mr Booth appeared around the side, wheeling his bicycle.

'Nurse May.' He came at once to help me, propping his bicycle against a tree and lifting the pram through.

'Thank you,' I said, a touch discomposed.

'Where are you off to?'

'The lodge and back, to post a letter.'

'But we're feeding the ducks first!' Millie cried.

'Is that so?' He set off walking with us down the track. Decca stayed by my side, while Millie and Saul fell into step either side of Mr Booth and his bicycle. Saul's lessons finished at one, meaning Mr Booth had been in the kitchen three-quarters of an hour. After he left each day, I noticed a slight and temporary improvement in Blaise's manner, before the sallowness descended again.

'Nurse May has been teaching us spellings with angry grans,' Millie told him, and boldly took his hand.

'Is that so?' he said again, puzzled. 'What is an angry gran when it's at home?'

'She means anagrams,' said Decca, as we drew up along-side them.

'That sounds like a splendid game,' he said. 'What can you spell?'

'Tree and wood and river,' Millie announced. 'And cat and bat and ball.'

'Those are baby words,' said Saul. 'I bet you can't spell Indian or pirate.'

'Not everybody has a tutor,' I reminded him.

'Did you have a tutor, Nurse May?' he asked.

'No. I went to school.'

'Can I go to school?' cried Millie. 'I want to go to school.'

Mr Booth caught my eye.

'Not today,' I replied.

'When, then?'

'My father is the schoolmaster,' Mr Booth cut in. 'He teaches lots of boys and girls before they go off to work.'

Millie frowned. 'Work where?'

'In the mills and factories. Like your father's.'

The children missed the slight thorniness in his tone.

'Do you work at the school?' asked Millie.

'No, stupid.'

'Saul!' I scolded.

'I work at people's houses,' Mr Booth told Millie. 'And there's nothing stupid about asking questions, so don't stop.'

'But that's enough for today,' I told them. 'Run along to the pond.'

Millie set off at a sprint beside her brother. Decca followed, and they raced across the bridge.

'It's a shame they won't school them,' Mr Booth said as we walked beside each other. 'There are girls with no shoes better educated than those two.'

To agree would have been disloyal, but he did not seem to expect a reply. I'd begun teaching them spellings with tiles from a word game, though it was not my duty. With Saul away from the nursery most mornings and Charley asleep, we made a schoolroom of the breakfast table using my spare copybooks from Norland. I hadn't told them to keep it a secret, though Decca said nothing to their parents, and their father kept them so occupied in the drawing room Millie was too distracted to boast. I knew it would displease Sim. Our training had been distinct: our job was to teach morals and manners, not arithmetic.

'I hope we haven't kept you,' I said to Mr Booth.

'Not at all,' he replied. 'I'm going the way of the lodge if you'd like me to post your letter. Save you the walk.'

'Oh,' I said. 'That's very kind.'

I took it from my cloak and passed it to him. He glanced at the front, and too late I realised my mistake.

'Writing home?' He slipped it into his satchel. 'Sorry, didn't mean to look.'

My heart quickened and I tried to seem cheerful. 'My sister,' I said.

'Older or younger?'

After a moment I said: 'Younger.'

'Well, I'd best get on. I teach at Laithe Hall in the afternoons. It's only over the hill. Have you been yet?'

'No, but the name's familiar. Mr England went there after church.'

'It's his brother-in-law's house. Well, mansion, really. Michael Greatrex.'

'Greatrex,' I said. 'So he's related to the mistress?'

'It's her brother.'

I frowned. 'The man I saw on Sunday didn't seem like her brother; she barely spoke to him.' Mr Booth said nothing and began walking again. 'Do they have two daughters and a son?'

'Anne, Enid and Master Michael, my pupil.'

'Then it was them. But . . . how strange.' I shook my head.

'*All happy families are alike; each unhappy family is unhappy in its own way.*'

'I beg your pardon?'

'Tolstoy. *Anna Karenina?*'

I shook my head.

'I'll lend it to you, if its themes aren't too scandalous for the nursery.' He gave a wicked smile. 'Good day, Nurse May.'

I watched him cycle away and turn right out of the mill yard towards town. Mr Booth was intelligent, clearly, far cleverer than I was, though good-natured and generous with it. He'd been kind to the children and held Millie's hand. But something about him suggested a deeper complexity: the comment he had made about their wealth carried more than a hint of resentment. Or was it disdain? My cheeks felt hot; I held my fingers to them and went to find the children.

Cotton drifted through the air like ash, landing on my cloak and making it seem as though I'd pushed the pram through a snowstorm. Like most of the water mills built a hundred years before, England Mill was a more modest enterprise than the glittering, thunderous constructions in larger towns and cities. Its three storeys each bore six windows, and a stout chimney stuck like a finger into the sky. The mill itself was not much larger than Hardcastle House, though outbuildings sprawled around it: there were the stables, above which Broadley slept with his grandson Ben, the groom, as well as five store rooms and a toll house, which collected a levy for the bridge. A warehouse and weaving shed completed the ensemble, and on the west bank the old boiler house was used to store wood.

Behind the mill the children threw their bread into the pond, and three or four ducks soon multiplied to a frenzy. I stood at a distance with Charley's pram facing the water; he sat up watching, clapping his hands in delight.

'Those ducks will be too fat to fly,' said a voice.

I spun around to find Mr England, who had approached from the path. I straightened my cloak.

'Good afternoon, sir. I hope you don't mind me bringing the children.'

'Of course not. I only wish I'd brought a loaf myself.' He chucked Charley under the chin, and the child squealed with pleasure.

'Father, can we go in the engine room?' Saul asked.

'Mr England is working,' I told him. A stray bit of bread landed on Charley's blanket, and I swept it up before it could reach his mouth.

'I don't see why not,' said their father. 'Nurse May hasn't seen the mill, after all.'

'Sir, there's no need on my account.'

'It wouldn't interest you?' he asked mildly.

'Oh, it would. Only . . . is it safe for the children?' I thought of what Sim would say if she knew I'd taken my female charges inside a manufactory, though privately I was intrigued.

'I admire your concern. It's very safe, I assure you. They've been before, haven't you, girls? They like watching the workers.'

'I like the snow,' said Millie.

'The cotton,' her father corrected, offering his arm to her as a gentleman might. I turned Charley's pram and followed, bitten by curiosity, and quite buoyed at the prospect of escaping mud and fowl for a short while.

He led us through a side door into a dark, narrow room stacked with sacks and ropes, and out into a cavernous hall, with a staircase extending up three floors. Cotton drifted freely, and a boy my brother Archie's age swept the floor into snowdrifts, only for another pale blanket to take its place. Years ago the paper mill in Balsall Heath had burnt down, and my brothers and I stuck out our tongues to catch the powdery bits of parchment that fell for days from the sky.

We passed along a corridor lit with lamps towards a great roaring sound and a sulphurous stench that made me want to pinch my nose. Saul skipped through, and I hung back with the pram.

'The engine room,' he announced.

'I don't like it in there,' Millie announced. 'It's dark and noisy.'

'I'll stay with you,' said Decca.

I drew the pram up at the doorway. 'After you, Nurse May,' said Mr England.

'I shouldn't, sir.'

'Nonsense. The pram will fit in. Here, let me. Come on, girls.'

To my astonishment, he took the handlebar and pushed it himself. The engine room was dark, shut away from light and air, with two raging furnaces manned by three filthy men in vests, slick as seals from sweat and coal dust. Their skin was charcoal, the whites of their eyes like lanterns. They did not stop their work to speak to us, shovelling coal from a bank against the wall into the greedy, gaping mouths of the stoves. Even if they had, we likely wouldn't have heard them, so noisy was it in there, and so intensely hot. Saul asked if he could empty a shovel into the fire, and his father helped him.

Overwhelmed by the heat and noise, Charley started crying, and with relief I manoeuvred him out to the cool stairwell. Decca and Millie followed, and a few minutes later the England men emerged, their faces shining with triumph.

'Better than feeding the ducks?' Mr England enquired.

'*I* don't think so,' said Millie. Decca said nothing; she spoke seldom around her parents, and even less in front of the servants and Mr Booth. 'Can we see the snow room?' Millie asked. 'Oh, please, *please!*'

'Very well,' her father said. 'You lead the way. Ah.' He remembered the pram. 'Young Charles, come with me.' And he leant over the pram and took out the baby. I followed, stunned, as we climbed towards the rhythmic pounding above. On the first floor, Mr England pushed open an enormous pair of peeling blue doors. The noise was deafening. Stretching the length of the mill, supported by iron pillars, was one of the vastest rooms I'd ever seen. The floor was thick with lint and light poured through the high windows, illuminating the blizzard of dust and fluff and fabric; it was like being inside a pillow, or a thundercloud, with all the noise and chaos. There were five machines on either side of a narrow aisle, with vast drawers sliding rapidly in and out so fast it made me giddy. Nine or ten workers attended them, but were either too preoccupied to notice us or had been told not to. We passed them unobserved, and it would have been rude to study them. Awkward with no baby in my arms or pram to push, I reached for Decca's hand and squeezed it. The windows were sealed for humidity, and condensation beaded the windows. With Mr England unable to speak over the commotion, I studied the components of the looms and found them unfathomable, with the yarn stretching like strings of dough between white rolling pins. I had the vague sensation of being watched, and turned to see a boy of fourteen or fifteen staring at me from beneath the brim of his cap. He was quite bold about it, and did not look away when I caught him, following me with his eyes. I put my back to him, and continued down the length of the room.

The children knew to keep away from the machines, and walked in single file. The youngest worker was a boy Decca's age. He wore white trousers, smeared with dust, and darted quick as a flash beneath a machine, disappearing from sight. The loom ploughed open and closed once, twice, three times, and eventually he crawled out and took up his post. Despite the oil and dust, his feet were bare, and as he picked his way across the floor I saw his soles were dark grey. Next to him stood a girl of around sixteen, who had a deep, mature cough. She covered her mouth and gave in to it, her body racking with the effort. Her hair hung down her cheeks in greasy strands. I realised I was staring at her, and turned away to examine a wheel, half reaching out and thinking better of it. Walking back the way we came, Decca slipped; her hand was still in mine and I gripped her tightly as she found her footing.

Mr England returned Charley to me on the staircase. I felt it would be polite to ask a question, and enquired how many looms he kept. 'Nineteen,' he replied, sounding pleased. 'There were sixteen when I took over. Did you visit your father at work as a girl?'

'We lived above the shop,' I replied, my ears ringing. 'So we were never really away from it.'

'What sort of shop?'

'A greengrocer, though it's a general grocery now.'

'A businessman. He and I have something in common.'

The two men were incomparable. I imagined my father sitting at Mr England's wide mahogany desk in his grocer's coat, dirtying the cream paper with soiled fingers. At the end of each day he would stand at the kitchen basin as the water turned a deep, earthy brown. I pictured him wearing Mr England's clothes, a glass of brandy at his wrist, cigar smoke curling above him in the lamplight. My father had never smoked in his life, and signed the temperance pledge before I was born.

'And how is trade?' Mr England asked.

'Good, thank you, sir.'

We visited the second floor, which was much the same as the first, and Mr England spoke with an overseer, who nodded at the children out of courtesy and ignored me. I wished to ask him the age of the youngest worker, but after my conversation with Mr Booth, thought it might be improper. Instead, I asked where the cotton came from.

'The Rochdale canal.' There was a pause, and he smiled

broadly. I laughed, not understanding, and returned Charley to the pram. 'Australia, nowadays,' he said. 'Though I'm one of the last remaining cotton manufacturers in these parts. Everyone else moved to wool, or the finishing of fustian: corduroy, twill, velveteen, moleskin.' He reached for my cloak and held the seam between finger and thumb. I felt my pulse quicken. 'This is serge, a type of twill. Perhaps it was made in this valley.'

We were standing outside in the yard. Looking tired suddenly, he removed a cigar from a silver travel case kept inside his breast pocket. I wondered at all the material inside; the place would go up in seconds.

'No smoking in the mill,' he said to me, as though reading my mind. 'A dismissible offence, even for me.'

I thought that was reasonable of him; it at least explained the frequency with which he smoked at home. I told him I found the tour interesting, and he looked pleased, and said I was welcome at the mill any time. Going back over the stone bridge and up the hill, I felt brighter, more lively; I had seen my master at work, a successful manufacturer who appeared good to his staff. Though I had no desire to work in a factory with roaring furnaces and greasy men, with wheels spinning and frames shuddering back and forth, there was something appealing about being a small, vital part of such a system, where everybody and every thing had its rank and occupation.

Most mornings I saw from the nursery window the workers arriving, trickling down the lane across the valley like a line of ants. The women were almost concealed by the trees, wrapped in plain grey and brown shawls. Nobody ever passed Hardcastle House, but at the top of the hill was a village, and once or twice I'd seen people cross the bridge and disappear into the trees on our side. The hill was exceptionally steep, with no clear footpath; it would be a hard climb twice a day, more so in winter. I thought of the coughing girl: who she lived with and what her house looked like. I looked at my white gloves, wrapped around Charley's fat legs, and wondered what she thought of me. I wondered if she knew we were not so different at all.

That evening I went to light the lamps in the night nursery and found something on my pillow: a sprig of flowers, with dark stems and white, cloudy blooms like puffballs, or rabbit tails. I picked it up to examine it, feeling quite strange and nervous, as though I'd done something sly. There was a noise in the corridor; Millie came looking for me, and I hid it beneath the pillow. Later, when the children were asleep, I took down Decca's encyclopaedia of botany from the shelf, searching its pages for a match and finding it under G: *gossypium hirsutum*. Cotton. I held it to the lamplight and stroked its snowy buds.

CHAPTER 7

Life at Hardcastle House settled into a rhythm, and the new became familiar. A full spring clean of both nurseries revealed the full extent of Nurse Nangle's neglect, or poor eyesight. No object or corner escaped me: I wiped toys and medicine bottles, washed the windows and walls, aired and mended clothes, and organised the press into sections for each child. I soaped hairbrushes, polished chamber pots and laundered curtains. The children helped where they could, dusting and tidying. I fell into bed exhausted, and one night Saul woke me to tell me there must have been a leak, for it had rained on his bed. My watch face told me it was seven o'clock; I'd overslept by an hour, and the water Blaise left outside had cooled. I went along with Saul's story, dressing quickly and taking his bedding to the scullery for Emily to wash, and asking for more water.

'Master Saul had an accident,' I told her, adding it to the washing basket.

'Oh, not again,' she said with sympathy.

'Does it happen often?'

She shrugged. 'Now and then.'

Blaise was in the corner ironing.

'Blaise, could you fetch more water, please?'

'I'll just do this first.'

'Is there a spare oil cloth?'

'Only the baby's.'

She pushed the iron over a petticoat and did not look at me. Asking for things was awkward at the best of times, but Blaise always succeeded in making me feel worse. Though I'd reached harmony with Mrs Mannion in the kitchen, Blaise's enmity remained, and Tilda and Emily said little to me. I felt as though she'd poisoned them against me. I didn't care that they talked about me in the kitchen; I knew they did, for they fell silent when I came through the swinging door. But I didn't like how deferential she made me towards them, grateful for the tiniest crumb they threw. I was lonely, and I only realised how lonely when a knock came at the nursery door later that morning. To my surprise, Mrs England entered with a letter in her hand.

'For you,' she said. She, too, had barely spoken to me, offering only the occasional greeting when I passed her in the house or asking benign questions when I took the children to the drawing room. It was as though they were strangers, and it unsettled me. Charley never reached for her and stitched himself to me. One evening I'd passed him to his mother in an attempt to improve their bond, but he writhed on her lap and almost tipped off, at which point Mrs England looked desperately at me and I took him back.

'Thank you, ma'am.' I accepted the envelope, and the sight of Elsie's writing sent my heart into a somersault. The envelope felt substantial, padded, as if my sister had written a dozen sides instead of her usual one. I must have smiled, for Mrs England hesitated, as though she wished to speak.

'How are you settling in?' she asked.

'Very well, thank you, ma'am.'

She glanced towards the table.

'The girls are writing a compendium of local plants.'

'Oh?'

It had been my idea, and we'd already gathered a dozen different species on our walks. On the table lay a range of species for Decca to copy, and she'd decided that when she'd completed flora, she would begin on fauna, starting with birds. I'd promised to take out a membership at the public library, and she was thrilled at the idea. She was devoted to her industry and had allowed Millie to help, though Millie had her own copybook. Her diagrams were unrecognisable, but Decca and I heaped them with praise.

'Girls, show Mrs England your work.' I hoped she would not mind the dirt on the tablecloth.

They pushed their copybooks towards her; she examined them obligingly and searched for something to say. 'What is this one?'

Decca brimmed with attentiveness. 'Hawthorn,' she said. 'Also called quickthorn, thornapple, May tree. May tree!' She beamed. 'Like Nurse May.'

'I'm not sure I care to share my name with a thorn,' I remarked, smiling.

Decca pointed to her next drawing. 'This is a male fern. Do you see how it coils?'

'I think it looks rather ladylike.' Mrs England straightened and looked about her. 'The nursery is spick and span.'

'We cleaned it yesterday,' said Millie, wishing to be praised herself.

'*You* cleaned it?'

'I helped.'

A hint of a nod; a ghost of a smile.

'Ma'am?' I indicated we step towards the fireplace. In a low voice I said: 'Master Saul had a minor lapse in the night.'

Her brown eyes searched mine.

'He wet the bed, ma'am.'

'Oh.'

'I should have asked the master, but I'd no time this morning. I don't know if he does it regularly.'

'He does,' Decca called from the table.

'Are there oil cloths for the children, or just Charley? Blaise seemed to think not.'

She opened and closed her mouth. 'I'm not . . . I don't know, I'm afraid.'

'Might we buy one? Only it takes so long to wash and dry the mattress.'

'I wouldn't know where to get one.'

'I can get one. I expect they're only a few shillings.'

She opened and closed her mouth.

'Or I could make one,' I said quickly. 'But it would take a few days to dry.'

'You must ask Mr England. Excuse me.'

She hurried from the nursery, leaving us in astonished silence. Even Charley, who had been banging a drum with a tin soldier, seemed bewildered. I smoothed my apron and took a seat with the children, folding myself into a tiny chair and craning my neck to look.

'Now,' I said. 'Who'd like to tell me what this is?'

While they worked I tore open Elsie's letter, eager for news from home, and went to the window to read it.

Dear Ruby,

I do not know where Yorkshire is but I will ask Miss Sellers to show me. I do not know when I will next go to school. My hands have been bad for a while. I dropped the teapot last week. It smashed and stained the floor. Father wrote to us this week, with a letter for all of us and one for you. I have put it in this envelope, it's up to you if you read it. Mother says you ought to. Archie has joined a football team. He practises with cauliflowers in the yard and it makes Mother angry. Ted is saving for binockulers, I don't know how to spell it but the thing you put to your eyes to see far away. Do you have your own bed there and can I visit if you do? Write soon please. Have the children got nice toys? I am thinking of giving Constance away. I am getting too old for dolls. If they want her they can have her. She needs a new eye.

    Love,
    Elsie

Beside my sister's letter was a small envelope the size of a block of butter, bearing my name. I plucked it from the envelope and held it between two fingers, feeling the weight of the words, and took it at once from the nursery. In the next room I knelt before my bed to open my crate, and found the little bundle of letters I'd wrapped in an old blouse. I shoved the letter inside the shoestring tying them together, and closed them in darkness once more.

'Shall we show Nurse May our trick?'

    'Yes!'

We were in the drawing room, and Mr England was in high spirits. He'd played two songs on the upright piano and now sat on the stool smoking. Cigar cuttings littered the carpet. His good mood was infectious; the children cheered and ran about, and Charley clapped on the rug. Their father stood with tense biceps, knees bent and his fists in the air like a strongman. Either side of him, Millie and Saul each locked their hands around his sleeves, and he lifted them clean in the air. They shrieked and squealed, dangling from his arms, their feet a foot or more from the floor. Then, reddening with effort, the cigar still clamped in his mouth, he lifted them up and down. I laughed, though if Millie lost her grip she could sprain an ankle; the same determination seized Saul as he clung on, his legs inches from the floor.

Before long Mr England roared with surrender and dropped them to the floor, where they collapsed in a giggling heap.

'How about that?' he said to no one in particular. Decca smiled shyly, too big to take part.

'That was marvellous, sir.' Usually I made myself inconspicuous and hovered by the door. Mrs England wore a vacant smile. I hadn't seen her since our uneasy encounter about the oil cloth that morning. An enormous portrait of her grandfather, Champion Greatrex, the manufacturer, took up most of the wall above the fireplace. Mr England had asked me what I thought of it, and I'd replied it was striking. The old man sat on a chair wearing Scottish plaid trousers and a frock coat with gilt buttons. His silvery beard reached his collar, and in his right hand he held a black cane topped with a silver beast. I'd asked what it was, and Mr England told me: an alpaca, for the wool he produced.

'Children,' he announced now. 'I have some news.' He waited for silence, and I collected Charley from the floor. 'The Mill Workers' Society for the Relief of the Sick have appointed me treasurer.'

'Will they give you treasure?' asked Saul.

'I'm afraid not. It means I'm put in charge of finance.'

'Oh,' said Saul.

'Congratulations, Papa,' said Decca.

'Thank you, Decca. My appointment means that some-body very special is coming to the house tomorrow. Can you guess who that might be?'

'A pirate!' cried Millie.

'No, half-wit! He said there *won't* be treasure.'

'Saul, don't insult your sister. A pirate is a very good guess, although incorrect. But it does begin with P.'

'A . . . a . . . popinjay!' was Saul's guess.

A blast of laughter. 'Where on earth did you hear that?'

'Mrs Mannion said it about the knife man. What is it?'

'Never you mind. Popinjay is not the answer.'

They trembled with anticipation. 'Who is it, Papa?'

'A *photographer*,' said Mr England, drawing out each syllable, 'is coming to take our picture.'

'Will we be in it?' asked Millie.

'Yes. The six of us.'

'Oh,' said Saul, though he was impressed. 'Cousin

Michael wants to become a photographer when he's a man.'

'Nurse May,' said Mr England. 'Please have the children ready at nine.'

'Yes, sir.'

He gave a warning look to each of them. 'I expect very best behaviour. And no dribbles of porridge on your clothes.'

The photographer and his assistant arrived after breakfast. I draped bath sheets over the children while they ate, and they made a great comedy of feeding themselves with exaggerated care and stiff, mechanical arms. From the window I watched two men unload their equipment from Broadley's cart and place a camera on the ground, draped in tarpaulin. The rich were inclined to have their pictures taken outside so they could show their houses, and the weather seemed in favour of the arrangement: the sky was a peaceable white. The children crowded around me to look out.

'Is *that* the camera?' asked Saul.

'Yes. Have you seen one before?'

'Yes. But it's tiny.'

'Have you had your picture taken?' I asked them.

'Yes, but I was a baby,' Saul replied. 'Do nurses have their pictures taken?'

'I've had mine taken, yes. I haven't seen any pictures of you in the house,' I added.

'There was a sports day at Greatrex,' said Decca.

'Is Greatrex a house?'

'It's our great-grandfather's town.'

I stared at her. 'He owns a *town*?'

'Yes, he built it around his mill, for the workers. There's a school and Sunday school, and a park and a public bath. There's even a hospital.'

'And a statue a hundred feet tall.' Saul thrust his hand in the air.

'It's not a hundred feet. There's also a railway station.'

If anybody but Decca had said it, I would not have believed them. The Greatrex family were like cool white draughts, smoothly monopolising a checkerboard.

'I should like to see the town called Greatrex,' I said, half to myself, clearing away the breakfast things.

I cleaned their faces and hands, then took Charley downstairs with me to ask if the photographers were ready. Mr England stood with his back to the house wearing a pale linen suit and claret cravat, his thumbs hooked in his buttonholes, discussing chemicals with the junior assistant. A few strides from the gate they'd erected a canvas tent for a darkroom, and the camera was placed on a flat wooden board facing the house. Its single round eye watched me. Mrs England was nowhere to be seen.

I hovered at Mr England's elbow, and after a moment

he turned. 'Nurse May, this is Mr Cleeve, Mr Harpenden's assistant and nephew. Mr Cleeve, this is our children's nurse.'

I nodded at the young man. 'Should I bring the children down, sir?' I asked.

'I think we'll soon be ready,' said Mr Cleeve, glancing at the tent just as a third man lifted the flap and stepped out. 'Mr Lowden,' Mr England addressed him. 'Enjoy the house at your leisure. We shan't be long.'

'I'll stay out here, sir,' Mr Lowden replied, cocking his head at the tent. 'Percy doesn't mind, if you don't.'

'Certainly not.' Mr England's moustache stretched into a smile. 'Nurse May, you might fetch my wife, too.'

'Yes, sir.'

'You may have to drag her out of the powder room.'

Mr Cleeve grinned in a placatory sort of way, and I took Charley inside. There was no sign of Mrs England downstairs; I went to the landing and knocked on her door.

'Yes?' The voice from within was strained.

'The photographer is ready, ma'am.'

The door opened, and I stepped back. Mrs England had a mouthful of pins and was fastening them into her hair. Behind her, draped over every surface, was a tailor's workshop of skirts, dresses, bodices, belts. She wore a beautiful dress of lavender silk and chiffon trimmed with lace.

'I thought they were arriving at ten,' she said.

'Nine, ma'am.'

She fled to her dressing table and sat on the stool to examine herself, then twisted around and began searching the bed for something, landing on a single silk glove the colour of cream. 'Oh, where is the other?'

'Lilian?' Mr England called from the hall.

'I'm coming, Charles.'

'Here, let me help you,' I said, at once combing the bed for the matching glove. Within seconds I located it beneath a creased silk belt and passed it to her. She crammed it over her fingers and turned to the wardrobe, lifting down hat boxes and batting at tissue paper.

'Lilian!'

Her discomposure alarmed me, and her memory; in the drawing room last night the master *had* said nine, and it was now quarter past.

Mr England appeared in the doorway. 'I thought you were wearing white,' he said.

She stood frozen by the wardrobe, holding a striped box.

'I wore this suit to match yours. If you'd said you were wearing lilac, I'd have put on my black wool.'

Mrs England spoke in a small voice. 'I can't find my white silk, Emily must have it. I could wear—'

He sighed. 'Never mind, I'll change. It won't take me a moment.' He disappeared into his dressing room next door. A door behind the washstand connected the two rooms and Mrs England eyed it as though expecting it to open, holding a wide cream hat like a tray in her hands.

I felt a stab of irritation, hot and sudden as a wasp sting. The children had been waiting half an hour; any longer and Charley would need his napkin changing. He roved about on the floor now and putting it to his mouth. I lifted him again and set him on my hip. How much smoother things would run if there was a housekeeper, I thought, not for the first time. The photographs would have been taken by now, and everybody dispatched to get on with their work.

I shepherded the children into the yard, and by the time Mr England had changed his suit and assembled the family, he noticed a curtain that needed straightening, and went to do it himself. Mrs England had recovered from her mania. She said a brief hello to the photographers and stood beside the children with her gloved hands clasped at her waist.

'I like your dress,' Decca said humbly. Her mother gave a delicate smile of thanks and brushed at her sleeve.

Mr Cleeve arranged the children. Decca held Charley and stood in the middle of Millie and Saul. Their parents sat either side on chairs brought from the dining room. Mr England shifted about before deciding the chair from his study had a better height. Mr Cleeve brought the item, and in all the fuss and delay Charley began crying, and I had to walk him around the yard, patting and shushing. At long last the Englands were ready, as were the plates. Mr Harpenden inspected the composition, stroking his moustache and stepping backwards. There was a brief, satisfied silence, and then Mr England said: 'Where should Nurse May stand?'

Assuming he meant while the photographs were taken, I offered to go inside.

'No,' he said, 'of course you'll be in the picture. Do you think behind Decca, Mr Harpenden?'

'That will be fine,' the photographer replied.

I found my feet quite unable to move. I had only a few seconds to think of some objection that would not appear rude or disobedient, but none came to me, and the opportunity passed.

'Nurse May?' said Mr England.

I realised everybody was waiting for me and, rigid with reluctance, crossed the cobbles. The third man, Mr Lowden, watched from a distance, a notebook tucked beneath his arm and a pencil behind his ear. Mr Cleeve conducted me to stand behind the little party at Mrs England's right shoulder. My mind whirred: I wondered why I was being included and not the other servants. The three men examined our configuration with pensive brows, then Mr Harpenden disappeared beneath the cloth.

After the photograph was taken and Mr Cleeve attended to the plates, I relieved Decca of Charley and she shook her arms with relief. At that moment Mr Lowden strolled over, a pencil held between his knuckles like a cigarette. He wore a shabby brown suit, and lead smudged his fingers. His notebook was well worn, and he put a thumb to his tongue and turned to a clean page.

'Can you tell me about the benefits of the Society, sir? Why should mill workers join?'

With a cold, sinking sensation I realised he was a journalist, and turned to the children to fuss with their collars.

Mr England nodded. 'From the day of entrance, members are entitled to fifteen shillings per week for the first six months of sickness, then eight for the next.'

Mr Lowden made a note. 'How does that compare with what you pay your male workers?'

'The benefit reflects the average pay of workers across the valley, with all levels taken into account.'

Mr Lowden noted it all down. 'And how do men apply?'

'How long must we stand here?' Millie moaned.

'Until Mr Harpenden and Mr Cleeve have finished taking our photograph,' I said quietly.

'When will that be?'

'When they tell us.'

'I should like to be a photographer, but I wouldn't take pictures of *families*,' said Saul. 'Cousin Christopher has a Box Brownie, but it's minuscule. Mine shall be much bigger.'

'Your brothers-in-law are president and vice-president,' Mr Lowden was saying. 'Remind me of their names?'

'Henry and Michael Greatrex.'

'Ah, yes. I tried for an interview with them, but they are busy men.'

'They are,' said Mr England, straightening his tie.

'And the children's names are . . . ?'

Mr England touched each child on the head. 'Saul, Rebecca, Millicent and the baby is Charles.'

'And your wife?'

It seems we had all forgotten she was there, including herself. She came to attention and replied: 'Lilian.'

'Formerly Greatrex?'

'That's right.'

'What's your name, miss?'

After a pause, I realised Mr Lowden was speaking to me.

'*My* name?'

He nodded, pencil poised.

'I'm afraid I'm nothing to do with the Society for Sick People. I can't even remember what it's called. Sorry.'

'No, miss.' Mr Lowden was a man with thin patience. 'For the photograph in the newspaper.'

There was an uncomfortable silence.

'Is the photograph going in the newspaper?'

'The *Halifax Courier*, next week's edition. Your name, miss?'

Sweat pricked at my armpits, and my heart knocked hard in my chest. 'Oh,' I said. 'Nobody will want to know who I am.'

'Nurse May is modest, and perhaps a little shy,' said Mr England.

'Nurse. May.' Mr Lowden stabbed at his notebook.

'Perhaps a photograph of the family would be better for the article? Without me?'

'Nonsense, we wish to show off our Norland nurse,' said Mr England. 'Write that down, Lowden, she's from the Norland Institute in London. The Princess of Greece has one, I'm told.'

Mr Lowden obliged, and Mr England took out his cigar case. 'Care for it?'

'I won't, sir, thank you.'

'I left my cutter inside, one moment.'

My mouth felt dry, my heart so loud I thought they might hear it. Oh, why hadn't I objected at all? Now I could hardly convince them, with the photograph taken and the plate developing. But I had to do *something*.

'Ma'am, could you hold Charley a moment?'

I passed him to his mother, who was too surprised to object, and hurried after Mr England.

'Sir, I should have said something earlier, but my principal, Miss Simpson, would be so cross if she knew one of us had appeared in a newspaper without proper uniform. If I'd known I was having my photograph taken I should have put on my cloak and gloves.'

'Then you must fetch them. We can't have you getting into trouble with the principal.'

'I shouldn't leave the children. Perhaps they can take another without me? I'd hate to hold everything up.'

'Nonsense. When else will you have the chance to appear in the newspaper? Fetch your things; I'll tell Mr Harpenden. The children can wait with their mother while you dash inside.'

113

I glanced over at them arranged around her; she was bouncing Charley rigidly, and Millie was stroking his feet. Sensing I was watching her, Mrs England's eyes found mine, and this time she did not look away.

CHAPTER 8

Having heard so much about them, I was intrigued to meet the Greatrexes. I assumed they would drop in often, that the coat stand would fill regularly with the cloaks and umbrellas of parents, cousins, aunts, but three weeks passed before Mrs England's extended family descended one Sunday for lunch. I peered through the nursery window at the ladies rustling up the track in their skirts, the men's canes tapping against the cobbles. The brothers looked as though they had hatched from the same egg: all were clear-skinned and fair-haired, varying in size, with golden moustaches and light, intelligent eyes. Also attending were her mother and father, Helen and Conrad, who were elderly and wore expensive-looking clothes. One of the first things I noticed about them was their voices: they dressed like gentry but had the same unremarkable accents as the local people. It was a curious contrast and quite distracting; assembled in the drawing room they might have been actors at a civic hall play.

All morning the children had been restless, asking when they would come. I dressed them in the clothes they wore for the photograph; a copy of the newspaper that featured Mr Lowden's article had been ironed for the guests. When it arrived Mr England had marched into the nursery and thrown it down in triumph, stabbing the picture with a finger. He bought copies for all the servants. I was relieved the image was quite small, though my name was there in black ink: *Nurse May, a graduate of the Norland Institute of Children's Nurses*. I shoved it to the back of a shelf in the day nursery.

The three older children were to eat with the family while Charley and I stayed in the nursery, though I took him down to be petted before the meal. Tilda and Blaise set the dining table with the best china, and Mrs Mannion was roasting a flock of birds. Judging by the cries issuing from the kitchen, it seemed such gatherings were infrequent.

'You must be the new Nangle,' said Mrs England's mother to me. She was tall and stately, with silver hair and blue eyes that landed softly, like snow. I smiled obligingly; the children gathered around her, nervy as colts. 'Do you speak?'

'Yes, ma'am,' I replied, remembering how Mrs Radlett

had scored my tact with visitors: very good, but not excellent. 'Pleased to meet you.'

'Do you have a name?'

'Nurse May, ma'am.'

'You're from that fancy place, aren't you?'

'Birmingham, ma'am?'

'No, not *Birmingham*,' she spat. 'The nursing college.'

'The Norland Institute, ma'am.'

'Institute, you say. Very grand. I told Charles he'd get a girl a third of the price from the village, but he insisted. What do they teach you at this *institute* then?'

'The fundamentals of children's nursing, ma'am. It's a mix of lectures and placements, academic and practical.'

'Academic!' She let out a high, cold laugh, and I hated her instantly. 'And how do you like the north?'

'A great deal, ma'am. It's a beautiful place.'

'Beautiful! Ha. Is that so?'

I searched for an escape, but Charley was well behaved, gazing about serenely. Decca had moved away to talk to a female cousin and Saul was missing, but Millie knelt at my feet fiddling with a coral necklace Decca had let her wear. Mr England was absorbed in masculine conversation, his wife absent. Mrs Greatrex appeared to notice this as the same time as I did, and said: 'Where has Lilian got to?'

I pretended to look for her. 'Perhaps she's delayed.'

'My daughter is a woman, not a locomotive. Make yourself useful and fetch her, will you?'

'Yes, ma'am.'

She reached for Charley, who sat frozen in her lap and stared at her in frightened fascination. I knew I only had a minute before he began to cry, and closed the drawing-room door behind me. The hum of voices and the tinkle of wine glasses carried through, and I allowed myself a moment of peace, closing my eyes and exhaling against the doorpost. The kitchen door swung open, and Blaise came through with a tray of water glasses. A moment later Tilda followed with the jug. I avoided their eyes and made my way to the staircase.

'She's so sour,' I heard Blaise mutter in the dining room. 'Sour little sow.'

The pair of them burst into laughter, and tears blurred my eyes. I wiped them with a sleeve and knocked on the mistress's door, which opened at once, as if she had been standing there. She was fixing a button at her cuff.

'What time is it?' she asked.

I checked the watch at my waist. 'Twenty-five minutes past twelve, ma'am.'

'What's the matter?'

I blinked and swallowed. 'Nothing, ma'am.'

'You're upset.'

'No, I . . . I have a slight cold.'

She pulled a silk handkerchief from her sleeve and held it to me.

'Oh, I have one, ma'am, thank you, there's no need.'

She stuffed it away again. 'Is everybody here?'

'I think so, ma'am.'

From the room came the whiff of talcum powder, and something else – a sharp, smoky scent, like an extinguished match.

'Are you going back down?'

'Yes, ma'am. The children are in the drawing room.'

'I'll come with you.'

I went down behind her, and she seemed to steel herself before opening the door, taking a breath and plunging inside, then pausing again, hovering on the threshold as though faced with a room full of strangers. I saw her mother's eyes travel neutrally over her, assessing her skirt, her bodice, as though she was a mannequin in a shop. What was it Mr Booth had said about unhappy families? Perhaps there weren't so many ways to be miserable after all.

After a lunch of ham sandwiches, I gave Charley a rusk and put him down for his nap. The nursery was quiet without the other children, and I was sitting in the rocking chair mending stockings when I heard the floorboard creak in the corridor. Nobody knocked, so I got up to investigate and found Mrs England in the night nursery, standing over the cot.

'Ma'am?' I said.

She was studying Charley, and seemed tired. I lowered my mending and set it on Saul's bed. 'Is something the matter?'

From below came the distant drone of voices; the nursery sat above the dining room.

'Am I needed downstairs, ma'am?'

At that she came to, as though hearing me for the first time. 'No, no,' she said. 'I thought I would check on the baby.'

This would not have been unusual for most mothers, but it was for Mrs England. I moved towards her and we watched him swim below the surface of sleep. 'I put him down ten minutes ago.'

She stood at the window and peered through the blinds, as though expecting, or fearing, more guests. Then she saw Herbie sitting on my pillow, and her face softened. 'Is that yours?'

'Yes. Well, actually he's my sister's, but she insisted I take him when I left home. She said he would take care of me.'

She took up the bear, lost in some faraway place, and rubbed his glass eyes. 'That's good of her. I wish I had a sister.'

I did not know what to say. 'Brothers are nice, too,' I offered. 'And their wives can feel like sisters.'

'Mmm.' She peered about the room, taking in the beds and pictures with a complex expression of fondness and grief. 'This used to be my nursery,' she said.

I was surprised. The house did not feel like hers at all; she seemed quite the stranger in it.

'You must have had some happy times here.'

'Yes,' she said flatly.

I stood, waiting, and after a moment, she sighed. 'Well. I should go back.'

There was a rustle of silk; her feet were silent on the floorboards and she closed the door gently behind her.

At half-past two I went down to collect the children. Lunch had finished, and Saul was in the dining room with the men. Cigar smoke filled the room, engulfing them in grey clouds. Saul was coughing when I entered and came without resistance. From the kitchen came the loud scrape and clatter of crockery. Across the hall I found Decca in the drawing room with the women, sitting on a cushion at the feet of her cousin Anne or Enid, I didn't know the difference, but she was a year or two younger than me and looked me up and down when I entered.

'We wondered where you'd got to,' the elderly Mrs Greatrex remarked. Her daughter sat beside her, and her three daughters-in-law were also present; one stood by the window, one sat on the piano stool reading music and the third perched beside her daughters. Mrs England had no teacup and clasped her hands in her lap. I noticed a strip of calico on her right hand, which she covered with her left.

'Rebecca would like to stay here with us ladies,' Mrs Greatrex said. 'Wouldn't you, Rebecca?'

Decca seemed uncertain, clinging to her cushion like a frog on a lily pad.

'Of course, ma'am,' I said. 'Where is Miss Millie?'

'Shouldn't you know?'

'She's playing with the young ones,' said Mrs England. She seemed drawn and weary, as though she couldn't wait to be alone again. I envied her for the calm sanctuary of her bedroom, her long, solitary baths.

'Thank you, ma'am. I'll find her.'

Saul and I searched the downstairs rooms, and met Frank Greatrex, the youngest of the three brothers, coming down the hall. He was round-faced and cheerful-looking, with the affable nature of those who enjoy the company of children. He ruffled his nephew's hair.

'Uncle Frank, do your pheasant for Nurse May!'

He obliged, sounding so much like the distinctive screech my mouth fell open in delight.

'Now the curlew!'

He fitted his fingers to his mouth and out came a curious, mournful cry.

'Now a grouse!'

Next he produced a comical retching sound, and I covered my mouth to laugh.

'Frank.' The tone was cold and clipped, and I felt a presence like a draught behind me.

Frank's eyes flicked over my shoulder, and his smile grew more determined. 'I was entertaining the children, Father.'

'They have their nursemaid for that.'

I bristled at the slight, though the likelihood of it being intentional was slim; Conrad Greatrex was unlikely to be intimate with the nursery hierarchy. It wasn't clear if they wished for me to leave or Frank was about to, so I said: 'Come with me, Saul,' and guided him to the back of the house. Frank gave an apologetic grin and moved past me to join the men.

Saul and I continued our search outside, though there was no sign of Millie in the yard or the trees surrounding the house. I grew anxious, and asked in the kitchen if they'd seen her, but nobody had. We hadn't checked upstairs, and I glanced in the bedrooms and bathroom with a rising sense of panic.

'Perhaps they are playing hide and seek,' Saul suggested.

The linen cupboard was empty, but then I heard giggles from the nursery wing; I'd left the door open to listen for Charley, and found Millie and two of her cousins in the first room, crouched by my bed.

'Miss Millie, I've been looking all over for you. Come away from there. Look, you've woken Charley. What are you doing?'

Millie's cheeks were red, and I moved closer to see what game they were playing. My trunk was open, and all my things laid out on the floor.

'You said you didn't mind me looking at your things!' she cried. 'You said I could!'

Half-blind with shock and fury, I snatched at whatever I could and flung them back inside.

'Who is this?' One of her wicked cousins was holding a photograph – my photograph. They had gone inside my tea tin and found the most private thing of all.

'Give it to me! Millie, you will go next door this instant; the rest of you, downstairs. Go, now!'

The two older girls slunk off in their petticoats, and Millie began to cry. 'I didn't want to look, they made me!'

'Go to the nursery, please. Saul, take your sister.'

Shining with glee, Saul took hold of Millie's arm and led her from the room, her sobs echoing down the hall.

I realised I was shaking. The photograph had creased, and in the corner was a smear mark left by a sticky finger. I rubbed it on my apron, feeling hot tears rise for the second time that day. Bits of newspaper were scattered on the rag rug, and Elsie's letters, and . . . I saw the word *Rhubarb*, and threw the bundle of letters to the back of the trunk.

There was a small noise at the door. 'Go away,' I said, wiping my cheeks with my sleeve. But silence followed, and I turned to see Decca clutching the doorknob, her brown eyes wide.

'Sorry, miss,' I said. 'I thought you were . . .'

'Saul told me what happened,' she said. 'Millie should never have done that, but Pamela and Sarah should have known better.'

She came and knelt next to me to help me tidy. She did not pause to examine anything or ask any questions, placing my hairbrush, button hook and a sheaf of magazines inside.

'Thank you,' I said, closing it and fastening the padlock. 'It's my fault for leaving it unlocked.'

'I don't think it is,' the little girl replied.

'Well, I've learnt my lesson. I shan't let Millie out of my sight again.'

A small smile. 'I don't know why she is so naughty.'

'If I didn't have one myself, I would find it hard to believe sisters could be so different.'

'Is your sister naughty?' Decca asked.

'No. But my brothers are. Or were.' I smiled. 'My youngest brothers used to hide in the neighbours' coal sheds and jump out at them. You could hear them screaming halfway down the street. They were always bringing things home that they'd found on scrap heaps or fallen off carts; I swear they used to pinch them when the driver wasn't looking. They even brought a dead cat home once. My mother had a fit. She said they were like terriers. My other brother, Robbie, he used to fix the things they brought back: metal and tins and broken things, bits and bobs. Lamps, watches, that kind of thing. He'd take them apart and put them together again.'

'Will you see them for a holiday? Once a year Mrs Mannion visits her brother in Scarborough and we have to eat cold food for three days.'

I slipped the key into my pocket and took up Charley from his cot. 'Perhaps. Now, let's find Millie before she drowns in a pool of her own tears.' At the door something came to me. 'Decca,' I said. 'Your mother was wearing a bandage. Did she hurt her hand?'

'Oh, yes,' said Decca. 'She burnt it on Papa's cigar.'

A heatwave arrived without warning, and I took the children to town for ice-cream. On the long, dusty walk from the house, I told them how we used to make our own in winter, leaving jam and cream on the doorstep overnight.

'For the foxes?' Saul asked in disbelief. I couldn't help but laugh, and he looked pleased with himself.

As well as visiting the ice-cream parlour, I wished to buy a picture postcard of the crags for Elsie. I chose one for myself of the waterfall we visited on our walks, that fell from the rocks like a lace curtain; it had the pretty name of Horseshoe Cascade, surrounded in the picture by misty black forest. I saw Decca looking longingly at them so bought her one, too. We strolled through the town, looking in shop windows, and walked home along the river, passing a cricket match at the club. I parked the pram, and we sat on a bench to watch, licking our ice-creams. The bench was at the edge of the pitch, and Saul became enthralled in the game, edging closer so that he was standing only a few yards from one of the players.

I called him back, thinking him a nuisance, and the player turned, too, at the sound of my voice. I recognised

126

him at once, but it took me a moment to place him. Then it came to me: he was the man from the park outside the church. He acknowledged me with a nod.

'Saul, come and sit down.'

'He's all right,' said the man.

When there was a break in the game he brought Saul the grape-coloured cricket ball. He showed him how to bowl, pivoting his arm in a wide circle. Saul copied and before long had to remove his jacket with the effort. Charley was asleep; I adjusted the pram shade and put my face briefly to the sun. One or two spectators dozed on the edges, their hats pulled low over their faces. Millie appeared to have most of her ice-cream on her chin and cheeks, and I took out a handkerchief and began wiping.

'Hello again,' said the man, coming over and leaving Saul to practise.

'Hello,' I said, shielding my eyes.

'You found them, then.'

'Found who?'

'The rest of the children.'

I did not smile. He scratched the back of his neck, which was the same reddish brown as his arms; his cricket whites made him look darker, and I noticed his hands were clean this time. He wiped them together self-consciously.

'Do you like cricket?' he asked the girls.

They were shy and said nothing.

'I don't think they've seen it before.'

'We have, at Greatrex,' said Millie.

'Ah,' said the man. 'You're the Greatrex children.'

'England,' I corrected him.

'Sorry?'

'Their surname is England, not Greatrex.'

'Of course. Is the little one hiding?'

'He's asleep.'

He squinted over at the players, who were drinking lemonade in the shade. 'What's that you've got?' he asked Decca, coming closer. She was clutching her picture tightly, as though afraid it would blow away.

'A postcard,' she mumbled.

He glanced at it upside down. 'Horseshoe Cascade. One of my favourite places.'

'We go there, too,' she said.

'I bet you haven't swum in the bottom of it. I wouldn't recommend it: it's shallow as a bath tub.' He pronounced it *shaller*.

She gave a begrudging smile.

'Those falls are named for my grandfather,' he went on. 'He made horseshoes for a living, like me.'

The girls stared at him, and Millie frowned. 'Horses don't wear shoes.'

He laughed. 'They do, but under their feet, so you can't see them.'

'What's the point of that?'

'To protect their hooves on the roads. You have horses,

don't you?' They nodded. 'You should look at their shoes next time you see them. Would you like to see them being made?'

Saul joined us, panting. 'See what being made?'

'Horseshoes. I'm a blacksmith. Have you ever been to a forge before?'

'Never. I'd like to go. Can we, Nurse May?'

'I'm not sure.'

'Not today,' said the man. 'Whenever you're free to. I live on the moor, not far from where you are. Close to the falls, in fact, on the Keighley Road – do you know it?'

'I can't say I do. And I'm not sure a forge is a suitable place for the children.'

'It's safe as houses. And I'll let you take a horseshoe home. They're lucky, you know.' He said this to me.

'Please, Nurse May,' said Millie.

'The little girl's eager. How about it? You could come tomorrow afternoon.'

'I shall have to ask their parents.'

He gave a nod of concession. 'I'm Tommy. Sheldrake,' he added. 'And if you like what you see, you might persuade your groom to come to me instead of old Travis at the crossroads. Tell him I'll do him a good price.'

I looked closely at Tommy Sheldrake and tried to take the measure of him. He wasn't bad-looking, perhaps thirty or so, without a ring on his finger. His hair was sun-bleached, his eyes dark, and as he was squinting at me I couldn't make out his true likeness. I wondered if he was flirting;

he was friendly enough but over-familiar and a little presumptuous, assuming that I should wander into the stables and strike up a conversation with Broadley about horseshoes.

'We'd better go,' I told the children, rising to a stand. 'Good day, Mr Sheldrake.'

'And to you.'

He raised his hand in a salute and watched us down the path.

Saul got his way that evening, telling his father about our invitation from Mr Sheldrake, while demonstrating his cricket bowl with a porcelain shepherdess from the mantle.

'I think it's a splendid idea,' said Mr England, as I knew he would. Mrs England was in bed with one of her heads. I hadn't seen her for a day or two, but that morning heard the quiet splash of water from the bathroom; she often bathed after breakfast, and was in there an hour at a time.

'Someone named the waterfall after his grandfather,' Millie announced.

Mr England regarded me with raised eyebrows. 'Is that so? And are all five of you going?'

'The thing is, sir, I'm not sure I'd be able to take the baby.' Remembering how tender Mrs England had been with him at the family lunch, I said: 'Perhaps the mistress could mind him for an hour?'

He gave a quick, tight shake of his head, discreet enough so the children did not see.

'Then I'll take him in the pram,' I said, hoping he would think the suggestion as ridiculous as I did.

'Wonderful. Then that's settled. I shall look forward to a full report at teatime.' He drew out a fresh cigar.

'I'm not sure I know the place, sir,' I said. 'He told me it was on the Keighley Road.'

Mr England held up a finger, indicating I wait, and left the room, returning a minute later with a map the size of a small tablecloth. He spread it over the top of the piano, and I went to look.

'Here,' he said, circling his index finger, compelling me to move closer. Hesitantly I did, and followed his finger north, out of the town. 'This is the Keighley Road. This is where we are.'

The scent of tobacco was powerful, though he had not lit his cigar. I felt warm suddenly, and wished for a cool breeze from a window. 'Turn left here and keep going uphill. I know of a forge, if it's the same one. I'd send you with Broadley but I've to go to Leeds tomorrow.'

There were inches between us and I was aware of several things at once: his breath stirring my hair, and his broad, powerful chest. His hands were large, and beneath the tobacco was a sharp, clean note of cologne. I went on staring at the map.

'Do you see how the road kinks here?' He showed me a little square signalling a dwelling. 'I think that's it.'

I sprang away. 'Very good, sir.'

To my astonishment, he winked at me. 'Capital.' He turned to the children, and clamped the cigar between his teeth. 'Who wants to play Prussian generals?'

CHAPTER 9

Mr England had been right: the forge stood at a bend on the highway that cut across the moor. We saw it half a mile off, sitting squat on the brow of a hill like a rock on a great empty seabed, with the watery sky above. The land here was barren, with barely a tree to divert the eye or stem the wind, which forced us to hold on to our hats. The children ran ahead, their frocks flapping behind them. A few farmhouses were dotted here and there, but the moor was sparse as far as the eye could see, as though life was not welcome here. I found it a strange, unnatural place, and wondered how to describe it to Elsie.

The yard was crammed with wheels and railings, and I knew it would be impossible to keep the children clean.

Mr Sheldrake stepped out to greet us, waving from a distance and grinning broadly. Out of his cricket whites he was almost unrecognisable, with grease smearing his face and a leather apron over his clothes. Attached to the forge was a low, ancient cottage, with windows like arrow-slits to guard against the wind. The house was isolated, almost vulnerable in its exposure; there was no other dwelling visible in any direction, though the road passed directly in front.

'Afternoon,' he said. A stray sheep looked on as we approached.

'Good afternoon, sir,' the children chorused. At that moment a sheepdog came hurtling out of the yard and straight towards us.

'Here, Sam.' Mr Sheldrake got hold of its scruff and pulled it away, but not before it stamped two muddy paw prints on my apron. 'Sorry about that. I hope you don't mind dogs.'

I didn't, and said so. Sam barked, wanting to play, and the children surrounded him.

'Before you come inside, wait there a moment.' He disappeared around the side of the forge, and returned with several cotton aprons, all of which were adult-sized and drowned the children, particularly Millie. Mr Sheldrake laughed. 'I thought that might happen,' he said. 'Come with me and I'll fix you.'

We followed him into the yard. Every inch was filled with scrap metal of all shapes and sizes, from long scaffold

poles to rusty ploughs and dented machinery. We waited
for Mr Sheldrake at the doorway and a moment later he
came out with a needle and thread between his teeth, and
within minutes had crudely shortened the hem of Millie's
apron. Saul wanted his doing next, but Decca's barely
grazed the floor. When he had finished, he tucked the
needle into the tool belt at his waist.

'Blacksmiths are also seamstresses, did you know?' His
accent was local, but seasoned with something else, his
words lilting up at the end of the sentence. I smoothed
down my own apron and pushed the pram inside.

The forge was dark, lit only by two narrow slits left
open to the elements and a cherry-red fire blazing in a
chimney that occupied most of the far wall. More scrap
metal was piled in the corners, and dozens upon dozens
of tools – the uses for which I could not imagine – decorated the remaining walls. On the dirt floor two chairs
and a table were dressed with a cheerful cloth before a
domestic fireplace, and Mr Sheldrake invited me to sit.
With the daylight shut out it felt like being inside a cave,
or a house in a fairy tale. The children walked about
examining things, their fingers coming away black. Mr
Sheldrake showed them how to pump the bellows to fan
the bed of coals. Saul had a turn and then Decca, who
did not react when a spark blew from the flames and
landed on her apron, but calmly watched it extinguish
itself.

Charley had fallen asleep on the way, oblivious to our

surroundings. I rocked the pram back and forth, and watched from a distance as Mr Sheldrake demonstrated how to make a horseshoe, holding a length of steel in the furnace, then curling it like dough around the end of the anvil. The children looked on, Sam panting at their feet as the shoe dulled from fiery red to glowing amber, then finally a dull grey. Mr Sheldrake worked rapidly, his hammer falling in deafening blows. I had never seen them so absorbed; even Millie pursed her lips in concentration. He returned the shoe to the fire, then took a chisel to it, slinging the hammer with precision, not seeming to care about the heat or impact. His hands, I saw, were like leather themselves, his forearms like the sinewy flank of a horse.

Saul cried: 'Nurse May, come and see.'

I got up to stand with them, holding them back from the furnace as the shoe was baked a final time. Mr Sheldrake allowed Decca to plunge it into the water butt, where it made a satisfying hiss.

'Is it safe to touch?' I asked as he returned it to the anvil.

He said it was, and all five of us stroked it; it was warm as fresh bread. 'Keep it,' he said, passing the little shoe to Millie, who clutched it to her chest.

'Can we do another one?' asked Saul.

'Certainly.'

'Why is it so dark in here? Would you not like more windows?'

'I need to see how the metal glows. It's no good working in daylight.'

'I prefer it dark,' Saul replied loftily. 'Sometimes there are too many things to look at.'

Mr Sheldrake took a bar of raw iron and held it between the tongs. 'Metal has a mind of its own, you see. You don't make it, you manipulate it. You train it to do what you ask of it, and you've a very short time in which to do it. I can't stop to answer the door or scratch my nose, otherwise it's ruined. It's a matter of timing and precision. This' – he turned the tongs – 'could be a bolt. It could be a poker, a knife. A spoon. It could be anything. But it's a servant, not a slave, and it'll do nothing against its will.'

Charley cried out from the other side of the room, and I went to give him his rattle. He sat up and gazed about, deciding he wanted to get down and reaching for me.

'No,' I told him. 'You must stay there.' That sent him into a rage, and his face grew as red as the fire as he screamed the place down.

I called for Decca, who picked her way through the gloom. 'Can you take Charley outside in his pram? I would do it myself, but I can't leave you all in here.'

'Yes, Nurse,' she said, though I could tell she was disappointed.

The daylight was blinding, and I closed the door behind her and returned to the others.

'The young master has asked for a knight's helmet,' Mr

Sheldrake remarked with a straight face. 'But I'm not sure that's the work of an afternoon.'

'A sword then!'

'I don't make weapons.'

The heat from the fire was uncomfortable, and Mr Sheldrake seemed to blaze with a similar energy. I took a step backwards, wishing for a cool flannel for my face.

'Why don't I fetch something to mend?' said Mr Sheldrake, looking about. 'I know. One moment.' He crossed the room and pushed open the door, dazzling us once again, and leaving a bright rectangular imprint when I blinked.

'We must go home soon,' I told the children.

'No, I want to stay here!' said Saul.

'Manners.'

'I should like to stay, if you please.'

'Mr Sheldrake can show you one more thing, then we must go home for tea – it's three o'clock already.'

'Can we come back tomorrow?'

'Mr Sheldrake has to work.'

'I can help him.'

I smiled. 'I don't think he needs an apprentice.'

Eventually Mr Sheldrake returned with a broken pitch-fork. 'Who knows what this is?' he asked.

'A giant eats with it,' said Millie.

'Good guess, miss, but it's something much more revolting. It's a dung fork.'

The children cried out in revolted fascination. 'This

came back with me from Australia and I've been meaning to mend it ever since.'

I spoke without thinking. 'You were in Australia?'

'I lived there almost ten years.'

'You scrape up *slops* with it?' Saul asked.

'Sheep, cow, horse, elephant.'

The children laughed.

'I'm not sure it's suitable,' I said.

'Sorry.' He pulled a guilty face, and the children laughed again.

'Is there something more appropriate for them to tell their parents about?'

'I'm sure there must be. Let's see what we have.' He fished around in the piles beside the chimney and came up with a toasting iron.

'That's dull,' said Saul. 'I want to mend the dung fork.'

'If you help me fix this, I'll let you take it home to give your cook. Do you know what they toast in Australia? Marshmallows.' The children were transfixed. 'If you're well behaved your nursemaid might buy you some. Then you can toast them in your nursery fire and pretend you're camping.'

'Nurse,' I said when he'd finished.

'Beg pardon?'

'I am a nurse, not a nursemaid.'

I'd spoken more harshly than I meant to, irritated still by when Conrad Greatrex made the same mistake at the house. Beside us, the fire cracked and sparked, and Mr Sheldrake was taken aback.

'My apologies,' he said, looking at me a beat too long.

Despite the makeshift aprons, dirt and dust streaked the children's clothes, and by the time we arrived home I had only fifteen minutes to wash and change them. I brought the water myself, expecting to find the children undressing as I'd asked. Instead they were poking the mended toast iron into the empty grate, while Millie galloped her horse-shoe across the floorboards. I hauled her wash frock over her head and began unbuttoning Saul's boots. Decca stood motionless by her bed, and I asked her to pass me the sponge. The water was black by the time I'd cleaned their hands and faces, and I cursed at the sound of the tea tray in the hall.

'Decca, pass me your things.' I put out a hand.

'If I change now, the tea will be cold,' she said.

'You can't have tea so dirty. It will only take a minute.'

'I don't mind staying dressed.'

'But you're covered in filth. Here, I'll help you.'

I got to my knees to untie her pinafore and tossed it on the heap by the door. Next I unbuttoned her dress and she removed it herself, folding it on top of the others and stepping into a clean frock I held out for her.

'Should I put the things in the laundry bag?' she asked.

'That would be helpful.'

'Shall I take it down to Emily?'

'That would be even more helpful. Thank you.' I was used to her assistance and took it for granted sometimes. I buttoned her up and she hurried off with the bag swinging.

In the next room I seated Saul and Millie, settling Charley into his high chair to serve their tea. Realising I'd forgotten his bib, I went through to the night nursery. Decca had returned and was posting something beneath her pillow.

'You were speedy! What are you doing?' I asked, taking a bib from the press.

To my great surprise, she looked worried or guilty, and pulled back her hand like she'd been burnt.

'Is everything all right?' I said.

Her ears were crimson. 'Yes,' she said.

'What have you put beneath your pillow?'

'Nothing.'

There was a beat of silence, then I held out my hand. 'Why are you acting strange? Give it to me.' Something passed between us, and I felt my amusement evaporate. 'Give it to me,' I said again. She was not a child who glared or retorted, nor was she contrary; this was the first time she'd shown me any resistance. We moved at the same time to the bed and she reached it first, darting her hand in and out, quick as a flash. I heard the rustle of paper, and she trapped it behind her back, pressed herself against the bed.

'What on earth have you got?'

'It's nothing.' She was frightened, reproachful, and I knelt on the floor before her. 'Is it yours?'

She bit her lip, shaking her head.

'Whose is it, then? Is it mine?'

Another shake.

'Decca, you must tell me.'

'I can't.'

I reached around her back and my hand closed over an envelope. She let me take it and I saw it was blank.

'Who gave this to you?'

She swallowed. 'Mr Sheldrake.'

A frown pulled at my brow. 'Mr Sheldrake?'

She said nothing, and her brown eyes were wide.

'Why would he give this to you? What is it? What did he say?' I made as though to open it, and her hand shot out to stop me.

'No, he said not to look.'

'Why not?'

She whispered the next words: 'It's not for me.'

'Who is it for?'

'Mama.'

The room was silent. From next door came the distant hoot and clatter of the others, and my watch ticked in my pocket. I licked my lips and swallowed.

'What did he say to you exactly? Decca, what did he say?'

'He asked me to give this to Mama.'

'When? When did he do that?'

'When I was outside.'

'Why would he not give it to me?' I asked her.

She said nothing, and the paper crackled in my fingers.

'I should tell your father at once,' I told her. But I knew I would not: letters were private. I understood that more than anyone.

'You can't,' she begged. 'Please, he said nobody else was to know.'

My mind buzzed with possibilities, but kept returning to one. Either Mrs England was not expecting a letter from the blacksmith Mr Sheldrake, or she was. In which case they were in correspondence. Which meant . . . What did it mean?

I tucked the letter into my pocket and took Decca's hands. 'Leave it with me,' I told her. 'I will speak with your mother, and I promise I'll tell no one else.'

Mrs England was present in the drawing room that evening, recovered from her head. She looked tired and faded against the rose-coloured sofa, but brightened when the children entered, sitting up straighter and stifling a yawn. I quarrelled with myself about the best time to speak to her, wondering if it was better or worse to raise it with her husband at home, where he might overhear. But who was I protecting? The envelope burned a hole in my pocket, making me feel guilty by association. I was convinced one of the other children would find it in my apron and draw it out, that my face would betray me.

'Well, children,' said Mr England, snipping a cigar. The tip tumbled to the carpet and came to rest against Mrs England's skirts. He held a match to his mouth and inhaled with deep satisfaction, as though he'd been waiting for this moment all day. 'Tell us about your outing,' he said through the smoke.

Mrs England looked at each of them, and Millie drew out from behind her the little horseshoe. Saul brandished the toasting iron like a sword.

'What do you have there?' she asked.

Her daughter held it to her in triumph. Decca remained by my side at the door.

'A horseshoe! Where did you find this?'

'Mr Sheldrake made it for us.'

There was a pause, in which Mrs England's smile seemed painted on, and she looked at her daughter. 'Who, darling?'

'Mr Sheldrake, the blacksmith.'

I watched her closely. There was a movement at her throat, as though she wished to swallow, but changed her mind. 'Who is that?'

'They met him yesterday, didn't you, children?' said Mr England, leaning against the piano. Behind him, Champion Greatrex gazed mildly from his frame into the room. 'He invited them to his forge, to show them how he makes things.' He coughed into his hand and took another drag. 'Jolly kind of him. What did you think of it?'

'It was *most* interesting,' said Saul. 'He let me fix this.'

'What is that?'

'A dagger!'

'It's a toasting iron,' Millie said. 'He asked for a sword but Mr Sheldrake doesn't make weapons.'

'Ha! A pacifist.' He tapped the ash into one of the large crystal trays frequented about the house. 'What did you learn, then?'

'That metal is more of a servant than a slave,' said Saul.

'How so?'

'You can train it but not force it.'

Mr England's moustache twitched. 'What did Nurse May think of that?'

I swallowed. 'I found it very interesting, sir.'

He nodded. 'Decca, you're quiet. What do you have to say about your excursion?' He waited, smiling. Decca wrung the front of her pinafore, and her mother sat entirely still, watching.

'It was very interesting,' she managed.

'Good!' her father declared. 'Did you bring a present home?'

'There was nothing for me, Papa.' She looked, then, at her mother, and an indefinable expression passed over Mrs England's face. She sank back into the couch and closed her eyes, as though she felt a headache coming.

'I'm to give this to Mrs Mannion,' said Saul unhappily.

'I should say every lad needs a toasting iron for camping in the wilderness. Mrs Mannion has a perfectly good toast fork,' said Mr England.

Saul looked relieved and returned the iron to his pocket. At that moment Charley crawled at lightning speed across the carpet and reached for the cigar nib; I leapt after him and prised it from his fist. Mr England held out the ash tray, heaped with cinders. I nodded my gratitude and moved towards him, aware of our proximity, and the letter in my pocket just inches from his leg. Burning with duplicity, I forced a smile and dropped it in.

I knocked on her door that evening, when Mr England was downstairs with his pipe. In the drawing room she'd told him she could feel her headache returning, and would take her evening meal in bed. I listened for the servants clearing the tea things and the click of the study door, and crossed the landing. Mrs England answered in her nightgown, her dark gold hair hanging over her shoulders, almost reaching her waist.

'Ma'am, could I come in a moment?'

The tiniest frown puckered her forehead, then smoothed itself. She opened the door wider, and I followed her inside. She sat on the edge of the bed like a child.

Gently, I closed the door and passed her the warm,

creased envelope. 'I found this in Miss Decca's possession, ma'am.'

She took it, turning it over and examining it. 'What is it?'

'It's from Mr Sheldrake.'

'Who?'

'The blacksmith, ma'am.'

Her dark eyes burned like coals.

'He gave it to Decca, without my knowing, and asked her to pass it to you. He said nobody was to know. Decca was very reluctant to show me.'

'I can't imagine what he would want. Did you read it?' she asked.

'No, of course not.'

'Well,' she said, her tone light. 'He's probably offering his services, but we have a perfectly good blacksmith.' She tossed it casually across the bed.

'Ma'am,' I said. 'I don't mean to pry.' Her expression was full of caution, and I spoke hesitantly. 'But if you don't wish to receive correspondence from him, I can tell him so. It was inappropriate of him.'

'How do you know Tommy Sheldrake?'

'I don't, ma'am. I've only met him a couple of times out with the children. He invited us to his forge to see him at work, and Mr England thought they would enjoy it.'

'I don't want them going again. Anywhere near him. Do you understand? And the same for you.'

'Yes, ma'am.'

She looked down at the envelope and ran her tongue

over her lips. 'I would appreciate,' she said, 'if you told nobody about this. I'm sure it's nothing either way.' A red patch had appeared on her throat.

'Yes, ma'am,' I said.

As I closed the door a thought arrived: in our conversation, only one of us had called him Tommy, and it hadn't been me.

I put Charley to bed and bathed the other children, weary with exhaustion myself, barely able to lift the steaming jugs. Decca had said very little since the events of that afternoon and slumped at the end of the tub peeling soap from the bar with a fingernail. She was shy at bathtime and tried to cover herself, sitting with her knees drawn up and her ankles pressed together. I vowed to begin bathing her alone, remembering how self-conscious I was at her age.

'What's that smell?' asked Saul.

I sniffed and detected a whiff of smoke. 'Perhaps the lamps need trimming.'

I soaped Millie's hair in silence, lulled by the quiet bedtime sound of splashing water, and got up to fetch the comb from the washstand. Mr England's shaving bowl had not been emptied, the water sitting grey and scummy against the porcelain, the blade dull. I took the comb and returned to the bath.

'Tangles, Nurse!' Millie shouted.

'Sorry.'

From a room beyond came the rise and fall of voices, male and female. Mr England's dressing room was next door to the bathroom, and Mrs England's beside that. Quickly it became clear their exchange was heated or frantic, and there was that smoky smell, woody in scent, unlike burning oil, or vapourless coal.

I got up to look out of the door. The landing was hazy, and I coughed and batted the fumes away, looking around. Mrs England's bedroom door was open, and Blaise appeared at the top of the stairs with a pail and made towards it.

'Why wouldn't you ask the servants?' Mr England's voice said. 'You've lit it all wrong. Where did you get this wood?'

'Is everything all right, sir?' I asked.

He leant out of the doorframe. 'Mrs England decided she wanted a fire, and that she would light it herself. Never mind, it's put out now.' There was the sizzle of water on hot logs, and he vanished again. 'What's this?'

I stood on the landing, listening hard, thinking how the sound was like the water butt at the forge, the hiss of the cooling iron.

Mr England spoke: 'Thank you, Blaise.' He'd said it rather coldly and closed the door behind her. She shot me a glance that was almost clandestine, as though she wished to roll her eyes, and took the empty pail downstairs. I listened another moment, but there was only silence.

In the bathroom, the children turned their faces to me like flowers in a tub.

'What was it?' Decca asked.

'Your mother wanted a fire.'

'I know how to make a fire,' said Saul. 'Papa taught me.'

'I'm cold,' said Decca.

I helped them out of the bath one by one, rubbing them dry and putting them in their night things. Chaperoning them across the landing, I instructed them to get in bed and went downstairs. Blaise was sitting at the large kitchen table eating a pastry slathered in butter. Mrs Mannion was blacking the grate, her hands and wrists stained charcoal.

'The children have finished their bath,' I told Blaise.

Crumbs fell to the table as she carried on eating. 'I'll do it in a minute.'

I waited for her to look at me. 'And Mr England's shaving bowl needs emptying.'

'I'll come up to the nursery, shall I, and tell you how to do your work?'

'Blaise!' Mrs Mannion exclaimed. 'Stop getting crumbs all over my table, will you, and empty the bath. And remember to keep the mistress's door shut else all the rooms will stink.'

Blaise wiped up the mess and dropped it in the waste pail. She moved languidly around the table and took the kettle off the range. 'I'll have a cup of tea first. Don't want to be disturbing anything.'

'What do you mean?' I asked.

She cocked her head at the ceiling. 'They're having a barney. And we all know what happens after.' She smiled unpleasantly, and looked directly at me. 'They go at it like two dogs in a ditch.'

CHAPTER 10

I wrote my postcard to Elsie, and the girls and I took it to the postbox with Charley in the pram, counting the squirrels we saw in the woods along the way. A carpet of leaves and acorns covered the ground, and the air was colder. I was slightly dreading the winter with its short days, when we could not be outside so much.

On our return, the hall was warm and welcoming, and I bundled the children inside. Mr England appeared in the doorway of his study.

'Good morning,' he said.

'Good morning, sir.'

Saul and Mr Booth were in the dining room; I heard the low drone of voices through the door. A week had passed since the incident with the letter, and the sudden plunge into autumn made it seem like a half-forgotten dream.

'Tramping through the forest again, I see,' said Mr England.

'We walked to the postbox, sir.'

'There is one here.' He indicated the gilded letterbox in the hall.

'I didn't know I could use it, sir.'

'Of course. Save yourself the walk.'

'Thank you.'

'Nurse May, would you bring Decca to the drawing room at eleven?'

A pause. 'Yes, sir.'

'Thank you.'

Decca stood mutely beside me. Her father closed the door, and she turned her face to mine.

'We'll take your shoes off down here, girls,' I said. 'I've just cleaned the carpet upstairs.'

I led them to the freezing little boot room at the back of the house where Mr England kept his hunting clothes. The walls were strung with coats that never quite dried and smelt like damp moss.

'Why does Papa want to see me?' Decca asked as I unbuttoned her boots.

'I don't know,' I said brightly.

'Why not Millie as well?'

'I expect we'll find out. I'm sure it's nothing to worry about.'

She had almost finished making her encyclopaedia of botany, piercing a pair of holes and tying the paper together with a red hair ribbon. The project came close to ruin when Charley upset a bottle of paste over the table, but most of it came off, and I cut out the soiled pages.

At quarter to eleven I put Charley down for his nap and set Millie up with some potato stamps at the table. Mr England had given me the money to buy an oil cloth for Saul, and I'd found an enormous one at the midweek market. I cut it in two, putting one half in the bed and the other beneath the tablecloth to protect the wood. Since his first accident Saul had suffered two more, but now changing the bed was the work of five minutes and saved him from embarrassment.

Decca and I went downstairs together. She held her compendium to her chest, her other hand travelling smoothly down the stair rail. That morning she'd put on the coral necklace her mother gave her for her tenth birthday, a pretty thing studded with pearls.

'Shouldn't I show them when it's done?' she'd said in the nursery, pressing a crease in the ribbon.

'We can tell them it's not finished. I'm sure they'd like to read it and see how hard you've worked. We could even make a ticket, like they have at the library, and ask them to sign it.'

Her cloudy expression cleared slightly, and I knocked once on the drawing-room door and pushed it open.

Mr England was standing before Champion's portrait with his watch in his hand, which he tucked smartly away at our arrival. Mrs England was seated at the opposite end of the room, beneath the large picture window. She'd pushed her hands beneath her wide silk skirts and was staring at the carpet, and did not look up.

'Please, sit,' said Mr England, indicating the hard little couch by the door. Decca obliged, arranging her petticoats nervously, and Mr England said: 'You too, Nurse May.' Stiffly, I lowered myself.

'You are to go to school,' he told Decca, with a little sigh of concession, as though he had lost an argument. 'It's all arranged. This weekend Broadley and Nurse May will take you to St Hilda's in Ripon. They were good enough to grant you a space at short notice, thanks to your grandmother's connections. Term started a few weeks ago, so you'll be a little behind the others. But you'll catch up in no time at all.' He attempted a smile of reassurance, but it was unclear who for.

On the front of her encyclopaedia Decca had written: *A Botanical Compendium of West Yorkshire by Rebecca England*; beneath she had sketched a daffodil and carefully painted it yellow and green. I stared hard at the daffodil, absorbing Mr England's words, and at once two things became clear to me: that Decca would be very unhappy at school, and that her being sent away was a consequence of something I did not fully understand. I glanced at Mrs England, whose face was set like a mask.

There was an awful silence. Then, in a small voice, Decca said: 'When will I be able to come home?'

'You'll come home at Christmas.'

'And after that?'

Her father put his head on one side. 'Heavens, you haven't even gone and already you want to come home. I thought you would be a bit happier about it. Think of all the friends you'll make, and the things you'll learn. You'll return a little lady, full of accomplishments.'

In a high voice brimming with emotion, Decca said: 'Can't I stay here? I don't want to go to school.'

'Every child wants to go to school! Nurse May is in favour of it, aren't you? One of the first things she asked me was about your education. I must say the discussion left me quite ashamed.'

Decca turned to me, stunned and betrayed equally. Her expression was unbearable.

'I admit your mother and I have neglected your schooling. Girls simply weren't taught in our day, but now things are different. It was your mother's idea, and I think a splendid one.'

He withdrew a matchbook from his pocket, and next the inevitable cigar. Mrs England's eyes remained on the floor.

'Tell her, Lilian, what you said to me.'

For the first time, Mrs England looked towards her daughter. 'That I wish I had gone to school as a girl.'

There were several seconds of silence, broken only by the carriage clock.

'What do you have there?' Mr England asked, nodding at Decca's lap.

'A book, Papa,' she whispered.

'Will you show me?'

The child was immobilised; I put it into her hands and gently pushed her. She walked stiffly to her father and gave it to him.

'*A Botanical Compendium of West Yorkshire*, eh? Looks impressive.' He leafed briskly through it and held it out to his wife. 'Look at this, Lilian.' He was agitated now, drawing on his cigar in short little puffs. I watched him with sympathy: he was a good father, doing the best he could for his daughter. By sending her to school, he was giving her a gift more valuable than any jewel or dowry. That she had such a happy home she did not want to leave was a credit to him. I told myself it was my own selfishness that made me so forlorn. I wished I could say something to comfort Decca, him, both of them, but I was compelled to sit in silence, worrying about how far behind the other girls Decca would no doubt be.

Mrs England crossed the room to take up the booklet, looking curiously blank. I watched her, thinking how unfeeling she was at times, how distant from her children. Was it so much to ask, for her to embrace her daughter? To tell her there was nothing to fear? I had tried my hardest not to pass judgement, but now it poured from me. As if she could sense it, she glanced at me, and just as quickly away.

158

'You'll go on Sunday afternoon.' Mr England appeared relieved to be back in the realm of logistics. 'It's a couple of hours to Ripon, depending on the weather.'

'But we haven't finished *The Wonderful Wizard of Oz*,' said Decca. 'And there's Blaise and Mr Booth's wedding.'

'I am sure they will save you a piece of cake.'

My nose stung with tears, and I blinked them back. I thought of my sister, and all the rows I'd had with my mother over her education. Several times I'd resisted the urge to put it all in a blistering letter when I had the sense from Elsie that she was lonely and unstimulated. I thought of her blacking the range and peeling vegetables, her future lowering like a ceiling above her. I tried to picture her as a young woman, sitting at a smart desk before a typewriter, trying her best to push the keys with her 'tricky fingers', as she called them, and it made me want to weep.

Sunday was in five days' time. I imagined locking Decca's trunk and waving her off at the doorstep, and something inside me constricted. I hardened myself against it, and sat up straighter.

Mrs England passed the booklet back to Decca. 'It's very good,' was all she said.

Decca accepted it, and shook beside me. I moved closer and put an arm around her.

'I told you they would like it,' I said.

'I must get to work,' said Mr England. He moved past us, through the solid silence, smoke trailing behind him.

Mrs England hovered by the piano and waited for the door to close.

'You'll have a happy time there,' she said. 'You'll learn lots of things.'

Decca gulped, and I rubbed the small of her back.

'Nurse May will take you upstairs now.'

I forced myself to stand and held out a hand, which Decca took automatically. Her skin was ice-cold, and I squeezed her fingers and led her from the room. We were on the stairs when she said: 'My compendium.'

'I'll fetch it. You go on.'

Mrs England was sitting on the piano stool, leaning forwards. Her knees supported her elbows, and she held her head in her hands. I noticed, then, that she had removed her bandage; a perfect circle was stamped on the back of her right hand, beneath the little finger.

I hesitated in the doorway. Decca's book lay on the floor by the hard little couch.

Slowly she took her hands from her face. Her skin was red and blotchy, her cheeks wet. Her mouth turned down slightly, and she looked so disarmingly like her daughter, my instinct was to comfort her. I hurried over and knelt at her feet. She tried to compose herself, making no noise at all, pressing her cheeks with flat palms as though trying to force the tears back inside.

'Don't cry, ma'am,' I said, offering her a clean handkerchief, though I was confused by how upset she was. Had it not been her idea?

She accepted the handkerchief, dabbing at her eyes and sniffing. Then she stood, tidying her hair and brushing down her skirt, leaving me to stumble up from the floor as she swept from the room.

Decca was distraught. I sat on her bed as she sobbed for an hour, wiping her face and stroking her hair. She cried so hard I feared she might be sick. Millie kept a grave vigil beside us, and Charley sat up in his cot. Millie thought something terrible had happened and frowned in bewilderment when I told her the cause of her sister's distress.

'I don't want to go! I don't want to go!' Decca sobbed over and over.

I shushed and murmured, trying to be encouraging as she wept and shook, soaking my handkerchief. 'The first few weeks will pass quickly, and soon you won't want to come home! You'll have a jolly time and forget all about us. You can take your paints, and Tedda. And just think how many friends Tedda will make with the other girls' bears! You'll have such fun. And I'll write every week, and send you your favourite things: sarsaparilla and glacé cherries, and almonds, and all your magazines. We can go to the stationer's tomorrow and buy all your books and pencils. How does that sound?'

The weeping subsided eventually, and by the time Saul came up from his lesson, she was sitting up in bed.

'What on *earth* was that racket?' he demanded, slinging down his books. 'I could hardly hear Mr Booth.'

'Miss Decca is going to a school in Ripon.'

'A school? I thought I was going to school first!'

'Decca is older than you.'

'Will she go instead of me?'

'Of course not. You will go when you are ten.'

Back and forth we went, with Saul asking questions I could not answer: how many girls went there? What lessons was she to have? Would she wear a boater? And so on, until I wished to crawl into bed myself.

I was Decca's age when Doctor Pike came for the first time. It was a winter evening; the shop was shut and the supper things put away. The youngest three were in bed, and I was letting down Archie's trousers; my brothers grew faster than my needle could stitch. The kitchen was warm with the heat from the range, and a candle burned at my elbow. Robbie sat at the far end of the table, tinkering with a clock he'd found on a rubbish heap, trying to get it to work again. There was a knock at the street door, and Mother went down to answer it. He came up the stairs, taking off his hat and saying good evening to all of us, holding at his side a large, shiny bag with a gold clasp. The floorboards groaned and shifted, and Father came out of the bedroom, clearing his throat.

His shirt was clean, and he'd tidied his hair with a wet comb.

'Hello, doctor,' said Father.

I lowered my needle then. A doctor had been only once, years before when Ted had mumps. I'd stayed home from school to look after Elsie while Mother nursed him; his medicine was so expensive she kept it on top of the wardrobe away from our clumsy fingers.

Doctor Pike placed his gleaming bag on the table.

'Ruby, Robbie, go to bed,' said Mother.

'But I haven't finished Archie's—'

'Do it in the morning.'

The bedroom was dark, and I settled in beside Elsie, a baby then, who slumbered, star-shaped. I lay awake, listening to the adults' low voices, gripped by fright. Archie had a slight cough, but no worse than he'd had before; none of us were ill, and all of us in bed, so I knew Doctor Pike must have come for my parents. But they seemed well, too. Perhaps it was an invisible disease, silent like the plague, or even leprosy, which we'd read about in the Bible at school. A long time passed before I heard the scrape of chairs, the creak of floorboards, the street door thudding below. I stared into the dark, my heart thumping. Mother and Father did not speak again, and I listened to the sounds of them going to bed: Mother putting away her shoes, Father setting his watch on the cupboard.

Doctor Pike returned a few months later. It was spring

then, and I was on the street playing hopscotch. I hadn't seen him go in but I saw him come out; it was his bag I noticed first. Dreading the worst, I ran upstairs to see what was the matter. Father was sitting at the table, Mother leaning against the dresser, her arms folded. They'd heard my feet on the stairs.

'Why was the doctor here?' I asked.

Neither of them would look at me.

'Coffee?'

Mr England and I were sitting in the study the day before Decca left for school. The week had passed in a blur of packing and organising, and my fingers were sore from sewing. I did not like coffee, but accepted a cup nonetheless. Mr England had asked me to visit him once my heavy morning work was done. Decca was minding the baby, and I was eager to go back upstairs: I missed her already, and she hadn't yet gone.

'Cream?'

I shook my head. 'No, thank you.'

The study was a small, handsome room, furnished in deep mauve and crimson. It was dark and fragrant, lit only by a green lamp, like a fortune-teller's lair. A glass-fronted bookcase ran the length of the wall opposite the fireplace. Beneath the window was a walnut desk the size of a piano, scattered with papers and paperweights, though no breeze moved through the room; the window was closed and the atmosphere heavy with smoke. It was a masculine space, which Mr England occupied naturally.

He leant on the arm of his chair. 'Well, Nurse May. You've been here a month, and I understand from your principal that a review is part of the procedure. She wrote to Mrs England last week.'

I thought of the wedding-cake houses on Pembridge Square, the steady stream of nurses going in and out at number ten, like cuckoos in a clock striking the hour. How distant it all seemed. Four children sounded like such a lot after baby Georgina. Now I was losing one of them, and three didn't seem enough.

'Firstly, we are extremely satisfied with your work, and will report as such to Miss Simpson.'

'Thank you, sir.'

'Can I ask a question regarding the agency?'

'The Norland agency? I shall try to answer it, sir.'

'Do you know how much commission it takes from your wage?'

'Only a small one. I'm not sure of the exact amount.'

'It makes sense, doesn't it, for you to have your full salary? Cut out the middle man, so to speak?'

I blinked in surprise. 'You mean leave the agency, sir?'

'I'm a businessman, you're a businessman's daughter. I am always thinking of ways to line the pocket. It's one of my worst habits; I'm afraid I can't help it. You'd be better off each quarter, would you not?'

'I'm not sure I can do that, sir.'

'Not sure if you can, or if you will?' His drew up his moustache in a smile. 'Think on it. I only suggest it for your benefit.'

I nodded.

'Nurse May, you look most put out. Of course, I'm not suggesting you do anything against your will. Stay with the agency if it pleases you. Only I recall you mentioning a poorly sister. How old is she?'

'Eleven, sir.'

'And what is the matter with her exactly?'

'It's her spine, sir. It affects her movements: her hands and legs. Sometimes she struggles to walk and pick up things.'

He narrowed his eyes in sympathy. 'Is she in pain?'

'She suffers, but she bears it well.'

He sighed and moved his saucer half an inch to the right. 'This is a delicate question – forgive me if I'm intruding – but . . . I assume you contribute to your family's finances? Doctor's bills, that sort of thing?'

'Yes, sir.'

'How much of your wage?'

I reddened and stared at my fingers. 'Half, sir.'

He nodded across the desk and I moved my coffee cup to my lap.

'And your first wage is due to be paid . . .'

'Next week, sir.'

He put an elbow on the polished wood and stroked his chin thoughtfully.

'I'm yet to send the money order. Would it help if I increased your salary by five shillings a month?'

My mouth fell open, and the cup slipped in my lap. Coffee splashed my apron, and I set the saucer on the desk to dab at the stain. 'I . . . sorry . . . I wasn't . . .'

'Consider it done.'

'Mr England, I . . .'

'This is not a discussion.' He smiled.

'Thank you, sir. I can't thank you enough.'

'Thank you will do just fine.'

I got up to leave. The scarlet silk cushion I'd been sitting against dropped onto the seat, and I propped it against the chair back. Down it slid again, and again I righted it. It happened over and over, making me increasingly hot and flustered, and after several attempts I wished to dash the thing against the wall. Meanwhile, Mr England observed, amused, from behind his desk. On my ninth attempt to set it right, it took mercy on me and was still.

'Stay,' said Mr England. 'Good doggy.' He grinned, and his teeth were white as pearls.

We all walked together down to the coach house, the Englands, the servants and me, followed by Broadley pushing Decca's trunk in a cart. Decca and I had stencilled R. England on it ourselves. When she hadn't been looking I took Herbie from my pillow and tucked him inside, beneath her nightdress. My stomach had been in knots all morning, and as much as I'd put on a jolly face for the children, I knew they saw through it.

Her parents said their goodbyes, her father dignified and composed, giving her a kiss on top of her dark head, her mother worn and tired, as though it was something she'd already done a hundred times. While Broadley secured Decca's trunk, I clambered in beside her. Millie and Saul waved cheerfully, and Blaise bounced Charley on her hip, flapping his wrist. The children would be without me until late in the evening, and I'd instructed their parents on how to put them to bed.

I'd warned Decca against eating all her lunch, and I'd been right to; she emptied her stomach three times on the way to Ripon, and sat so still and white-faced that if I didn't know about the blackberry jelly, I'd have thought her sickening for something. She spent the journey looking silently out of the window, resting her head against the leather trim. It was a grey, drizzly day, and the weather grew worse on the moors, but she fixed her attention on the dreary sky without seeming to see it. I pointed at sheep in the fields and kites circling over-head, but she was unresponsive. I wished I had some words of comfort, a promise of when I'd see her again, but I'd wrung myself dry of positivity, and did not want to make vows I couldn't keep. I knew I'd find her different the next time I saw her and dreaded it already. The other girls would shape her, colour her; she wouldn't be made of dough much longer.

St Hilda's Ladies College was a grey, turreted building set behind a high wall with elaborate gates. Mrs Maurice, the headmistress, met us at the door. She was in her fifties or sixties, wearing an old-fashioned black gown and a crucifix brooch at her throat. The hall was hushed and dim, with the strong scent of lilies and furniture polish. Stone cherubs flanked a wide central staircase, overlooked by an enormous stained-glass window depicting various biblical scenes. Dark doors led off in all directions, and distantly a bell chimed.

'Welcome to St Hilda's,' said Mrs Maurice. She spoke quietly, as though we were in church. 'You are Miss England's nurse, I take it? May I offer you refreshment?' I looked over at Decca, who appeared only to be a pair of dark eyes in the gloom. Mercifully her pinafore was clean; she'd had the foresight to put her head out of the window to vomit.

'No, thank you, ma'am. I'd best be getting back.'

'Very well. The young lady, being one of our younger charges, will be paired with an older girl, called an aunt. If you'd like to come with me, miss. Is this everything?'

Broadley had finished putting Decca's things in the hall; as well as the trunk there was a small suitcase and a hat box for Sunday best. In addition to Herbie, I'd tucked in her picture postcard of the falls, a bag of sarsaparilla and the latest issue of *Girl's Realm*.

There was no reason for me to stay, and I hugged Decca tightly. 'You write to me whenever you want to. And I'll write to you,' I spoke into her hair. 'We'll save *The Wonderful Wizard of Oz* until you're home for the holidays.' She submitted, too stricken by what was happening to embrace me back. I tidied her hair and unfastened the top button of her cloak just to touch her, not knowing when somebody else would.

'Do you know the address?' she whispered.

I replied yes, and that I'd write once a week at least, at a different time than her parents so the letters came separately. Then I was leaving, thanking Mrs Maurice and stepping into the steel-coloured daylight. Broadley had taken up his seat at the reins.

'All right, Nurse?'

'Yes, thank you, Broadley.'

'Rain's on its way. It'll take longer going back.'

I climbed into the sour-smelling cab, more upset than I had a right to be. Little girls went off to school all the time: they learnt how to play the piano and arrange flowers and speak French and other nice, proper things that made them good wives and daughters. Accomplishments, like Mr England had said. She would make friends, who might invite her to their country houses in the summer, who might open up her little world. Every parent on Longmore Street in the flats stacked like matchboxes above the shops would have given their best candlesticks to send their children somewhere like St Hilda's; they would have been unable to comprehend the tears and resignation. I settled in Decca's seat, which was still warm, rested my head against the leather and watched the sky all the way home.

CHAPTER 11

The crash came from the landing at breakfast time. I was peeling grapes for Charley when a noise startled us, like a cabinet falling from a great height. Saul, Millie and I stared at one another, and though I told them to stay, they followed me to the door. The landing was a wreck, the floor littered with broken china. Tea steamed from the stone flags, glass glittered and egg trembled in pearly fragments. In the midst of it all was Blaise, flinging everything onto a silver tray.

'The bloody door's locked!' she exclaimed. I knelt beside her and helped her collect the worst of it. 'I went sideways into it, thinking it were open, and lost my balance.' Her cheeks were red with embarrassment, and her right hand was bleeding.

'Stop, I'll do it. Why was it locked?'

'Blaise?' Mrs England called from behind the door.

Blaise rolled her eyes and said loudly: 'I can't get in, madam. You'll have to open it.'

'*I* haven't locked it.' The emphasis was on the first word.

'Well, I've no key for your room.'

Two pale faces watched us from the nursery.

'Saul,' I said, 'can you see if your father's home?'

'Why?'

'Please do as I say.'

Off he darted down the stairs as Blaise and I scooped broken crockery into our aprons.

'Is the cut bad?' I asked.

'No.'

'I'll get you something from the medicine cupboard.'

She glanced at me from the corner of her eye. 'Thanks.' And after a moment, 'Did you have medical training at that school?'

'We do three months in a hospital on a children's ward. The rest is theory from *Cassell's* and journals, that sort of thing.'

'Suppose you have to be good at reading to learn about medicine.' She sounded resentful, but it was a general resentfulness and not the direct kind she usually reserved for me.

We cleared away the worst of it and emptied our aprons into a towel Blaise took from the airing cupboard. Beneath the sound of tinkling china, I asked quietly: 'Why is her door locked?'

Blaise looked uneasy. After a pause, she said: 'He locks her in at night.'

'Why?'

Her eyes flicked towards the bedroom door, and she spoke in a whisper. 'He's found her wandering about before at night.'

'What's wrong with that?'

'She nearly started a fire in the kitchen once. She took the baby downstairs when Mrs Nangle was sleeping. And another time he . . . he found her in the woods. He's afraid she'll hurt herself.'

I thought of the coin-shaped burn beneath her little finger.

At that moment Saul bounded up the stairs two at a time. 'Papa's at the mill,' he cried.

'Thank you. Now finish your breakfast.'

'I'm not hungry.'

'Saul.' With a sigh he disappeared. 'What was she doing in the forest?' I whispered.

Blaise pulled a face. 'Who knows? She looked like she'd been walking: her dress was covered in mud. She didn't say anything to me and I didn't ask.'

We were standing by Mr England's dressing room. The door was ajar, and through it I saw the curtains were tied back, the narrow bed neatly made. The door to his wife's bedroom was beside the window. A pile of books sat on a stool beside the bed, a crystal tumbler balanced on top like a paperweight. Before I knew what I was doing, I walked inside and found myself lifting the glass, inhaling the scent of brandy.

'What you playing at?'

'The key might be in here.'

On the carpet was a blackened nightlight that needed cleaning. A frock coat hung on the press door.

'You can't just go in the master's room.'

'Why not? The mistress is locked in; the key must be here somewhere.'

'One of us will have to go to the mill and tell him.'

'I can't leave the children.'

We stared at one another, then Blaise sighed and untied her apron. 'Looks like I'm going, then.'

When she'd gone, I took a last look around the narrow room before stepping out onto the landing. Glass crunched beneath my feet, and I stood for a moment, alone with the portraits. Mrs England's door was a wall of silence.

'Mrs England?' I said.

'What?'

Her voice was much closer than I expected, and I took a step backwards.

'Blaise has gone to fetch the master.'

There was movement through the wood, the rustling sound of skirts. Air pushed through the keyhole, brushing my hand like feathers. Then there was stillness, cool and heavy as a lake.

On Blaise's last day, Mrs Mannion made a lemon sponge cake, and the household gathered in the kitchen to bid her farewell. We ate standing up from little crystal bowls, and Mrs Mannion passed around glasses of sherry for the adults. I accepted one but did not drink it. Mr England gave a generous farewell speech, teasing Blaise about being far better suited as a tutor's wife than a maid, and everybody laughed, Blaise included. She fanned herself with a napkin, rosy from all the attention. I wiped ice-cream from the children's faces and told them they could have no more, but Mr England kept spooning little curls into their bowls and winking at them. Mrs England listened to a tale of Mrs Mannion's with a faraway smile on her face. Emily stood beside her, casting nervous glances at Broadley's grandson, Ben the groom. He was a year or two older than Emily and spoke with a squeak, and slept above the stables with his grandfather. His appearances at the house were like single coals thrown on a smouldering fire; she glowed and twinkled at him, and he didn't know where to look.

'Nurse May,' Mrs Mannion prompted. 'Do you want to fetch the gift from the children?'

'I'll get it!' Millie cried, and everybody laughed. I brought Charley with us to the nursery, where a bouquet of wildflowers stood in a porcelain vase. The children and I had spent the afternoon picking them, assembling a pretty bunch of orchids and meadowsweet, with some glossy fronds of fern and sprigs of myrtle. I'd tied it with a length of lace from one of Charley's baby gowns. Millie presented it to Blaise, who was radiant with delight. All night she had not stopped smiling; it quite transformed her face, making smooth apples of her cheeks, and her dark eyes shone.

'We wish you a long and happy marriage, Blaise,' said Mrs England. 'Thank you for your years of service, and all you've done for us.'

'Thank you, madam.'

'Best of luck for tomorrow. I'll go up now, if you'll excuse me.'

'Of course,' said Blaise. 'I'll see you at the church. I've pressed your dress for you. It's hanging in the wardrobe.'

Mrs England opened her mouth, then closed it and smiled. 'Thank you. I'm not sure I'll come tomorrow. I'm a little under the weather.'

'Oh, you won't miss my wedding!'

'Of course she won't,' said Mr England. 'The whole family will be there.'

'Except Miss Decca.' Blaise pouted theatrically. 'How's she settling at school?'

'Very well,' said Mr England.

She hadn't yet written to me, though I'd sent a letter the day after she went. 'Has she written to you, sir?'

'Not yet,' said Mr England. 'Though the headmistress has.'

With a sense of unease, I checked off the things I'd packed in her trunk. Her new pens and stationery had gone in, and a booklet of stamps. Perhaps they could only write at set times, I thought, though five days had passed.

At some point Mrs England had left the room, the door swinging soundlessly behind her.

'Right,' said Mrs Mannion. 'I'll clear up and we'll go to the Lanterns, shall we?'

The others began collecting bowls and sherry glasses, and Mrs Mannion took out the jar of soap jelly and poured some into the sink. I filled a jug for the children and took Millie's sticky hand to lead them up to bed.

'Are you coming, Nurse May?' Mrs Mannion called across the kitchen.

Mr England was holding the door for us, and I paused beneath his arm. 'Coming where?'

'To the Three Lanterns. We've having a celebratory shandy for Blaise before the wedding tomorrow. Just one, mind.'

'Oh, no, I won't, but thank you.'

'There's no harm in a shandy, Nurse May, when the children are in bed,' said Mr England. 'I only wish Mrs Mannion had invited me.'

'Oh, give over,' said Mrs Mannion, waving soap suds over the floor. 'Blaise said to invite you.' To my surprise she spoke to me.

'She did?'

I glanced at Blaise, who was leaning on the counter beside a battered suitcase that somehow held eight years' worth of belongings. She was deep in discussion with Tilda and had not heard.

'Go to the pub,' said Mr England. 'Put the children to bed and Broadley will bring you and Tilda back.'

It was an order, half-concealed, but still an order. I nodded.

'What time are you going?'

'Twenty minutes,' said Mrs Mannion. 'I'll just finish here.'

Mrs Mannion lived in a cottage on the edge of town and walked to and from the house each day. Emily lived at home, too, which meant that from tonight Tilda would sleep alone above the scullery. I wondered if she minded, but I knew nothing of her character at all.

Blaise caught my eye and gave a quick smile, then returned to her conversation. I put the children to bed; the baby went down easily, heavy with ice-cream, and Saul got himself undressed while I washed Millie.

'Where are you going?' she asked.

Since Decca left, she'd been full of questions. I'd let her sleep in my bed the first night, when she missed the warmth of her sister beside her.

'The public house,' I said.

'What's that?'

'It's a place where people meet after work.'

'And drink beer,' said Saul.

'Not me,' I said.

'What's beer?' asked Millie.

'A drink for grown-ups.'

'Can I try some?'

'Ladies don't drink beer, but perhaps when you're older your father will let you have a sip.'

'I've tried it,' said Saul. 'It's dreadful.'

'Have you now?'

'Yes, it tastes like soil.'

I was only half-listening, anxious, somehow, about the evening ahead with the servants. I thought about faking a headache or pretending Charley wouldn't settle, but at this point any excuse would be transparent. There might be other people at the pub, friends and acquaintances of Blaise's, who would want to chat, and I'd have to come home with Tilda in the carriage. What on earth would we talk about? And if she wished to stay longer than I did, I doubted Broadley would do two trips, and besides, I couldn't leave her alone at the pub. Nor could I sit quietly with the silent, sullen Emily, who was too young to come with us. Oh, why did Mrs Mannion have to invite me? It was much simpler at Norland, where the students only mixed with each other and there was no hierarchy to speak of. At Perivale Gardens there was only Cook and Ellen, who never went out at night or suggested anything social. They visited the shops on their half-days and a treat for them was tea at a corner house.

The children watched me change into my single smart outfit: a white blouse that needed pressing but would have to do, and a navy wool skirt with a black trim and buttons. Putting on my own clothes felt odd; I had worn uniform every day since arriving at the Englands', and neglected to take my half-day on a Sunday – another thing Sim would be displeased by. But here it was nothing like London, where I could saunter anonymously. I had no wish to sit alone in a tea room on the high street and be drawn into conversation with servers and patrons. The people here were almost *too* friendly, unfamiliar with the concept of minding their own business. Nobody at Hardcastle House noticed I hadn't taken my half-days, or if they had, they hadn't mentioned it. Or perhaps they thought I *did* take it, that the children occupied themselves for five hours while I read a book.

Mr England was still in the kitchen. He'd removed his jacket and sat in his waistcoat and shirtsleeves, which he'd rolled up his arms. 'Ready for a night on the town,' he said over his cigar. The smile did not reach his eyes, and he was looking at me in a way that pinned me to the floor. I fumbled with my waistband and went to stand with the others, who had changed, too, out of their service uniforms. Already I longed to take off my hat and go upstairs to the sanctuary of the nursery and read in the flickering lamplight, with the children safe around me.

Blaise was in high spirits from the sherry and tucked a flower into her hair. 'Shall we go?'

I followed the others through the scullery, but Mr England called me back.

'Is the nursery locked?' he asked, tapping ash from his cigar.

'Yes, sir.'

He nodded. 'Have fun.'

The Three Lanterns stood by the old stone bridge in the centre of the town, plainly furnished with stone floors and whitewashed walls. It flooded every year when the river swelled and immersed the shops and pavements in freezing brown water, so no fuss had been taken over its appearance: it was a modest drinking place for working people, and few ordered the fine wines and spirits advertised. Inside, two front rooms stood either side of a central bar, with a billiards hall at the back and a storehouse and yard beyond. Though it was my first time in a public house, I found it quite comfortable and familiar, with its low ceilings and pictures on the walls. In the room to the right a group of men sat around a little table, laughing and shouting over one another. They knew Blaise and called her over, and she waded through hats and jackets with her suitcase and flowers, and dropped onto the lap of a man sitting on a bench. I realised it was Mr Booth, and watched with astonishment as they kissed full on the mouth, Blaise holding her hat, crushing the bouquet between them. There were roars of encouragement and applause, and one or two got up to make room for us, fetching stools and chairs from the corners.

A young man in a flat cap and shirtsleeves offered me a stool beside him. Mrs Mannion and Tilda accepted seats beside the others, flustered and smiling, pulling down their jackets and straightening their hats. I hadn't known it would be like this, that we would sit with men: men who had been drinking. The one in shirtsleeves introduced himself as Alan Shawcross. He was bright and pink-cheeked, with straw-coloured hair and a gap between his front teeth.

'I'm Ruby,' I said.

'Are you a maid like Blaise? How many have they got up there?'

'No, I'm the children's nurse.'

'A nurse!' He was impressed. At that moment Mr Booth stood to fetch a round of drinks for the women, moving with difficulty through legs and stools towards where Mr Shawcross and I sat beside the empty fireplace.

'Nurse May.' He sounded pleased. 'I didn't expect to see you here.'

'Me neither,' I said. Mr Booth was holding a glass of beer.

'Would you like a drink?'

'Nothing for me, thank you.'

'You must have something. A glass of wine? Shandy?'

'I've already had a sherry at the house.'

'Sherry it is, then.'

Blaise was laughing at something.

'Mrs Mannion.' Mr Booth clamped a hand on the cook's shoulder. 'Can I interest you in a brandy?'

Mrs Mannion shrieked. 'Oh, not a brandy, Mr Booth, I only take a very weak shandy.'

'And Tilda?'

'I'll have a glass of beer, please.'

'That's the spirit.'

He clapped Mrs Mannion on the back and disappeared through the doorway. I turned back to Mr Shawcross, eyeing the clock on the chimney breast. Broadley was returning at ten, in two hours: an unbearably long time. An oil lamp hung from the ceiling, and with all the tobacco and fumes from the ale, and all the men drinking in close quarters, I felt as though I was in the belly of a ship. I had to ask Mr Shawcross to repeat himself.

'I said: what does being a nurse involve?'

'Do you have children, Mr Shawcross?' I'd noticed his wedding ring.

'Yes, a little lad. He'll be seven months next Tuesday.'

'Well, I expect my duties aren't that dissimilar to your wife's.'

'If only someone paid her for it,' he said, with a note of wistful resentment. 'You've a funny accent. Where are you from?'

'Birmingham.'

'The Black Country! I applied for a job at the *Post* a long time ago.'

185

'The *Birmingham Post*?'

'Aye.'

'Are you a journalist?'

'A reporter at the *Halifax Courier*, same as John.' He pointed out the man two or three seats away, and I found myself looking at Mr Lowden.

'Hello again,' he said.

'Hello,' I returned.

'Nurse May, wasn't it? You never did give me your first name.'

'Did I not?'

'She gave it to me,' said Mr Shawcross. 'What's it worth?'

'Did you see the article?' Mr Lowden asked me.

'I did.'

'We have to give the Greatrexes a tickle every now and again, at the *Courier*,' said Mr Shawcross. 'You never know when you might need them.'

'More like the other way around,' Mr Lowden cut in. 'Did you hear about what happened at Colden Mill on Monday? A lad got his arm ripped off in a loom. Fourth death in a Greatrex mill in as many years.'

'One sherry, one shandy, one beer, one brandy.' Mr Booth set down four glasses in front of us and distributed them to the servants. 'Which was yours, Ruby?'

Mr Lowden's eyes found mine, and something in them made me go cold. My own expression appeared to confirm it to him, and he sat back. I watched as his face shifted into a facsimile of an expression I knew all too well, and wished to leave at once. There was a cab rank at the station, five minutes' walk along the canal. The clock on the wall told me it was fifteen minutes past eight.

'You're not leaving already!' Blaise had removed her hat, and her cheeks were pink.

'I think I had too much ice-cream,' I said, hearing how pathetic I sounded. She knew I was lying; her dark eyes narrowed in suspicion, but she said nothing. Tilda had wandered off somewhere with the man she'd been talking to, and Mrs Mannion had her back to me, deep in conversation. I slipped out, shoving my way through the bar into the cool night.

I set off at speed to the station, standing aside for the tram to go clanging past before crossing the road.

'Nurse May! Ruby!'

A male voice shouted again, and I quickened my pace, glad it was dark so I could disappear. Footsteps caught up with me, and Mr Booth appeared to my right. He shoved his hands in his pockets. 'What's the matter?'

'I ought to get back for the children.'

'You've not been out an hour. Did they not say you could stay, at the house?'

'I shouldn't, really. I have duties after the children go to bed.'

'I'll walk you.' He began crossing the road.

'That's all right, I'll go to the station for a cab.'

'You'll not get one now – they clear off about seven after the Leeds train.'

'Please, Mr Booth. I insist you go back.'

'*I* insist you come back. You left in a hurry.' He looked closely at me beneath the street lamps.

'I'm not feeling well.'

'I'll take you. It's only up the road.'

'It's two miles!'

'You can't walk through the woods on your own.'

'Please go inside.'

'Then come back with me, wait for Broadley.' I didn't move. 'Now I know where Master Saul gets his stubbornness,' he said. 'Come on, then.'

He fell into step beside me as we trudged uphill. The road curved around the side of the valley, hemmed in by a low stone wall with a vertiginous drop to the river below. The water sounded faster at night, and I wondered if Mr Booth would take me all the way to the house. I had only crossed the bridge once in the darkness before, with Mr England on my first night, and that had been with a lantern.

Mr Booth switched sides automatically to put himself by the road and I asked him to swap.

'You don't like heights?' he asked.

'No.'

'I used to sit on this wall and fish when I was a boy.'

'It's forty feet! All you'll catch there is your death.'

He laughed and we walked on.

'You must be excited for tomorrow,' I said.

'What's happening tomorrow?'

'I should push you in,' I said. 'You know what I mean: your wedding day.'

'*Here is the golden close of love, All my wooing is done.*'

I said: 'I should hope so.'

He laughed. 'Lord Tennyson. One of my favourites.'

'Never heard of him.'

'You've never heard of Tennyson?' He groaned. 'Oh, I'm envious. One of our greatest poets and you have it all to come.'

'When am *I* going to read poetry?'

We passed beneath more amber street lights, and, as we ascended, the town glowed in miniature.

'Do you hope to be a blushing bride, Nurse May?'

'I would like to get married one day.' To my embarrassment I did blush, and hoped he couldn't tell. 'How do you know Mr Lowden?'

'Oh, you want to marry *Lowden*,' he teased.

'No!'

'I thought he might have said summat to offend, you shot up that quick. So he's nothing to do with you feeling unwell?'

'No, of course not. He was asking rather a lot of questions, though.'

'Natural, in his line of work. I've known Lowden since school.'

'Is he a friend of the Englands?'

'I don't think anybody's a friend of the Englands.'

'What do you mean by that?'

'Wazzies don't have *friends*. Only us proles do.'

'What are wazzies and proles?'

He laughed. 'Bourgeoisie? Proletarian? You're green as grass, Nurse May. I told Blaise she was wrong about you.'

'Why, what did she say?'

He fell silent, as though in regret, and passed a hand over a tortoiseshell cat sitting on a wall outside a house.

'She'd kill me for telling you, but I suppose it doesn't matter now she's leaving. She said you thought you were better than them.'

Hot and indignant, I replied: 'I don't at all.'

'That's what I said. I think she took offence that you're from London. She reckoned you'd have all these airs and graces.'

'I don't have them. And I'm not from London, I just worked there.' We continued in silence, and then I said: 'She decided she didn't like me before she met me.'

'She can take a while to warm up,' he said. 'But her heart's in the right place. She's a good person.'

Somehow his loyalty stung more. I wondered how it would be to have somebody defend me like that.

'She went for the job of nursemaid, you know.'

'*Blaise* did?'

He nodded. 'And Mr E turned her down. She hadn't the experience. She's not bitter, though. She's quite happy being an housemaid. Was,' he corrected.

'That explains a lot,' I said bitterly.

'At least her name suits her, don't you think?' he said next. 'A fiercely burning fire.'

I couldn't help but smile. 'It does, rather.'

'That's our house down there, by the packhorse bridge.' He pointed to the mass of glowing windows below. 'Spring Grove. We move in on Monday. Blaise wants me to paint the door bright red.'

I smiled. 'And will you?'

'What do you think? It'll be like living inside a cherry.'

'I expect it will be strange for her at first, not working,' I said.

'She wanted to stay on, but . . .'

'But what?'

He shrugged. 'It's not proper, is it?'

'Mrs Mannion's married.'

'She's an honorary Mrs.'

I blinked in surprise. 'Well,' I said, 'I suppose being a wife is work in a way.'

'How do you mean?'

'Somewhere between a mother and a serving girl.'

'Good heavens.' He stopped and looked around. 'Am I about to marry my mother?'

I laughed. We were already halfway home, leaving the lamplit windows of the road for the dark mouth of the woods.

'I'm afraid I'll have to leave you now,' he said.

'Oh!' I said.

'I'm joking.' He took my arm, and a bolt of lightning seized me. 'Are you all right, Nurse May?'

'Fine, thank you. I'm sorry you had to leave the others.'

'They'll be there when I get back. I'll go down with Broadley.'

The forest closed in either side of the bridleway, and I looked through the solid blackness across the valley towards the house, where Saul, Millie and Charley were asleep.

As though sensing my thoughts, he asked: 'Do you miss Decca?'

'Very much.'

'You're alike as two peas in a pod.'

I frowned. 'I haven't heard from her. I didn't think to ask the headmistress how often they were allowed to write.'

'Perhaps she's not much to say yet.'

I nodded and we walked in silence for a moment. 'Earlier,' I began again, slowly, 'when you said about Mr England having no friends . . .'

'Mmm?'

'Why does he have no valet? No footman? There aren't any male servants at the house.'

'Why do you think?'

'I haven't thought about it until now.'

'He likes to be the only cockerel in the coop.'

'Meaning?'

'Oh, I don't know. Just a few things Blaise has told me.'

I longed to speak with him about the other day at breakfast when we'd found Mrs England locked in, but discretion prevented it. Already we were straying towards impropriety, and with reluctance I steered us back to safety. It was the most candid conversation I'd had in a long time, and I wished it wouldn't end. Already I'd gone from being someone who'd never been alone with a man to walking arm in arm with one at night. I was confused, used only to the company of brothers.

We approached the stone bridge and crossed it together. 'I can go from here,' I said, turning to face him.

'I'll walk you to the house.'

'There's no need.'

We were standing close together.

'Best of luck for the morning,' I said.

'I'll need it.'

'You won't.'

His face was cast in shadows, but I knew he was smiling. 'I'll see you at church, Nurse May. Ruby.'

'Thank you for walking me back, Mr Booth. And thank Blaise for me.'

'Call me Eli. The others do. And it's no bother.'

I watched him go, and it was like he took a lamp with him, for now the darkness seemed to creep closer, and with it the knowledge that Mr Lowden was still at the pub with Blaise and the others, and the conviction that he knew who I was. I should have been more worried, but rising to the surface was another thought, a traitorous one: how glad I was that Blaise had left her employment, and how pleased I was that Mr Booth would stay.

CHAPTER 12

It was the perfect day for a wedding. The October air was crisp, the sky a sunny blue. Inside, Hardcastle House was chaos, with servants' tempers fraying, silk ties sought and discarded, boots furiously polished and an outfit change for Millie, who had spilt her breakfast. Tilda flew from room to room like a whirligig; it seemed Blaise had been more organised than the household gave her credit for. The Englands were not replacing her; they had appointed Tilda general housemaid, and she was completely overwhelmed.

I returned the nursery breakfast tray myself and, crossing the landing, heard raised voices from Mrs England's room. A moment later it flew open, and Mr England stepped out. I caught the end of his words: '. . . going alone with the children.'

He gave me a glowering look, but it was one of complicity. 'Tilda?' He barked down the stairs. 'Tilda!'

I passed Tilda puffing up in her best dress. She had curled her fair hair in ringlets and wound it into an attractive roll.

'Tilda, help Mrs England get dressed, please. We must leave in half an hour. Is Broadley ready?'

'I think so, sir.' She disappeared into the mistress's room.

I took the tray to the kitchen, where Mrs Mannion was clearing the breakfast things. She wore a fitted black jacket and skirt, and had fastened an amber brooch at her neck. I was the only member of staff wearing uniform.

'What a palaver,' she cried. 'Tilda doesn't know if she's coming or going, Emily's disappeared to sort her hair and I'm getting soap all over my skirt.'

'Do it later. I can help when Charley's napping.'

I hurried upstairs to arrange the children, and at half past ten had them standing by the front door, with Charley in my arms wearing a long white dress I hoped would not get dusty on the drive. Next down was Mr England in a dark suit with a silver-topped cane, his moustache bristling. The servants were meeting us at the coach house, so of course Mrs England was last. She came tripping down the stairs in a state of disorder, wearing a gown the colour of violet cream filling. She'd looped her silk handbag over her arm.

To my surprise, she reached out and passed me a letter. 'This arrived for you yesterday,' she said. At once I recognised Elsie's handwriting. Mrs England did not explain why she was only handing it to me now. I thanked her, shoving it into my pocket, and led the children from the house.

We were among the last to arrive at the church, which was not the same one the Englands attended, and a different denomination. I helped the children up the steps and followed the master and mistress to a reserved pew at the front. Almost every seat was taken, and the guests turned to watch us down the aisle. Mr Booth was sitting at the front beside his family, glancing around and waving now and again. He caught my eye and smiled, and I felt myself turn scarlet.

Mrs England sat beside me, wearing an enormous hat that obscured most of her face, and staring at her spotless gloves. Mr England took Charley onto his lap and the baby showed great interest in his moustache, tugging at it and making the guests laugh. Before long the organ started up, and we stood as one as Blaise came down the aisle with two bridesmaids. She wore a simple cream dress with short sleeves and elbow-length gloves, and clutched a spray of white hellebores. A veil covered her neatly rolled dark hair, and a smile split her face in two. I found that I could not look at the couple as they exchanged vows, so stared instead at an arrangement of pink roses and the heads of the people in front. Mrs England, too, was making me anxious, fizzing with a frantic sort of energy and fidgeting worse than her children. She opened and closed her hymn book and shifted in her seat, and did not stand when we rose to sing.

Within half an hour the couple were proclaimed Mr and Mrs Booth, and we exited into the slow-moving traffic of the aisle. Mr England spoke to many people and shook many hands. It took us five minutes to reach the doors, and by the time the vicar approached in his slim black coat, Mrs England had vanished.

'I don't believe we've met,' he said, shaking Mr England's hand. 'Reverend John Blackley.' He was small and meek-looking, and wore gold-rimmed spectacles.

'Charles England. Pleased to meet you, Reverend.'

While the two men spoke, I looked about for the mistress's distinctive hat among the sea of brown and black.

'Can we find Mr Booth?' asked Saul.

'Yes,' I replied. 'I can see them over there. Why don't you wish them congratulations?'

'Can you come with us, Nurse May?' said Millie.

Looking about for Mr Lowden, I took them towards the little crowd circling the bride and groom. Somebody gave Millie and Saul a handful of rice each, and everybody laughed as they threw it at rather than over the newlyweds. Mr Booth pretended to have been shot, which made the children laugh harder. Charley was getting heavier by the week; I wished he would cry so I could retreat to a quiet wall, but he gazed about, absorbed by the festivities.

'Congratulations,' I said brightly.

'Thank you,' Mr Booth returned. Blaise was talking to an older woman; she looked over and gave a brief, dismissive smile. My eyes fell to the gold wedding band on her finger. I turned again to Mr Booth, but it seemed after the previous night we'd run out of things to say. I felt colour rise again to my cheeks, and longed for a glass of water.

'Where is the wedding breakfast?' I asked him.

'At Crossley's. Nothing fancy, only a ham and egg tea for two dozen.'

'Lovely,' I said.

'Not sure where the sense is calling it a breakfast when it's after dinner.'

'I think it's because it's your first meal as man and wife.'

'Is that so?'

I felt that he knew this and was looking for something to say. I thought about our tramp through the forest, his arm locked through mine. How I hadn't wanted our conversation to end. I was relieved when Charley wanted to get down.

'I'll leave you to your guests,' I said.

'You take your nurse for a walk, young man,' he told Charley. 'Thank you for coming, Ruby.'

I led Charley along a path that cut through the burial ground and let him toddle about between the gravestones.

'Hello,' said a male voice from behind. I turned and looked into the face of the last person I was expecting.

'Mr Sheldrake.'

The blacksmith was standing with his back against the stone wall of the church, smoking a cigarette. He was the smartest I'd seen him, in a brown suit and cap.

'You look as though you've seen a ghost,' he said.

I wrenched Charley up onto my hip and stood so I was facing him. 'What did you think you were doing, asking a little girl to run your errands?'

He stared at me a moment, then looked at the ground and threw down his cigarette.

'Yes, I know all about it,' I said. 'Don't worry, Decca didn't break your promise. In fact, she didn't tell me, I found it myself.'

'Did she give it to her?'

'I did.'

He took a lungful of air and exhaled slowly, with relief.

'I can't think what business you have writing to the mistress, but I'll thank you not to involve me or the children in whatever it is. You know their address: if you want to write to the Englands I suggest you buy some stamps.'

'Nurse May.' Mrs England was standing on the path behind me. 'The other children are looking for you.'

'Yes, ma'am.'

I swept past her, expecting her to stay and exchange a word of warning with Mr Sheldrake, but a moment later I heard her feet on the path behind me, and then she was at my side, her little bag swinging between us. The crowd outside the church began to thin as clouds gathered. The weather in this county was changeable, and a blue sky in the morning made no promise for the afternoon.

'I'll find Broadley,' said Mrs England. She was unreadable, unruffled; I recalled the disorderly woman who'd left the house two hours before.

We found the carriage and climbed in, and arranging Charley on my lap, I felt my sister's letter against my thigh.

'Miss Decca would have loved today,' I said. Mrs England gazed out of the window. 'Have you heard from her?'

'Not yet,' she replied.

'I expect she'll write soon. Blaise looked well,' I said in an attempt to lighten the mood. 'I think I saw some of our myrtle in her bouquet.'

'She's started showing,' said Mrs England.

I stared at her. 'Showing what, ma'am?'

I think it was the first time I'd seen her smile, and she looked almost fondly at me. 'Blaise is expecting.'

I was overcome with shock, and found myself speechless.

'Expecting what?' asked Saul, who missed nothing.

'Expecting good weather all afternoon,' I told him after a moment.

Mrs England turned back to the window. With the finger and thumb of her right hand she played with her wedding ring, moving the band back and forth beneath her glove, as though trying to work it free.

Dear Ruby,

Thank you for the postcard, I did not know they had waterfalls in Yorkshire. I have put it in the parlour on the wall. Ted asks how big it is compared to the Niyagra one in Canada, he says he should like to visit there one day. Mother says have you read Father's letter yet. She also says when are you due your wage it must be soon. The doctor wants to do the magno-electric machine on me again. I still hate it but I suppose I am used to it by now. There is no sign of my plum tree in the yard, perhaps it needs more soil. Please send another postcard if you have any money left.

Love,

Elsie

There was a knock on the nursery door and Mr England opened it, filling the frame. He always seemed larger in these rooms, or them smaller with him inside.

Charley was standing against Millie's bed, his fat legs planted on the floorboards. He turned at his father's voice and reached up a hand.

'He has the posture of a general,' said Mr England with pride. 'Nurse May, there's a party at Crow Nest next weekend – Lilian's grandfather's home – for the fiftieth anniversary of Greatrex Mill. It's only five or six miles, so we shan't stay the night.'

'Yes, sir. Will the children go?'

'They will. You've met some of the family, but a warning: there might be some extra children to mind. Some waifs and strays. They can get rather giddy at these things.'

'Yes, sir.'

'Did you enjoy the wedding?'

'I did, sir. It was a lovely day.'

He nodded at Elsie's letter on my bed. 'News from home?'

I nodded and felt my heart quicken.

He grinned. 'I didn't think you the type to have a sweetheart.'

'I don't, sir.'

'Your private life is none of my business, but I hope we shan't lose you to the institute of matrimony for a while yet. Which brings me to say' – he sighed and set a hand on Saul's bedpost – 'I appreciate your tact with Lilian. You are very kind, Nurse May, to all of us.'

'Thank you, sir.'

'If you have any concerns,' he said, looking closely at me, 'I hope you would come to me.'

A beat of silence. 'Yes, sir.'

Millie came running in, shouting: 'You said you would help me with my puzzle!'

'I will, miss.'

Mr England ruffled her hair. 'Has nobody told you it's rude to interrupt?' He picked her up and threw her on the bed, tickling her with great violence, and I smiled as the little girl dissolved into helpless laughter and screamed for him to stop.

Crow Nest stood on the brow of a hill surrounded by woodland, four or five miles from Hardcastle House, and a palace compared to it. The house itself was vast, with two wings standing either side of a central dwelling. The windows were the size of railway tunnels, the front door guarded by velvet ropes. There was a lake, a lawn and terraces, flower gardens, vineries, a winery. A banana house stood to the west of the glass winter garden, and alpacas and llamas roamed the grounds, looking like creatures from another world beneath the grey Yorkshire sky. As well as the innumerable Greatrex family, hundreds of their workers – managers, clerks, weavers, sorters, spinners, engine-tenters, messengers – sat down to an elegant luncheon, having received their invitations in the summer on thick cream card. White canvas tents covered yards of tables groaning with beef, mutton, pigeon pies, roast duck, grouse, partridge, plum pudding, tartlets and jellies, with ice-cream for the children.

There were scores of children. Sitting with my charges and their cousins, of whom there were too many to count, only then did I comprehend the size and influence of Mrs England's family. And at the heart of it, Champion

Greatrex, the Scotch-plaided, gilt-buttoned, silver-bearded octogenarian, who wore fifty years of power and prosperity as lightly as a silk dressing gown. At any given moment there were twenty or thirty pairs of eyes on him, as though his guests could not quite believe he was flesh, this man who produced nine children and owned forty mills, who had steered his business through boom and bust without closing a single factory. He roamed around the little groups clustered on the lawns, his slim fingers gripping a slim black cane crowned with a silver alpaca.

When we left the house that morning, I hadn't expected a tenth of the grandeur, simply picturing a picnic in a large garden. In their splendid clothes, the England children looked ordinary and discreet among the snowy wash of frocks and sailor suits of Yorkshire's finest families. Nursemaids and governesses tailed the Greatrex children, milling about and exchanging niceties. One or two admired my uniform and asked questions about Norland. They talked freely, familiar with one another and their charges, congregating on woollen blankets and wiping cake crumbs from their mouths. Watching the infants race across the grass, I wondered how Sim would manage it; most likely she'd clap her small white hands and herd them into a crocodile. Despite the mayhem, the change of scenery was enlivening; standing in the fresh open air, I hadn't realised how close and gloomy it felt in the valley.

Much of that day I watched Mrs England. She was like a butterfly, delicate in a pale rose linen dress and matching jacket, with a black satin bow at her throat, flitting around the edges of conversations, never committing to one. She stood with her brothers on a little slope of lawn, and before long her parents drifted over, her father in sombre black, her mother in dove grey, with long gloves and a hat piled with ostrich feathers. Within a minute, Mrs England had drifted from the group and returned to her place at the empty table. She looked cold, clutching at her sleeves and twitching her foot. She turned in my direction, but gave no smile, looking past me towards the lake.

Saul came towards me, high-coloured and panting, asking for lemonade. I poured a glass for him, leaving him with Charley, who was tearing out fistfuls of grass, then sat down beside them. I was tired and had ached to sit for a while. Saul had wet the bed again, and changing the sheets in the middle of the night disturbed Millie and Charley, who wouldn't settle back down. I'd spent the hours before dawn in the day nursery, pacing the floor-boards with the baby and trying to get him to sleep.

We watched the sack race at the bottom of the hill, and I spotted Millie among her cousins, twisting her ring-lets.

'Can I play now?' asked Saul.

'Yes, but mind you don't go too fast, there are too many people about.'

'I won't.'

He tore off like a hunting dog, and I took Charley's chubby fist and led him over to where Mrs England was sitting. The tables were a riot of savaged tartlets and melted ice-cream, their sugary scent hanging like a sickness in the air.

'Are the children enjoying themselves?' asked Mrs England. There were dark circles beneath her eyes; it seemed she had not slept either.

'Yes,' I said, stifling a yawn and settling Charley on the grass by my feet. He, too, was tired, and I knew it wouldn't take much to tip him into a tantrum. 'I enjoyed your grandfather's speech.'

'Did you?'

'I liked what he said about the community of a mill, and each one being like a town.'

Mrs England gave a hollow laugh of contempt. 'And he the Lord Mayor.'

We watched the revellers. Further down the lawn, two men had removed their shirts and begun a wrestling match. A tug of war took place by a copse of rhododen-drons, and a group of children petted a sand-coloured llama wearing a leash like a dog.

'What a remarkable place to live,' I said. 'It's like an amusement park. Was your father raised at Crow Nest, ma'am?'

'Yes. Viper Nest, I call it.'

I resisted the urge to raise my eyebrows. Charley found an errant spoon and we watched him bang it on the grass, neither of us noticing Helen Greatrex gliding over.

'Good afternoon, Lilian.'

'Good afternoon, Mother.' Mrs England did not stand to kiss her, and the older woman looked over her eyeglass at me.

'Good afternoon, Mrs Greatrex,' I said.

She ignored me and took the seat beside her daughter.

'It's like the old days,' she said. 'All the children here together.'

Mrs England said nothing.

'I asked Charles how he managed to get you to come to one of these things. I can't remember the last time you came to see your father and me at Reddicliffe.'

'It's difficult to get out with the children,' said Mrs England.

'What've you got her for if you can't leave them?' She jabbed her hat in my direction. 'I'm almost fifty-nine, Lilian. I can't be juddering about in carriages all the live-long day.'

There was a loud laugh from the party assembled on the lawn. It had come from Mr England, who fitted so smoothly into the group he could have been a Greatrex himself if it wasn't for his dark colouring. Several of the men had canes like Champion's, two of which had been requisitioned by a pair of boys who were fighting a duel.

'Charles has asked to speak to your father later,' said Mrs Greatrex.

'They are speaking now,' Mrs England replied.

'In private.'

'What about?'

'Business, I should imagine. No doubt he wants another loan.'

'Does Father not benefit from lending? I can't imagine he offers them interest-free.'

'Best leave it to the men, I say.' After a stony silence, Mrs Greatrex went on: 'Your grandmother would have loved this.'

'All these people spilling beer on her lawn – what isn't there to love?'

'You might involve yourself a little more. Why are you sitting up here? You're like lint swept into a corner.'

'It's more sheltered.'

'Are you unwell? You look peaky.'

'I'm fine.'

The old woman peered around her daughter's hat, fixing me with icy eyes. 'Is your nurse having a break?'

I shot up as though something had stung me.

'Sit down, Nurse May. Charley is fine, as you can see.'

'He'll be getting stains on his suit.'

'I'll buy him another one.'

I was taken aback by her curtness. Her mother was difficult but Mrs England was being downright rude, her retorts like vinegar, acrid and sour.

'How is Rebecca faring at school? I hope it's worth the fees. It's pointless, if you ask me, putting girls in formal education. A waste of money. I did tell Charles you were lucky to find her a place at short notice. I hope you've sent Mrs Audley a thank-you note.'

'Not yet.'

Decca still hadn't written to me; she'd now been at St Hilda's for two weeks. I'd dropped a second letter in the gilded box in the hallway, which Ben emptied and took to the postbox at half-past four each day. I pictured her hunched over a desk, her dark hair falling like a curtain. I wondered who brushed it at night, who would cut her fingernails. I hoped the other girls were kind to her, but I knew how these things could go. How it came naturally to some children to be cruel to the gentle ones.

'Caroline is expecting,' Mrs Greatrex moved on. 'No doubt she'll be hoping it's her last. She's forty-four in December.'

Her daughter said nothing. The atmosphere crackled, and wondering how best to extricate myself and Charley, I noticed a little crowd had gathered by the sack race. A child broke off and ran to where the Greatrexes were standing further up the lawn, and a moment later Mr England hastened away with him, striding across the grass. I got to my feet at once.

'Mr England has run down there.'

'Where?' Mrs England frowned, scanning the party.

'Down there, by the sack race.'

She stood to see where I was pointing, and Mrs Greatrex peered through her eyeglass. 'I can't see a thing. What's happening, Lilian?'

'Watch the baby, Mother.'

We hurried down the hill together, holding our hats. A

dozen people were gathered in a ring around Saul, who was sitting on the grass with his head between his knees. I thought at first he was crying.

'Saul?' His mother had genuine fear in her voice, and bystanders scattered to let her through.

'He's short of breath. It's his asthma,' said Mr England, who was kneeling at his side. His hat lay discarded on the grass. 'Is there a doctor here?'

I crouched down beside him. Only the crown of Saul's golden head was visible, and his little shoulders heaved up and down like a piston. 'Master Saul, I'm going to move you so you can breathe a little easier. There's no need to panic, just put your head up for me and I'll take off your jacket. There's a good boy.'

Seeing what I was doing, Mr England helped with the other sleeve, and next I loosened his collar. He gulped desperately, like a fish on dry land.

'There's a thousand people here, there must be a doctor,' Mrs England cried. 'Can somebody find one, please!'

Several men hurried in different directions. A wrestler had come to see the fuss, sweat glistening on his bare chest, and more people were arriving, some with beer bottles and fruit from the buffet. Saul buried his head in his arms.

Mrs England fell to her knees beside her son, as though to shield him. Mud streaked her skirt and her hat lay on the ground.

'Let's take him somewhere quiet,' I said. The house was a hundred yards away, and Mr England lifted him easily and carried him up the lawn. A serving girl unfastened the velvet rope, and I followed them inside.

CHAPTER 13

'Upstairs,' said Mrs England. She led us along a dim, tiled hallway, past several white doors into a central atrium the height of three houses. Daylight poured through a domed glass roof and a staircase climbed three of the walls. On the first floor was a pillared gallery, leading to dozens more doorways and endless corridors. Mrs England hesitated at the top, looking in every direction before settling on one. She took us down a narrow hall, hung with pictures, to a light, spacious bedroom overlooking the back lawns. There was a can-opied, old-fashioned bed, and the air was stale: the room had not been ventilated in a while, and I couldn't have hazarded a guess as to when it had last been cleaned thoroughly.

'Are there any iron beds?' I asked. 'Only these get quite dusty. Preferably close to the servants' staircase.'

We returned to the warren of corridors and came to a halt in a narrow room with a single bed and bulky mahogany press. Mr England lowered his son onto the eiderdown and I removed his shoes and arranged the pillows so he was sitting upright. Several things were unnerving me: as well as the sight of him struggling for breath, there was a high, whistling sound coming from his throat, and a private resignation in his face that I found alarming. Mrs England opened the window, and I sat on the edge of the bed.

'Saul,' I said. 'I need you to slow your breathing, if you can. It's difficult, I know, but just try to breathe in for a little longer, and out the same.' I turned to his parents. 'What do you usually do when this happens?'

'Keep him rested,' said Mr England. 'The doctor massages his neck and chest. He hasn't had a turn like this in a long time. I can't imagine what's brought it on.'

'I . . . can't . . . breathe . . .'

'Shh, Master Saul, don't speak. Just focus on breathing . . . in . . . out . . . slowly, that's it . . . in . . . out . . .' To Mr and Mrs England, I said: 'We need bowls of boiling water. Several, for the steam. It's bronchial asthma he has, isn't it?'

'Yes.'

'The bowls need to go all around the room.'

'Steam?' said Mr England. He ran a hand through his hair, and was quite discomposed.

'Yes,' I said. 'It moistens the air and opens the throat. I will go to the kitchen and ask for some.'

'I'll go, I know where it is,' said Mrs England. 'How many?'

'As many as they can bring.'

'Ten? Twenty?'

'Five or six should do for now. Make sure it's boiling.'

Mrs England disappeared, closing the door behind her. Mr England came to stand beside me, and we looked at Saul. He was clutching the bedclothes, his knuckles bone-white. Red patches of exertion bloomed at his cheeks, and his mouth was open and slack. I said nothing, only rested a cool hand on his, and a few minutes later came the sound of feet in the hall and a cane tapping. Champion Greatrex himself entered the room, accompanied by another elderly man with a short silver beard and tremen-dous whiskers.

'Powell will see to him, Charles,' said Mr Greatrex, resting both hands on his cane. I hazarded a glance at him, noticing how short he was, and slim as a boy, though his long beard made him appear wizard-like.

The doctor made for Saul, clutching his wrist with a liver-spotted hand and frowning at his watch. He drew his mouth into a suspicious pucker. 'Too much cake, I expect. Gastric asthma is a common side-effect of spas-modic croup.'

STACEY HALLS

'The boy has bronchial asthma, sir,' I said.

The doctor ignored me. 'Plenty of rest, boy. There isn't anything else for it. You should lie down to aid digestion.'

'Would a cigar help?' asked Mr England.

'It would do no harm, but it might stimulate the senses. Better not.'

Mr England returned the silver case to his jacket. 'Our nurse has instructed my wife to bring bowls of hot water.'

The doctor examined him over his spectacles, as though I was not there. 'What for?'

'The steam is easier to inhale, sir, and opens the lungs,' I replied.

'Nonsense. It will only sweat out a fever, which he does not have. Stomach acid is the cause of this; he won't be the only child here to fall ill, with all the indulgence.' He closed the window with a decisive thud. 'I don't have my bag with me but I'll go home and come back within the hour.'

The old Mr Greatrex had been standing mutely in the doorway; he held it open for the doctor and the two men exited.

In a low voice, I said: 'Sir, you know it isn't gastric. Indigestion doesn't cause this type of asthma.'

'The doctor said he should lie down,' Mr England said.

'Sir, he was wrong to say that. Master Saul should be elevated, so that air can circulate in his lungs.'

'Wrong?' Mr England did not conceal his surprise.

'Doctor Powell is Mr Greatrex's surgeon. He's served the family for forty years.'

'I don't mean to deny him, sir . . .'

'And yet you do.' There was the trace of a smile beneath his moustache. 'Tell me, Nurse May, what is your medical training?'

I swallowed. 'I worked for three months on a children's ward, sir, at Charing Cross Hospital.'

He looked thoughtfully at his son. 'Three months,' he repeated. 'And does the root of the cause matter?'

'Yes, sir. The master should sit upright so oxygen can circulate, and steam will help him to breathe. In the meantime, the room should be well ventilated until the water arrives. With all that, it should pass in an hour or two.'

I heard myself, how contrary I was being. Only in a matter such as this would I have dared to speak to him that way. While Saul laboured on, Mr England watched me arrange the pillows behind him, my heart beating hard. At that moment Mrs England returned, quiet as a mouse, looking stricken.

'Doctor Powell said no steam,' he told his wife.

She froze in the doorway.

'But Nurse May disagrees with him.'

She looked from one of us to the other.

'He also told us Saul should lay down. Again, Nurse May thinks she knows better.' He gave a rueful grin, though the situation was far from comical. 'What do you think, Lilian? Should we obey the doctor with forty years' experience? Or the nurse with a month?'

Several expressions flitted across her face, while I stood mutely at the headboard. She opened her mouth, but said nothing, and stared at Saul with hungry, desperate eyes.

'Son, I'll leave you with your nurse and mother,' said Mr England, stroking his head. 'I hope you feel better soon.'

His footsteps receded down the landing, and Mrs England and I stood in silence. The distant sounds of jollity drifted in through the window, which I'd reopened as far as it would go, and decided that if I were to lose my position, at least the child's life might be saved.

'I'm going to get it wrong,' said Mrs England.

'How do you mean, ma'am?'

She crossed the room to sit beside her son and hold his hand. It was the most intimate I had seen her be with him.

'Why do you disagree with the doctor?'

'Ma'am, of course I know he has more experience than me. But he said Saul's symptoms were caused by over-indulgence, when I saw what he ate at lunch: he only had a bit of beef and some potatoes. He was too excited to eat.'

'Doctor Powell is my grandfather's doctor,' she said. 'He's known us for years. I think we should take his advice.'

I closed my eyes. 'If we lie him flat he won't be able to breathe.'

'What do you know?'

'Not as much as Doctor Powell, ma'am. But the hospital I worked at treated children with respiratory diseases, and steam and fresh air was what they used. There was a sanitorium, like a sort of hot house, where they would go if they were bad.'

She looked at me as though I was speaking a foreign language. A moment later there was a knock, and a servant arrived with the water.

'Don't send it back,' I told my mistress. 'We should increase the humidity, I promise it will help. It's worse here with the coal smoke; it's a wonder anybody can breathe.'

Two female servants set down basins and mixing bowls of boiling water; everything else was in use for the party, so they had gathered what they could from the bedrooms and scullery. Now they were here, I fastened the window, and steam clouded the glass instantly. I found two chairs in nearby bedrooms for myself and Mrs England, and we sat by Saul's bedside, opposite one another. She clutched her son's hand and said very little, watching his face and smoothing his wheat-coloured hair from his forehead. His condition didn't improve but it didn't worsen either, and it felt like no time at all had passed by the time Doctor Powell returned with his kit bag, accompanied by Mr England. He glanced at the bowls, which the servants had already replenished once, and his mouth disappeared beneath his moustache.

'Get rid of these,' Doctor Powell demanded.

I hesitated, and Mr England noticed.

'Nurse May, you will remove the bowls at once.'

I took the one closest to me into the hall, fighting back tears, and met, coming from the servants' staircase, a kitchenmaid with the kettle. Passing her the chamber pot, I asked her to take them away. She blinked in confusion, but did as she was told, and while Doctor Powell rummaged in his bag, I lined up the rest outside the bedroom door. Saul lay flat on the bed, writhing in breathless agony as his father held down his arms. I was lifting the last pail when Doctor Powell positioned the tip of a large syringe at Saul's white throat.

'No!' I cried out without thinking.

The doctor turned in astonishment, meeting my eye for the first time, before diverting his shock to Mr England.

'Nurse May, leave the room at once,' he ordered in a tone I'd never heard him use. He glared at me, but I took a step towards the bed.

'Sir, my place is with the children.'

'Your place is wherever I say it is,' he barked. 'Go down-stairs.'

I glanced at Mrs England, who was standing beside her son, wearing the same mute expression of disbelief and horror.

'Do not look to your mistress, go!'

'I . . . want . . . Nurse . . . May . . .' Saul gasped.

'*Please*, sir.'

'I must have no distractions!' cried Doctor Powell.

'What are you injecting?' I pleaded.

'Nurse *May!*'

The doctor stabbed the syringe into Saul's neck, making a sickening puncture sound that silenced us at once. Saul choked, then gasped noiselessly as Doctor Powell eased down the barrel, his eyes bulging at the ceiling. After what felt like several minutes, the doctor withdrew the needle, glistening with dark blood. My head swam, and I reached for the wardrobe to steady myself.

'The results should be instant,' said Doctor Powell, wiping the needle with a handkerchief. 'I've injected a diluted solution of cocaine, which will diminish pain in the lungs and stimulate the brain to produce more oxygen.'

Saul clutched at his throat and swallowed, but made no noise; it was as though he'd forgotten how to breathe. Doctor Powell held a compress to the puncture wound and instructed Mrs England to take over. His briefcase stood open on the floor, gleaming with bottles and instruments, and he fastened it with a snap.

'I'll return in an hour, once the full effect has taken hold. Meanwhile, take care to see he's comfortable.'

'Thank you, doctor,' said Mr England. Without another word, and without acknowledging me or his wife, he showed the doctor out, closing the door firmly behind him.

In the silence that followed, the sound of the festivities started up again. I had quite forgotten there was a party outside. I put my hands beneath Saul's armpits and carefully brought him to sitting. He gave no resistance, and breathed in little shuddering gulps.

'The doctor said—'

'Mrs England, not once have I heard of cocaine being injected into a child's throat. Cocaine is used for pain relief and fever, not asthma.' I was close to tears; seeing this, she fell silent. I moved the chair closer to the bedside, watching him intently.

'What did they do at the hospital for asthma?'

'Steam, ma'am, as I've said.'

'Then let's try it again.'

I stared at her. 'But Mr England—'

'Damn him! I'll lock the door if I have to, just tell them to bring it now.'

I delivered the message to the kitchen, apologising to the harassed maid who had only just removed the basins one by one. The kitchen stairs were at the end of a long hallway, where a marble bust of Champion Greatrex sat on a plinth before a picture window overlooking the grounds. The party guests were little smears of brown against the green landscape, and I realised with a jolt how long it had been since I'd seen Millie and Charley. I hurried upstairs and asked Mrs England if she wished for me to return to my duties with the others, but she shook her head. The kitchenmaid arrived with a full pan, followed by another girl, who had spilt scalding water over her arms. I helped her set it down, and the pair of them made two more trips. When they'd brought the last of them and the air was thick with warm vapour, I took up my post again, and saw Mrs England glance at the door. She got up, taking her chair with her, and put it beneath the handle, before sitting down again with her back to the door.

'He won't . . . bring the . . . needle . . . back?' Saul gasped.

'No,' I told him. 'He won't.'

Eventually, while I wiped sweat from his damp hairline, Saul fell asleep. The sky outside darkened, and we had no lamp, but I dared not ask Mrs England to move from her post. We kept our vigil as the light faded.

'I didn't want to come today,' she said after a while.

I shifted in my seat. 'You weren't to know this would happen.'

'Something always happens.'

'I should have watched him more closely.'

'It will be my fault,' she said, with no self-pity. 'Sometimes I wonder if I am cursed.'

I wondered why it would be her fault, and could not imagine Mr England accusing her without a reason. There were so many things I wished to ask her – what Mr Sheldrake put in his letter; why her husband locked her in her room. Why she had such disdain for her entire family; why she was, as her mother put it, like lint swept into a corner, brittle and lonely. Why nobody came to the house; why she never left it.

'I don't believe in curses, ma'am,' I said.

'You went against him.'

'The doctor?'

'No,' she said.

'I'm sorry, ma'am. I felt I had to do what was right.'

She narrowed her eyes, but not unkindly; she was looking at me in a sort of wonder, as though I was a tricky puzzle to solve.

At last the revellers disbanded and the great clear-up began. The guests seeped from the grounds back to their trams and trains, pulling tired children along and thinking of their beds and what remained in the pantry.

The doctor returned in the early evening, attempting to enter the room and finding it locked. He asked to be let in, but I told him the boy had recovered and was sleeping, and to try again in half an hour. He accepted this and shuffled off.

When he was breathing deeply, Mrs England said, without taking her eyes from him: 'I want to stay here with him.'

'Should I go outside, ma'am?'

'No, I mean, I wish to stay here at Crow Nest. With Saul.'

'Of course. You mean for me to go back to Hardcastle House with the others?'

She nodded, biting her lip and looking at her son, whose eyelids flickered as he dreamt. In a low voice she said: 'I've already lost Decca. I can't go through it again.'

'But, ma'am, Mr England said it was your idea to send her to school.'

She looked directly at me. 'And you believe that?'

'I'll find the others,' I said, standing and tightening my apron behind me.

'Charles will listen to you, if you tell him. Make it seem like his idea.'

'Ma'am?'

She said nothing more and went on gazing at her son.

Lamps and torches lit the tents and made them eerie. I found Millie making shadow puppets with her cousins, and Charley asleep in an aunt's lap. Several people enquired after Saul as I moved through the chairs towards Mr England, finding him seated with half a dozen men. Bottles of wine and brandy lay open before them, staining the tablecloth dark red.

'Sir,' I mumbled, standing beside him.

'Ah, Nurse May,' he exclaimed. 'Gentlemen, this is Ruby May, our children's nurse.'

The men regarded me, and some nodded. I felt their eyes slide downwards and pretended not to notice.

'We got her from the Norland Institute in London. A ladies' college for nurses – have you ever heard of such a thing? Nurse May keeps us all shipshape, don't you?'

'Sir, may I speak with you a moment?'

'How is my son?'

'Master Saul has improved slightly,' I replied, conscious of the group's attention. 'But Mrs England is worried that a journey home tonight could be dangerous.'

'What did Powell say?'

'That it would be a risk,' I lied.

Mr England considered, and the surrounding moustaches twitched. *Make it seem like his idea.*

'Why not have him stay here a week or two? What do you fellows think?'

'Seems reasonable,' said one.

'What about Mrs England?' I asked.

'Well, I suppose she should stay, too, for a while.'

'If you wish, sir. I will arrange to send their things.'

He tapped his cigar into the dregs of a wine glass. 'Then I shall be quite the bachelor without my lady wife,' he mused. 'You will come back to Hardcastle, of course, with the other two.'

'Yes, sir.'

'The steam did the trick, then?'

I blinked and met his gaze, which was smooth and neutral.

'It appears so, sir.'

'Gather the children, Nurse May, and I'll send for the carriage.'

CHAPTER 14

When I was nine, the funfair came to Balsall Heath, and Father took me and my brothers. It was cold, late autumn or winter, and dark by the time we left the flat. Mother stayed at home, big with Elsie. The fair occupied the cricket ground by the railway bridge, and flaming torches lit the crowded stalls and attractions. We did a lap together, then Father gave us a penny each to spend how we wished. I bought a toffee apple and my brothers scattered like marbles to play games. There was a carousel, gleaming and spinning in the firelight, the painted horses mesmerising in their rainbow coats. Father and I stood for a long time watching. I reached for his hand and looked up to smile at him, to reassure him I didn't mind that I couldn't ride it, that it was enough to look. His fingers were limp in mine, and he stared forwards with the blank expression he wore more often now, as though he'd forgotten how to smile. His eyes glistened, and horses danced inside them.

I woke as the carriage drew to a halt. Charley was asleep on my lap, and Millie's head lolled on my shoulder. Mr England smiled as I came to my senses.

'I'm sorry, sir.'

'No need to apologise. It's late.'

He extinguished the ceiling lamp and we climbed out.

'Want me to take you up with the lantern, Mr E?' Broadley asked.

'I'll do it, Broadley, thank you. Goodnight.'

'Night, sir.'

He picked up Millie, who sunk back into oblivion, her arms dangling at her sides, and took the lantern from Broadley. I followed him over the river and up the dark hill, yawning myself, Charley a deadweight in my arms. Tilda had left a single nightlight in the hall and gone to bed. The household felt depleted; first Decca had gone, then Blaise, now Saul and Mrs England. Carrying the baby upstairs, I had the uneasy sense of having forgotten something, and wondered how long it would take to adjust to having two charges instead of four.

Mr England went before me into the nursery and laid Millie on top of her bed. He removed her shoes, and I undressed Charley, who whimpered softly before falling to sleep. I closed the curtain above his cot and moved to

Saul's bed. His brown wool bear slumped against the pillows, and I set him upright again.

As I neatened the sheets, Mr England sat on the eiderdown. He'd fallen asleep first in the carriage, within minutes of departing Crow Nest. I found myself moved at the sight of him: his mouth open beneath his moustache, his face slack and peaceful as a child's.

'I can manage from here, sir,' I told him.

'When is Saul coming back?' Millie asked sleepily, taking off her own stockings.

'Very soon,' I told her, going to help.

'Has he gone to the same place as Decca?'

'No, Miss Decca is at school, you know that. Master Saul and your mother are staying at your great-grandfather's house until he is better.' I pulled a nightgown over her head and coaxed her into the covers.

'Why is Papa in here?'

I pulled the blankets to her chin. 'He wished to see you to bed.'

'Goodnight, Papa.'

'Goodnight, Millie.'

Satisfied, the child turned on her side to face the wall.

'You are very attentive, Nurse May,' said Mr England in a low voice. 'I'm afraid the children have forgotten Nurse Nangle altogether.'

Another wave of tiredness crashed against me. I smiled and smoothed my apron. I wished he would go to his room so I could hang my clothes up and sleep.

'Nurse May?'

'Yes, sir?'

'Am I a good master?'

This melancholic tone surprised me. I glanced at Millie and spoke softly. 'Yes, sir.'

He picked up Saul's bear. 'Am I a good father?'

'Of course, sir.'

'Was your father good to you?'

A pause. 'He was, sir.'

He sighed, and looked weary. 'My father resented me.'

'I'm sure that's not true, sir.'

'My mother died the day after I was born. My birthday always brought such sadness for him. I was ten years old when he married again. My stepmother was just eighteen; a child herself. She didn't know how to be a mother to me, and then her own children came along.'

I listened for Millie's breathing and was relieved to hear it was deep and slow.

'When I came home from school, she wouldn't let me play with my brothers and sisters. It's an unfortunate thing, to feel unwelcome in your own home. To be a burden. I gave my brother James a whistle for his birthday once, and she threw it on the fire. Said whistles were for dogs. She died when I was twenty, in childbirth. My father never recovered.' His brow furrowed, his dark gaze fixed on the wall.

'I'm sorry to hear that, sir,' I said. 'What became of him?'

'He married a third time. An older woman, a widow. I

invited him to the house, to see the children, but he never came.'

Millie shifted and sighed.

'Look at them,' he said. 'Oh, to be that peaceful. Safe with their nurse in the nursery.'

'I should go to bed, sir,' I said, stifling a yawn.

'Would you do one thing for me, Nurse May? Would you put me to bed?'

The yawn died in my throat. I thought I hadn't heard him correctly. 'I beg your pardon, sir?'

'Put me to bed, Nurse May.'

I swallowed. 'I'm not sure what you mean, sir,' I whispered.

His eyes burned with intensity, and the nightlight flickered inside them. 'I wish you would attend to me, like you do the children. Don't be afraid. I only want to be cared for. You're so good at it.'

There were several seconds of silence, and a slow sort of horror drenched me as I realised he was serious.

'Please.' The single word was low and deep, like the first key on a piano.

An age passed, in which we stared at one another. I knew he had been drinking, but he did not appear drunk. I thought of Mrs England, miles away at Crow Nest, and Tilda asleep above the scullery; the servants' quarters were not part of the main house.

Slowly he passed me the nightlight, and with a trembling hand I took it. I was no longer tired, but filled with an alert focus as I led him from the nursery across the dark landing to his dressing room.

I stood on the threshold and said: 'Can I get you anything from the kitchen, sir?' How calm I sounded, when my heart beat so fast.

'Hot water and whisky, please. Just a dash.'

'Where do you keep the whisky, sir?'

'In my study. The cabinet on the right.'

I took the nightlight downstairs to the dark kitchen. Mrs Mannion had left dough proving beneath a cloth on the side; her household book was closed on the counter, splattered with stains. I stood with chattering teeth, waiting for the water to boil, hugging my arms as my mind raced. The house was silent, the floorboards still. I crept through to the dark scullery, above which Tilda slept alone. A flight of stairs scaled the back wall, and quietly I climbed them and tried the door. Like every door in the house, it, too, was locked. I knocked gently and whispered Tilda's name, but heard only silence. I rapped again, and waited half a minute, but either she was fast asleep or had sneaked out. I retreated to the kitchen, where the kettle was bubbling, and filled a tin mug, going next to the study to search for the whisky. There the lamp threw its paltry light over creamy paper, glossy mahogany, crystal ash trays as I moved to the cupboard in the far corner. A key sat inside the lock, but the door was ajar; I found the decanter and tipped a measure into the mug, wrinkling my nose against the smell. Shadows crowded at the edge of the nightlight, and I thought of Elsie, and what I would tell her to do.

'Put the drink outside the bedroom door and say a firm goodnight. Then go to the nursery and lock it.' The steadiness of my own voice brought some comfort. Passing the great varnished desk, I paused, for something had caught my attention. I raked my eyes back over the mess of papers and lighted on it: a single line of cramped writing, peeping out from beneath a large black volume. I tilted my head to see more closely, and it was as though somebody poured a glass of cold water down my neck. Before I could set down the mug to move the book, a creak above my head made me freeze. I froze for two seconds, three, four, my ears ringing, then hurried from the study to the hall.

'Nurse May?' Mr England stood at the top of the stairs with a lamp.

'Coming, sir.'

He'd changed into his dressing gown. He watched me climb the stairs and led me across the landing to the bedroom, where I stopped again in the doorway.

'Here you are, sir.'

'Just put it there.'

He gestured to the stool beside his bed. I set it down with caution and retreated with the nightlight. 'Is there anything else, sir?'

'Earlier you told me that Doctor Powell said it would be a risk to bring Saul home.'

I swallowed, and saw the trace of a smile.

'That isn't how he told it. He claimed you denied him access. That the boy was asleep, and you did not wish to disturb him.' He waited. 'Did my wife ask you to tell me that, Nurse May?'

I said nothing. The nightlight flickered, throwing shadows at the wall.

'Does my wife often ask you to lie to me, Nurse May?'

'No, sir.'

He sat down against the headboard, and brought his legs up. 'Please, sit,' he said, gesturing to the foot of the bed. I lowered myself so we were sitting like nurse and patient.

'I think she was worried for Master Saul, sir.'

He nodded. 'Do you know, I named him for the King of Israel. I thought it would give him strength.'

'I'm certain he'll recover, sir.'

Mr England looked closely at me. 'You defied me today.'

Several seconds of silence passed, in which my heart thumped against my ribcage, and I didn't know where to look. *You went against him*, Mrs England had said. Sim's face swum to the front of my mind; she would have supported me, I know she would. *Above all else*, she said, *it's your job to keep them alive.*

'I'm glad you did,' he went on in a low, intimate voice. 'I'm not afraid to admit defeat. You just might have saved his life. My children are lucky to have you.'

Relief flooded me, and I gripped the lamp with both hands.

'You showed backbone today, Nurse May. Where do you get it from, I wonder?'

'I don't know, sir.'

I'd set the mug on top of the pile of books on his bedside stool; he lifted it now and took a sip, sliding the uppermost book from the stack and returning the mug to the pile.

'When we spoke on your first day, and you told me of your interest in shaping children into good human beings, you said something about marble. Or was it canvas?'

'Both, sir.'

'Remind me?'

'My principal said the child's mind is a material more precious than canvas, more exquisite than marble.'

He smiled. 'Extraordinary. I am interested in the matter of minds myself, and the debate surrounding nature and nurture. Are you familiar with the polymath William Dalberg?' He held the book aloft.

'No, sir.'

'His principals examine the origin of our personalities: whether we are born impressionable – the canvas you speak of – or whether we are predisposed to certain . . . behaviours. Take criminals, for example.' His eyes glittered. 'Dalberg believes nature is the chief agent in our development from birth, that some of us are more inclined to criminality than others. His research shows that parents contribute one quarter each, and grandparents a sixteenth.'

I waited.

'That would suggest that convicts breed convicts. Do you follow?'

'I think so.'

'And that, in order for the convict's offspring to live a life free of crime, that individual would have to turn three-quarters of its being against the quarter that is . . . *bad*.' He whispered the word, and a chill whispered through me. 'That must be difficult. Not impossible, but difficult.' He sipped his whisky. 'You are perplexed, Nurse May.'

'I don't have the head for science, sir.'

He smiled. 'Apologies. I am in danger of boring you to death.'

'Not at all, sir.'

'I only raised it because of your interest in alienism. What did you think of Crow Nest?'

'I thought it splendid.'

'Have you ever been anywhere quite like it?'

'No, sir.'

'I was around Saul's age when I saw it for the first time.'

'Did you know the Greatrexes as a boy?'

'My father was their lawyer. I became a sort of cousin to them. I spent many a happy afternoon there, running about in the grounds.' He was in a sort of reverie, and I found my mind wandering, thinking of the cluttered desk in the study. 'You're tired,' he said. 'I'm sorry to keep you.'

'That's all right, sir.' All the fear and trepidation of the last few minutes drained from me. I was paranoid: of course he was not writing to my father. It was a letter from somebody else I had seen downstairs. Of course it was possible that two men, ten, a thousand, could have similar handwriting. My mind was showing me things that were not there. All Mr England had asked of me was to bring him a bedtime drink and sit with him a while; there was no reason for me to wake Tilda. Imagine if she had come to the door! What would I have told her – that the master wanted a nightcap? I was delirious with tiredness, and stood up to leave.

'Aren't you going to kiss me goodnight?'

I smiled, thinking him teasing, but his dark eyes did not move from my face. I thought of him asleep in the carriage, him reading in bed while his wife slept next door, having nobody to discuss his books with. I pictured him as a boy, racing across the lawns at Crow Nest, arriving home tired and happy, only for his stepmother to splinter him with a cruel word, a sharp glance. Before I knew what I was doing, I crossed the room and dropped a chaste kiss on his head. He smelt of hair oil and cigar smoke, and something stirred in my stomach. He did not move, or seem to breathe, and slowly I drew away, stiff with shock at what I'd done. I could not bear to look at him, aware only of his dark eyes, which were alive with an energy I did not understand.

'Goodnight, sir.'

I scurried back to the nursery, locking the door behind me and wishing I could swallow the key.

'Are you a deep sleeper, Tilda?' I asked as she unloaded the breakfast tray the next morning.

'I'm dead to the world,' she replied. 'Why, did you knock?'

'Yes,' I said, cutting Charley's toast. 'I was . . . just looking for something in the kitchen.'

She swivelled the tray to her hip. 'Sorry,' she said. 'The knocker-ups have to use a sledgehammer on my window.' It was the first time she had joked with me, but I could not raise a smile. 'Mrs Mannion told me about Master Saul,' she added. 'I hope he's all right.'

'He will be. That reminds me, could you pack a case for the mistress and I'll do one for Saul? Broadley will take them to Crow Nest this morning.'

'I'll do it now. Did you find it, then?'

'Find what?'

'What you were looking for?'

'Yes, thank you.'

'Well,' she said after a moment. 'Best get on with it.'

I'd unlocked my trunk in the pale dawn light, before the children woke. The first thing I did was open my tea tin and search for the envelopes, which were still there, sealed and tied with a shoelace, untampered with.

Postmarks spread like bloodstains in the corners. Next I took out a sheet of clean writing paper and got into bed; the nursery was cold but the fire could wait ten more minutes. *Dear Miss Simpson,* I wrote. I sat for the time it took for a bead of ink to form on the pen nib.

'Nurse May, I need a *little*,' said Millie from her bed.

I crumpled the paper into the grate and drew out the chamber pot.

After breakfast I wanted to be out of the house. I waited for the sound of the front door, peering through the blinds to watch Mr England striding across the yard in his hat and coat. I'd half-hoped, half-dreaded he would come to the nursery; listening for every creak and murmur, I'd dropped the ash pan on the hearth, and had to clean it while Charley screamed in his cot.

I put the children in their outdoor things and settled Charley with a rusk in his pram. On the path, where I always struggled getting out of the gate, a voice travelled across the yard.

'Why don't you use the back door?'

I leapt out of my skin. 'Mr Booth, you startled me.'

He came to help, lifting the pram through the narrow space and down the step.

'The children use the front door,' I told him.

'Says who?'

'Me. I'm afraid Master Saul isn't here.'

'Oh. Where is he?'

I burst into tears.

'What's the matter?'

Millie rushed to my side, her eyes wide with concern.

'Sorry.' I fumbled for a handkerchief. Mr Booth passed his, and I thanked him, and pressed it to my face. It smelt of coal tar soap, and an image came to me of Blaise attending to their laundry, humming to herself in a sunny kitchen.

'It's his asthma,' I said. 'He fell ill at the party yesterday, so he'll stay at Crow Nest a week or two. I'm sorry, I should have sent a note.'

'But a doctor's seen him?'

'Yes, yes, though I hope he won't come again,' I said, tucking away the handkerchief. 'He'll be fine. Sorry,' I said again. 'I shouldn't cry in front of the children.'

'Why not? Children cry more than anyone.' He turned to Millie and said, in a merry voice: 'Miss Millie, why don't we take your nurse for a walk to cheer her up?'

'I'm sure you have better things to do.'

'Well, you'd be wrong. My lady?' He held out an arm for Millie, who took it, giggling, and we set off walking together.

'Where shall we go?' he asked.

'The waterfall!' cried Millie.

'Oh, it's quite far,' I said.

'The waterfall it is.'

We passed through the mill yard, and I glanced up at the windows.

'How was the party?' Mr Booth asked.

'Um,' I said. 'It was . . .'

'Lost for words this morning?'

I smiled. 'It was unlike anything I've been to. The scale of it was immense; I can't imagine how much food they ordered.'

'And what happened with the master?'

I stopped walking. 'What do you mean?'

'You said it was his asthma.'

'Oh.' I gave him a summary, leaving out the part about the injection, and what happened after that.

We left the bustle of the mill behind and passed the pond, where pairs of ducks floated in idleness. 'Can we feed them?' asked Millie.

'We don't have any bread,' I told her. 'Maybe next week.'

We moved away from the coal smoke into the sanctuary of the woods, where the air was fresh and cold.

'He won't have his bath chair,' said Mr Booth. 'I'll take it over to Crow Nest.'

'That's good of you. I'm sure he'd like that.'

Millie ran ahead to look for toadstools, and Mr Booth chucked Charley's chin.

'I hear you're going to be a father.'

He raised his eyes to meet mine, then looked away. 'I am.'

'Congratulations,' I said, but it came out hollow.

'Thank you.'

'How is Mrs Booth?'

'Mrs Booth. My mother's the first person who comes to mind when you say that. She's well.' The sunny kitchen; the laundry. I pictured Mr Booth coming home with his satchel, planting his hand on her stomach, his lips on hers.

'When are you expecting the baby?'

'February.'

I was surprised. 'Not long.'

'Not long,' he said. What was it he had called me the night before the wedding? *You're green as grass, Nurse May.*

We walked along the flattest part of the riverbank. Around us, the forest was changing colour, the trees losing their leaves to the ground, where they pasted themselves to the pram wheels. Each time we went walking, I had to clean them in the boot room afterwards, but I found a grim satisfaction in removing all the dirt.

We reached the stepping stones, like great flat teeth in the river's wide mouth. Without Saul to compete with, Millie pounced across at leisure, and after a while Mr Booth joined her. He pretended to chase her and she leapt, shrieking, from rock to rock.

'Be careful,' I called.

'Nurse May, come and jump with us,' cried Millie. She was enjoying having me to herself, and I, too, ought to have found pleasure in giving her more attention, but part of me felt like the other two's absence was my failure. Jittery and irritable, I stood on the bank, jiggling the pram.

'Come back now, please, Millie.'

242

'It isn't deep!'

Mr Booth reached the other side and turned back, skip-ping over the steps and launching himself into the little sandy bay where we sometimes looked for minnows.

'Millie, come back, please.'

She slipped and screamed, but didn't fall, and within seconds Mr Booth was beside her. He lifted her easily, carrying her over the current, and set her down on the riverside.

'I told you to come back,' I shouted, feeling heat flare at my cheeks as I brushed at her petticoats, which were dry. 'You could have drowned.'

'I didn't fall in,' she wailed.

'No, but you could have.'

Mr Booth winked at her. 'No harm done, eh?'

I turned my back on them, pushing the pram upstream. Horseshoe Cascade roared over the steady gush of the river, tumbling over crags and jagged rocks to join the water further down. The ground surrounding the falls was a mass of shattered stones, as though somebody had taken a great hammer to them, and I thought at once of Tommy Sheldrake.

'Mr Booth,' I said as we watched Millie pick her way over the rock pools. 'How do you know Tommy Sheldrake, the blacksmith?'

He pulled his mouth down at the corners. 'I don't, really. Think he's courting one of Blaise's cousins. Why do you ask?'

'No reason. He invited the children to see the forge a few weeks ago.'

'Nice of him.'

'Who is Blaise's cousin?'

'A girl called Lucy. She's a cashier at the bank.'

I let the matter drop and fell into pensive silence.

'You're not yourself, Ruby.' He'd waited for Millie to move further away before using my name, and I felt something collapse inside me.

I sighed. 'I'm just confused.'

'About what?'

'About lots of things.'

'Go on.'

'I'm worried about Decca, who still hasn't written to me. And Saul. I should have been watching him carefully but I was miles away when it happened. I should have stopped him from tiring himself out; I should have stayed with him.'

'There's nothing you could have done. You haven't eyes in the back of your head, and you said yourself he'll be all right,' he insisted. 'You're worried, that's all.'

'I just have a feeling that . . .' I watched Millie leap between the rocks, her arms spread like wings. 'Never mind.'

'A feeling that what?'

'That something's not right here.'

I was aware of Mr Booth's eyes on me, and he seemed to hold his breath. 'What do you mean?'

'In the house. With the family.'

'Oh.' The word landed like a stone.

'What did you think I meant?'

He looked very hard at me, reminding me so much of Mr England the night before that I shrank away from him.

'Is everything all right, Ruby?'

'No,' I said. 'But I don't know what I can do about it. I can't leave my position.'

'Why not? Not that I want you to go, of course.'

There was an awkward pause. 'I promised my principal I would stay no matter what. I fought for this job. She didn't want to send me here – she didn't think I could cope with four children – but I practically begged her to let me come, and now two of them aren't even here . . . And, in all honesty, I'm not sure I should leave them anyway.'

'Why do you say that?'

'A frog! Nurse May, I found a frog!' Millie's jubilant cry brought me to my senses.

'Forget I said anything.'

Mr Booth took a step towards me. 'Ruby, I—'

'Nurse May!'

'I'm coming,' I called. I left Mr Booth with the pram and took a few steps towards the rock pools, turning back for a moment. 'Sorry, what were you saying?'

An indefinable expression passed over his face and was lost. 'Nothing,' he said, and gave a smile as false as my own.

CHAPTER 15

We waited in the drawing room until half-past five, at which point it became clear Mr England was not coming to see the children. I stood at the window, but there was no light in the yard, no lantern bobbing up the track. I held Charley's hands and led him through to the kitchen.

'Mrs Mannion, do you know where the master is?'

'He said he'd be out until the evening, so I'm just doing a light supper for when he gets back.'

Soup bubbled on the range and she sprinkled in pepper, wiping her hands on her apron and taking down the biscuit tin. She passed both of the children a ginger snap, and Millie said thank you.

'He didn't tell me he was going out,' I said, trying not

to sound as disappointed as I felt. 'I got the children ready.'

'That's all I know, I'm afraid. Here you are, take another one to bed.'

She gave them another biscuit and took up her place at the range again. I let Charley toddle to the foot of the stairs, then remembered something and directed him back to the kitchen.

'Mrs Mannion, has any post arrived today?'

'Not that I know of; the mistress does all that. Ask Tilda if anything came through. She'd have put it on the table, I'd imagine.'

Besides the usual vase of dried banksia, the hall table was empty. We passed the study, and I recalled what I'd seen the night before.

'Millie,' I said. 'Would you take Charley into the drawing room for me?'

She grabbed his hands like a puppet master and led him away. When she'd turned the corner, I tried the smooth brass knob of the study door; it was unlocked.

The room was always gloomy no matter the time of day, with the green light filtering in from the woodland. From the doorway I saw the desk was tidy, the surfaces free of paper; the black volume was nowhere in sight. I took a hesitant step inside when a crash came from next door, followed by a great wail.

In the drawing room Charley was splayed on the carpet beside the overturned piano stool, screaming.

'He wouldn't sit still! He kept trying to get down!' Millie cried.

'All right,' I said, lifting the baby and bouncing him. 'There, there. I'm here now.'

The front door slammed. 'That will be your father,' I told the children, overcome with relief that he had missed me looking in his study by seconds. But there was no sound of footsteps, no easy whistle. I went into the hall and saw Mr England standing at the front door with his hat in his hands. His dark eyes were troubled, and a wave of complex emotion broke in my chest.

'Good evening, sir,' I said.

'Good evening.' He looked up the stairs, and I followed his gaze to see Mrs England ascending. There was a beat of silence.

'Did we forget to pack something, sir?'

He shook his head.

'Papa!' Millie clung to him.

I felt cold, suddenly. 'Is it Master Saul?'

'No. Nurse May, could you take the children to the nursery? I'm afraid I can't keep our appointment this evening.'

'Yes, sir. Right away, sir.'

The kitchen door opened and Broadley came down the hall carrying a trunk on his shoulder.

'Would you like it upstairs, Mr E?'

'Thank you, Broadley.'

I peeled Millie from her father and ushered the children

to the night nursery, where I put Charley in his cot and knelt at the fire to stir it. The coal scuttle was almost empty, and I asked Millie to get into her night things while I went downstairs. On the landing, Mrs England's door was ajar.

'Tilda, is that you?' came her soft voice.

'Nurse May, ma'am.'

'Could you ask Tilda to draw a bath for me?'

'Yes, ma'am.'

'Thank you.'

I scurried downstairs, passing Mr England's study on the way to the kitchen. The door was open, and I stopped in my tracks. The master was sitting at his desk with his head in his hands. He appeared not to have heard me, and I watched him, immobilised, with the coal scuttle loose in my hand.

He pulled his hands down his face, as though wiping off all the day's dust and grime. I found that I still couldn't move, and we looked at one another. He managed a smile, though it appeared to cost him great effort.

'Can I get you anything, sir?'

He shook his head and got up from his desk, coming to stand before me. 'You're very good to me,' he said, and closed the door gently.

I wanted to weep; I longed to know what was causing his despair. Gathering myself, I went down to the cellar for the coal, then went to find Tilda, who was polishing the silverware in the dining room. She was quite absorbed, humming to herself, and didn't hear me come in. I decided not to disturb her; I would draw Mrs England's bath myself.

I settled Millie in bed with a storybook, then began the laborious task of filling the bath from the copper, carrying the water upstairs and emptying it into the tub. I tested the temperature with my elbow, like I did for the children, and put out a new cake of soap and a clean towel. Finally I tidied Mr England's shaving things on the washstand and turned the wall lamps down to a pleasant glow before going to the mistress's room.

The door was still ajar, and I knocked and told her it was ready.

'Thank you, Nurse May,' came her soft reply.

I lingered, longing to ask what brought her home, why Saul had not come with her. The day before it felt as though something had shifted between us; perhaps it had only been the change of setting, because Mrs England had shut herself like a book once again. Beside me, the door to Mr England's dressing room was closed. I imagined what she would say if she knew what had happened, how hurt she would be. My skin crawled with guilt, and something less familiar, more dangerous, made itself known deep down inside my body, in a place I hadn't felt anything before.

'How is Master Saul, ma'am?' I looked through the gap at the iron bedstead, the cream eiderdown. *They go at it like dogs in a ditch.* I shook my head.

'He's much better. He'll come home in a fortnight.'

'I'm glad to hear it, ma'am. If you need anything else, let me know.'

'Thank you.'

In the nursery, Millie had fallen asleep sitting up. I removed the book from her lap and put it beneath the bed, noticing the fire was dying, and realising I'd left the coal in the scullery. Fetching it now would be better than in the morning.

On the landing I met Mrs England on her way to the bathroom. She was clutching the dado rail, as if for support, with one hand on her stomach. At once I forgot myself and went to help her, offering my arm. 'Ma'am, are you all right?'

'I'm fine. I suffer each month.' She was so frail; I hadn't noticed how thin she'd grown.

'Mrs Mannion is making soup, if that might help.'

She gave a wan smile. 'Maybe later. Thank you.'

She closed the door, and I stood on the landing, hearing the distant tinkle of Tilda's spoons. I fetched the coal, but before I closed myself inside the nursery for the evening, I couldn't help but pause at the top of the stairs. There was something not right; a miasma in the air. I crept on tiptoe to the bathroom and lowered my right eye to the keyhole, closing my left. I saw the roll top of the bath, the little stool with the towel and the soap. Mrs England's pink dress – the dress she wore to the party – lay in a heap on the floor, and first one white foot, then the other, lifted from the tiles.

I glanced behind me and knelt. Coal shifted in the bucket, and I held my breath. There was a gentle splash of water, and I saw a leg, a bottom, a back. She moved with difficulty, easing herself down, clutching the sides of the tub. Her skin was the colour of milk, and her hair wound down her back like a gilded curtain. Like a waterfall.

I pulled away. What on earth was I doing creeping around and spying at keyholes? I thought of what Sim would say if she saw me, and felt sick with shame.

Dear Elsie,

Did you get my last letter? I asked if Mother received the postal order. I trust it arrived. The clerk at the post office said it would. If it hasn't I will go in and ask. Here is another postcard, as promised, of Hardcastle Crags. The house is named for them, I think. You can't tell from the picture but they are toffee-coloured, and very high. The children like to play on them and hide in the holes. Sometimes they leap out and give me a fright! I haven't opened Father's letter, but you would let me know if it was something important, wouldn't you? Please write by the same day's post, so I know you have the money.

The family I work for had a party at the weekend, and there were alpacas for the children to pet. They are funny-looking creatures: quite soft and furry, with long necks and squat bodies. I believe they come from Peru. I hope you are feeling well enough to go to school soon. I should hate for you to fall behind the others.

All my love to you and the boys,

Ruby

Charley's crying woke me, bringing me to the surface from some murky dream. Not a breath of air stirred the curtains, but the river chattered faintly below. Already Charley had fallen silent and rolled back into sleep. I turned onto my front, pushing away the silt of thoughts and memories that deep sleep disturbed. *You're very good to me.* I thought of his lamplit dressing room, the mug steaming on the side. The rustle and shift of his dressing gown, the scent of his pomade. I turned the pillow over, and the cotton was cool on my cheek. He took my hand. *Ruby, I . . .* No, that had been Eli by the river. What had he been about to say?

Charley coughed. I was facing the wall and opened my eyes, aware, now, of a sulphuric smell, like a gas pipe left on. The scent was faint, mixing with the cool air from the window, and disappeared when I sat up in bed. Frowning, I knelt to examine the wall bracket above the headboard, putting my nose to the glass shade. The odour was no more powerful; there was no telltale hiss. I unlocked the door and checked the lights in the corridor and day nursery. All the valves were closed, the pipes quiet, but the smell was unmistakable. I hurried through to the main house.

On the landing, the stench of sulphur hit me square in the face. I rushed to each of the wall lamps and the ceiling fitting; every one was off, and the same in the bathroom. I hammered on Mr England's dressing-room door, shouting, and next the mistress's bedroom. Mr England came first, flying on to the landing in his nightshirt, pulling on a dressing gown. In his hand was an unlit lamp.

'No, sir!' I snatched it from him and set it on the sideboard. 'Ma'am?' I battered the door again.

'What on earth is it?'

'The gas, can you smell the gas? I don't know where it's coming from.'

'Good God.'

Mr England disappeared into his room, and I watched from the doorway as he reached for the dial on the ceiling light, sniffing and turning it on and off again. 'It's not this one.'

'The mistress's room, then. Or it could be downstairs.'

I hurried through to the spare bedroom at the front of the house. The room was dark and cold, with a little flurry of fallen soot at the hearth. Moonlight streamed in through the open curtains.

I ran back to the landing and banged on the mistress's door. 'Mrs England, wake up! Don't light a lamp.' I did not care that I was standing in my nightgown before the master with my hair unmade, shouting like a madwoman. 'You need to open the door, sir.'

Comprehension flooded his face, and he ducked into

the dressing room. The scent was growing stronger. I got to my knees and put my nose to the crack beneath the door, wrinkling it at once.

'Mrs England!' I coughed and tried not to inhale.

A moment later Mr England was upon the lock, fumbling with a small brass key and flinging open the door. The room was thick with the stench of gas, enough to make me feel sick and giddy; my head swam, and I put a hand to my mouth. The mistress was asleep, her slight form barely making a mound beneath the covers.

'Lilian.' Mr England shook her, but she was limp as a rag doll. 'Lilian, wake up.'

He threw back the eiderdown and lifted her as I hastened to the wall brackets. The fitting on the wall opposite the bed was hissing quietly, indistinguishable from the sound of the river; mercifully, Mrs England slept with her window open. I turned off the tap and threw the sash wider.

Mr England carried her from the room and I closed the bedroom door behind me, going next to the linen cupboard and bunching a bed sheet at the bottom of the mistress's door. Then I opened every window upstairs.

Millie woke at the squeal of the sash and sat up, her face creased with sleep and confusion. 'What are you doing?' she asked.

I checked on Charley, who was dreaming peacefully, his fists thrown over his head.

'Shh,' I told her. 'Go back to sleep.'

'You always tell me to go back to sleep.'

'That's because it's night-time.'

'Why is the window so far open? I'm cold. Can we have a fire?'

'Not tonight. I'll close it soon, but you must go back to sleep first.'

I took the eiderdown from Saul's bed and lay it on top of hers, thinking all the time of Mrs England and her rag-doll body. How she'd slept for hours by a leaking gas pipe. And her stiff journey to the bathroom earlier, as though every step was causing her pain.

My watch was in the pocket of my apron, hanging from the peg; it was half-past eleven. The nights here were so long and penetrating. The Radlett house wound down like a mechanical toy, creaking and sighing itself to sleep as the square shut off its windows one by one, but in Yorkshire the silence was instant, the darkness dense.

Millie nestled into me and I thought again of Decca, miles and miles away in an unfamiliar bed. Was she lying awake, thinking of us? In the days that followed, I'd regretted not going with her to the dormitory and helping her to unpack.

Millie's breathing deepened. Already the stink was dissipating, and I shuddered at what might have happened if Charley had not cried out. When Millie was asleep, I settled her beneath the covers and crept out to the landing. There was no noise anywhere in the house, no sign of where Mr England had taken his wife.

I found her in the drawing room, lying on the couch in her nightdress. She was awake and bleary-eyed, blinking up at me in the dim moonlight like a creature from underground. There were footsteps at the end of the hall, and Mr England appeared from the kitchen with a glass of water.

'Are you all right, mistress? Should I wake Tilda?'

'No need, I'll send for the doctor in the morning,' Mr England replied, handing the drink to his wife. She took a shaky sip. 'Are the children fine?'

'Yes,' I said. The next question hung like cigar smoke in the room. Who had left the gas on? Tilda lit the lamps at night, but neither of us had been expecting Mrs England, who, I was certain, had gone to her room before Tilda could prepare it. I hadn't been inside, had only spoken to her from the landing. Had it already been leaking then? Perhaps Tilda did it when Mrs England was in the bath and, distracted, forgot to close the valve. Broadley had taken her trunk upstairs; would he have turned on the lights?

Mr England stood anchored to the carpet, unnatural with his hands unoccupied. I knew he itched to strike a match, to put a cigar to his lips. Aside from at Crow Nest, it was the closest to discomposed I had seen him.

'I've opened the windows upstairs,' I said.

'Thank you.'

Mrs England shifted and winced.

'Should I prepare you a bed down here, ma'am?'

'I'll do it,' said Mr England. 'But you might fetch her dressing gown and slippers in the meantime.'

'Yes, sir.'

I found her apricot gown draped over the bedpost and, shivering, looked about for her slippers, but the floor was bare. The trunk Tilda had packed that morning lay beneath the window. I knelt before it and swung it open. Most of the clothes were neatly folded, and I found the bedroom slippers tucked in a corner, underneath a sheet of paper covered with coloured squares. I looked closer, holding them up to the moonlight, and saw that they were postage stamps, and one was missing. Stamps seemed a strange thing for Tilda to include. I returned them to the trunk, folding a sleeve over and shutting her things in darkness.

The mistress was ill the next few days, and a doctor visited the house and diagnosed her with gas poisoning. He said there was nothing for it but rest and clean air. She was sick and dizzy, and Tilda travelled back and forth to the scullery with chamber pots covered with cloth. We aired the house for twenty-four hours, and an engineer attended to check the pipes for faults, but found none. By the time the fires and lamps were lit the following evening, the children and I were wearing twice as many clothes as usual.

No post arrived from Elsie, nor from Decca, and I began to feel uneasy and nauseous, as though the gas had poisoned me, too. The doctor returned to examined me and the children, pressing his cold stethoscope against my shift, and told Mr England to send for him if any of us worsened.

On the third day, I waited until Mr England left the house before going to the mistress's bedroom with Charley. She answered my knock, and I found her sitting up in bed, an untouched breakfast tray beside her.

'Good morning, ma'am,' I said.

'Good morning.' She was pale and tired-looking, though she slept most of the day. I recalled Mrs Radlett's early symptoms, her peakiness and the aversion to cooked food. My mind raced ahead to what would happen if she had a fifth child. A monthly nurse would have to be found, but where would she sleep? There was no room for another bed in the night nursery. But she had said her monthlies caused her pain, so she couldn't be expecting.

'Did you want something?' she asked.

'I wondered if you were fit enough to visit the nursery today, ma'am.'

'What for?'

'I thought you might like a change of scenery.'

She glanced about the room, considering it. 'I suppose it wouldn't hurt.'

'Only if you are well enough.'

'I'll come later. Would you mind asking Tilda to run me a bath?'

'Of course, ma'am.'

At a quarter past eleven, Mrs England appeared in her silk dressing gown, fiddling with the sash. Millie grew shy at once and closed her copybook, where she'd written the word *bear* a dozen times beneath my questionable drawing.

'I thought we could play story sacks,' I told Mrs England, who took a seat in the rocking chair.

'What's that?' she asked.

'I want to show her!' Millie reached for the pillowcase she'd crammed with objects from the nursery; she'd made me shut my eyes as she went about collecting things, and shrieked if she thought I was peeking.

'We put objects in at random and shake it, then take them all out and tell a story that connects them all,' I explained. 'Millie, would you like to start?'

First she drew out a wooden soldier. I took my place at the hearth, with my back to the fire, and clasped my hands together. 'There was once a brave soldier named Sergeant Redcheeks,' I began. Millie laughed and thrust her hand inside the bag, bringing out a poker.

'Who was challenged to a fearsome duel with . . .'

Out came a miniature teacup. 'The Queen of Teacups! The Queen had to be very careful, because she was made of porcelain, and could break easily, so she ordered all her most fearsome teapots to fill themselves to the brim with boiling water and wait on the ramparts for Sergeant Redcheeks to approach. He came over the hill with his poker . . .'

I motioned for her to take another, and frantically she pulled out . . .

'A puzzle piece! What Sergeant Redcheeks didn't realise was the *ground* was one gigantic puzzle, and at once the pieces all began moving this way and that, trying to trick him. He hopped back and forth and got entirely lost, when . . .'

Millie reached into the pillowcase again.

'An enormous spinning top went whizzing past and cried: "All aboard!" So Sergeant Redcheeks climbed astride with his poker and rode the top like a horse. But the problem was it only span around and around, and he was more confused than ever, so . . .'

Next she took out a pencil.

'The Queen of Teacups took pity on him, and said that she would make him her new corporal, if only he would sign the bill. He did so with a flourish, and . . .'

Out came the piece of cotton Mr England had given me. I faltered and fell silent. Two pairs of eyes fixed me to the spot, Mrs England's even wider than her daughter's. Charley stood in his pen, gripping the bars and gurgling.

'Nurse May, you can't stop!'

'Oh, don't stop.' Mrs England gave a shy smile. 'What happens next?'

I swallowed. 'Ah. The cotton . . . Oh. Deary me. He had a smart new cotton suit made in the royal colours, ah, blue and white. But then he was left in the rain and rusted, and that was the end of Sergeant Redcheeks.'

'But I have more things!' Millie cried.

'The End means The End, Miss Millie. That's enough adventure for Sergeant Redcheeks.'

'Bravo!' Mrs England clapped and beamed. Her colour was high and feverish, but she seemed enchanted. 'That was wonderful, Nurse May. Do you really make it up as you go?'

'Yes, ma'am.'

'Where did you learn to do that?'

'At home. It was something for all the children.'

Millie approached her mother. 'Do you want to do one?'

'Oh, no. No, I couldn't.'

'Why not?'

'I'm not . . .' She faltered. 'I'm afraid I don't have a good imagination.'

Millie looked blank.

'Imagination. It's, ah . . . it's when you go somewhere in your mind, and it feels as if you were really there.'

'Like making things up?'

'You might put it that way.'

'Nurse May says we shouldn't make things up,' Millie said in a solemn voice.

263

'And she's right. But sometimes it's all right to do it, if it makes you feel better.'

Charley flung a wooden brick from his pen, and I crossed the room and lifted him. 'Would you like to take him, ma'am?'

'I'm not very good at holding him.'

'He's quite sturdy, ma'am. You can't hurt him.'

'I'm afraid I'll drop him.'

'You won't, ma'am. And if you do, he'll survive. He's going to be a big, strong boy.' I raised him over my head and he squealed, kicking his fat legs.

'Not like his brother.' She was looking at the space the bath chair had occupied, until Mr Booth took it to Crow Nest.

'Master Saul is strong, in his own way,' I said.

She nodded and seemed distant once more.

'Would it be all right if we wrote to Master Saul?'

'Of course.'

'Shall we write to your brother?' I asked Millie. The sprig of cotton lay on the carpet, and I collected up the items and returned them to the pillowcase.

'Yes,' said Millie. 'And I would like to write the words bear and apple.'

'I'm sure he'll be very glad to read them. I'll fetch my stationery. Would you like to write him a letter, too, ma'am?'

Something in the mistress seemed to fade. 'I will this week. I'll sit here and watch, if you don't mind.'

'Of course not.'

I retrieved my writing things from my trunk, and Millie and I sat at the low table. Mrs England took Charley onto her lap and rocked him. He fastened his right thumb in his mouth and nestled into her, and before long fell asleep. Millie and I worked on either side of the table, me as the scribe, her the dictator. The pen scratched and rain pattered the windows. By the time I got up to put more coal on the fire, Mrs England had fallen asleep beneath Charley, with one hand fastened around his middle, the other gripping the arm of the rocking chair. I watched her and thought of my mother, who fell asleep often after she had Elsie, and couldn't feed her herself. I wondered if Mrs England had been a nursing sort of mother, tried to imagine her propped in a nest of snowy pillows, a silver tea tray at her side.

Elsie's birth had gone badly. There were others in-between the five of us, but we never mentioned them. I thought of them sometimes, the other babies, relieved that they had gone to heaven, yet guilty for it, because there was no room for them at Longmore Street. Elsie survived, somehow. She was yellow and sickly but clung stubbornly to life, staring up at us with eyes like brown buttons. I was thrilled to have a sister. Father loved her, too; he would tickle her nose with a feather and make her sneeze. She slept in the bedroom drawer when she was tiny, and I had nightmares about shutting her in. I started taking her into bed with me, nuzzling into her smell of warm milk and washing. At night, when she woke, it was me she cried for, me she wanted. Me she trusted.

There were stars that night. The rain had stopped and the sky was full of them as I lay on the ground looking up. I was cold and wet, and my hair dripped down my neck, but I didn't shiver. I couldn't feel my body at all.

'What's your name?' they asked me.

'Where's Elsie?' I replied. So the newspapers said. I couldn't remember myself.

CHAPTER 16

I spent the morning at the window, waiting for the postman on his bicycle.

'What are you looking for?' Millie asked.

I decided to make it a game. 'Whoever sees the postman first wins,' I told her. 'Could you keep watch while I clear these breakfast things?'

On my return from the kitchen, Millie came flying down the stairs. 'I saw him! I win! He's here!'

The postman stepped back from the doorstep in surprise. 'Good morning, miss.'

'Good morning.'

He handed me three letters, and I thanked him, closing the door rather abruptly. All three were for Mr England.

'I won!' Millie shouted again.

'Yes, you did. Well done.'

'Can we play again tomorrow?'

'Good idea.'

I put the letters on the hall table, remembering how Mr England had said his wife distributed the post, and remembering, too, how she had handed Elsie's letter to me on the morning of Blaise and Eli's wedding, a day or two after it arrived.

The mistress was in her bedroom, sorting through her clothes. I knocked and stood in the doorway.

'Pardon me, ma'am, but there isn't any post for me, is there?'

She looked at me over her shoulder. 'What do you mean?'

'I'm expecting a letter but it hasn't arrived.'

She shook her head. In her hands was a pale blue military jacket with cream-white piping; for somebody who went nowhere, she had the most attractive clothes.

'Have you asked the postman?'

'I saw him just now.'

'Perhaps there's been a delay.' She turned her back to me.

'That's a pretty jacket, ma'am,' I said.

'This?' She examined it with her head on one side and returned it to the rail. I hesitated. I'd left Charley in his highchair smeared with toast and butter, and thought for a moment I could hear him cry out.

'Miss Millie and I are having a spinning top competition this morning, if you'd like to take part.'

She smiled. 'I'd like that.'

There was nothing in the evening post and not a bean the next morning. I slept fitfully, pestered by bad dreams and scenarios, and after breakfast asked Mrs England if she minded me going to the post office. To my relief she said I could, and even offered to look after Charley. I left them in the nursery and took Millie with me, buttoning her quickly into her coat and gloves.

Mr England was in the mill yard speaking to a gentleman.

'Papa!' Millie ran to him before I could stop her, and I hurried to catch up.

'Miss Millie,' I called, 'your father is working.'

I found her hand and drew her back, but Mr England seemed pleased to see us. The other man turned at the distraction, and I looked into the pale blue eyes of Conrad Greatrex. Millie grew shy and clung to her father.

'Good morning, Millicent,' Mr England said. His jaw was set tightly. 'Where are you off to?'

'The post office,' she replied. Her grandfather made no acknowledgement of her, glancing about as though he had somewhere else to be.

'Would you like Broadley to drive you?' Mr England looked for the pram. 'Where's Charley?'

'With Mrs England, sir.'

He appeared to almost say something, then thought better of it. 'Are you sending a parcel?' he asked.

'No, sir. I'm expecting to hear from my sister but haven't yet, so I was just going to enquire about any delays or see if they had anything there for me.'

'I see.' He seemed annoyed about something; beside him, Conrad Greatrex radiated impatience. 'Nurse May, I'm not sure it's my wife's responsibility to mind the children so that their nurse can stay on top of her correspondence.'

There were several seconds of silence. I opened my mouth to speak and found myself indefensible: he was right. My skin coloured with embarrassment, and I made myself look him in the eye. 'I'm very sorry, sir. I'll go back to the house.'

'That's quite all right. Take the carriage and come straight back.' He placed a large hand on his daughter's head. 'And no dragging Nurse May into the toy shop.'

I was hardly aware of my surroundings, barely heard his parting words as the two men left us, walking smoothly into the mill. I was so humiliated I thought I might cry.

The trip to the post office proved fruitless: the clerk was busy and impatient, and insisted there were no delays or backlogs. He reached over my head for a parcel from the person queuing behind me, signalling our conversation was over. I went, blinking, out into the street and stood for a moment with Millie, looking blindly up and down for Broadley and finding him parked where we left him, in front of the haberdasher's. What had I been thinking, sending pretty postcards and thinking everything was fine, when the last time I heard from my sister was . . . when was it? She didn't date her letters, and I threw the envelopes away. It must have been a fortnight at least. I thought of the cream envelope nestled in beside her letter, and what it might contain.

On the journey home, I stared out of the window as the forest streaked by. Millie was quieter than usual, tracing the flowers around the edge of her handkerchief, and I realised I ought to have sent a telegram to Robbie. Now I would not have another opportunity to, unless I brought both children on the four-mile round trip to town.

A quarter of a mile from the mill, we passed Mr Booth on the bridleway. He raised his cap and looked surprised to see me through the window; I was late to wave, and a moment later he'd gone. I was too preoccupied to wonder what he was doing near Hardcastle House, with Saul at Crow Nest.

It's up to you if you read it. Mother says you ought to. That's what she had said. I felt cold suddenly and gathered my cloak around me. I hoped Mr England would not be at the house.

'Nurse May, you look sad,' said Millie.

I forced a smile. 'I'm not sad,' I replied.

'Were you looking for Decca's letter?'

'No, although it would have been nice to have one. Should we write her another this week?'

'Yes. When is she coming home?'

'Not for a while. She'll be home for Christmas.'

'Christmas is a long way away. I'm not sure I want to sleep by myself until then.'

'You'll be so used to your own bed by the time she comes back, you won't want to share.'

She did not reply, and looked through the window, her little chin pointing up.

Mrs England was sitting on the carpet in the day nursery beside Charley, building towers from coloured bricks. One collapsed as we entered, and Charley let out an excited scream.

'Oh dear,' said Mrs England, smiling. Her face fell at the sight of me. 'They didn't have your letters?'

'No, ma'am. I'll just put the coats away.'

I went into the night nursery and closed the door, hesitating for a moment before locking it. Shivering, I went to kneel at my bed, and dragged out my trunk. I took out the black tea tin, an old Horniman's design that we used to sell in the shop. On the lid, a woman with red hair regarded a steaming cup, as though trying to decipher something in the vapour. I opened it on the rag rug and lifted out the bundle tied with a shoelace. I'd never counted how many letters there were, but now I did: fourteen, including the latest. Almost two a year.

I slid the uppermost one from the stack. There was no

postmark, just a single word on the creamy paper. *Ruby*. I recalled his shaky columns, the numbers he said squirmed and wriggled before him. He never learnt the correct spellings of things: cauliflour, carotts, brocoli. Not that they mattered so much.

With shaking hands, I pushed my thumbnail into the corner and heard a little tear. I smoothed down the tiny flap and rubbed, as if to reseal it. Then, in one swift motion, I ripped it open. The letter was folded inwards; shadows of words pressed at the paper, and I pinched it to determine how long it was: perhaps two or three sheets. Finally, I drew it out and opened it.

Dear Ruby.

I felt my head swim, and closed my eyes against it. When the sensation passed, I forced them open and scanned the first page, but the words flew at me like birds, and made no sense beside one another. I held the paper at arm's length and skimmed it. Trembling hard, I turned it over and scanned the next page, then moved to the final one, signed: *Yours Faithfully, Arthur, your father.*

I glanced through it all again, to make certain I had missed nothing. Then I sat back against the bed and closed my eyes. It had been unwise to read it with the children next door, my duties stretching before me until night-time. I felt like sitting there in my cloak on the floor until the grey sky faded to black and it was time to crawl into bed. I don't know how long I sat there. I was numb: too empty to cry, too exhausted to feel anything at all.

'Nurse May?' Millie's voice came from the corridor. She tried the door and found it locked. The handle turned again, and a moment later: 'Millie, come back. Leave Nurse May for a moment.' Footsteps receded down the hall, and the nursery door closed.

I put my head on my arms and closed my eyes. *Disease of the kidneys.*

I don't know how long I sat there. After two minutes, three, four, I tore the envelope to pieces and put the scraps in my cloak pocket. I didn't know what to do with the letter. When it had been sealed, its words unread, I could pretend it didn't exist with all the others. But now, with the ink bleeding over the page . . . *Disease.* There was no hiding place for a word like that in the room; it was poisonous, like the gas leak, and would suffocate me eventually.

A tiny knock came at the door, followed by the mistress's voice, low and private: 'Nurse May, would you like me to take the children out?'

My mind returned at once to Mr England's admonishment at the mill, his dark expression. I opened my mouth and closed it.

'No, ma'am,' I managed.

'I don't mind. Just pass me their things and I can take them for a walk.'

I peeled myself from the floorboards and unlocked the door. Mrs England was standing in the dim hall, looking worried.

'I'll come with you,' I said, though it was the last thing
I wanted. I wished to burrow beneath the covers and sleep.

'You don't look well.'

'I'm fine.'

Leaving the house with the baby had its own routine, and
I went through the motions, fastening Charley's outdoor
shoes, though he seldom put a foot on the ground,
buttoning him inside his coat and finding a hat he hadn't
squashed. Millie got wordlessly into her jacket. She knew
something was wrong; it was strange enough that her
mother was coming with us. I fetched the pram from the
boot room and laid down some fresh blankets, for the
vestibule was shady and cold, and anything left in it went
damp. I brought a rattle, a teething ring and a clean napkin
and towel for emergencies, plus a little corked bottle of
water. Millie insisted on bringing the card game Happy
Families, tucking the pack in her coat pocket, and Mrs
England said it was like we were going away for a week.

The four of us set out in a little party, Mrs England in
a handsome blue wool coat and a straw hat with a broad
white ribbon. I expected we would take the usual path to
the mill, but she turned right out of the house, and we
followed a discreet footpath up the wooded valley, sharing
the bulk of the pram where it got stuck. On the flat brow
stood a village, pinned to the moor by a jet brooch of a

church that had somehow withstood a century of harsh northern winters. The village streets were narrow, the houses made from the same charcoal-coloured stone as the road, so that everything had a dank, rain-washed appearance. Moorland surrounded it, lapping against the outermost cottages in a great flood of bleakness. On the main street, a group of dirty-faced children stood by a water pump. A little boy clung monkey-like to the lever, wrenching it up and down, sending wasteful streams over the ground. They stared at us as we passed, at the silver-crested pram, the honey-coloured mistress and her nurse in blue. A dark-haired woman scrubbing her doorstep turned to follow us with her eyes. Behind the low cottages, a graveyard wrapped around the church, and I thought how desolate it must be, to look out at gravestones and the lonely moor beyond.

We soon left the village behind, and all that was before us was land and sky. With no shelter, the wind charged at us from all directions, and the sky was a darkening grey.

'Where will we go if it rains?' I called out.

'We'll go down soon,' said Mrs England. Her cheeks were pink, her hair blowing from its pins. There was a vivacity I hadn't seen in her before; I felt as though I'd lost the pale, sad creature of the house, and before me was a changeling.

Before long we descended into the valley, wrenching the pram with difficulty down the steep hillside, avoiding the jagged moss-covered rocks sticking up from the ground, and sooner than I expected, we heard the rushing, gushing sound of water that grew louder with every step.

'Is that the river?' I asked.

'Horseshoe Cascade,' said Mrs England. It always came as a surprise when I remembered Hardcastle House was her childhood home. She seemed the very last person to be intimate with the forest, but she navigated the paths and clear little streams as though she knew it well. In almost two months I'd only known her to leave the house a handful of times, and I'd accompanied her for most of them.

Soon we reached the valley floor and the brown, fast river. There was a fragile-looking wooden bridge I had not seen before. I was hot and weary from pushing the pram through damp leaves, and stopped on the riverbank.

'Are we to cross it?'

Mrs England smiled. 'Are you afraid of trolls?'

'Is there another way? I'm not sure it's safe for the pram.'

'There isn't another bridge for half a mile. This is the way to the crags. The pram will be fine – look, it's wide enough.'

I wondered why we had gone such a long-winded way instead of the simple one, past the mill and along the bridleway. Millie scurried across alone and waited at the other side. With her blonde hair and brown coat and hat, she blended into the forest as though in a photograph. I looked at the swift water, swollen by rainfall.

Mrs England took the pram handlebar and said: 'I'll push it.'

'Are you sure it's safe?'

'I've crossed it a hundred times. Unless you would rather go back.'

I thought of what Mr England would say if his wife told him I was unwell again and unable to look after the children. I gripped the handlebar, but she batted my hands away.

'I'll do it. That way if we all fall in, it will be my fault.'

I made myself go first. The boards were slippery, covered in moss, and a third of the way across I stumbled, but held tight to the handrail and recovered myself. I stared at Millie, focusing on her round, pink face, her fawn-coloured jacket, her little straw hat, the river rushing like a merry go round beneath me. Within seconds it was over. I would insist, I decided, on going the usual way home.

We climbed up through the woods and reached the vast toffee-coloured crags, surrounded by flat grey slabs that lay in tablets, overgrown with moss and ferns and ivy, like a temple left to ruin. My thighs ached, my arms screaming in protest as we scaled the narrow path leading through the rocks. Mrs England saw and took over the pram again.

'I think we should leave it here and carry him,' she said.

'Are we going all the way up, ma'am?'

'We ought to. We've come all this way.'

She lifted her baby from the blankets and put him to her shoulder, and he looked around in surprise.

'Is it safe with the children?'

'Very safe. I've come here since I was a child.'

I sighed and followed her, and eventually the treetops lowered so that we were above them, spreading before us in a great brown carpet that was skeletal in places, patchy gold and chestnut in others, with an army of evergreens covering one side of the valley. Bracken and lilac-grey heather concealed the sharp edges where the crags dropped off to thin air. We stuck to the weaving path and finally reached the top, where an enormous rock balanced precariously on the peak.

In all my life, I'd never seen a view more pleasant. We'd reached an immense height, with the entire valley before us like a painting, lit by sunlight. A great chasm lay between the crags and the moor beyond, as though two deep cuts had been made in the landscape, and a narrow slice removed. I took off my hat and felt the wind cool the sweat at my hairline.

'Do you miss home?' Mrs England asked as we looked out.

'No,' I answered. 'I miss my sister and brothers. I miss watching them grow. They look different every time I see them.'

'When was the last time?'

'More than a year ago.'

She was silent, and then she said: 'We can't always be there for the ones we love.'

I thought about what she meant, and then she said: 'It must be so different here compared to Birmingham. I can't imagine living in a city.'

'It is,' I replied. 'Though we lived on the outskirts. I've never been anywhere like this. I have to say it's not what I expected at all.'

'What did you expect?'

'I'm not sure, ma'am. I didn't have long to think about it.'

Millie peeled away from me and began picking heather. I told her to be careful and stay well away from the edge. Mrs England kept a tight hold of Charley.

'She's like a little magpie,' said Mrs England, watching Millie. 'Always collecting things.'

We followed her around, picking tough little sprigs of heather, and I saw Mrs England look out once or twice at the uncultivated hills that reached in every direction. A gust of wind caught her off-guard and stole her hat from her head; she shrieked and flung a hand after it, but it flew over the edge of the crags, down into the treetops.

She turned to me, her face wiped clean with shock, and I burst out laughing. 'I'm sorry, ma'am,' I said. 'I don't mean to laugh at you.'

A broad smile split her face, and within seconds Charley was shaking in her arms, looking bemusedly from one of us to the other as we hunched over in our corsets.

'What's funny? What?' Millie tugged at us, making us howl even harder.

Mrs England wiped her eyes. 'Oh, well, never mind,' she said. 'At least it wasn't one of my favourites.'

'Should we go down and find it?' I asked.

'No,' she replied, laughing. 'The crags have claimed it now.'

We began the descent, Mrs England ahead of me with Charley, while I took a firm hold of Millie's hand. At the top of the path I took a swift glance backwards, to look at the magnificent scenery one last time. A black blot on the landscape caught my eye, on a distant bit of moorland across the valley. I saw the packhorse trail winding before it, and what looked like a long, low yard beside it. From the miniature chimney coiled a wreath of blue smoke, and I realised it was Tommy Sheldrake's forge, alone and lonely on the scrub. I watched it a beat longer, as if at this distance I might see him come outside in his leather apron, and put a hand to his brow.

Below me, Mrs England strode away in her neat blue coat and grey skirt, her pretty hat claimed by the woodland, her dark blonde hair coming loose in the wind.

CHAPTER 17

'Thank you for drawing the bath the other night,' said Tilda. We were in the scullery, sorting the laundry while Charley had his nap. 'I wish they'd get another maid. I could do with some help.'

'Oh, it was nothing,' I said, hanging clean stockings off my left arm. 'Why don't they?'

'Don't know. Money, I expect. I asked Mr E, but he said I'd have to make do for the time being.'

The two of us spoke more often now, pausing in doorways and lingering with our trays and cloths and chamber pots, though we were still tentative and courteous to one another. I knew it wouldn't have happened if Blaise still worked at the house.

'She seemed out of sorts that night,' I went on. 'Said she suffers with her monthlies.'

Tilda passed Emily another load of washing. 'She hasn't got her monthly,' she said.

I looked at her. 'The other day?'

Tilda plucked a pair of frilly cotton drawers from a pile and held them up. 'Clean as a whistle.'

Emily stirred the copper with her back to us, her mousy hair escaping from her cap. I frowned and went on layering stockings.

'Oh, I meant to say,' said Tilda. 'Did you ask Mrs E to look after your post?'

I stared at her. 'No. Why?'

'I found a stack of it in her bedside cabinet.'

My heart began thudding. 'What do you mean?'

'A bunch of letters in the drawer next to her bed. Swear it was all for you. I thought it was strange, but then I reckoned you might want to keep them away from the children. You've not much privacy, have you? Not that the young ones could read them, mind.'

The scullery seemed to warp around me. Tilda saw my expression and frowned. 'Has she kept them from you?'

I tried to recall how many times I had asked Mrs England if there was any post for me: it was at least once. Emily went on stirring, and soap powder hung in the damp heat, scratching at my nostrils.

'Why would she do that?' Tilda asked.

'Are you sure they were for me?'

'If your name's Ruby May.'

I clattered out of the scullery, through the kitchen, into the hall and up the stairs, shedding stockings on my way. From the dining room came the scrape of cutlery, the rustle of a newspaper; Mrs England was in there eating lunch. Her health was recovered now, her appetite returned. On impulse I went straight to her bedside drawer, flinging it open, not caring who followed or caught me. Inside was a mess of trinkets: bookmarks, pen nibs, handkerchiefs. A slim diary from the previous year, a broken hair pin, a small cotton bag of dried lavender. And beneath it all, as though to conceal them: a stack of envelopes in differing sizes, five or six of them, all addressed to me at Hardcastle House. I drew them out cautiously, as though my eyes were playing tricks on me. There was Elsie's writing, and Sim's clear, swift hand, and Elsie's again. And . . . My eyes brimmed with tears. 'Decca,' I whispered, stroking her untidy writing. A fog of confusion descended, rolling and thickening. How long had they been there? Time had a habit of standing still at Hardcastle House; the only sign it moved at all was the chill that intensified each morning, and the deepening carpet of leaves on the ground.

All the letters were sealed and untampered with. I held them, dumb with incomprehension, when a noise startled me. The door was slowly opening, and a moment later a golden head appeared.

'Millie!' I sighed. 'You gave me a fright.'

'Charley is awake and I'm hungry.'

'I'm coming.' I shoved the letters back into the drawer and closed it.

'What are you doing in Mama's room?'

'Looking for Charley's rattle.'

'It's in his cot.'

'Is it? Thank you.'

Bludgeoned by bewilderment and by relief that Elsie was well enough to write to me, I straightened and smoothed my apron. Were there more? I looked about the room, wondering about other hiding places. The idea that she had hidden them from me . . . it was too immense for words; too immense to be reasonable. I considered the possibility that she had put them there to give to me but forgotten every day. Or had she kept them from me for a reason?

I asked Millie to wash her hands and she skipped off to the nursery. Before I knew what I was doing, I fell to my knees and looked beneath the bed, then stood and went around to the other side. There were only a few things in the drawer of the left-hand cabinet: coins, a pocketbook and a tin of hair oil indicated Mr England had at one time slept there. On the dressing table was a neat display of crystal bottles, pretty little jars, hairbrushes, combs, a boot hook. A pink rose swelled inside a paperweight.

I was trembling with rage. The Englands knew about my sister, about her health, her disability. They ought to have known paper and envelopes and stamps were not free to us, that every letter we posted hoped for a reply. I had written to Elsie in a panic, which would have confused and worried her. I got to my knees again and dragged Mrs England's trunk from beneath her bed, determined to uncover something else, anything else. Perhaps she knew about everything; perhaps she had known all along. The trunk was unlocked and still held her clothes from Crow Nest. I rifled through them, searching through silk, cotton, linen for the cool smoothness of paper, the sharp corner of an envelope, but there was nothing. By the time I'd finished, her clothes lay in a jumbled heap and I slammed the lid.

I had opened the letter from my father for no reason. Eight years of distance, of space and separation, had been broken for no reason, the layers I'd so carefully, so purposefully, wrapped around myself were now in tatters. I'd torn them off myself. Trembling, I kicked the trunk back beneath the bed and left the room, making more noise than I cared to, and stood at the top of the landing, listening to the ordinary sounds from the dining room: their hushed chatter, the tinkle of cutlery. The scale of her betrayal was incomprehensible. I felt quite violent towards her, and willed myself calm. I had kept a secret for her, one I didn't fully or even vaguely understand, but still I kept it. I knew about secrets, and I knew, too, how one led to another. I was a fool for thinking she'd have no more.

The weather was too poor for a walk, so that afternoon we stayed in the nursery and performed a puppet show for Charley. One rainy morning the children and I had made a miniature theatre from old shoeboxes and decorated it with Decca's paints. I knew Mrs England would come to the nursery – she visited now every day – and at half-past one I heard her tread in the corridor. I listened for her knock; she never waited for a response and let herself straight in.

'Pardon me,' she said, seeing what we were doing, and smiling. 'Is there room for one more person in the audience?'

'Yes, ma'am,' I said, feeling a sudden rush of fury. She settled in the rocking chair behind Millie and me. The two of us were kneeling at the low table, while Charley watched from the carpet on the other side.

I'd had an hour or so to think about things, but failed to reach a conclusion, let alone an explanation. Meanwhile, it was as though Elsie and Decca were in the mistress's bedroom, calling me. I pictured them locked in, like Mrs England had been. I'd always thought her sane and trustworthy, if reticent and somewhat useless as a wife and mother. But now I wasn't so sure. Perhaps Mr England was the only person who understood her, who knew her better than anybody.

He had been avoiding me since the night of the party. Once or twice I'd seen him through the blinds approaching the house or leaving it. I was tormented by the feeling I'd done something wrong, that what happened in his room had been my fault. That I ought to have controlled myself, that I behaved with impropriety. Though I had the sense that his changeable mood was only partly to do with me; he seemed busy and preoccupied, as though something troubled him.

I couldn't concentrate on the puppet show, but Millie either didn't mind or notice, and went on playing undeterred. She had two parts in our drama: a princess and a fairy, having given me the roles of the king and the sailor. All I could think of was the wall I'd spent eight years building, reduced to rubble now. *Disease of the kidneys.* The knowledge of it was a responsibility, and I already had enough of those.

'Nurse May, you aren't doing the voice!'

'Perhaps the sailor should kiss the princess now,' said Mrs England.

Millie pushed the paper puppets together and I pulled the cord, fashioned from an old cushion, that drew the curtains.

'You are so inventive, Nurse May.' Mrs England's voice was full of warmth. 'I wish I'd had a nurse like you as a child.'

'Did you not have one, ma'am?' I asked stiffly, moving to tidy the game.

'Only a governess, shared with my brothers.'

I lay the puppets flat in their box and returned them to the cupboard, rearranging the games and toys inside at random so I wouldn't have to look at her.

'Still no post for me, ma'am?'

'Not that I know of, I'm afraid.'

'Only,' I spoke slowly, and my voice was thick in my throat, 'Tilda mentioned she saw a letter addressed to me in your personal things.' My mouth was dry, and I licked my lips. 'She thought you might have mislaid it, perhaps.'

There was a beat of silence. 'In *my* things?'

'Nurse May, can we play prowling tigers?'

'Yes, Millie. Let me tidy first.'

'One of your letters?' Mrs England asked.

'That's what she said, ma'am.'

'Did she say where?' She was puzzled, perplexed.

'The bedside table, I think.' I kept my tone neutral, but my heart was beating hard.

At once she got up from the rocking chair and went to look. I wiped Charley's chin and put him in his pen. He screeched in protest, so I passed him his teething ring and he sucked, watching me. A minute later Mrs England returned with the little bundle of post. I knew there were six envelopes, and she had brought them all. She wore on her face an expression of pure astonishment.

'I don't know how these got there,' she said. 'I must have put them there and forgotten about them.' Her cheeks were pink, and the tops of her ears.

'Thank you, ma'am.' I took them from her and tried not to sound as bitter as I felt. 'Six of them. That's my sister's handwriting. And Decca's. I thought it wasn't like her not to write.' I tried to sound unfussed, unruffled, but Mrs England didn't seem to be listening. Her eyes were glazed, and a little frown puckered between her brows.

I waited for her apology; she realised this and looked me in the eye. 'I'm sorry, Nurse May. What must you think of me?'

I took a breath. 'That's all right, madam. No harm done.'

'No, but the agony you went through waiting for them. And from Decca as well.' She blinked in confusion. 'She hasn't written to me.'

Mr England had thanked me for being kind to his wife, and now her brown eyes were so afflicted I felt a pang of sympathy. After all, it made no sense that she should withhold letters from her own daughter. Why in this house did it feel as though the ground was always shifting? Why did I not know where I stood from one day to the next?

'I expect this is for all the family,' I said, tearing it open. 'What does she say?'

Decca had written just one side. 'She says that they have macaroni on Fridays, and she is learning French. She likes the French teacher, Mrs Patrice.'

'What else does she say?'

Her penmanship had improved ever so slightly and I felt a tug in my chest. 'Not much.' I reminded myself that no matter how I felt, she was Decca's mother, and I had no claim to the child. 'Perhaps the other one will say more.'

It was even shorter and ended with the sentence: *I hope Christmas comes soon.*

Mrs England wrung her hands and scanned my face anxiously. 'What does it say?'

'You can read it, ma'am.'

Her eyes jumped back and forth across the paper. 'Oh dear. She says very little.'

The subtext made it obvious how Decca found St Hilda's. *This was your idea*, I thought. A coil of resentment glowed white-hot inside me, and I had the intense desire to be away from Mrs England, to go somewhere private and read my sister's letters. After so long, and with what I knew about Father, it was worse than an itch I couldn't scratch. Even poor Decca paled in significance, though I knew later I would read her letters properly and feel wrung out with helplessness. I recalled the first days at Norland, when everybody but me seemed to have a friend. Starting term late, when the girls had had weeks to form alliances and arrange hierarchies, was guaranteed to have counted against her.

I sighed. 'Would you like to keep them, ma'am?'

'No, they are addressed to you. This is what I dreaded,' she added in a low voice.

'What did you dread?' Millie asked. She was kneeling at the low table, giving her dolls tea.

'Nothing.' A smile flickered across her mother's face, then went out.

'Is there a letter for me?'

'Decca wrote to all of us,' I said brightly. 'She misses you very much.'

'When can we play tigers?'

'Soon, miss.'

'Can I have some milk?'

Charley was playing contentedly in the corner. 'I'll get you some if you'll watch Charley for me.'

Mrs England straightened and brushed down her narrow waist. 'I'm going to Crow Nest this afternoon.'

'Should we come with you?'

'Maybe next time.' She looked me in the eye, and her gaze was calm and bold and steady. 'I'm sorry about the letters.'

I found I believed her, and was more confused than ever. 'That's all right, ma'am.'

'Do you know where the postbox is?'

'The one downstairs?'

'No, the one at the end of the bridleway. In the wall by the lodge.'

'Yes, ma'am.'

'I would use that, if I were you.'

I frowned.

'Nurse May, I'm thirsty!'

I stroked Millie's hair. 'I'll get you a drink.'

I followed my mistress out to the landing, and she went inside her bedroom and closed the door.

In the kitchen, Mrs Mannion was latticing a gooseberry pie.

293

'Mrs England is going to visit Master Saul,' I told her, pouring milk into a glass.

'How long for?'

'She didn't say.'

The cook rolled her eyes to heaven. 'A bit of notice would help. The master won't eat this on his own.'

'Mrs Mannion, did Mr Booth call at the house earlier?'

'No, why would he?'

'I don't know. I saw him coming from the mill.'

Tilda came through the swinging door with a duster.

'Don't be bringing that into my kitchen,' Mrs Mannion warned. Tilda flapped it in her face and the cook shrieked. 'Get out of it!'

'Mrs England is going to visit Saul,' I told Tilda.

'Oh, right,' she said. 'Did you get your letters?'

I nodded, not wishing to speak of it in front of Mrs Mannion. 'She didn't say whether or not she'll stay at Crow Nest, but I noticed her trunk is packed.'

Tilda fixed me with a frown. 'What trunk?'

'The one under her bed.'

'I unpacked it the night she got back.'

'What are you two wittering on about?' said Mrs Mannion. 'This is a kitchen, not a mothers' meeting.'

Tilda accompanied me to the kitchen door. 'Do you know why she came back?' I whispered.

'No idea. She only mentioned something about Saul being well cared for where he was, and that she felt a bit useless.'

She pushed open the door for me, and the two of us almost collided with Mr England, who was standing on the other side. He wore his hat and coat, and his expression was unreadable.

'Tilda,' he said. 'Could you light a fire in my study? I'll work from home this afternoon.'

'Of course, sir.'

'Thank you.'

I expected he would say something to me like usual, throwing a brief comment or aside my way, but he didn't even glance at me and went off whistling down the hall. Tilda pulled a face and followed him into the study. I felt as though I'd been reprimanded, though he hadn't said a word. I decided I would speak to him later. It would be the decent thing to do, to apologise for leaving the children with their mother, plus I could show him Decca's letter, perhaps ask if there was anything he wished to put in a reply. It would displease him to know his wife had kept my post; it would unite the two of us, if only briefly. I imagined telling him, and his brown eyes filling with worry and alarm. I could comfort him, reassure him that it didn't matter now I had them, that no harm was done. In a few hours I would take the children to the drawing room, and we would all be together again; he would play the piano with Millie sitting on his knee, while Charley tore around like a fat balloon, screeching with pleasure. After the gas incident, when the mistress was ill, Mr England had asked me to keep the children from coming into the house in case there were traces of it. Tilda delivered this message to the nursery, and the disappointment had struck me like a blow. No matter; his wife had been unwell, and he was concerned. It was understandable, but normal life could resume now she was recovered. She was lucky to be married to a man as considerate as him.

CHAPTER 18

B ut it was not to be. At four o'clock Tilda came to the nursery with bread and butter, baked apples and a message: the master was busy working, and would not see the children today.

My dismay must have been obvious, for she said: 'The mistress will see them, though.'

'I thought she went to Crow Nest?'

'She didn't in the end. They're going together tomorrow.'

'Where is he now, Tilda?'

'In his study.' She left with the tray.

Millie looked at me. 'Papa doesn't want to see us again?'

'Of course he does. He just works so hard he can't find the time at the moment.'

'Can we see Saul tomorrow?'

'I'll ask.'

The children spent an hour with their mother in the drawing room, and at five minutes to six I heard Mr England leave his study and go to the dining room. Cigar smoke drifted through the door as I gathered up the picture books, and Mrs England kissed them goodnight before going to join her husband. One of the double doors was open, and I heard the chink of crockery, and her soft greeting.

Upstairs, Millie attempted to drag out the evening as usual, chattering as I brushed her hair and asking me to tell her again about the London trams that moved without horses, and the staircase in Harrods that glided upwards of its own accord. My letters winked at me from my pillow. From the moment I'd been left alone I found I was unable to read them, half-dreading what news they brought. They'd waited weeks already, and could wait a few more hours. I'd propped them on my bed, glancing at them constantly in case they disappeared again.

'And now you must go to bed,' I told her.

'Why must I go to bed every night?' she complained. 'It's so boring.'

When she finally settled, I turned down the lamps and went softly downstairs. There were no sounds from the dining room. I looked in and found the table empty, the candles extinguished. The drawing room, too, though warm and invitingly lit, was vacant. I knocked at the master's study.

'Come in.'

My stomach turned over as I let myself into the dim room. Mr England seemed to have taken up where he'd left off before dinner; papers and pen nibs littered his desk, and a ledger stood open at his left elbow.

'Nurse May.' His expression was neutral in the shadowy light from the desk lamp. 'How can I help?'

'Sir, I wanted to apologise for the other day.'

He blinked.

'For leaving Charley with his mother.'

He gave a deep, long sigh. Then he wiped at his face – a habit of his, I'd noticed, when he was stressed or uneasy – and gestured to the chair with the scarlet cushion before the desk.

'Thank you, sir,' I said, hoping he would ring the bell and ask for coffee. But I was being foolish; of course he would not. I was not his equal, nor his confidante, and even though it was idiotic, I felt as though I had been, and had fallen from favour.

He stretched, and his shoulders cracked as he rolled them. 'Would you object to me pouring a brandy?' he asked. 'It's been a long day.'

'Of course not, sir.' My own shoulders sank with relief.

He bent and reached into his cabinet, standing upright with a crystal decanter. The pleasant glugging sound of the amber liquid relaxed me, and I sat more comfortably against the cushion.

'It was a nasty business, this week with the gas pipe.

STACEY HALLS

We owe our lives to you. If anybody had lit a lamp . . .
Well.' He returned the decanter to the cabinet and locked
it with a little brass key. 'You are extraordinarily perceptive,
Nurse May. I imagine you've already drawn a conclusion
as to why I prefer the children to be in their nurse's care
at all times.'

My heart beat a little faster. 'I understand, sir.' Was he
accusing her of leaving the gas on? *I don't know how these
got here.* Her ears had been red: she was embarrassed or
lying. Forgetfulness was one thing, deception another
entirely. I didn't know what to believe, and then there had
been the strange comment about the postbox . . . Perhaps
Ben hadn't been able to take the mail lately. I thought of
the woman who had stood next to me on the crags; she
had been different there, not at all like someone who
forgot things, who left valves leaking and misplaced her
servants' post. There, she'd been *whole.* I didn't know her
well enough to declare she was herself, but I felt that I
had seen, that afternoon, the closest thing to it. For she
was not the pale moth glancing off the edge of conversations, was not the preoccupied, distracted creature
inspecting her gloves at church. For something had
revealed itself to me on the crags, or, more accurately,
emerged fully formed, as if from behind a screen: Mrs
England was desperately unhappy.

'I wish there was a way I could repay you.'

'You don't owe me anything, sir.'

He regarded me over his moustache and said nothing.

I realised I was afraid of him and yet drawn to him at the same time. I was afraid of what he might say to hurt me, afraid that he did not think me up to the job. And yet . . . I wished very much to sit all evening with him in this smoky little room. I would be content just watching him at his work, filling his glass, blotting his papers. Sometimes, in the lonely hours, and never without guilt, I thought what a disappointment his wife must be to him. He deserved someone bright and rosy and shimmering, who took an interest in her home and in him. Instead, he slept alone and shut himself in his study. Charles England was handsome and sociable, rich and warm and dynamic; he ought to be at parties every other night, race meets and hunting days and theatres. How he would have loved London, where he could roll from box to club to restaurant. How different things would be if we were married. I would be there to take his coat and brush the cotton from his shoulders in the evening; I would be there to cut his cigars. We would go to bed together . . . To think of it, I felt myself redden from the inside out. Perhaps he didn't know it was ordinary for man and wife to share a bed, that keeping separate rooms was strange and unnatural. Perhaps his stepmother kept away from his father and that's how he thought it should be. *I wish to be cared for.* Again, his face, that haunted face, came to me. We could care for each other.

Suddenly the image came to me of Sim's letter waiting on my pillow, and another of her phrases sprung immediately to mind: *one act of self-control is worth eighty of enforced obedience.* Of course she had been referring to children, but I often found her maxims to be more relevant than they seemed.

'Where did you go on your walk the other day?' Mr England asked, settling in his chair.

'The crags,' I replied. 'I hadn't been to the top before.'

'You need quite the head for heights up there.' He smiled.

'Yes, sir.'

'Breathtaking, isn't it? Lilian and I used to go up there often.'

'Don't you anymore, sir?'

His eyes fell to some lost, faraway memory. 'Things get in the way.'

I glanced at the columns in the ledger and felt a brief surge of anxiety. 'I shan't keep you any longer, sir. Thank you for your time.'

'I'm sorry I wasn't able to see the children.'

'That's all right, sir. They aren't going anywhere.'

His moustache twitched. 'I'm not sure you can say that of Charley.'

I knew I should go, but I did not get up. 'Tilda said you and the mistress will visit Master Saul tomorrow.'

'Yes,' he said. 'Something to look forward to.'

I waited to see if he would invite me and the children, but he was distracted, and perhaps did not think of it. It had rained for two days, making walks impossible and confining us indoors; a drive to Crow Nest to see Saul would be a lift for all of us.

'He is very much missed, sir.'

'He'll be pleased to hear it. I'm sure he finds it terribly dull there with nobody to boss about. No doubt he is pining for his nurse.' He sighed again and placed both elbows on the table, momentarily clutching his head before taking up a piece of paper. I got up from the chair and set the cushion straight. This time it stayed.

'Thank you for your time, sir. Oh.' I swallowed. 'I ought to have said: there was a mix-up with the post. My sister had written to me after all.'

He was tidying his desk, moving books and papers. 'A mix-up?'

'Well, er . . .' His eyes travelled up to meet mine. 'Mrs England misplaced the letter and forgot about it.'

'Misplaced it?' he repeated. 'Where was it?'

'In her bedroom, sir.'

His brows lowered, and he looked very hard at me. 'How long had it been there?'

'I don't know, sir. A week or so.'

He drew his lips inwards as though he wished to say something, but thought it better not to. 'I hope there were no repercussions from the delay.'

'No, sir. Nothing like that.'

'Your family is well, I hope?'

He wouldn't understand why I hadn't read them. 'Yes. Thank you.'

I thought that would be the end of it, but he said: 'She isn't malicious, you know.'

I blinked in surprise. 'I know that, sir.'

'You might wonder why I've never called a doctor, but we all know what would happen if one were to come. I have no wish to go down that road. She's better off at home.'

There was a silence as I considered his words, and the candor of them. I nodded.

'Good. Well, I am determined to make sense of these figures before I retire.' He yawned. 'I feel as though I am going out of my mind.' He looked so tired, and his eyes watered from the effort of yawning. 'Excuse me. Nurse May, you look as though you're desperate to say something. What is it?'

'Nothing, sir. I don't pretend to know anything about business, and I don't mean to tell you what to do, but perhaps if you're tired it might be better to start fresh in the morning, when you've had a good night's sleep.'

'I can't remember what one of those is. But you are right, of course.' He smiled, and this time it reached his eyes. 'What would we do without you?'

Warmth flared inside me and sustained me for the rest of the evening. I sat in the day nursery in the rocking chair, letting down Charley's petticoats, trying to ignore the pull of the past, but when it was quiet, when my hands were working and my mind free to wander, it could be so persistent. *I'm going out of my mind.* I shook my head:

a coincidence. But my mind kept catching on his words, pulling them like a loose thread.

I recalled the warm, bright day in April when my father disappeared. He'd been in the shop all morning as usual, and counted out Mrs Parker's change for the flour and raisins she'd bought. Mrs Parker thanked him and he walked around the counter to hold the door for her. The bell trilled, but instead of closing it between them, he followed her and turned right, striding down Longmore Street in his spotless overalls. Mrs Parker thought nothing of it, supposing he had an errand. She caught the tram outside the bakery to visit her sister, and when she returned home that evening Mr Parker commented over his paper that Emma May was looking for her husband.

'Arthur May, the grocer?' Mrs Parker asked, puzzled. 'I was only in there today.' She recounted this to us at the kitchen table half an hour later, clutching her handbag on her lap.

'And he didn't say where he was going?' Mother asked. The five of us bunched around her in silence; I had Elsie on my hip.

Mrs Parker shook her head. She was a portly, respectable lady in her fifties and worked as a seamstress from her house in Sherbourne Street.

'Soon as Albert told me, I come straight here.'

Mother had been ironing when a customer called up the stairs from the shop below, wanting service. She looked for Father in the storeroom and the yard, the scullery and the privy, but he was nowhere to be found. She served the customers herself and returned to find a scorch mark on her shift, and Elsie playing with buttons in the corner; mercifully she hadn't reached for the iron. My mother flipped the door sign to closed as panic consumed her.

By the time my brothers and I finished school, there was still no trace of him. He hadn't left his overalls, not even a note, and Mother was beside herself. We rarely had visitors to the flat; once or twice a year Aunt Doris came, always bringing with her a little parcel of coal. But all my grandparents were dead, and Mother and Father were too busy for friendships. It was a strange and memorable thing to see tidy Mrs Parker sitting at our table with a string of stockings drying above her head.

'Ought you go to the police?' she asked.

Mother shook her head. 'I don't want him getting in trouble.'

'Mrs May, what if he's already in trouble?'

Mother sent the two older boys out to look for him, and they returned after dark. None of us slept that night, and it was Robbie's suggestion to leave a candle burning at the window, so Father would know we were awake.

Just after six the flat door opened, and I sat up in bed at once. 'Robbie,' I whispered.

My brother stirred on the mattress opposite, propping himself on an elbow and frowning in the early light. The candle had gone out; he saw this and looked at me. From the next room came the creak of a floorboard.

'Father,' I mouthed, and we leapt at once out of bed. Before we could turn the handle, my mother's voice came from their bedroom.

'Arthur, where have you *been*? You've had me worried sick.'

There was a low, inaudible mumble.

'What do you mean, looking for work? Where've you been all night? It's six in the morning! You left without a word, without closing the shop, without— I was upstairs, Arthur. What the hell did you mean by it?'

Robbie and I clung to the door like barnacles. Though he was home, fear stirred in my stomach. More mumbling; I heard the words 'factory' and 'motorcars'.

'You went to Longbridge? That's ten miles away.'

'Eight.'

'You have a business here; what on earth would you do that for? You aren't looking for work, you've got it.'

There was the scrape of chair legs and a dull thud as Father sat.

'You've got your head in the clouds, Arthur. I'm barely holding it together here; I feel like a string about to snap. I can't cope no more.'

There was a horrible sound, and I realised Father was crying. More footsteps, creaks, a rustle. 'Shh,' said Mother. 'That's enough. You'll get a couple of hours' sleep if you go down now. You must have been walking all night. Here, let me take your boots off.'

Robbie and I were facing the same direction, looking

at the wall. Neither of us moved until we heard Father's boots being set on the floor, and the bedroom door closing behind them. What did she mean: she couldn't cope? Couldn't cope with what? My heart thudded, and my stomach churned. Robbie crouched below me, and I stared at the cowlick on the crown of his head, where his straight brown hair grew wavy.

He turned to look up at me. 'Why was he crying?' he whispered.

'I don't know.'

We got back into bed and I drew the curtain against the daylight. Elsie had rolled into the space I'd left and was fast asleep. I lifted her gently and edged in beside her, feeling cold, though the room was warm and stuffy with five sleeping bodies. Mother said that to a burglar, an open window was as good as an open door.

My bed was closest to Mother and Father's room, the headboard resting against the thin wall. Robbie and I stared at one another, and after a while he turned on his side and went to sleep.

After an hour's mending, I heard Mr England's tread on the stairs, slow and defeated. I realised I had waited for him to go to bed before I went myself. I put away the mending and turned off the lamps. In the other room, where the children slept, I nestled down beneath the covers, set the nightlight beside the bed, and finally reached for the envelopes.

Dear Ruby,

We received the money, thank you for sending it. I needed new winter boots and Mother is taking me to Ballards on Saturday to get them. Archie got a job at Belgrave Works stuffing wire mattresses. He comes home with bits of feathers on him and we do a clucking sound, which he hates! There was a fire in the next road on Sunday night. We could see it from the window. The fire engine didn't fit and we thought the entire street would go up. But then it did fit, thank goodness. Mother says I shouldn't waste a half penny stamp if I have nothing to say. If you wished to send some money in your next letter that would be all right with me, so I can buy more stamps.

Love,

Elsie

Dear Ruby,

I did reply to your last letter, I hope you got it. We got the money thank you. And thank you for the postcard. I'm not sure I like the crags, they look quite fritening. But I like the boat at the bottom with the lady in the pretty hat. I wish I could go to a party. Please reply.

Love,

Elsie

The relief was immediate and all-consuming. I found myself weeping and smiling at the same time, and pressed the heels of my hands to my eyes to gather myself. I sniffed and sighed, and set Elsie's letters on the eiderdown, reaching next for Sim's and feeling so much lighter.

Dear Nurse May,

I trust things are well in Yorkshire and that you are settling in. I write with an invitation at the eleventh hour and hope very much that you will oblige. The annual Speedwell Ceremony takes place on Thursday week at the Steinway Hall in Marylebone, and this year twenty-four nurses will be awarded with badges for five years' service. The ceremony will be followed by tea in the winter garden, and several of our investors and clients will be in attendance. Mrs Ward will distribute the badges on stage, where she is to be joined by an assembly of nurses of varying degrees of experience. As one of our scholarship students, I should like it if you were one of them, and if you would join us for tea and supper afterwards to share your experience of being a scholarship student with the friends of the institute.

Please accept my apologies for the short notice: Nurse Gilbert, the scholarship student scheduled to take part, has come down with measles, and for her replacement you came promptly to mind. If agreeable, I shall write to Mrs England asking, as a great favour, for you to be in London for the event. You may take the time (two days will suffice) as annual leave. Please reply at your earliest convenience and I shall make the arrangements.

Believe me to remain,

Your most sincere friend,

M. Simpson

Dear Nurse May,

I write in hope that my letter of 23rd October reached you. If it did not, I reiterate my invitation for you to attend the annual Speedwell badge-giving ceremony at Steinway Hall in Marylebone. We can provide train fare, accommodation at Pembridge Square and board for your visit. If this is agreeable to you, please respond with immediate effect, as the ceremony is in six days' time. If your family can't spare you or find a replacement, I shall make other arrangements, but I should be grateful if you could let me know either way.

Yours sincerely,

M. Simpson

Though it was late, I wrote at once to Miss Simpson, explaining there had been a delay at the post office and how sorry I was to miss the Speedwell Ceremony. It was only half a lie. I missed London, with its brilliant street lights and busy pavements, its rush and buzz. But it was a distant world to me now: the college, the bustle of the refectory and the lemon pie on Fridays, the neat girls with their embroidery circles and violet-scented writing paper.

Even the speedwell badge itself, engraved with the Norland motto *fortis in arduis*, and something I had coveted deeply, seemed little more than a frivolous token of vanity. As though nurses were soldiers, as if we had fought in wars. Even the institute itself could be conceited: after our graduation ceremony, the founder, Mrs Ward, had called us 'powerful agents of the state, character-builders, Empire-makers'. Did Empire-makers rinse chamber pots and wipe porridge from dribbling mouths?

I considered Mr England's offer to work independently and claim my full wage. If I accepted, I would be better off, and so would my family. I doubted very much that any of the Speedwell nurses had to buy boots for their siblings and pay their medical bills. I doubted very much that their brothers stuffed mattresses. Their fathers were superintendents, surgeons, solicitors; they were proud of their papas, affectionate towards their mothers. Nobody asked about my family, and I didn't offer. Perhaps they caught the whiff of tragedy on me; perhaps I reeked of it.

It was late by the time I finished writing. I tidied everything away and checked my watch: half-past nine. Yawning, I took my wash bag from the bedpost and put on my slippers to use the bathroom. Mrs England had had a late bath; the water sat greying in the bath tub, and a cake of soap had been left carelessly on the floor. I picked it up and set it on the washstand, and then I saw something in the mirror.

It had steamed up in the heat from the bathwater, and someone had written with a finger in the vapour. I frowned and took a step backwards, too close to read it. My face appeared in fragments. The trace of vapour clung in rivulets, the glass almost cleared, but the message was unmistakable. Streaked across the mirror in clumsy writing was a single word: *whore*.

CHAPTER 19

Mr Booth was in the mill yard the following morning, climbing off his bicycle as we crossed the bridge.

'Good morning,' he said brightly, setting it against the wall. 'Off to feed the ducks?'

'Not today,' I replied. 'Just a walk.'

In the silence that followed I noticed his satchel.

'Why are you here?' I asked.

'I'm teaching a literacy class for the workers, just until Master Saul returns.'

'That's good of you,' I said. 'Was it your idea?'

'Mr England's. They work through their dinner hour, mind, but they seem to enjoy it. And at least I'm not twiddling my thumbs in the mornings, getting in Blaise's way at home.'

'Are you still teaching at Laithe Hall in the afternoons?'

'I am.'

I looked about the yard. Voices drifted over from the open door of a loading bay, and Ben was sweeping the carriage house, making little piles of hay on the cobbles.

'I need to ask you something,' I said.

Mr Booth nodded expectantly.

'It's about Tommy Sheldrake.'

'Oh, aye. Are you sweet on him?'

'No, of course not.'

'Why of course?'

'Mr Booth, I need a favour of you. Can you find out why he came back from Australia, and when?'

'You can ask Blaise.'

'I can't do that.'

'Why not? Pay a visit on her, she'd like that. She only has her mother and mine calling around all hours of the day. She could do with new company.'

'I can't take the children to your house. It wouldn't be appropriate.'

He withdrew in mock offence.

'I'm sorry, I didn't mean it like that. I only meant I'm not sure what the master would say.'

'Do you have to account for your every move?'

'No.'

'Well, then. It's not like they don't know me. You forget I've been around a lot longer than you.' He adjusted the satchel across his chest. 'I'll finish here at half-eleven; we can walk back together. Blaise will love seeing the little'uns.'

Charley gazed mildly from the pram. Millie was on the bridge throwing sticks into the water, and I told her to come away. She skipped towards us brandishing a dirty twig.

'Would you like to pay Blaise a visit and have dinner at our house?' Mr Booth asked her.

'Blaise the maid?'

He laughed. 'The very same.'

'Yes!' she cried.

'Yes, please,' I corrected.

'Yes, please.'

'That would be nice,' I said. 'If you're sure.'

'I'll meet you here.'

That morning Tilda had brought breakfast to the nursery as usual. She was as pleasant as ever, and I made no reference to the writing on the mirror, which I'd hastily scrubbed off with my sleeve. I'd washed and changed quickly, feeling as though I was being watched, feeling as though the word had rubbed off on my arm and made it dirty. I had no idea who the message was for, or who had written it. *It's for you*, said the voice in my head. But based on what? My woodland walks with Mr Booth? My evening appointment with the master in the study? It sickened me, and I had a fitful night's sleep.

I was conscious of it, strolling with Mr Booth along the bridleway, and found I had nothing to say.

'Why do you want to know about Blacksmith Tom, anyway?' he asked to fill the silence.

'You can't tell Blaise that's why I'm coming.'

'Isn't it?'

'Yes, but I don't want her to read anything into it.'

'I doubt you'll pull the wool over her eyes.'

He was right, and I sighed.

Spring Grove was a presentable row of terraced houses, three storeys each, blackened with smoke from the mills. Mr and Mrs Booth lived at the end house with the cherry-red door and ivy climbing towards the upstairs windows. The river rushed at the end of the street, fifty yards away. Mr Booth let us in with his key and said the pram would be fine outside. I hesitated, then decided I had already offended him once; the blankets would wash if they grew dirty with the soot. I lifted Charley from their depths.

The front door led directly into a small sitting room, and a second door stood open to the kitchen-scullery beyond. 'Is that you, Eli?'

'I've brought some visitors.'

Blaise appeared in the doorway, wiping her hands. Her stomach was round beneath her apron, like a pudding in a bag. 'Blimmin' heck,' she said, but she seemed pleased. 'You're the last person I expected.'

'Hello, Blaise.'

'Is it all right if they stay for dinner?'

'Course. Look at you, Miss Millie!' She held her hands out. 'You must have grown three inches since I last saw you.'

'I lost a tooth!' the child cried, poking her tongue through the gap.

'So you have. Did the tooth fairy come?'

'Yes, she left me a penny.'

'You must have been a good girl, then. And look at Master Charley, all buttoned up.'

She reached for the baby and I passed him to her. From the kitchen came the smell of fresh bread and oxtail soup, and my stomach rumbled. The sitting room was dim and humbly furnished, but immaculately clean. Against the staircase wall was a draw-leaf dining table draped with a length of salmon-coloured velveteen, from which Blaise was making curtains. A sampler hung above the scullery door, stitched in scarlet.

Blaise arranged the table and the four of us sat as she set out bread, cheese and bowls of hearty soup. As she took her place, settling her sizeable belly behind the cloth, I couldn't help but stare at the way she rubbed and petted it. I couldn't help but notice, too, the easy familiarity she and Mr Booth had. It shouldn't have come as a surprise; they were, after all, married. But I hadn't ever met a couple who'd set up home so young and occupied their roles so readily. Blaise seemed a changed woman to the sharp, sarcastic one I knew. She looked well; her dark hair was thick and shiny, and beneath her apron she wore a pretty embroidered blouse.

After we'd eaten and I'd given Charley his milk and broken off bits of bread for him to eat ('Like a duck!' said Millie, and everybody laughed), Mr Booth took Millie to the river to throw stones. Charley explored the two downstairs rooms on his hands and knees, and, satisfied, fell asleep in the armchair. Blaise and I carried the dinner things through to the back room and began washing up. There was still an awkwardness between us, but it had shifted slightly; I felt none of the old hostility. In its place was a curious sort of toleration.

'You have a lovely home,' I said, meaning it.

'Thanks. It's all a bit cobbled together, but we've been lucky with hand-me-downs. Once I have a mangle, I'll be happy. How are things at the house?'

I was silent for a moment, then decided that if there was anybody I could be honest with, it was Blaise, who knew the household better than anyone.

'I'm not too sure,' I began. 'A few odd things have happened.'

'Like what?' Blaise handed me the soup pan, and I dried it and put it on the rack.

'Was anything of yours ever . . . withheld?'

A frown creased her forehead. 'Such as?'

'Post.'

She laughed. 'No one ever wrote to me. They kept your letters from you?'

'Mrs England had them in her bedside drawer for a fortnight.'

'That is odd. Why would she do that?'

'I don't understand either. She was very apologetic, said she must have put them there and forgotten. But I'm not sure I believe her.'

'She read them?'

'No, they hadn't been opened.'

Blaise pulled a face. 'Perhaps she did forget, then. Can't imagine why she'd bother if she weren't going to read them.'

'I suppose,' I said, though I was still uncertain. I had to tread cautiously with the next bit. Trying to sound indifferent, I went on: 'Mr Sheldrake's a nice man – the blacksmith who was at your wedding. Eli said he was a friend of yours.'

'Oh, yeah, Tommy? He's not a *friend*, as such, but my dad knew his before he died. He's just one of them faces you say hello to.'

'Eli mentioned something about your cousin.'

'I don't know if anything's happening there. Lucy's seen him down the White Horse a few times. I think she was hoping he'd be more interested.'

'What's he like?'

'What do you mean?'

I felt my neck turn red. 'Is he nice?'

'What is it you're really asking me?' She looked across at me, and I blushed. 'Don't be sly, Nurse May. You sweet on him?' A smile twitched the corner of her mouth.

'I hardly know the man. I met him once or twice in town, and he invited me and the children to his forge to make horseshoes. Mr England thought it was a good idea, so I took them up there. It was a while ago now, before Decca went to school.'

She waited, stirring the water with her wrists. The word in the mirror appeared again. I couldn't tell her, couldn't imagine saying it out loud. I pushed it from my mind.

Blaise was still staring at me. 'Go on,' she said.

'He wrote a letter to Mrs England,' I said. 'He gave it to Decca without me knowing and told her not to tell me or anyone. I don't understand why he wouldn't have written to her the normal way, unless there was something . . . unnatural in it.'

'*Tommy* did? Tommy Sheldrake?'

I nodded.

'Did you read it?'

'No, I gave it to her. That's why I wondered if you knew him well.'

'When was this?'

'Late September. Before you left.'

Her eyes narrowed. 'Was that the night she started the fire?'

'It might have been.'

'I saw something in the grate. It could have been that letter. She might have set it alight to get rid of it. The master saw it too and asked what it was, but she said it was an old bit of paper.'

My eyes widened. 'Did either of you see what it said?'

'No. It was practically cinders by the time he arrived. I thought there was something odd about it: she never lit her own fires, and it was warm that night anyway.'

She fell silent and looked conflicted. Then she dunked a bowl beneath the water and began to speak. 'I saw him once in the trees near the house. I was cleaning the mistress's room, and when I looked out the window there he was. I called out to him, asked what he was doing. He said walking to the village, but I've never known no one to go that way through the woods when the path's just below it. Besides, he wasn't walking. He was standing still, looking at the house. I didn't tell anyone, and I never saw him again until Lucy introduced us, though I didn't recognise him straightaway.'

The two of us were quiet for a moment, then I said: 'Do you think . . . do you think he has something over her? I can't imagine what, but why else would it be such a secret?'

'No. He's not like that.'

I agreed with her; Tommy Sheldrake didn't seem the blackmailing type.

'Perhaps they had a . . .' Blaise faltered, failing to land on the word. She handed me a spoon. 'Who knows.'

'And you never saw him again?'

'Not around the house, no.'

'When was this?'

'Maybe six, eight months ago. It was spring, if I remember, not long after he moved back.'

'He said he'd spent some time in Australia.'

'About ten years. He got cheap passage out there. Blacksmiths did in them days, or anyone who had a trade. I think he worked on the sheep stations. Don't ask me why you'd go all the way out there, thousands of miles, just to work with *sheep*. We've plenty of them here.'

'Why did he come back?'

'His father died, so he had to take over the forge. Plus his mother's a sickly thing. Did you meet her?'

'No.'

'She's in bed with some wasting disease, poor thing. He had to come back to take care of her. His brother's a waste of space, apparently, always down the pub and doing sly deals down the canal. He's a bit of a wrong'un.'

'That's sad. Look, I'd appreciate if you didn't tell Lucy what I've told you.'

'About the letter?'

I nodded. 'Or anyone. I don't want anyone getting into trouble.'

Blaise smirked. 'Sounds like she already could be.'

'What? Are you saying . . . ?'

'I'm *teasing*. You don't have to take everything so serious all the time.'

I swallowed. 'She wouldn't do that to Mr England. Not when he looks after her so well.'

'I wouldn't worry about him. He's paid for it.'

'What do you mean?'

She shrugged.

'Blaise.'

Her fingers danced in the soap suds. 'Tilda was cleaning the study once and he'd left one of his ledgers open. The Greatrexes give him a sort of salary. A fortune, really. What it's for and where it goes, God knows.'

'How much?'

'More than eighteen hundred a month.'

'*What?*' I was astounded. 'That's over twenty thousand a year. What on earth for?'

'Don't ask me. I shouldn't have told you. You'll not let on to anyone?'

'Only if you don't.'

There was a glimmer of our old mutiny, and we half-smiled.

'You see things when you're a maid,' said Blaise. 'Too much, at times.'

'Meaning what?'

'I don't want to be putting ideas in your head. But perhaps she and Tommy did have something going on. And perhaps it's over now.'

'But a *blacksmith* . . . and she's married!' I remembered what Mr Booth had said, that I was green as grass. 'I can't see it,' I added, trying to sound cynical.

Blaise shrugged. 'That doesn't stop people. Anyway, I can't imagine it's owt you should be worried about. She barely leaves the house, and she's no chance of sneaking out at night, not while he locks her in her ivory tower.'

'I thought you liked her.'

'I did. I do. She is difficult, though. Like catching smoke. I used to wonder if she's more clever than she makes out.' She passed me another bowl. 'She made it very clear she didn't want a lady's maid. She never let me dress her, you know. Did her own hooks and eyes, buttons, everything.'

I fell into a pensive silence. Blaise made a pot of tea and we took it through to the sitting room, where Charley still slumbered clutching his cloth mouse. While she poured, I wrestled with the idea of telling her what I'd seen in the mirror, but decided against it. I'd already revealed too much. Worst of all, I'd broken the promise I'd sworn to Decca, who'd begged me to keep Tommy's letter a secret.

Feeling paranoid suddenly, I worried about Millie being alone with Mr Booth; they'd been gone a long time. If anything happened down by the river, and Mr England found out I hadn't been with her, but was sitting with a servant drinking tea . . .

I stood quickly and reached for my hat.

'Heavens, you in a rush?' said Blaise.

'I'd best check on Millie.'

'She'll be fine, don't worry.'

'Thank you for the soup. And the tea.'

'You've not had it yet.'

At that moment the front door opened and Millie and Mr Booth crammed inside, bringing a blast of cold air and looking thoroughly pleased with themselves. I rushed towards her, cleaning her hands with a handkerchief.

'See, what did I tell you?' said Blaise. 'Sit back down, I'll get another cup. Oh look, Charley's awake. He'll have a bit of tea in a saucer, won't he? You sit there, miss, next to your nurse, and I'll fetch you a slice of brack. Eli, could you nip to your mum's for some more milk? I'll put another pot on.'

She continued like this, talking and fussing over the children, and I remembered what Mr Booth had told me, that Blaise had wanted to be their nursemaid. She would have been good at it, too, I thought, watching her dangle a handkerchief in front of Charley, and wondering if it wouldn't have been better if she'd got the job after all. Our conversation had made me uneasy, and I sat on the arm of the couch feeling full of dread, as though I was approaching some kind of crisis, only I had no idea what it was.

Back at the house their voices carried through the drawing-room window: two men shouting, their indistinct forms pacing behind the glass. I eased the pram through the gate and up the path, shuffling Millie inside and closing the door softly, aware of a tightening in my chest. Mrs England was hovering on the stairs looking frantic, and flew towards us at once.

'I've signed the deed, Dawson witnessed it himself!' Mr England cried, but before he finished the second man barked: 'Dawson should have spoken to me first.'

The silence that followed was deafening. Trying to cause as little fuss as possible, I lifted Charley from his blankets, but he murmured and kicked for me to let him down. I held him tightly and pushed the pram towards the boot room, but Mrs England stopped it with a hand and whispered: 'I'll do it. Take them upstairs.'

The second man spoke again. 'I'm sick and tired of cleaning up after your reckless behaviour. If it wasn't for me, you'd be ruined.'

'I am not one of your *children*, so don't speak to me like one.' I had never heard Mr England so angry.

'That's exactly what you are.' The second voice moved closer to the hall, along with smart, polished footsteps. I gripped Millie's wrist and pulled her up the stairs.

'It would be a shame to let the arrangement we've had all these years go to waste.' Mr England's tone was light but dangerous.

'Meaning?'

'Meaning it would be a shame. That's all.'

There were several seconds of silence. And then: 'I don't take threats from blackguards. Consider our agreement terminated.' There was something in the icy coldness of it that made me know instinctively that it was Conrad Greatrex. I was right: he stalked into the hall in a flash of silver and black, slamming the front door behind him. The coloured glass rattled, and in the shocked silence that followed there was an enormous crash, of splintering glass or china.

I ran into the drawing room and found Mr England standing before the fireplace, panting as though he'd been in a fistfight. On the floor by the window were the remains of the elegant blue vase from the mantel. Slowly I dragged my head towards Mr England, who glared at me, his expression murderous, and I shrank from the violence in it. Charley began crying, and I realised I was still holding him in my arms. I knew I had to remove him but my feet were stuck to the floor.

Mrs England spoke from my shoulder; I hadn't heard her approach. 'Should I go after him?' Her voice was calm, placating. It was the voice of someone entirely unsurprised by what she saw.

'No.' Her husband brought a hand to his moustache and wiped it, then he reached inside his breast pocket for a cigar. Shaking, he brought out his cutter and snipped off the end. 'Pick it up.'

I almost took a step forwards, but his eyes were on his wife. Mrs England hesitated, then crouched towards the carpet. I had seen enough. Every fibre of me was screaming to get the children inside the nursery, when, to my horror, there came a stifled sob from behind. Millie was in the doorway in her coat and hat, her face red and crumpled. I rushed towards her and ushered her from the room, just as the shock drained from Charley and he, too, began to wail.

'Nurse May,' Mr England barked from the fireplace. 'Bring me the children.'

I froze in the hallway. Tilda was standing by the kitchen, her expression a mirror of mine. Time suspended itself, though the long-case clock ticked beside me.

'Nurse May.'

'Charles, please . . .'

Millie looked at me with terror and squeezed my hand. I wondered what would happen if I ignored him, if I took the children to the nursery and locked us inside.

'Nurse May, bring them here at once.'

Tilda was like a statue. I peeled my eyes from hers and slowly walked the children back into the room. Mrs England's eyes were like warning lamps as her husband strode towards me in one swift movement.

'I'm taking the children out,' he announced, reaching for the baby and plucking him from my arms.

'I thought we were going to see Saul,' said Mrs England.

'We are, aren't we, darling?' He did not look at me, and spoke to Millie, whose small hand was now fastened in his.

'I'll fetch my gloves,' said Mrs England.

'You will stay here,' he replied calmly, not looking at her and moving past us to the hallway, taking his hat off the stand.

Mrs England held herself very still, as though she was afraid of spilling over. 'When will you be back?'

Shaking, I went out after him and gripped the pram handlebar to turn it, but Mr England held it still. 'You will stay at home.'

I blinked in surprise. 'But my place is with the—'

'Take the afternoon off. Why don't you return to your friend, Mr Booth's? The two of you get on so well.' He kept his cold black eyes on mine, and there was nothing friendly in them. 'There's no need to be frightened, Nurse May. A father is quite at liberty to take his children out. Is he not?'

He looked closely at me for two seconds, three, four, to make sure his meaning had landed. Then, with Charley clamped in one arm, he gave Millie a gentle push, sweeping after her and closing the door. The stained glass shuddered again, and their blurry shapes retreated. The walls seemed to lurch and slide around me, and I thought I might faint.

'Nurse May, what's the matter?'

I sank to my knees, reaching for the solid stone flags with both hands.

'Tilda? Tilda!' Mrs England cried out.

The housemaid came running from the kitchen. The two women helped me to the stairs, where I sat and trembled against the wall.

'Send for a doctor; Nurse May is unwell.'

'You must go after him,' I pleaded. 'You must stop him.'

'Who?'

'Mr England!'

'Why?'

'Come in here,' said Tilda, lifting me up as easily as if I'd been an empty pail. She led me through to the drawing room and I sank into the cushions and put back my spinning head.

'Fetch her a glass of water, Mrs Mannion.'

The cook's pink face and white cap waltzed in and out of sight. She retreated again, and the drawing room came into focus. Two concerned faces peered down at me, and I closed my eyes.

'A brandy might be better; there's some in Mr England's study.'

I'm going out of my mind, he'd said. His words had a haunting significance to those I'd spoken eight years ago, the same ones that were plastered over the newspapers, fossilised in black ink: *He was the very best father, until he went out of his mind.* I kept a copy in my tea tin, the headline faded now, below the picture of Elsie and me with the policemen who found us. I kept it to remind myself of what I'd overcome in my darkest moments, when I felt weak and sentimental, half-mad with the urge to tear open all my father's letters, postmarks blooming like bruises on the envelopes: stamped in the corners with the Broadmoor Criminal Lunatic Asylum.

There was a glug of brandy, and I remembered how Millie had reached for his hand, saw their outline in the squares of coloured glass – red and blue and green.

I looked at Mrs England and said: 'You must stop him.'

The room began to spin again, and I was falling backwards. The sky was inky black, and the last thing I remembered was the stars.

CHAPTER 20

I was twelve years old when my father tried to kill me. Mother and I were cleaning the oil lamps when Father came out of the bedroom. He'd been ill for a few days, and Mother and Robbie had been keeping the shop going while I looked after the young ones. We'd eaten supper and cleared it, and Mother and I sat at the table with the lamps and a little dish of vinegar and water between us.

Father wore his hat and coat. Around his neck was the brown muffler I'd made him one Christmas. He said: 'I'm taking the kiddies out.' He often spoke without looking at us, as if he preferred for us not to see him. His cheeks were hollow; his face had lost all shape. He'd got better that spring, briefly, washing each morning and tying on his apron to open up downstairs. But then he got worse. He was like a phantom trapped on this earth. He didn't live with us, he haunted us, sitting in his chair or on the end of the bed, staring forwards, rarely speaking, never laughing, forgetting to tie his boots. He didn't eat much, and went days without food altogether. Mother said he was poorly. That's all she ever said.

'Where?' Mother didn't look up from the *scrape*, *scrape* of her knife. She seemed more and more tired lately. Sometimes she'd blink and glance around in surprise, as if coming up from a dream. Then the weariness would descend again, closing her face like a curtain.

'To see my cousin,' said Father.

'Which one? Bert?'

Father said nothing, his expression unreadable. Well, he was dressed. That was something, and I was glad he felt well enough to pay a visit.

'Ruby will look after you,' said Mother. 'Won't you?'

'I'll come, Father,' I said. 'Why don't we take Elsie?'

So Elsie and I went.

We took the tram to New Street and boarded a train, then another, arriving just before eleven o'clock at night. Father had brought us an apple each, peeling Elsie's in the carriage with his penknife, wiping it first on his trousers. He said little on the journey, and the late hour meant there was nothing to see from the windows; the dirty glass only reflected the feeble light from the ceiling lamp.

The railway station was a cavern of brick and glass, and I waited with Elsie while father enquired about trams. It was raining hard, and we dashed out into it, seeing with relief a tram waiting at the stop. Father asked the driver when the last car returned to the station. I was tired and confused, but I kept quiet. At that age I'd learnt what was helpful and what wasn't, what a child might ask and what an adult wouldn't. *Ruby will look after you.* There was the trace of vinegar, still, on my fingers.

It was the first time I'd left Birmingham. I didn't know Father's cousins, but as we rattled and swayed through the dark, a picture developed like a photograph in my head of a large, comfortable family with plenty of tumbling children and two dogs. Elsie leant on me and dozed; it was hours after her bedtime. If I'd known the journey would be this long, I would never have suggested we take her. Father kept his eyes on the windows, where the rain zig-zagged down the panes as the car climbed upwards. The driver called the last stop and we got out.

We were the only passengers to disembark. Father spoke again with the driver, but the sound of rushing water drowned the two of them out. I led Elsie a few steps further, and we looked out at a great black powerful river, wide as three fields and stretching out in both directions as far as the eye could see. Behind us was a vertical screen of rock. It was still raining hard. Father picked up Elsie, and I followed him beyond the terminus, with the river on our left. Soon we arrived at a flight of steps cut into a high stone wall. They appeared to lead into a forest or park, but it didn't occur to me to ask if Father knew where we were going, and I followed him like a lamb. We stumbled about, sheltered from the rain but also the moonlight, and eventually came out on a footpath climbing upwards onto the brow of a hill. It seems we had scaled the rock; the sound of the river receded, and the night sky opened out above. We carried on uphill, circling about a bit and turning left, then right. I was relieved when we approached a little tollbooth with a friendly lamp in the window. Father asked the attendant what time the bridge closed.

'Doesn't close, sir,' the man replied, giving me a wink.

I could see no bridge in the dismal glow of the street lamps, only a large stone tower, like a fortress, thirty yards beyond. Father fixed his handkerchief around my neck to protect me from the rain, though I was wet already. My hat kept the worst of it off my face. Elsie rubbed her eyes, and we moved on. Halfway to the tower, Father paused to fasten her inside his coat, buttoning her against the driving rain. That's when I asked if his cousin's house was nearby.

'Not far, Rhubarb,' he said.

We sheltered beneath the tower, shivering, and soon Elsie fell asleep, her mouth disappearing behind Father's collar. My own tiredness made me numb, and I was vaguely worried about what we would do if the rain didn't stop, but said nothing more. A policeman passed and lifted his hat.

'Dreadful night to be out,' he remarked.

Father nodded, and the constable walked on. The road was long and straight, swallowed by mist in the distance, encased by colossal iron railings running along both sides. On the other side of the bars, protected from traffic, were two footpaths, studded every now and again with street lamps that battled with the darkness. Father kept his eyes on the furthest point where the road disappeared, as though he was waiting for someone to appear. One or two carriages came past, trundling along in the mud.

We moved on, going around the side of the tower to take the path to the left of the road. The rain made it hard to see, but we passed a hotel or some other grand building, with a hundred glowing windows and wide lawns. Its chimneys threw out silvery smoke even at this hour, and I thought how nice it would be to work in a place like that when I was old enough, setting cutlery on white tablecloths while glamorous ladies dripped with jewels in wing-backed chairs.

We'd been walking for several minutes when Father turned back.

'Father?'

I watched him retreat with Elsie, his head bent against the weather. He hesitated, then turned on his heels and came back to me. I felt the smallest tug of anxiety in my stomach. He was acting even more peculiar than usual, and I was beginning to doubt if he knew where his cousin lived at all. Here we were in a strange city, in the middle of the night, in the pouring rain, with no map or address to speak of. He'd asked about a bridge, but I couldn't see one, and the river had vanished from sight.

When he changed direction a third time, heading back towards the tower, I said: 'Father, where are we going?'

'I'll carry you.'

I could barely see his face beneath his hat.

'But you've got Elsie.'

He picked me up and held me to him, and I saw that he was crying. He buried his face in my hair, and the knot turned to a fist in my stomach as he sobbed and sobbed.

'Father, why are you crying? Are you lost? Don't worry, we can ask the policeman how to get there.'

Elsie woke, crushed beneath my weight, and whimpered in protest. I moved to get down, but he clung to me, weeping as if his heart would break, his arms binding mine so I couldn't move.

He carried me to the edge of the path where a white painted parapet ran along the length of it. The top of the railing came to his shoulder, and he heaved me up so I was sitting on it, with my heels fitting through the gaps. I peered out at nothing; we seemed to be on the edge of a park or a cricket field, with only yawning blackness beyond. The hotel lights glittered like stars, and there was something odd about them, about the position of them. That's when I realised they were below us. For a giddy moment I felt as though I was swaying, as though we were suspended in mid-air, and beneath the path was nothing at all.

I looked at Father and he at me, and I was aware of an odd sensation, of fright, or fear, for Father seemed to me like a stranger. Though he was clutching me, there was something distant in his eyes, as if he was already beyond this moment, looking back at it over many years. Elsie peered out from his coat like a wet woodland creature, her brown eyes wide.

'Can I get down now?' I said.

He put his head in my lap, his entire body convulsing as he wept. His coat smelt of damp wool, and his arms were tight around me. Then Father pushed me with both hands.

I woke in the nursery. There was a cool, damp weight on my forehead, and Mrs England was sitting on my narrow bed, looking worried.

'No, don't sit up,' she told me as I struggled. 'You must lie down.'

'Where's Elsie?'

'Elsie? Your sister?' Her pretty face was full of concern. 'As far as I know, she's at home.'

'Where are the children?'

'The children are fine.'

'Where are they?'

'They're with their father.'

'We have to find them.' I ripped off the cold compress and pushed myself up. The light was dim, the blinds closed against the afternoon. I fumbled for my watch, and Mrs England put a firm hand on my wrist.

'You must lie down, Nurse May. You've fainted, and now you need rest.'

'There's no time for rest.'

'Take as much time as you need,' she murmured.

At that moment the door burst open and Tilda swept in with a tea tray. 'Welcome back to the land of the living!' she declared, setting it on Millie's bed. 'You were talking some right nonsense down there. Milk? Sugar? I don't know how you take it.'

'I'll do it, Tilda,' said Mrs England.

The maid came closer to examine me. 'You do look peaky. Perhaps there's summat going around. Could be that gas still. My dad won't have it in the house.'

'Thank you, Tilda.'

She closed the door behind her. I watched Mrs England for a moment, thinking about how Mr England had looked at me, and what he'd said. My mind was in scraps, thoughts fluttering like confetti, impossible to make sense of. The broken china, the row with Mr Greatrex . . . It must have been about money. It was always about money. Mrs England dropped two spoonfuls of sugar into the steaming cup and passed it to me.

'Earlier you said something strange,' she said. 'You thought that . . .' She shook her head, as though she was being silly. 'You thought Charles was going to . . .'

I sipped, and the sweet liquid revived me. 'I must have been delirious,' I replied. She stared at me, but I kept my eyes on the teacup in my hands. 'Please, forget I said anything.'

'Why did you say that?'

'I don't know. I'm sorry, ma'am.'

'He wouldn't do anything to hurt the children.'

'No,' I said.

Somehow I had grabbed hold of the parapet. Before I fell, I'd been clutching the painted rail, and my right hand reached out instinctively. That would have saved me if it had been an accident, if it had all been a terrible mistake. I dangled like a petticoat on a peg, too shocked to scream, too frightened to comprehend what was happening. My feet flailed beneath me, trying to find purchase. Elsie whimpered. Father sobbed. He crouched down and a flame of relief ignited in me. *I will be safe*, I thought. Then Father placed his large hand around mine, the same hand that had stroked my hair from my feverish forehead, that held mine across the road. And he loosened my fingers, one by one.

My eyes were closed, but sleep wouldn't come. I heard Mrs England's neat shoes on the floorboards, the key in the lock. From the outside came the searching cry of a rook from a nearby branch A few moments later my mistress returned, closing the door again. I heard the rustle of paper, and the bed sunk down. She gave a sigh, a small, contented one, and I opened my eyes just as she finished tucking something into her bodice. She brought a hand from her collar and brushed down her sleeve. She was unruffled, her gaze steady and calm.

'Do you know what one of the most skilled jobs in a factory is?' she asked me.

I shook my head.

'A piecer. It's their job to repair broken threads when the machines are in motion. They have to watch the yarn like hawks, going between the looms and checking for flaws. When they find one, they have to fix it while everything's still moving. It's dangerous work. And piecers are always children, because of their size. They can get under the machines more easily.

'My grandfather began working as a piecer when he was seven, in a mill at Bradford. When my father and his brothers turned the same age, he made them do it, too, for a fortnight, as a sort of rite of passage. Really, it was to teach them how to identify faults. Flaws. Imperfections. And how to fix them quickly, so it becomes instinctive. They're all experts now at fixing broken threads. It's one of the lowest-paid jobs in factory work, but in some ways it's the most important. It keeps the whole operation going.'

I waited for her to go on, but she fell into silence. I didn't understand what she meant by it, what message she was trying to convey, and searched about for the right remark, the appropriate question. But nothing came, and the moment passed.

Father threw Elsie after me. The pair of us whistled through two-hundred-and-fifty feet of nothing, smashing into the dark water below.

Two miracles happened that September night. The first was that we both survived the fall; the second, that we landed within feet of a pill boat called the *Mazeppa*, on its way upstream to escort a vessel from the port to the coast. The rain fell hard and visibility was poor, but the crew heard the first splash, followed by what they assumed was the piercing cry of a gull. Then a second splash. They circled around and pulled us both on deck – Elsie first, three years old, the size of a large doll, gasping and crying and clinging to them. They pulled me out next, thinking I was dead.

The *Mazeppa*'s crew were aware of the tortured souls who fell like raindrops from the vast, glittering bridge into the river, had seen them being scraped from the muddy banks when the wind pulled them away from the water.

But children? They hadn't seen anything like it before. At once they took my sister and me to an inn on the bank and roused the landlord. Elsie was hastened to a surgeon, while two of the crew attempted to revive me, as they had done on the boat, emptying my lungs of the tar-black water, breathing into my mouth. Neither could believe it when a sound came from me like a plug being pulled, followed by a cascade of water. I had been dead, and now I lived.

'Where's Elsie?' I had said, lying on the path with my petticoats clinging to my bones.

Of course I remembered none of the rescue. I read about it in the papers, like everyone else. They printed a picture of Elsie and me with our saviour, the pilot. He was a kind old man, with a white beard and small brown eyes, and he took a shine to Elsie. He visited us both in hospital more than once, bringing chocolate and nuts. When the time came for us to go home, he was loathe to part with her, and when he left there were tears in his eyes.

For the photograph I wore a fawn-coloured coat with fur trim belonging to the photography studio, and an enormous hat. Then they made a postcard of us, assembled with the pilot and the constables. We wore matching black dresses with white lace collars. Elsie held a doll and sat on the pilot's knee. She couldn't stand on her own; the fall damaged her spine, and she had to learn to walk again. Her injuries would cast a long shadow over her life.

I was unscathed, but the guilt was worse than any pain I'd known, and though the doctors were hopeful and told me I would go on to live a normal life, I knew even then that I'd never recover.

'Nurse May?' Millie swam into view beside my pillow. The room was warm, with a fire popping in the grate, and the lamps lit against the fading light. The nursery looked so attractive in the evenings, like a scene from a picture, or a dream.

Mrs England knelt before the fender with Charley, playing with a wooden horse. The remains of a nursery tea sat on a tray beside them.

'Shh, Millie,' she said. 'I asked you not to wake her.'

'But she missed tea!'

'It's all right, miss, I'm awake.' I sat up straighter. 'Ma'am, I'll see to the children.'

'You'll do no such thing. When was the last time anybody looked after you?'

I shuffled back against the headboard. 'Did you see Master Saul?' I asked Millie.

'Yes,' she said. 'I saved you this.' She passed me a currant bun.

'That's very kind, thank you. How is he?'

She shrugged, and I looked at her mother.

'I believe he's well,' she replied.

The children had returned, which meant their father was in the house. A knot twisted in my stomach, and I watched Mrs England play with her son, galloping the horse across the rag rug. *He knew who I was.*

I thought back to my first night at Hardcastle House, when he'd collected me himself from the station. Had he always known? My mind whirred and clattered like one of his looms, and I remembered how strange it was that Mrs England hadn't been expecting me. How she always got the time wrong, barely ate, left the gas on. How she seemed to despise her parents, and was locked in her room at night like a child. He had thanked me for being kind to her, and with a slow, dawning comprehension, I realised I had been complicit.

There was a knock at the door and Tilda returned for the tea tray. I didn't wish to go through another inquisition, however gentle, so I closed my eyes and feigned sleep.

Over the clatter of china, Tilda said in a low voice: 'That be all, ma'am?'

'Yes, thank you. I think Nurse May just needs to sleep,' Mrs England replied. 'Tilda,' she said as the maid retreated. 'Could you ask Mr England to come to the nursery?'

My heart pounded: *no, no, no.*

Within minutes there were footsteps, measured and polished on the boards. A breeze stirred across my face, and his presence filled the room like a scent. I recalled how he dwarfed the narrow beds, the child-sized objects, and made everything else seem to shrink, including myself. My heart knocked loudly against my ribcage, and I willed myself still. There was a brief silence as he took in the little scene before him.

'Is she no better?' he asked.

'No, Charles.'

'Well, should I send for a doctor?'

'I don't think that's necessary. He'd only prescribe rest.'

Charley gurgled and clashed two horses together.

'I think someone ought to stay with Nurse May tonight. She can't care for the children in this state.'

'I thought she only fainted.'

'She's still dizzy. I don't want her to get out of bed and risk falling.'

'Tilda can do it.'

'But Tilda wakes at six to make the fires.'

My watch ticked in my pocket, and the fire cracked and spat. It was as though they were having some unspoken conversation, one I couldn't interpret without seeing their expressions, their body language. I knew he was looking at me; I felt his eyes prick my skin.

Why had Mrs England come home from Crow Nest early? Why did she hobble to the bathroom as though every step caused her pain? *They go at it like dogs in a ditch.* What if that wasn't what they were doing?

'Mama, *you* sleep with us,' cried Millie.

Her mother shushed her at once, and the floorboards shifted. There were several seconds of silence so thick I could taste it. I remembered what she said to me at Crow

Nest in that narrow little bedroom, when she wanted to stay with Saul. *He must think it's his idea.*

'Well, how about it?' he said.

'How about what, Charles?'

'You staying in here tonight with them.'

His wife appeared to consider it. 'Nurse May cares for us so well, I suppose I ought to return the favour.'

'Right,' he said. 'Then that's that.'

When he'd gone, I opened my eyes and saw Mrs England lift Charley in the air. She searched his cot for his nightgown, finding it under the pillow, and sat with him on Saul's bed. She unfastened his buttons with inexperienced fingers, lifting away his layers and removing his stockings.

'Ma'am?' I spoke without moving my head from the pillow.

She looked up from the bed, her son's fat little feet in her hands. He squealed with pleasure, and her smile froze on her face when she saw my expression.

'You didn't take my letters, did you?'

There was a pause. She gazed at me, and her head made the slightest movement. *No.*

They found Father in the early hours, wandering near a railway station. He was soaked through and delirious; at first the constable thought he was drunk. In his coat pocket were a few shillings and a letter from an auctioneer, confirming an appointment to visit the shop at Longmore Street and value the contents. He told them his name and address, and the policeman handcuffed him and took him to the station. He surrendered without resistance, and they walked together along the quiet, dark streets. At the station they made him hot beef tea and called the doctor. The following morning there was a hearing at the magistrate's court. He made no statement, only a request to visit Elsie and me at the infirmary. His request was denied, and I never saw my father again.

And now I dreamt I was alone in the mill, standing before a deafening loom. The yarn crashed in and out like waves threatening to seize me. Sunlight slanted through the high windows, and all around cotton drifted like snow. At the far end of the vast space was my brother, Robbie, a young man now. He called out with a hand cupped around his mouth, but the thunderous noise made it impossible to hear him. He pointed, and I turned to see my father striding through the machines towards me. He appeared as he had that night on the bridge, in his soaked wool coat and hat, wearing the muffler I'd made him for Christmas.

'Ruby.'

Before me was a lamp, and a small white hand. Above

the warm light was a round, pale face with hair falling down.

'Where's Elsie?'

Then I realised where I was.

'I'm sorry,' I said.

'It's all right. You were shouting.'

'The children are safe, ma'am?'

'Of course,' she whispered. She was kneeling beside my bed, and her breath was sweet on my face. 'You were talking about your father. You sounded afraid.'

'He's dying.'

'Is he? Why didn't you say so? You must go to him.'

'I can't.'

'Why not?' The lamp flickered and trembled in the silence. Then, after a moment, she said: 'I'm sorry I have to do this now. I wish it didn't have to be like this.'

'Do what, ma'am?' I was only half-listening, still thinking about my dream, the looms and my father marching towards me.

She spoke again. 'Promise me you'll keep the children safe? You won't leave Millie and Charley?'

My brain felt like cotton: damp and swollen. 'What do you mean?' I whispered.

Beyond, in the darkness, Millie breathed thickly.

Mrs England shivered, though her dressing gown was wrapped tightly around her. 'You'll be all right now?' she asked, though she was the one who was white and trembling.

'What will we do in the morning?' I asked.

'All will be well,' she said. 'You mustn't worry.'

'I must lock the door,' I said.

'I've already done it. Go to sleep,' she told me, tucking the eiderdown back over me.

I burrowed down beneath the bedclothes, sinking back into exhaustion and letting it carry me away.

CHAPTER 21

Charley's crying woke me. The room was dark, the night full and thick; without looking at my watch, I knew it was one or two o'clock. I lay in the warmth for a moment, waiting to see if he would settle, but he moaned again and pulled himself up to standing. Yawning, I pushed myself from the sheets, padded over to the window and quietly pulled back the curtain, opening the blind so moonlight could streak in. I lifted Charley and sniffed. I kept a little stack of napkins in a wash bag at the end of my bed and began wiping and changing him, shushing him softly as he burbled, so as not to wake the others. Mrs England had gone to sleep in Saul's bed, Millie in her own, though she had wanted to sleep with her mother. I peeled Charley's wet nappy from his legs and threw it in my chamber pot, then reached for the jug on the washstand. Soaking the towel in water, my eyes adjusted to the darkness. I noticed the eiderdown had slid off Millie's bed and bent to replace it, lifting it and frowning. The bed was empty. I looked across the room, trying to make out two shapes in Saul's bed. It, too, was empty, and the nursery door open. Charley watched from his cot as I patted the bedclothes and lifted the pillows, as though Millie and her mother might be hiding. How had I not heard anything? I put out a hand to close the door, and found the key in the nearside lock. My forehead creased with not understanding. Somehow I got the nightlight going, though it took three or four strikes of the match. The hallway was black and silent as a tomb, the main door to the house closed. I went barefoot to the day nursery. Unoccupied and without sunlight to colour them, the toys and furniture looked half-sinister, crouching in the gloom. I shivered and returned to the bedroom.

'A-gone,' said Charley.

I blinked in astonishment.

'Charley?'

He said it again, holding up empty palms. 'All gone.' His first words. He waited for my reaction, but I wanted to sob. Mrs England had asked me to look after Millie and Charley. So where would she have gone? I kept the key to the nursery in my apron, hanging on the peg, but Mrs England had locked up that night, and must have left it in the door. Perhaps she'd wandered back to her own bed.

But what about Millie? I settled Charley back in his cot; mercifully he made no fuss and rolled on his side to sleep.

On the landing I stood still for a moment, listening. The long-case clock in the hall ticked, and there was no light downstairs. The bedroom doors were all closed, including Mr England's dressing room; light snores came from behind the wood. My bare feet took me across the stone floor to the mistress's bedroom, which was unlocked and empty, the bed made. The spare room, too, was unoccupied, as were the bathroom, water closet, linen cupboard . . . I padded downstairs with my lamp, looking in each of the rooms with their clinging scent of tobacco and furniture polish. On the threshold of the drawing room I stepped on something small and hard, and almost cried out: another cigar end. I rolled it in my hand, thinking hard.

Mrs England would not have taken Millie out at this hour, even in the carriage. Tentatively I tried the front door, turning the brass knob gently, and to my amazement it opened. A slow, icy feeling of horror seeped over me. *I wish it didn't have to be like this.* If Mrs England had left, and Millie had followed and was lost, or worse . . . It was unthinkable. I looked out into the dark yard and listened to the wind stroking the trees, and the river, rushing with the same boundless energy, never tiring. I had no decision to make, I had only to accept it, which I did with straightforward clarity. I closed the door and went upstairs for my cloak.

The rain was coming down, but it was soft and gentle, almost apologetic. Leaving the feeble nightlight on the hall table, I took the lamp instead and lit it on the doormat, slipping from the house and tossing the used match behind a flowerpot.

The woods were a hard, unbroken mass reaching towards the cloudy night sky. I would avoid venturing into them if I could help it, thinking of the slippery, tangled roots and the sodden ground that tumbled and plunged with no warning towards the river. Halfway down the track, I called out for Millie. Waking the master was an option I couldn't consider; my charge was missing and I had to find her. The thought of Mr England's fury was enough to keep me away: those cold black eyes burnt inside my brain like an image from a nightmare. I shook my head, my breathing shallow, and quickened my pace.

'Millie?' I called louder, hoping the rustling trees would conceal my voice from the house. The forest reared up either side of the track, straining towards the light. All those hiding places, all those thick trunks and little ledges from where somebody could watch me. Suddenly the woods seemed vast and terrifying in a way I never considered during the day. My feet carried me forwards, but every part of me yearned to turn back. I argued with myself: the proper thing to do would be to wake Mr England, rouse Tilda, call a policeman. But Mrs England had not gone missing: she had escaped. Most likely she did not want to be found. But for how long would she be gone? An hour, a night, forever? Another alternative, and the least appealing of all, was to recognise this and return to bed, where I could wake in the morning and pretend to discover them gone. *I'm sorry I have to do this now.* My mind raced with possibilities, but kept getting stuck on one.

'Millie?'

The river seemed louder at night, and I paused on the ancient bridge, the water amplified beneath it. Clinging to the balustrade, I made my way across with the lamp, praying I wouldn't see a small white nightgown snagged against a rock, being tugged and whipped by the current. But there was just water, black and glittering, rushing on its tireless journey. On the other bank, the mill loomed dark and silent, its chimney reaching into the night. I passed the stable, taking some comfort from the warm creatures sleeping in their straw, Ben and Broadley above them.

I put as much space between the mill and myself as I could, moving over the slick cobbles, still calling Millie's name as my mind worked frantically. *Had* she taken her? Doing so would guarantee a search. According to the law, children belonged to fathers, not mothers. If her design was to run away, she would be a fool to have taken her daughter. Mrs England was a Greatrex, the daughter of a family whose mills were scattered like coins for miles around, the granddaughter of a man so rich he'd built a town. It would be front-page news, a scandal in black and white. I shuddered at the thought of it, the intrusion it would bring on the house, because I knew all about it. When Father went to Broadmoor, Mother considered moving us from Longmore Street. But attempted murder was good for business, and A. May's busier than ever. The customers would glance at baskets of turnips, tins of coffee, before their eyes slid inevitably to the door behind the counter, hoping for a glimpse of the May girls. Mother made us stay upstairs or in the storeroom, kept us occupied with housework and stock-taking. Neighbours, strangers, friends, they all asked after us, wondering how we were. Were we damaged, nervous, distraught? Perhaps we were angry; perhaps we'd end up in the asylum like our father. I didn't know how I felt myself until the word came to me one morning as I lined the chickens' boxes with newspaper and saw it halfway down a column of tiny words: betrayed. People said it was a miracle that we survived, but it didn't feel that way to me.

I took my lamp into the trees. The rain fell softly and made the rotting leaves wet and slippery. I crunched through twigs and fungi, muddying my nightgown. I'd thrown my cloak over the top, but it did little to warm me, and my legs were bare above my boots. Just then there was a sound, very faint and keening, like an animal. Like a child.

'Millie?' I cried, standing still, straining with every fibre to listen. The sound stopped, and then started up again:

a low moan, a whimper. I began to run, thrusting the lamp in all directions. That a child I loved and cared for was really out here at night – it was beyond comprehension, beyond reason, and just as I'd convinced myself it was impossible and that she was installed in the leather womb of a carriage with her mother a long way from here, I saw a white shape among the darkness. Charging ahead I lost it, my arm growing weak with the effort of holding the lamp aloft, then suddenly, into its path, staggered Millie in her nightdress. Dirt streaked her face and feet, which were bare, and her wet hair clung to her. I cried out, an involuntary, guttural wail that came with such force I dropped the lamp, which promptly smashed and extinguished, rolling down the bank.

The little girl was sobbing. I shushed her, collapsing to my knees and pulling her towards me, rocking with her to comfort us both.

'You're safe,' I told her. 'You're safe.' I said it again and again, a dozen times as she clung to me, unable to speak. After a few minutes, her sobs reduced to little gasps and hiccups. I gathered her into my cloak; I hadn't thought to bring anything warm for her.

'Where's Mama?' I asked her.

She said nothing and wiped her nose with a sleeve.

'Millie, did you come out with Mama?'

She whimpered and shook her head.

'Did you see her? Where is she?'

She trembled and moaned. At least I had found her,

and she was alive. I stood and lifted her to my hip to retrace my steps to the river, which would lead us home. Millie clutched at my plait like a rope. Her weight seemed to increase with every step, and she was shaking. I set her down and put my cloak around her, then lifted her again. Our progress was slow, and it was only when we'd left the cover of the trees and the mill stood black and menacing before us that I tried again.

'Millie, where is Mama?'

'I don't know,' she whimpered.

'Did you leave with her?'

She shook her head.

'Why did you leave the house?'

'The door was open and Mama wasn't in bed.'

'Did you hear her go?'

Another shake.

My back twinged with sharp shocks of pain that I knew I would pay for in the morning. I went carefully across the cobbles, through the squeaking gate and up the path to the door. Blessedly, it was still unlocked, and I closed it behind me, collapsing against it with a sigh. The dim glow of the nightlight welcomed us, and the clock ticked gently halfway down the hall, which never felt empty even when I was alone, with the Greatrexes watching from their gilded frames. With no key to lock up and no clue where it was kept, I carried Millie with difficulty upstairs.

Charley was sleeping, an arm flung up beside his head, his rosebud mouth open. I resisted the urge to lift him up and hold him to me; instead, I tucked his blanket around him and let down the veil. Millie trembled, and I peeled off her nightdress and took a clean one from the press, dressing her and wrapping a blanket over the top. I sat on her bed and took her onto my lap.

'Where did your mother go?' I whispered into her hair as we rocked back and forth. 'Did she ask you to go with her?'

She shook her head and wiped her face with the corner of the blanket.

'Can you tell me what happened?'

'I woke up,' she said, with little gasps between each word. 'And Mama was gone. And I went to see if she had gone back to bed, but the door was locked. Then I found the key on the floor, so I opened it. But her bedroom was empty, and she wasn't in the house. Papa said she walks in her sleep, so I thought she might be doing that. Then I found the front door was open, so I went into the yard to look for her because I thought she might be lost or in the woods. I didn't want her to be frightened. And then I got lost.'

'You were very brave,' I whispered. 'I don't know any other little girls who would have done that.'

'I'm not afraid of the woods, only the dark.'

I nodded and held her close. 'So you didn't see her wake?'

She shook her head. 'She read me a story in my bed, then she got in Saul's. She was crying before she went to bed. She kept kissing me and Charley and squeezing us.'

We were silent for a moment as I took this in. Then, as if she could read my mind, she said: 'Is Mama coming back?'

We were sitting against the wall as Mrs England had done earlier, our feet dangling over the bed. I'd watched them from my pillow, bathed in lamplight, and thought how lovely they looked together. And then I'd fallen asleep and woke to Mrs England asking me to look after the children. I thought about all the signs, obvious now: her mysteriously packed trunk, the sad way she held Charley, how she'd asked me to keep the children safe.

'Of course she is,' I said smoothly as my heart pounded in my chest. 'And I'll be here to look after you. Now,' I breathed. 'You must go to sleep.'

'Will you sit with me?'

'Yes.' I laid her down and smoothed her hair, and tried not to think about the morning.

Climbing stiffly into my bed, I rested my head against the wall and listened to the faint ticking of my watch in my apron. Beneath the soft taps there was a single *thunk*, like the hour hand of a large clock, or a door . . . Frowning, I got to my knees and put a hand between the blinds, prising apart the slats.

Mr England was walking down the path, away from the house. He closed the gate and strode with purpose across the cobbles, disappearing down the track into the trees. He hadn't taken a lamp with him. I stared at the spot where he'd vanished, but the blackness was blinding, pooling into the edges of my sight. Charley gave a small sigh behind me, and I turned to look at him and his sister, both fast asleep. A streak of moonlight split through the blind, making my silver-backed hairbrush gleam on the dresser. I stroked it, feeling how heavy it was, how expensive. When Sim gave it to me, I felt part of something for the first time in my life. I closed my eyes and pictured her hunched over her desk, writing. *Fortis in arduis*, she'd told us on our first day, clutching the podium in the lecture hall with both hands. *Strength in adversity*. I thought of the blue vase in a broken heap on the carpet, Mrs England's white face. How calm and steady she was, though her husband made out she was weak, mad, dangerous. I knew, then, where she was.

Quietly, so the children wouldn't wake, I sat on the edge of the bed and laced my boots a second time.

CHAPTER 22

The woods at night were far from silent. Nightjars and owls called their strange solos, and my boots crunched on the stones littered across the track. All around was the sound of water: noisy little brooks and streams made their ceaseless descent to the river, bubbling, chattering, murmuring. The rain had stopped, and the moon peered out from behind her misty veil. I pulled my cloak more tightly at the neck, closing my shawl around my face.

The way was easier without a lamp, which rendered everything beyond its range even darker. The glimpses of moon were guidance enough, and my eyes adjusted without difficulty. I left the mill yard and paused on the bridleway that passed the outbuildings, looking left to the moors and right towards town. I turned left, passing the millpond, its smooth and glassy surface like a mirror held up to the night. Pines climbed the hillside above the track, which wound like a ghostly ribbon along the valley, and I tried to remember how to reach the low, lonely cottage on the moor.

I'd locked the children in the nursery; this time there would be no escapes. All being well, I could slip inside, unnoticed. If I returned after the master . . . No, I told myself, *don't think about it. Just keep walking.* My legs carried me upwards, the crags looming like a spectre to my left.

'Ruby?' A hiss, unmistakable.

The shock almost tripped me. I froze, looking out at the slim trunks and black branches. I could hardly hear above the blood pounding in my ears. Seconds later it came again.

'Ruby? Is that you?'

The voice was female.

'Who's there?' I whispered, my voice cracking. Then, more loudly, 'Who's there?'

It had come from the left, from the crags. From *above*, as if the person was standing on a tree branch, looking down.

'Mrs England?' My voice was quiet and feeble, and I tried again. 'Mrs England, it's Ruby. Are you there?'

'I'm up here.'

'Where?'

'On the crags.'

'Are you alone?'

'Yes.'

I hurried back to where I thought the footpath was, climbing the grassy verge between two high rocks that acted as gateposts. The trees thinned out as I ascended, picking my way between the large black hunks of rock. The shadows of the woods fell away, opening into a bright, moonlit sky. There was no wind, and beneath the breath in my lungs I heard the bare branches creak and shiver. Towards the top, where the ground levelled out, a slender column detached itself and came towards me.

'Ruby.' Mrs England was wearing a hooded cloak. She'd tied her blonde hair back beneath it, and her face loomed pale in the silvery light.

'What are you doing?' I asked.

'I can't stay any longer.'

'Does he know you're coming?'

She was blank for a moment. Then she said: 'No. I didn't know when I could get away. Charles can't know I'm there, though.'

'No,' I said. 'Why are you here, on the crags?'

'He sleeps so deeply at night, and I can't risk waking his mother. I'll wait here until dawn.'

'When will you come back?'

Her eyes burned in her silver face. 'Ruby, I'm not coming back.'

'But why?' My voice was small and childlike.

'I can't live there any longer.'

'But the children . . . you can't leave them. They need you.'

'I will send for them.'

I shook my head in disbelief. 'Send for them where? You're going to live *there*, with him? They can't live there. Besides, their father has a right to them; the law means they'll have to stay with him.'

'Trust me, I will. It will all become clear now I have it.'

'Have what?'

'I need to get away from him because he will kill me when he finds out.'

'Finds out what? Mrs England, I don't understand. I want to help you but you have to tell me.'

'I promise, you just have to trust me.'

'Why didn't you tell me you were leaving?'

'I did it to protect you,' she said.

'*Me?*'

Sympathy softened her face. 'You can't see it, can you? How he has you as his pet. Anything I told you he'd get out of you.'

'He wouldn't.'

'Yes, he would.' She gave a thin smile. 'You don't know how controlling he is. He's doing it to you, too, keeping your letters and taking you under his wing. He makes you feel special and then he isolates you, he slowly suffo-cates you, so that you feel as though you have no one, that you're all alone. I've put up with it too long now; I *had* to escape.' She paused, and seemed to realise something. 'But why are you here? Why did you leave the house?'

'She brought me.'

Mr England was standing on the path behind us, silhouetted against the moonlight. He stepped slowly, leisurely towards us, his boots ringing on the flat sandstone, and I felt as though I was dreaming, watching in mute horror as he approached. The two of us were pinned to the rock, our exit blocked and only whistling space behind us. The ground seemed like silt beneath my boots; with nothing to hold on to, I closed my eyes and tried not to think about how high we were.

'Finally, you escaped.' He addressed his wife, whose face was a ghostly mask, white as paper beneath the hood of her cloak. 'I must say it was a stroke of genius, pretending to be concerned for your nurse's welfare like that.' He moved closer, with deliberate steps, and I saw he was wearing his green wool hunting suit with high, polished boots. This disturbed me more than the fact he'd come out at all: the idea of him dressing in his bedroom, fastening his breeches in the darkness.

Mrs England turned slowly towards me, and I shook my head as my blood ran cold. But I had led him to her.

He put an arm on her sleeve. 'I'm afraid this has to be the last time. You must come home now.'

'No.' Her voice was low and pleading, and struck me straight in the chest. I took an involuntary step forwards.

'Don't move.' Mr England's impressive moustache

concealed his mouth, and his eyes fell like stones upon me. 'If you take another step, I will have you charged with neglect. Don't think I didn't see you return earlier with Millie. I would ask you how my five-year-old daughter found her way outside alone in the middle of the night, but I'll save that conversation until the morning.'

'Millie?' Mrs England whispered.

I almost whimpered, and closed my eyes, trying not to cry.

'I knew I couldn't trust you.' He looked directly at me. 'I wonder if, in all your conversations, you have found the time to tell your mistress you are the daughter of a murderer?'

The forest sighed around us.

'No? How perplexing. I thought you would have had enough time by now to disclose it. It's something I certainly wish I had known when I employed you. Never mind, I shall write to your principal and give a full explanation as to why the position is no longer tenable.'

'My father isn't a murderer,' I cried, tears of anger spilling over my cheeks. 'He's a sick man.'

'Criminally insane is the term, I believe. Now then, Lilian, would you like to tell me where you were going? Either myself or the doctor, whoever is first, I don't mind. I notice you didn't use his name, but I will find out soon enough.' He looked meaningfully at me. 'I assume it has something to do with Decca's father.'

I thought I hadn't heard him right, but he watched me, waiting for his words to settle.

'You didn't know? What *did* the two of you talk about? Decca is not my daughter. The Greatrex family has always kept her father's identity a fiercely guarded secret, so I can only imagine it's somebody entirely unsuitable. Even more unsuitable than a lawyer's son.'

I was wiped clean with shock. Mrs England stood for several seconds, glowering at him, then, with a trembling hand, reached inside her cloak, fumbling between her shift and her corset. There was the crackle of paper, and I remembered the sound from earlier, when she'd left the nursery briefly before sitting down on my bed. She reached across the chasm that separated her from her husband, who closed it in two quick strides and snatched it from her. Meanwhile, I glanced about, trying to find the edges of the crags where they bled into darkness.

'What is this?' he asked. He shoved a large hand inside his pocket and brought out a matchbox; there was a scrape and a flame leapt to life. Mrs England waited, her terrified brown eyes flicking between the paper and his face. 'What is this?' he said again, frowning in the meagre matchlight. 'A marriage certificate?' He spoke with unguarded surprise. 'From August eighteen ninety-three. Why is your name on this?'

Mrs England said nothing.

'Who is Thomas Sheldrake?'

I watched her, and it felt as though the crags were moving gently, swaying like a boat in a dock.

In a quaking voice, she replied: 'I am married to him. I have been married to him for eleven years.'

Mr England gazed at her, dumfounded, and in a voice full of wonder said slowly: 'St Michael's, Harrogate. This is a trick. You're playing a trick on me.'

'He brought it back from Australia.'

'It's forged.'

'It isn't.'

'Then . . .' He stared at her, calculating. 'The children . . .'

'Are illegitimate.' Her voice cracked. 'Yes.'

Slowly he straightened, with an expression of utter disbelief.

'And they will come to live with me,' his wife said quietly.

'I don't believe you.'

'It doesn't matter. Tommy and I are married.'

'Tommy.' The gentlest of frowns puckered his forehead, then his expression cleared. 'Not the blacksmith?' His moustache spread across his face, and he began to chuckle. 'Oh, Lilian. Now I know why your family threw you at me like a rag. I did always wonder.'

Tommy was Decca's father. I was shaking violently, only half aware of what was taking place before me: Mr England ripping the certificate into tiny pieces and sending them fluttering like ash, like cotton, from the crags; Mrs England gasping like a drowning woman.

'It doesn't matter,' she said. 'We can prove it if it comes to it.'

'If it comes to it? Lilian, this won't even make it to court. You think a blacksmith will take on the Greatrexes? All that money and power? He will weasel his way back into whatever hole he's been hiding in, just as he did all those years ago.'

Tommy in the trees, Tommy at the church, Tommy in the graveyard: I saw, now, the signposts directing me to the realisation that Decca's father had been hoping for a glimpse of his daughter, his wife, all this time.

Mr England took hold of his wife's wrist and gazed at her. 'That's why you wanted her at school, wasn't it?'

'Charles, that was *your* idea, don't do this again. You twist everything, you make me feel as though I'm going mad.' She wrenched her sleeve from his grip but he gripped it again.

'Our children,' he said softly, in a disbelieving whisper. 'All bastards. All *bastards*, Lilian!' He shook her violently, and dragged her across the rocks. *Whore.* I saw it in the mirror. All this time he had known about Decca, and all this time he had punished both of them for it.

'No, Charles,' she was screaming as the two of them struggled, and my head began to spin. All around were jutting rocks, mean, jagged shapes that disguised the fact we were fifty, sixty, seventy feet in the air. The crags were a different place in the darkness; there was no sign of the friendly clumps of heather, the beds of bracken Millie made into a bouquet. *They're bastards, Lilian.*

Mr and Mrs England battled as one great shape, twisting and mutating in the darkness. I was vaguely aware of the noises they were making: him grunting, her whinnying and panting, their boots scrabbling on the smooth rock. Already the moment seemed like a memory, one I was observing from a great distance.

He's going to push her. The thought was clear and instant, like the moon sliding out from behind a cloud.

I led him here, and now he's going to push her.

I stood frozen, my arms limp at my sides, as Mrs England writhed and screamed and sobbed, as his arms encased her. He clung to her, like my father had clung to me, holding me closely in the rain.

It's your job to keep them alive.

My feet moved by themselves towards them, and with all my strength I brought the hairbrush down, glinting and flashing like a blade of moonlight. There was a sickening, crunching sound, followed by a second or two of pure silence. He staggered forwards and put a hand to his dark hair, looking with astonishment at the blood coating his fingers, and then at me, as if to say: *Oh.*

Time stopped entirely, and we stared at one another, illuminated in the silver light. Then Mrs England pushed him.

Everything happened in slow motion, and the moon revealed it all to us, concealing nothing: his hand closing around thin air, his other swinging behind him to reach for something, anything that would right him as he folded over at the waist. His boots lost their purchase on the uneven stone; his throat arched gracefully as he threw his head back, his face turned up to the sky. For a moment he was perfectly suspended, and then he was falling, looking up at the stars. Though it felt like a lifetime, it was over in a moment, as though he'd never been there at all.

CHAPTER 23

Three weeks later

'I can't find the blasted key.'

Mrs England was standing behind the desk in the study with one hand on her hip.

'I'll look for it,' said Decca, helpful as ever.

'I bet *I* can find it first,' said Saul.

All six of us were in the study, packing its contents into crates. Though December was around the corner, no fire was lit and the window and door were open, letting the crisp air in. A remarkable change had come over Mrs England. In the weeks since her husband's death, she'd gained a vibrancy about her, despite the sombre mourning dress of ebony silk and crepe. Her dark eyes shone, and her hair seemed spun with gold, as though it, too, had lightened. She'd packed away her pearls and diamonds,

377

and two little jet stones hung from her ears, set off by a handsome brooch at her neck. Except for the linen sling binding her left arm where she'd broken her shoulder, widowhood suited her very much.

She threw some papers into a crate and raked her eyes over the desk once again. The children picked and prodded about the room, opening cupboards and searching between books for the missing key. My gaze fell on the spine of a heavy black volume in one of the crates.

'Do you know, ma'am,' I said, 'I thought I saw a letter from my father in here once.'

'Your father?'

'Mmm. It was the night of the . . .' I fell silent and looked at Saul, combing through the items in a crate with great diligence. His time at Crow Nest had changed him and put meat on his bones. Unused to catering for children, the cook there took it upon herself to fatten him, sending up porridge with cream, pies, cakes and sandwiches all day long. Every day a servant wrapped him against the cold and pushed him around the grounds in his bath chair until he was well enough to take exercise himself. He'd never been lavished with such attention, and was put out to be one of four at home again. He was there almost a month in total, returning the morning after his father's funeral. Immediately after delivering him, Broadley had set out again for Ripon to collect Decca from her school.

'Remind me of your father's name?'

'Arthur, ma'am.'

'I might have seen an Arthur, though I'm not certain.' Mrs England made for the crates, lifting books and papers with her free hand to peer at the contents beneath. With so much to go through, the children and I were helping her. They had adapted well, considering, all of them draped in black like their mother. Even the doorknocker had been wrapped in bombazine as a mark of respect.

The verdict of death was misadventure. When Tilda found Mr England's room empty in the morning, she wasn't concerned; it was like him to miss breakfast and go early to work. But when the master failed to show for a board meeting at the mill and nobody could account for his whereabouts, the overseer sent a boy to the house, and his wife confirmed they hadn't seen him since the evening before. When he didn't return at noon for dinner, Tilda sent Ben for the constable, and a search was organised. His body was found before nightfall at the foot of the crags, with a blow to the head sustained on his descent.

The coroner, an old friend of the Greatrexes, conducted an inquest, with which Mrs England fully cooperated. She explained that her husband was a paranoid man, who often left the house in the middle of the night to check the mill was secure. Could he, perhaps, she asked, have been in pursuit of a thief or an opportunist? It was easy to get lost in the forest, no matter how well you knew it, and if the cloud cover was considerable . . . Well, said the coroner, it was certainly a possibility, and surprising that there hadn't been a death on the crags until now. The wider Greatrex family discreetly absorbed the sorry state of Mr England's finances, paying off mortgages, reimbursing creditors and sweeping everything out of sight.

Dozens of calling cards were left in the bowl on the hall table, from well-wishers pushing them through the door. I watched them from the nursery window, a parade of furs and taffeta rustling over the cobbles in observance of the curious mourning rituals of the rich. Mr England's widow made a singular appearance at the funeral in a floor-length veil of ebony lace. The service was very well attended, with what Mrs Mannion claimed was the whole town packed into the church. Employees of England Mill sat cheek by jowl in the pews with the numerous Greatrexes, who descended from all over the West Riding, the men distinguished by their solemn arm bands, the women in their dark gowns, like a cloud of butterflies from a strange, night-time world. I didn't go with the servants, and stayed at home instead with the youngest children, preparing for the elders' return.

My reunion with Decca after many weeks apart was a happy one. Her mother and I watched from the windows, and when her little figure appeared in the trees, accompanied by Broadley and his faithful carriage, we tore down the path to greet her. The only thing she would tell us about her time there was that she didn't care for school. Her absence had changed her, too, and returned her a little woman, dignified and serene. She was relieved to be back among her mushrooms, and on her first afternoon at home the two of us went for a walk. Mrs England stayed with the other children, and waved us off from the window with the baby on her hip. We were out for hours, tramping through the woods and taking cuttings for the little basket she carried. On the riverbank she found a lantern, broken and rusting, and we gave it to Broadley for scrap. Muddy and content, we returned home for crumpets and a fire in the nursery, where she spent the evening making observations in her exercise book. Her grief appeared as a tight, contained thing, like a box she carried with her. She did not mention her father at all, and comforted her brother and sister, who wore their sorrow openly.

That first night I bathed her separately from the others.

'Nurse May?' she said to me.

'Yes?'

'How did Papa die?'

I paused, soaping her back, and sighed. 'He suffered a fall.'

'From the crags?'

So she had heard it somehow. I was glad I had told her the truth.

'Yes,' I said.

The child was thoughtful, hugging her knees, her dark hair streaming down her spine. On our walk, I'd asked her if she wished to sleep in the nursery still or have her own room beside her mother. She replied that she wished to sleep wherever I was.

'I didn't know the crags were high enough,' she said.

'Well, that doesn't really matter. Tripping down the stairs can be fatal.'

'Millie said something strange earlier.'

'Hmm?'

'She said: "Did you see where Nurse May found me?"' She half-turned towards me.

I carried on soaping her hair, separating it gently with my fingers. 'I'm not sure what she meant by that.'

'She said you came to get her when she was out looking for Mama at night.'

'Sometimes dreams can be so realistic.'

There was a pause. 'I thought Papa might have gone out looking for her and fallen, and that's how he died.'

I glanced at the bathroom door, which was closed. Mr England's shaving things had all been put away, and the washstand looked decidedly more feminine. Tilda had made up little jars of cut blooms from some of the extravagant sympathy bouquets that arrived at the house. On the washstand was a sprig of dried baby's breath, a single rose planted through it like a stake.

'Sometimes,' I said, 'when people we love die, we have all sorts of thoughts to try to cope with it better. We try to imagine their last hours and what we might have done differently. Your father loved you all very much, and I'm sure if Millie had gone into the woods at night, he would have been the first person to look for her.'

There was the gentle splash of water, and I took the

comb from my lap and began on her hair. She was old enough to do it herself, but the ritual was necessary for both of us.

'My father lives in an asylum,' I said.

'Does that mean he's . . . ?'

'He's unwell,' I supplied. 'I think about him often, and I miss him sometimes. I haven't seen him for eight years.'

'Aren't you allowed to see him?'

'I am, but I don't.'

'Why not?'

'Because I don't want to. And that is a good enough reason not to do something. Saying no can be ten times harder than saying yes, but it makes you feel a hundred times better.'

Decca fell into a brooding silence as I untangled her hair.

'When I was not much older than you, I had an accident. It didn't cause me great pain in my body, but it did in my mind. I was very sad for a long time. It made my spirits low, and when your spirits are low it's hard to see the point in anything. Nobody understood how I suffered. Everybody told me I was lucky to be alive, that it was a miracle. They expected I'd be happy, but I wasn't, and that made everything seem worse. I felt very hopeless and alone.

'I read the same old newspaper over and over, and in it was an article about a school for children's nurses in London. The article talked about the blue dresses they wore, and frilly aprons, and badges they earned for years of service. It made it sound like a club, like . . . a family. Something to be part of. I loved school and wished I could go back more than anything, but my mother decided to keep me at home. The more I thought about it, the more I wanted to be one of those nurses, to work with children and make them feel safe and loved. But I was too young to go there, so I had to wait until I was eighteen. The time finally came, and I sat the exam and passed it. I don't know what I'd have done if I hadn't won the scholarship. I was lucky, really, that the other girls could afford it. They were much cleverer than me. Sometimes I wonder what would have happened if I hadn't set my mind on that college. Sitting the exam was the first thing I ever did for myself. What I'm saying is: I've managed just fine without a father, and I know you will too.'

I squeezed her hair with a towel and helped her from the bath. She seemed lighter, somehow, as though a part of her had come away in the water.

Later, when all four children were in bed, Mrs England asked me to join her in the drawing room. At first, it was strange to see her occupy the house – her own house – but that, too, seemed natural now. We spoke about the funeral and the children, and then fell into a peaceable silence.

'Ma'am,' I said. 'Do you think Decca knows Mr Sheldrake is her father?'

'I don't think so,' said Mrs England. 'Does she?'

'I'm not sure,' I replied. 'Did your family force you to marry Mr England?'

'My mother arranged it. I managed to keep the fact that I was expecting a secret, but eventually she grew wise to it. She confronted me, and the next day I was engaged to Charles. I told her Tommy and I were married, but she didn't care. She said as we weren't married in our faith, it wasn't valid.'

Her eyes glazed over. 'I never liked Charles, even as a girl. He was always *there*, chasing after my brothers, wanting to be one of us. His father was my father's lawyer: a cold, calculating man. Charles came to my room once, when I was changing. I opened the door and there he was, spying at the keyhole. I must have been thirteen.' She sniffed. 'My mother called it a marriage of necessity. It was necessary to everybody but me.'

I was silent. Then I said: 'What became of Mr Sheldrake?'

'He left for Australia shortly after. I never heard from him again. I asked him not to write to me, and he never did. When his father died, he had to come home to take over the business and care for his mother. His brother wanted to sell the forge, but it meant so much to his father. It's been in the family more than a hundred years.' She smiled. 'He was a nice man, Tommy's father.'

'You must have been young when you met Mr Sheldrake.'

'Seventeen,' she said. 'I used to ride a lot when I was younger, and I passed the forge one day. He offered my horse a drink.' She looked deep into the past, her expression vacant.

'I've never seen you ride, ma'am.'

'I haven't in years. Perhaps I'll start again.'

'And Mr England didn't know that he was Decca's father?'

'My mother told him some tale about me being compromised. She made out I had no say in the matter, but he worked out for himself that it was more than that. That it meant something to me. He held it against me all these years. He hated me for it. I never told him who her father was, but Lord knows he tried to get it out of me.'

'Why, when all that time had passed?'

She shrugged. 'Because I didn't belong to him as much as he'd have liked me to. Because there was someone else before him. He made me come home from Crow Nest, you know, because I was out walking. He couldn't find me when he arrived and didn't know where I was. I was out posting a letter; thank goodness he didn't find me with it. I could never be free of him, even there. Even if I went out walking, I had to pass the mill and wave to him or someone, and the same on the way back. I felt like one of his workers, so eventually it just seemed easier to not go out at all.'

I sighed. The idea that Tommy had known all along, and returned to the town where his daughter lived . . . I would never have guessed in a million years why he invited us to the forge that sunny afternoon, nor, it seemed, had Mr England.

'When did you and Mr Sheldrake start speaking again?' I asked her.

'Soon after he came home. Though it was so infrequent; he couldn't write to me at the house because Charles controlled the post, and sometimes the postman left it at the mill if he caught him. It's like he was waiting for something like this to happen; he knew, on some level. I think part of him always worried I would leave him, then the money would dry up and everything that came with it.'

'You mean divorce him?'

She shook her head. 'No, not divorce. I'd have to prove adultery, and of course I couldn't. And he would keep the children. Besides, my family would never allow me to do something so unholy, and obviously I've no money of my own. All of it was his.

'Tommy promised to give me some, enough to set up somewhere new. Do you remember when Decca brought the letter from him?' I nodded. 'It was the certificate, but he wrote me a note as well. I was terrified Charles would find it, so I burnt it in the grate. It made all that smoke, and before long the whole house knew about it. He saw the ashes in the fireplace; he knew I was hiding something. That's why he sent Decca to school.'

I blinked in surprise. 'To punish you?'

She nodded, and her face was tight with resentment.

'There were so many punishments. He sold my horses. He told me I cried out my lover's name in my sleep, so I was afraid even to go to bed with him next door. And the children preferred him.'

'I'm not sure that's—'

'He made it that way. I didn't dare show my affection in case he started doing it to them, too. To protect them, I've had to ignore them all their lives.' Her eyes glistened with tears. 'He hated me talking to you. He thought you were his.'

I was, I thought with a great heaviness. If I examined it closely, I knew I would fall apart.

'That's why he put my letters in your room,' I said.

She nodded. 'You can't have believed I would do such a thing.'

'I didn't know what to believe.'

She leant towards me from the rose-pink couch, and her black gown rustled. 'It's done now,' she said.

We found no letter from my father among the hundreds of pieces of correspondence in Mr England's study, though of course there was no time to go through them all. I decided it wasn't important; perhaps he had written to Mr England, perhaps he hadn't. I realised I didn't care how Mr England came to know who I was.

'Your poor mother,' Mrs England had said. Then: 'I

don't understand how a parent could . . . I don't understand why parents do lots of things.'

'My poor mother never let us speak of it again,' I replied, trying to keep my voice even. 'She went on as if nothing had happened.'

I didn't tell her she visited my father twice every year, with a little parcel of goods from the shop and a letter from all but one of his children. I didn't tell her that when it happened, she went to the prison before the infirmary, to see him before us. When she finally arrived at the ward, where Elsie and I were screened from the other patients, she didn't touch me, only sat in a chair at the foot of my bed and looked at me with fear and disapproval, as if I'd thrown myself from the bridge, as if it was my broken mind that had broken our hearts.

'I told you to look after him,' she said.

Much later, during another blazing row when I refused to write to or visit him, she asked me why I was the only one who couldn't forgive him.

Why couldn't I? I asked myself the same question. It was different for her: it was as though she was released by what happened, freed from her role as a sick man's wife. He was no longer her burden, and I resented her for it.

'Are we taking *all* of this to Melbourne?' asked Saul.

'None of it, I should imagine,' his mother replied.

'Where will it go, then?'

'The solicitor will keep some of it, and we'll sell the books and furniture.'

'We won't sell any of our things?' Millie asked with concern.

'Nothing of yours, no.' Mrs England turned to me. 'I don't suppose you've decided yet?'

'I'll let you know tomorrow, ma'am.'

She nodded.

CHAPTER 24

In the morning, the children and I walked to the postbox. Halfway down the bridleway, I saw a figure approaching on a bicycle, and my heart skipped. But this man wore a uniform, and I knew before he reached me that he was a messenger, and the message was for me. Sure enough, rather than tipping his cap and continuing, he slowed to a stop, his tyres crunching on the rough stones.

'You from the England house, miss?'

'Yes.'

'Ruby May?'

I nodded.

'I was just on my way to you. This arrived about ten minutes ago.' He passed me an envelope marked urgent.

'Thank you,' I said.

He nodded and rode away in the direction he had come.

'What is it?' Millie asked.

'A telegram.'

'What's that?'

'It's a sort of letter, sent through wires.'

'Are you going to open it?' asked Saul.

'Yes,' I said. After a pause, with clumsy fingers, I did.

FATHER DIED TUESDAY NIGHT STOP
SERVICE AND BURIAL FRIDAY AT B CHAPEL
STOP WE ARRIVE WOKINGHAM STATION
1151AM STOP.

'Who is it from?' asked Millie.

I searched for the sender: Emma May.

'My mother,' I said.

'Did she not sign it?' Millie peered over my shoulder.

It was the first I'd heard from her since my birthday in March. A red squirrel bounded across the track further down. I watched it spiral up a beech tree and vanish, and tucked the telegram inside my cloak.

That morning, I'd left Decca supervising breakfast, and found Mrs England in the study, writing a letter at the desk.

'Ma'am,' I said, closing the door. 'I've thought about your offer, and I'm afraid I can't come with you to Melbourne.'

She put down her pen with a sigh. 'Can't or won't?'

'Both. I can't be that far from Elsie or the boys. They're almost grown up now, but they're my responsibility if anything should happen to my mother. I won't abandon them. And if there's a chance my father recovers and is allowed home one day . . .' I swallowed. 'I should be close by. I'll stay until you go, though. For the children.'

She nodded, though her brown eyes were full of sorrow. She put her head on one side. 'Of course I understand, though I doubt the children will forgive me for taking them away from you.'

I smiled. 'They will, ma'am. Have you found a house yet?'

'Yes. I'm writing to the agent now. I had a letter from him yesterday. He's sending some photographs through the post, but they'll probably arrive after we've left. Anyway, it sounds perfect. It has a large garden with a view of the bay, and a *veranda*, of all things.'

'It does sound perfect. I'll send my resignation to my principal and catch the morning post, if that's all right.'

'Be my guest. I've invited Mr Booth to the house to inform him of the plans and give him his notice. Shall I tell him you're resigning, or do you want to?'

'I'd be grateful if you could tell him.'

The Booths had attended the funeral and left a card for the mistress. She was in the hall when it fluttered through the letterbox, and opened the door to call after them. I saw them come back across the yard beneath an umbrella and waved from the nursery window. Mrs England served them tea in the drawing room for the first time. I thought Blaise might call at the nursery, but she seemed eager to leave the house, marching across the yard and leaving Eli fumbling on the path with the umbrella.

Sending my resignation to Pembridge Square tipped me into a sort of depression. The five of us reached the lodge, and I let Millie post the letter into the wall. Before writing it I had checked my testimonial book, finding the paragraph that read: *Any Nurse or Probationer who fails in three situations will be asked to withdraw from the Institute.* In a little under two years, I'd left as many positions. To make matters worse, I'd also lost the left glove from my smart pair, and had no desire to visit the shops for a replacement.

We ambled back to the house. Winter had settled over the valley, which seemed to be in hibernation, though the busy waters gushed on. I'd laundered and packed the children's summer clothes, and brought out the serge and wool, the hats and scarves and wrappers, explaining to them that in Australia they had summer at Christmas, and winter in the middle of the year.

Tommy Sheldrake hadn't gone to the funeral, but read his newspaper in the park outside, as he had on the Sunday I met him, hoping for a glimpse of Lilian and her daughter. A week after the funeral, she went walking in the woods on her own. I took her meaning and watched from the window as she disappeared down the track. When she returned there were two pink spots of colour on her cheeks, and she shut herself in her bedroom.

She told me about her plans to emigrate the same evening. We were sitting in the day nursery in the lamplight with a fire going, and I had a pile of mending in my lap. I wasn't surprised in the slightest by her announcement; it was clear to me she couldn't stay, though unclear where somebody like her would go. Australia made sense: it was far from her family, as well as being a youthful, exciting country, with a hint of glamour, a promise of adventure. Moving there with the children would be like beginning a new diary, with all the pages clean.

'Might Mr Sheldrake go back to Australia, ma'am?' I asked, trying to sound casual.

'I doubt it,' Mrs England replied. 'He's built his life here now.'

'Just as you're leaving,' I said.

'I never thought I'd leave. I've lived in this house all my life. But now I can't imagine staying.'

'So the two of you aren't . . . ? Sorry, ma'am. I don't mean to pry.'

She gazed into the fire. 'I thought I still loved him, but we've rather outgrown each other. There's nothing to be done.'

I hid my surprise, wondering if Tommy felt the same. Before she became a widow, she'd been prepared to run away with him, but it wasn't easy to picture her as the wife of a blacksmith.

She looked at me, as if coming out of a dream. 'Will you come with me?'

I unpicked a faulty stitch. 'I don't think so, ma'am.'

'Will you think about it?'

A pause.

'Take a couple of weeks.'

'All right.'

'What would you do instead?'

'I don't know,' I said, but as soon as I said it, I knew instantly: I had holiday to take, and the Norland Institute leased a cottage on the south coast for quarantine after hospital training. I wished to go there and have the salt and wind wipe me clean, but I was uncertain how Sim would receive my resignation. I'd known I would leave even before Mrs England told me about Australia; my staying was untenable. Just as I'd longed to leave Longmore Street, though I loved Elsie and my brothers, it was possible for two people to have shared too much.

I felt weary and numb returning to the house with the telegram in my pocket, and shabby with my plain gloves. I already knew I wouldn't go into mourning for my father: nobody here knew about him, and I had no wish to attract attention. I decided I would not tell Mrs England either.

Just then, I realised I didn't want to return to Hardcastle House. I asked the children if they'd like to play in the woods, and they dashed at once through the trees, howling and prancing like savages. I stood on the side of the track with the pram, half-watching, half in thought. Before long there was the tinkle of a bicycle bell, and a grinding of tyres.

'Ruby.'

'Mr Booth.'

He jumped off his bike and wheeled it towards me. Though I was dull and lethargic, my stomach did a somersault as he came to stand beside me.

'How are you?' he asked.

'We're fine, thank you.'

He patted his satchel. 'I've brought some books for you. Saul mentioned you were a reader.'

'That's kind of you. Now they're all home, though, I'm not sure when I'll have a chance to get to them.'

'You can keep them.' He tightened his grip on the handlebars, his knuckles flaring white. I found myself unable to look him in the eye.

'Are you teaching at the mill?' I asked brightly.

'Mill's closed.'

'Oh, yes, of course. I knew that.'

'It's up for sale. Apparently some hotelier from Bradford has a mind to turn it into a skating rink.'

Now I looked at him. 'You can't be serious.'

He nodded. 'Oh, yes. Tea room, dancing, that kind of

thing. Weaving's no good no more. Too many factories and not enough to do in 'em.'

'I suppose it's a pretty spot.'

'I've been summoned by Mrs E,' he said after a moment.

'Oh, yes. I knew that too.'

'I don't suppose you have any idea what it's about? She told me to leave off tutoring while Saul's in mourning. I've a feeling I'm about to lose my job, either way.'

'They're moving to Australia.'

He gave a long, low whistle. 'Well, I wasn't expecting that. When?'

'As soon as they can. Before Christmas, if they're able to.'

'Australia. You can't get much further than that. And you're going with them?'

'No. I've just handed my notice in. It's four weeks.'

'What? You don't fancy being a pommy?' He was incredulous. 'I'd be biting her hand off if I were you.'

'Would you?' I half-smiled at him.

'Oh, would I? I'd already have my bags packed. A new life. Fresh start and all that.'

'That's the idea.'

'As long as you've two hands and a head on your shoulders, you've as good a chance as anyone to make something of yourself over there. I wouldn't even look at this place on a map again, let alone miss it.' He gave a wistful sigh. 'Maybe in the next life, eh?'

'You and Blaise could go.'

'She wouldn't leave her family. Never mind, eh?' Another

sigh, this one without self-pity. 'Anyway, what will you do next?'

'Find a new family, I suppose.'

'Shame you're leaving when you've only just started. Horrible business, that,' he went on in a low voice. 'I don't blame her for wanting to get away. She never seemed right happy.'

I said nothing, though my heart quickened. When I least expected it, the memory came to me of us sweeping through the woods in our cloaks, looking for his body. I'd never known terror like it, not knowing if he would be there or not, not knowing if he had survived or was lying in wait for us. When we eventually found him, nestled at the bottom of the crags as though sheltering, I'd pressed his neck for a full five minutes searching for a pulse.

'Blaise couldn't believe it when we heard. She was in shock; I've never seen her so quiet. I'm not one for gossip, but I suppose you haven't heard what they're saying in town?'

I swallowed and pulled down my cuffs. 'What are they saying?'

'That old Conrad cut him off before it happened. That he . . . you know. Did himself in. He was in dire straits, apparently, with his finances. I shouldn't entertain it, as you and I know there's nothing in it.'

I shivered. Another reason I had no desire to visit town was because the only way there led past the shut-up mill, which stood still and silent in its nook at the bottom of the valley. Without the relentless hum of machinery, the clatter of carts and thump of bales, without smoke pouring from the chimney, it was eerie, almost sinister. The wind played quietly across the cobbles and piled the leftover cotton in miserable drifts.

'My father's died,' I said, surprising myself. 'I just got the telegram.'

He was quiet. Then he said: 'Ruby, I'm so sorry. I shouldn't have spoken about Mr E like that. I didn't mean to—'

'I know. It's all right. I haven't said it out loud yet. It feels strange to hear it.'

He waited, his knuckles white above his handlebars.

'He wasn't well,' I found myself saying. 'He's lived in a sort of hospital a long time, so I haven't seen him. Now I suppose I never will.' I began to cry.

He fumbled about for a handkerchief, but I got there first, using my single glove to wipe my face.

'I know, Ruby.'

I stared at him, incredulous.

'I know who your father is. Who he was. John Lowden told me. He recognised you from a picture or something.'

'So you've known all this time?'

He nodded.

'Does Blaise?'

He shook his head. 'I haven't told her. It's not my story to tell.' He looked intently at me, and I saw his brown eyes were flecked with green. 'It's unspeakable, what happened to you, but there's no shame in it.'

I gave a deep, shuddering sigh, and wondered if Mr Lowden had been the one to tell Mr England, or whether he'd found out some other way. Most likely it had been the journalist: he would wish to ingratiate himself with such a family. No doubt he would have asked my master for an interview too. I was interested to realise I didn't care at all.

We watched the children chase one another with sticks.

'You've put colour in them,' said Eli.

'Have I?'

'They were like rice pudding before you arrived. All pale and lumpy.'

I laughed, for what felt like the first time in weeks. It bubbled up like a secret brook and felt just as clear and lovely. Then, after this, came more tears, as profuse as they were surprising. Eli found his handkerchief this time and pressed it into my palm.

'I don't know why I'm crying,' I said.

'I do – your bloody dad's just died. Don't be so hard on yourself.'

I felt better afterwards, wiping my nose and shoving his handkerchief inside my pocket, where it nestled beside the telegram.

'I wanted that back, actually,' he said, making me laugh again.

We set off walking together, and I was glad to have his

company through the ghostly mill yard, where the crags loomed beyond. A sale sign had been pasted to the door.

Back at the house, Broadley and Ben had their sleeves rolled up, decommissioning the outbuildings. Mrs England had given the old man the carriage as thanks for three decades of service; he planned to set up in business as a cab driver once the family had moved. All the servants were provided for: Tilda and Emily were being redeployed to Greatrex houses, and Mrs Mannion was retiring with a generous nest egg. She vowed to keep baking, selling bread and cakes from her cottage.

'I expect you won't return to Yorkshire,' said Eli as we drew up to the gate. I'd sent the children to the boot room ahead of me and hung back with the cumbersome pram, he with his bike, each of us nudging them gently back and forth like two nurses in Kensington Gardens.

'I expect not,' I said.

'Then I suppose this is goodbye.'

'I suppose it is.'

Charley watched with interest as he held out a hand. 'Ta-ra, Ruby May. And good luck.'

I took it. 'And to you, Mr Booth. I've appreciated your friendship.'

Neither of us shook; we held hands for a moment, like two people calling a truce. I let go first, and he clenched his fist as he dropped it, as though squeezing something inside. I battled with the pram through the gateposts, and he helped one last time. I thanked him, pink and flustered and overcome with too many feelings all at once, and closed the door between us. As usual, he went around the side.

Later, on the hall table, I found the books he'd left me: a Brontë and a Dickens, both of which I'd read, and a slim volume of Tennyson's poems I knew I wouldn't. I imagined him weighing up this last gift, whether to include it, what I would interpret from it. I took it anyway.

CHAPTER 25

The doorbell jangled, but the woman behind the counter did not look up. She crouched at a shelf, fetching a packet of table jelly for the older woman standing with her basket. The two of them were deep in conversation, and I took a seat and looked around. Outside, above the large window, the 'green' in greengrocer was no longer; the painted sign read: *May & Sons, Family Grocer*. There were no boxes of carrots or piles of shining apples; new shelves had been fitted and stacked four-deep with flour, custard, oatmeal, toffee, tinned milk, raisins and everything else a pantry could want. The walls were bright with posters and advertisements, and neat mahogany drawers had been installed behind the counter, with brass handles in the shape of shells.

My mother stood and saw me. She froze for a second, then took up the thread of her conversation. She gave the customer her change and they exchanged goodbyes. The other woman nodded to me on her way out, approving of my smart uniform, my spotless new gloves. The bell rang again, and suddenly it was the two of us, and slowly I got to my feet.

'I hardly recognised you,' she said. She did not smile. Beneath her apron she wore a black skirt and cream blouse with wide sleeves. There was more silver than brown in her hair now, and I noticed she had gained weight.

'The shop looks different,' I said. We stood at a distance in the small space, neither one of us moving forwards.

'I'll close up and we can go upstairs. Robbie's gone to the bank; he'll be back before long.' There was a length of silence, then she said: 'Are you staying for lunch? Archie and Ted come home at half-past twelve.'

'I'm going to London this afternoon. I can only stay an hour or so. Is Elsie home?'

My mother wiped her hands on her apron and put her head through the door. 'Elsie?' she called, tilting her head towards the ceiling.

A moment later, I heard her feet on the stairs. It was not the thumping clatter of a young person rushing down, but the careful sound of someone descending step by step, with the accompanying tap of a cane. I waited, my breath shallow in my throat, and a tall, slim girl appeared in the doorway. She wore an old blue blouse of mine, and a skirt that nipped her narrow waist. Her dark hair tumbled down in pigtails. She had the same anxious mouth and solemn brown eyes as I did, and now her mouth fell open and her eyes grew wide as she dashed around the counter with her stick, limping slightly.

'Ruby! You never said you was coming.'

I breathed in her scent, of pencil shavings and perfumed soap, and held her at arm's length so I could look at her, before embracing her so hard I thought I'd crush her bones.

'I thought I'd surprise you.'

'Are you staying? Please say you'll stay.'

'I can't, I'm going back to London.' My accent strengthened without effort, as easy and comfortable as putting on an old coat.

'One of the boys will sleep on the floor. They won't mind, will they, Ma?'

'She said she can't stay, Els. Take her upstairs and put the kettle on; I'll bring some biscuits up.'

Elsie went first up the narrow stairs, and when the familiar homely smell met me in the hall, I was glad to feel her close to me, warm and safe and alive. I'd grown used to large houses with vast kitchens, high ceilings and separate rooms for eating, resting and studying, so the little airless room where we did all our living and cooking, our mending and airing, seemed smaller and more forlorn than ever.

While Elsie made tea, I opened the door to the boys' bedroom. Elsie slept with Mother, and my brothers had our old room to themselves. That seemed smaller, too, half the size of the Englands' night nursery, with the beds unmade and the floor a quagmire of boots, socks and braces. Archie and Ted were both at work, and I folded a jumper on Ted's bed, lifting it to my nose and closing my eyes. I looked out of the window into the yard, where weeds sprang in tufts between the flagstones. Damson's lean-to and the chickens had long gone, though their coop remained.

Elsie swept crumbs from the table and draped over the tablecloth with yellow flowers that we saved for best. Our mother joined us with a tin of Peek Frean biscuits and shook a few out onto a plate. She untied her apron and laid it over the back of a chair, sitting with a great creak and a sigh. I'd left the boys' bedroom door open and the winter sun filtered through, throwing a rectangular patch of light onto the butter-coloured wall.

'How was the funeral?' I asked. I decided not to remove my hat, cloak and gloves.

'It was fine. Very respectable.' Mother scratched her hair and swilled the tea in her cup.

'Was it a religious service?'

'They don't go in for much of that in those sorts of places. The chaplain was a pleasant fellow, though. He said some nice things about your father. They sent a coach to pick us up at the station – all very grand. We waited for you. We didn't know if you were coming. Would have been nice to have you there, pay your respects.'

I sipped my tea and set it on the table. 'And he's buried there at the asylum?' I asked.

'In the cemetery. It was quite pleasant, wasn't it, Elsie? Trees, flowers, that sort of thing. Nice view of the village. Not a bad resting place.'

At that moment the door to the street downstairs slammed shut, and I scrambled out of my chair, startling my mother and sister. Boots trudged up the stairs, and a male voice bellowed: 'Why's the shop shut?'

'Robbie!' I rushed to embrace him. He was a man now, nineteen years old, stooping through the doorway. His brown suit fitted him well, and he slung his cap on the table.

'Not on the clean cloth,' Mother scolded, and Elsie poured him tea, smiling.

'That's why!' he exclaimed with a broad grin. 'Rhubarb! What you doing here?'

He changed into his shop clothes with the bedroom door half-open, talking and asking questions through the gap. Soon he had to go downstairs to serve customers, and in no time at all an hour had passed and I had to depart to catch the train.

'Don't leave it so long next time,' said Mother, without conviction; both of us knew I would.

I helped Elsie to clear the things and asked her when she'd last seen the doctor.

'Not for a while, when was it?' Mother answered for her. 'She's been all right the last few months, though her legs were bad last winter.'

'Can you go back to school?' I asked Elsie directly.

'We need her here,' said Mother. 'Robbie and I are in the shop, and the boys come home for their lunch hour.'

'Could she prepare it and leave it here for you? It seems unnecessary for her to stay here all day just for that.'

'Perhaps.' The reply was insincere, disinterested. I felt the old resentment rise and looked automatically for my gloves, then remembered I was wearing them.

'I'd best be off,' I said, kissing my mother on the cheek, breathing in her floury scent.

Downstairs, I embraced Robbie, saving the longest embrace for my sister, who stood at the door to the street. As I waved, the pavement was busy with shoppers and Elsie appeared in snatches, her plaits bouncing, waving hard.

I had said goodbye to the Englands that morning. Probate had delayed the family's passage to Australia, but Mrs England's solicitor, a well-mannered, thorough man from across the border in Lancashire, was working tirelessly to sell the house and book their passage before Christmas. I offered to stay until they left, but nobody knew for certain when that would be, and I was glad when Mrs England insisted she could manage alone. All the children had cried, even Saul, and so had I, clinging to the baby for longer than was necessary. The eldest three gave me presents. Decca had made me a book of Yorkshire flowers and written a poem about the moor, Saul gave me his precious pheasant feather, and Millie bequeathed me one of her dolls, wearing a frock I had made from one of her baby gowns. Mrs England handed over my testimonial book last. I would have left without it, quite forgetting I'd asked her to write an account of my time at Hardcastle House. I fastened it inside my portmanteau; my trunk would follow when I had a new address. It was raining by the time the carriage was ready, and Broadley came with an umbrella to fetch me.

A week or two after my glove disappeared, Emily handed it to me in the scullery. She had found it in the laundry in one of Decca's pockets. I thanked her, quite overcome with surprise and tenderness, and returned it to the pinafore. Before I climbed into the carriage, it was Decca I hugged the hardest, Decca I regretted leaving the most. I hoped happiness lay ahead for her, imagined her as a young woman sitting on a shady veranda with a fan and a novel in her lap, a glass of lemonade at her elbow, looking out at a glittering bay. I had left her some of my books, and she promised to write with their new address the moment they arrived. The five of them stood beneath large umbrellas, the servants alongside. As the carriage slid out of the yard, I pressed myself to the window to wave for as long as I could. Mrs England stood slim and upright in deepest black, holding Charley on one hip. How solid she seemed now, made of jet instead of crepe.

Pembridge Square was all change. Number seven was being renovated, with builders and decorators tramping up and down in front of the house. I stepped aside on the pavement to allow a workman to pass with an armful of rollers; he thanked me and loaded them into a cart. Pausing at the gate, I looked around and thought how different the square looked in winter, with the milky sky and white houses.

We sat in Sim's apartment. The principal made coffee on the stove, and we each had a slice of pineapple upside-down cake, warm from the kitchen. I hadn't expected what a comfort it was to be back among the nurses in their blue dresses and frothy aprons. Stepping through the glossy black door, I felt like a bird rejoining its flock. A maid delivered my things to a bedroom – private, this time – and I followed Sim upstairs to the top of the house. I hadn't had the privilege of visiting her private rooms before, and looked around with interest. The principal occupied the attic, where the ceiling sloped and two small windows overlooked the square. China plates covered the flocked walls, drapes were tied beside the fire, and a pair of velvet-backed chairs sat before it. It was fussier than I expected; somehow I did not think of Sim as a woman at all, and could not imagine her filling her spare time with the usual things.

'You may have seen the works at number seven,' she commented. She looked just the same as ever, with her frizzy fringe and ramrod back, her ink-stained fingers.

'Yes,' I said, grateful that the niceties were over, but more than a little confused. I had arrived at Pembridge Square expecting to be chastised, or at least reprimanded. But she seemed to have detected a significant change in me; she was delicate and attentive, almost deferential. I found it unnerving, having braced myself for a ticking-off that it seemed was not forthcoming.

'Has a new family moved in?' I asked.

'No, it's ours, actually. We're expanding.'

'Oh?'

'Norland nurseries opens in a few weeks. The work will be finished in the New Year. We have six suites, each with beds for three children, and already the waiting list is full.' She spoke with great satisfaction and pride.

'Goodness,' I said, impressed. 'Where do they come from?'

'They're mainly children of the Empire: Indian officials and so on. Some will be here short-term, while their parents are abroad.'

'That sounds wonderful.'

'But we are here to talk about you, Nurse May.' Sim sat forwards. 'Now, what is it about you that makes people want to emigrate?'

After a startled pause, I gave a weak laugh, and Sim glowed with good humour; she was in a cheerful mood that I could not match. Well, I had not come to be jovial; I had come to explain. I took from my pocket the postcard of Elsie and me with the pill pilot and the policemen, and passed it to her. She accepted it with a leftover smile, thinking I was showing her a family picture. The smile turned to confusion as she examined it, and next I passed her the newspaper clipping from the *West of England Advertiser*. I watched her eyebrows knit together and the lines around her mouth grow more prominent as she read. Within a few seconds her expression had changed completely, and by the time she reached the second paragraph, the sharp intake of breath told me she had found my name.

'This is you.' She gazed at me in disbelief.

I sat quietly, feeling more emotional than I'd expected to. For a long time I'd struggled with people's sympathy. They would always insist on giving it to me, but it was so heavy, and I had no wish to be burdened with it.

'Oh, Nurse May.' Her eyes were full of tears. My own blurred in response, and I looked away.

'I didn't show this to you so you'd feel sorry for me. I showed you so you'd perhaps understand why my placements keep failing.'

Sim leant over and took my hand. She read the rest of the article like that, and when she got to the bottom, gave a deep sigh.

'How I wish you had told me this earlier. I understand why you didn't, but I wish you had.'

'I didn't want anyone to know.'

'Of course. And your sister Elsie? How is she?'

'She's fine. I saw her this morning, before I came here.'

She nodded. 'Your placements aren't failing, Nurse May. But I can't help but think I've failed you.'

'Of course you haven't, Miss Simpson. But I'm afraid I've come to ask for another one.' I gave a dry laugh. 'A placement, that is. My third. I promise it will be my last, and if this one fails, too, I shall withdraw from the institute, as per the rules.'

'You will do no such thing.' Her tone was sharp. 'I wouldn't dream of it. Now . . .' She gave a brisk sigh. 'I might as well come out with it. A deposit was made in your name to the company account last week, and the funds cleared yesterday. The secretary alerted me to it, and I wrote to the benefactor immediately to ask if they had made it in error, but they assured me they had not, and said they hoped it was not an inconvenience for us to transfer it to you.'

'What deposit? Who made it?' I was quite light-headed and tried to work out how many weeks it had been since my father died.

'Forty pounds, from Mrs Charles England. I wrote to her at Hardcastle House, and she replied straightaway.'

'Forty pounds?' I was astonished. 'But that's a year's salary.'

'Indeed. I'll admit I've never known a bonus to be quite so generous.'

I sat back in a daze. 'You're certain she meant to leave that much?'

'Naturally I enquired, and the amount was confirmed.'

I sank, overwhelmed, into the chair. I could secure Elsie the best medical help there was. I could pay for a char-woman, even a maid, to keep the family. I could find a separate house, so my sister didn't have to use the stairs. They could lease the flat above the shop and use the income to open another one . . .

'I can see you are quite overcome, and rightly so,' said Sim. 'But without wishing to confound you even further, I'd like to talk to you about something else, something that I have already mentioned. The nurseries.'

'Sorry?' I came up, blinking.

'I am hiring a team of nurses to work at number seven. They'll take care of the children and train the probationers. I need six in total, one for each suite. I'm also appointing a matron, for which I've had several exemplary applicants, and there will be a vacancy for a head nurse, but both of those positions require more experience than you have. That's by the by; like I say, there are six roles available. I should like you to consider applying for one of them. I understand, of course, if you would prefer a placement with another family, but I think you would make an excel-lent teacher, Nurse May. You have just the temperament for it, and you know I'm of the opinion that character has more bearing than qualifications in this line of work. Of course, you wouldn't *only* be a teacher, you would be a nurse, too, so it will be nursery and schoolroom. Twin pillars of equal weight. I'd like you to think on it, though, of course, your windfall changes things quite considerably and offers you the option of having a break from employment altogether. However, I wouldn't recommend it. It's good to keep occupied. Idle hands and all that.'

I sat for a long time in silence, digesting this and watching the fire. After a while, I said: 'If I may, Miss Simpson, I'd like to go to the cottage by the sea. If there's room for me, that is. I need some time to think, and I liked it so much there.'

'There is, and you may. It's usually unoccupied over Christmas. I'll have the housekeeper make up a bed for you. Take as much time as you need.'

'Thank you.'

'Nurse May, I'd like to say something. Before you go spending that money on someone else, or bettering another person's circumstances' – I looked at her in surprise, and was met with her cool, steady gaze – 'sit with it for a while. It's yours. Nobody needs to know about it other than the two people in this room. And another thing: I had no idea you'd experienced such tragedy, but I must say you've overcome it remarkably.'

'Thank you, but—'

'Let me finish. These things are always a part of us, in one way or another, and I'm not suggesting you'll ever

put it behind you. But I'm yet to meet a student or probationer who embodies *fortis in arduis* more than you. I
admire you very much. Now, shall we take these coffee
cups down? Or Cook will have my guts for garters.'

Two days later, on a steam train bound for the south coast,
I sat with the heavy black testimonial book on my lap,
looking out of the window at the fields. I took off my
gloves and stroked the leather, daydreaming and thinking
of the letters I would write when I arrived: to Decca,
describing the chalky cliffs and the pebble beach; and to
Mrs England, thanking her for the money; and Elsie, too.
I had taken Sim's advice and decided to make no decisions,
waiting instead for the answers to land at my feet. I had
a job offer, and in the meantime the prospect of no work
at all. I had money in the bank, and a cottage waiting for
me, with a housekeeper, and a little window overlooking
the beach. The year was ending, and I wished to see it
off from a distance, and look at nothing but empty sky
and endless sea. For the first time in my life, I was in
charge, and I would savour every moment.

I opened the testimonial book, skimming past my
photograph, the rules, my certificate and Mrs Radlett's
tidy entry. That all seemed so long ago now, from a
different life altogether. I came to the second item,
admiring the elegant hand, signed with a flourish: the lacy

L, the curling E. Tucked into the spine was a small folded note I hadn't noticed before. With a frown, I opened it carefully, and found inside a short message in the same handwriting: *Thank you for bringing us back to life*. I closed the book and rested my head against the seat to watch the countryside streak by, thinking back to the morning I left, when Mrs England handed a letter to me on the landing. It was from Elsie.

'I'm sorry, I forgot to give this to you,' she said.

I looked at the postmark, dated three days before, and put it in my apron. She smiled, and her jet earrings danced.

ACKNOWLEDGEMENTS

Writing a novel during a global pandemic has been a strange experience. I started the first draft of *Mrs England* in January 2020, weeks before we went into the first lockdown. I was already in my own sort of lockdown, living alone in Hebden Bridge, working and only leaving the house for daily walks and weekly trips to the supermarket. I'm grateful to my friends and family for visiting me and keeping me company; something I've learned over the last year is how necessary human contact is for me, for inspiration and energy, for variety and rejuvenation. Those weekends stomping across moors with friends and evenings doing jigsaws with my cousins were wonderful, and sustained me through what would turn out to be more than a year without either.

My editor, Sophie Orme, had her work cut out with this book. It usually takes me at least two drafts to even work out what is happening in the story, but Sophie, you are such a skilled, encouraging and kind editor, and you never make me feel as though I'm handing you the brain dump my first drafts always are. I feel so lucky to work with someone who brings out the best in me, and I am endlessly grateful to be paired with someone so talented. Thank you to the wider Bonnier team – Francesca Russell,

Clare Kelly, Eleanor Stammeijer (please god let us eat sandwiches on a train one day soon), Margaret Stead, Katie Lumsden, Stephen Dumughn, Felice McKeown, Kate Parkin, Elise Burns, Vincent Kelleher, Stuart Finglass, Mark Williams, Stacey Hamilton, Jenny Richards, Nick Stern, Alan Scollan, Robyn Haque, Jennie Harwood, Jeff Jamieson and Perminder Mann. Thanks also to Patrick Knowles and Lucy Rose Cartwright.

As ever, thank you to my agent, Juliet Mushens, for having my back, doing the most and keeping Joanie in the lifestyle that she deserves. Thanks, too, to Liza De Block, Kiya Evans and Den Patrick for keeping the home fires burning.

I'm very grateful for the help and guidance of Dee Burn, Dr Janet Rose, Christopher Jones and Kate Morgan at Norland College, and Mark Stevens at Berkshire Record Office.

Thank you to my family and friends for always supporting me. There've been no reserved seats this year, but you'll always have front row in my heart. And thank you to my husband, Andy, who was happy for me to move 250 miles away to write this novel. Neither of us could have expected three months apart would result in a year of every day together. Thanks to you, I've loved every single one.

So many people have lost so much this year. Last but by no means least, I'm beyond grateful to the NHS and the key workers who have given their time and lost their lives during the COVID-19 pandemic.

AUTHOR'S NOTE

Mrs *England* is a work of fiction, but the character of Ruby May is based on Ruby Browne who, along with her sister Elsie, was thrown from Clifton Suspension Bridge by her father, Charles Albert Browne, on the night of 18th September 1896. Both girls survived the fall of 245ft (75m). Though at first Ruby was not expected to survive her injuries, both girls were discharged from Bristol Royal Infirmary a few weeks later. Their father, Charles, a grocer from Balsall Heath, Birmingham, was admitted to Broadmoor Criminal Lunatic Asylum (now Broadmoor Hospital). He was discharged in December 1899 into the care of his wife.

READING GROUP QUESTIONS

1. *Mrs England* begins when Ruby moves from London to an isolated Yorkshire town. How do the landscape and setting influence the story in this novel?

2. How does training as a Norland nurse affect the trajectory of Ruby's life?

3. What did you make of Mrs England as a character? How did your perception of her change throughout the book?

4. How does the novel explore the theme of marriage?

5. What similarities can you see between Ruby's family and the Englands? How does Ruby's upbringing influence her behaviour?

6. How does the novel look at gender and gender roles at this point in history?

7. What is uniquely Edwardian about this novel? How do you think the story might have played out differently if set at another point in time?

8. As a nurse, Ruby's class position is complicated. How does the novel examine the role of class and money in someone's life?

9. What do you think Ruby feels for Mr Booth?

10. Why do you think Ruby's father did what he did?

11. What do you make of the novel's closing paragraph?

Dear Reader,

I hope you've enjoyed reading *Mrs England*. If you'd like to receive more information about it, and about my previous two novels, *The Familiars* and *The Foundling*, you might be interested in joining my Readers' Club. Don't worry – it doesn't commit you to anything, there's no catch, and I won't pass your details on to any third parties. You'll receive updates from me about my books, including offers, publication news and even the occasional treat! You can unsubscribe at any time. To register, all you have to do is visit **www.staceyhalls.com**.

Another way of reaching out to me is via Twitter @Stacey_Halls or Instagram @StaceyHallsAuthor. I hope to hear from you soon, and that you continue to read and enjoy my books.

Thank you for your support,
Stacey

Please turn over for more information about
the Norland Institute, exclusive to this edition

RULES FOR NORLAND NURSES

1. Meals.—Nurses are not supposed to take their meals with the servants, but the presence of a nursery maid at the nursery meals should not be objected to. Where there is no Day Nursery the Nurses are not allowed to take meals in the bedrooms. It is hoped that employers will see the hygienic importance of this rule, not only for the Nurse but also for the children.

2. Sundays.—The Nurse should be permitted to attend her own place of worship once on Sundays, and without the children.

3. Holidays.—Nurses are entitled by the rules of the Institute to four weeks' holiday a year, to be taken at the convenience of the employer, either all at once, or in periods of not less than one week at a time. It is suggested by the Principal of the Institute that the best arrangement for many families would be to give the month's holiday at one time and obtain a substitute from among the Probationers of the Institute. This could generally be arranged by the Principal.

4. Washing is to be paid for by the employer.

RULES—*Continued.*

5. Travelling Expenses.—It should be understood that when a Nurse is engaged, the employer under-takes to pay in the first instance the travelling expenses to the new situation.

6. Notice.—Four weeks' notice on either side shall termi-nate the engagement. A written intimation of such termination should be sent at once to the Principal by the employer.

7. Exercise.—It is hoped that employers will see the importance of allowing the Nurses, whenever possible, to take daily exercise in the open air when the children of the nursery are delicate and unable to go out regularly. Half-an-hour's walk would be sufficient for the Nurse, and cause little or no inconvenience to the employer.

8. Salaries.—The salaries of the Nurses are paid through the Secretary of the Institute quarterly. The employer will receive every quarter day an account stating the exact amount due to the Institute.

9. Title.—The Norland Nurses are called "Nurse," adding, if preferred, the Christian or Surname.

10. Duties.—The employer is asked not to expect the Nurse to scrub floors, clean grates, or carry coals.

RULES—*Continued.*

11. Uniform.—The Nurses wear the Uniform of the Norland Institute on all occasions when on duty. The uniform consists of: —

> Black or brown bonnet, according to the time of year. A simple white or brown hat should be worn in the summer in the country or at the sea, and on very hot days in town.
>
> Dark grey or brown cloaks, according to the time of year.
>
> Light blue serge dress.
>
> Pink and white-striped Galatea dress for morning or heavy work.
>
> Fawn coloured drill dress for summer.
>
> White linen aprons.
>
> White cambric ties. Coloured ties may be worn with the drill dress.

12. Testimonials.—The employer is asked to write a testimonial in the nurse's book on the completion of each year's work, and also when the nurse leaves her situation, and to affix the date when the testimonial was given.

Reproduced with permission from Norland College

*The first cohort of Norland Nurses, 1892, reproduced
with permission from Norland College*